T0396469

Red Clay

Red
Clay

Charles B. Fancher

**BLACK
STONE**

PUBLISHING

Printed in the United States of America

First edition: 2025
ISBN 979-8-212-40869-1
Fiction / Historical / Civil War Era

Version 2

Blackstone Publishing
31 Mistletoe Rd.
Ashland, OR 97520

www.BlackstonePublishing.com

In memory of my late father,
Dr. Charles B. Fancher Sr. (1920–2020),
a man of outstanding professional
accomplishment in the field of higher education,
whose generosity of spirit, deep humility, and
infinite grace touched everyone
who had the privilege to meet him.

Part One
ROAD'S END

Chapter 1

Third Baptist Church, the biggest Black congregation in Red Clay, Alabama, was packed for Felix H. Parker's funeral. Church members, friends, and family, including some distant cousins from Birmingham, had gathered to say farewell on a brisk Wednesday morning in mid-December.

They were wearing their Sunday best. The women preened with hair freshly pressed and curled beneath feathered and flowered hats, their faces covered by lacy veils and their shoulders draped with fur stoles, little head-on fox pelts attached nose to tail, staring with unseeing beady black eyes. The men were distinguished in their suits with high-waisted pants, hand-painted ties over starched white shirts, Stetson hats resting on their knees, and spit-shined Johnston & Murphy shoes on their feet.

From the front pew reserved for immediate family, Eileen Epps looked over her shoulder at the sea of black, brown, and "high-yellow" faces and smiled. *Grandpa would have loved this.* She knew exactly what he would have said: "White folks put us down, but damned if we don't know how to look good when we come to church." And despite her grief, the recollection of the man who lay in the casket in front of her aroused a moment of perfect joy, untethered to the physical world.

She wondered, *Is this what the old ladies at church feel when the spirit moves them?* She could see them in her mind's eye as they would leap from their pews, throw their hands into the air, and shout "Jesus! Jesus! Help me, Jesus!" before collapsing into the arms of the ushers, those white-dressed, stern-faced women with ribbons and silver badges of authority pinned above their mighty bosoms, the women who swooped in with funeral home fans and tissues to comfort those overcome by the presence of the Holy Ghost.

"Watch this," Felix would whisper to Eileen whenever Eula Jean Wilkins got the spirit. Eula Jean was an unprepossessing woman, lean and nearly six feet tall. She had gray eyes, surprising in her dark-chocolate face, and thick white hair that she straightened on Saturday nights with a hot comb and hair grease in the kitchen of the little house she had shared with her husband thirty years earlier, before he was killed in a lumbering accident when they were still in their twenties. She had never remarried. She cooked and cleaned for a white family over in Demopolis.

The spirit didn't descend on Eula Jean precipitously. It enveloped her slowly, until it overtook her completely, usually about midway through the preacher's sermon. First, she would sway from side to side and then rock backward and forward, matching the tempo of the preacher's oration. When he reached a crescendo, with his voice soaring up and out through open stained-glass windows, like the voice of God from the burning bush, the spirit in Eula Jean would erupt.

"Here it comes," Felix would whisper and nudge his granddaughter in the ribs with his elbow. Eula Jean would shoot to her feet and her whole body would shake with her mouth open and her eyes rolled back in her head. Then she would sit down again, as if the fit had passed, before springing to her feet and stepping into the aisle to dance. She would prance to the altar, arms flailing and hat askew, and then dance to the rear of the church, following choreography known only to her, set to music that only she could hear. And when she was spent, Eula Jean would drop into her seat at the end of the pew and clutch her heart while the ushers fanned her and wiped her brow. If Felix would have been disappointed in any part of his send-off, Eileen thought, it would be because Eula Jean couldn't get the day off to attend his service.

Eileen remembered the last time she'd seen Felix alive, on the Saturday after Thanksgiving. She had been at home in Red Clay for the holiday, in her room packing to return to Montgomery, where she was a sophomore at State Teachers College. She heard footsteps behind her and turned to see Felix standing in the doorway.

"Grandpa, I really wish Luther could have been here," she said. Two years had passed since Japan's attack on Pearl Harbor, and her brother, drafted into the army after the US declared war, couldn't get a pass to come home for the holiday.

"Yes, baby, I missed him too, but I came in here to ask you a favor," he said. "You think you can get back to college by yourself? To tell the truth, I'm feeling kind of poorly . . ."

For the first time she noticed that he seemed older. His voice was raspy, and his gray hair was thinning. As a younger man, he had stood tall, muscular, with calloused hands as big as catcher's mitts, but that day he seemed smaller, stooped. The lines in his saddle-brown face were deeper.

"Of course," she said. "Don't worry about it. Are you and Mama going to be all right? Mama's old, and you're well up in your eighties now. I worry about you."

Felix stood straight, flexed his muscles, squared his shoulders, and said, "Girl, I'm the strongest man you know. I can handle anything that comes along, better'n any of them young 4-F boys at college with you." Then they laughed and sat quietly in her room as the sun began to set over the brick-colored hill across the road from the house Felix had built with his own hands.

"I'll be fine, baby. I'll be fine," he said and patted her on the shoulder as the last rays of sunlight slipped from view.

Outside, pine tree branches rustled in the wind, and raccoons and possums and foxes and all the other hungry creatures began the nightly hunt for food. In the distance, a rabbit shrieked as it was snatched and carried away in an owl's powerful talons, and all across planet Earth, the parade of life strutted in a never-ending cavalcade of triumph and defeat.

A few weeks later, Eileen was studying in the college library when one of her Alpha Kappa Alpha sorority sisters delivered the message: Come home. Felix H. Parker is dead.

———

A few white people sat in the rear of the sanctuary for the funeral, mostly men for whom Felix had worked. But as Eileen scanned the crowd, she saw one white face she didn't recognize, that of an elderly woman—very old, about ninety, Eileen guessed, and tiny, barely five feet tall, and frail. She wore a black dress, and her thin, wispy white hair was pulled back into a bun topped by an old-fashioned black silk bonnet. Eileen was sure the woman weighed no more than eighty pounds.

"Do you know who that old white woman is?" she whispered to her brother Luther, leaning across their mother, Maybelle, who sat between them.

Luther, home on leave from the army for the funeral, looked over his shoulder and turned back to Eileen. He shook his head and mouthed the word "No."

When the service ended and the pallbearers moved forward to carry the casket to the waiting hearse, Eileen noticed that the woman had disappeared, a phantom vanished without a trace.

The next morning Eileen woke early. Luther and their mother were still asleep in their rooms, exhausted by the strain of greeting mourners who had visited to express condolences and to consume mountains of fried chicken, potato salad, collard greens, cornbread and yeast rolls, cakes, and pies prepared by the ladies of the church and delivered to the house on Jefferson Street. They had meant well and were appreciated, but Eileen and her family had been relieved when they all left.

Among the last to depart was Edna Mae Daniels, a stylish elderly woman whose smart outfits rarely failed to make her a standout at church on Sunday mornings. "She ought to be ashamed—old woman like her trying to dress like a young girl," huffed Henrietta Foster, head of the church's usher board, as the rest of her claque vigorously nodded their agreement.

Edna Mae had spent most of the reception sitting alone, wiping her eyes and staring into space. When Eileen brought her a plate of food and a cup of coffee, Edna Mae grabbed her sleeve and whispered, "Your grandfather was a fine man." Her eyes bored into Eileen's with an intensity that caused the younger woman to turn away.

"Mama, what was Edna Mae Daniels to Grandpa?" Eileen asked as the last visitors were leaving.

"Daddy and Mama knew her, and we used to see her at church. They were friends, but now that you ask, I always thought there was something a little off in the way she and Mama got along." Maybelle might have said more, but she was pulled aside for a last hug by one of the departing guests.

Eileen stepped onto the front porch clutching a mug of steaming hot coffee. It felt good in her hands on that cold December morning, when frost held the grass in the front lawn at icy attention against a breeze that ruffled the pine needles overhead. At five feet, seven inches tall and barely a hundred pounds, Eileen felt the chill more sharply than most, especially this morning, when death lingered like an unwelcome guest. It hung in the air like dust and coated every surface.

She closed her eyes and tried to imagine the house without Felix. She had lived there for most of her life, beginning when she was five years old. Her father had died suddenly, and her mother had been left alone in Birmingham to fend for herself and the children. Felix, still grieving the death of his beloved wife, Zilpha, gathered them up the day after the funeral and moved them to his house in Red Clay.

Immediately, he had become the most important man in Eileen's life. As a girl, she had loved spending hours in Felix's workshop as he crafted fine furniture for customers. He talked while he worked, explaining why he used certain wood for one thing and not another and how to deal with customers. "They always complain about how much I charge, but I tell them, 'I use the best material, I tend to the details, and if it fails, I will fix it.' They know I'm right, so they pay."

She liked it best, however, when he talked about his mother and father and life on the plantation as an enslaved child. She had learned, though, not to press him when, in the middle of a story, he would stop talking, his shoulders would sag, and his brow would furrow, as if some memories were simply too painful to recall.

"What's wrong, Grandpa?" Eileen would ask.

"Nothing, baby. You don't need to know about all that slavery times stuff. Just make you sad. Tell you what; you go up to the house and ask your mama if you can ride with me to deliver this table. We'll stop at the store on the way home and get us a sugar cane joint and maybe a bag of roasted peanuts. What do you think about that?"

Over the years, however, Felix had revealed a great deal about his life, and Eileen treasured each bit, like fine pearls kept inside a velvet bag, brought out only for special occasions.

She was about to go back inside when she heard a car pull into the yard. Not just any car, it was a 1940 Packard 180, one of the most powerful and luxurious automobiles on the road, a fact known to Eileen only because Luther talked about them incessantly and had shown her a picture in a magazine. "I'm going to have a car like that one day," he said.

The big burgundy sedan rolled to a stop, its headlights cutting through the early morning shadows, its powerful inline eight-cylinder engine rumbling like the low growl of a jungle cat. Eileen's first impulse was to run inside to awaken Luther, but she remained frozen in place as the driver's door opened and a tall, caramel-colored Negro man with a sharply trimmed mustache stepped out, wearing a black suit and white shirt with a black tie and a chauffeur's cap. He nodded to Eileen and walked around to the other side of the car, opened the back door, and stood aside as his passenger emerged.

It was the elderly white woman from the funeral. She wore a black wool coat and leaned heavily on a cane as she shuffled toward the house.

Eileen remained motionless. "May I help you?" she asked.

"You are Eileen Epps, the granddaughter of Felix Parker," the woman replied. It was a statement, not a question, and her tone suggested that she was unaccustomed to being wrong—or being challenged when she was. "We need to speak." She continued to make her way toward the house, stopping when she reached the steps. "May I come in?" she asked.

Responding to her signal, the chauffeur helped her up to the porch before returning to the car.

"Please," Eileen said and opened the door.

The old woman entered and looked around, taking in the living room, the modest but tasteful furnishings, and the high ceilings that gave the space an open, airy feel. Eileen saw her eyes linger on the debris from the previous night's visitations.

"I must apologize," Eileen said. "Last night's guests left quite late."

"It's not important," the woman said.

"I've just made coffee," Eileen said. "May I offer you a cup, Mrs. . . . ?"

The old woman pulled herself up on her cane. "I am Miss Adelaide Parker," she said, "and a lifetime ago, my family owned yours."

Too stunned to reply, Eileen stood frozen.

"This is a shock, I'm sure," Adelaide Parker said. "I can imagine that you might not be happy to be here with me, but we need to talk." She paused, and then she added, "*I* need to talk—about your grandfather. About Felix."

"I'll get Mama and my brother up," Eileen said. "They should hear whatever you have to say."

"You could do that," the woman said, "but perhaps you should allow them to sleep for now. They can join us later."

Eileen searched the older woman's face, seeking clues for what she really wanted. Finding none, she gestured to the sofa. "Please have a seat, Miss Parker, and I'll get a cup of coffee for you," and without another word she headed for the kitchen.

When Eileen returned, she found the old woman settled at the end of the sofa, softly caressing its intricately carved, polished wood arm. "Felix made this, didn't he?" she asked.

"Yes, ma'am, he did," Eileen replied. "He built the house and almost everything made of wood inside."

"I'm not surprised," she replied. "He once made something especially for me many years ago. I can tell you about it if you like." She accepted the cup of steaming coffee and smiled as Eileen settled into the other end of the sofa with a cup of her own.

"We had not spoken or corresponded for many years, but Felix was important to me, and I know what you and your mother meant to him. I can tell you things about him that I think he would want you to know, and it would mean a great deal to me to hear what you have to say about him. That is, if you are willing."

"I want to hear all of your stories, Miss Parker, and I'll be glad to tell you what I can. Grandpa was a talker, but he was closed up about some things, and I'd like to know whatever you can tell me," Eileen said.

Adelaide Parker sipped her coffee, looked directly into Eileen's eyes, and, satisfied that she had found a willing partner, began to speak. "I am eighty-eight years old, young lady, and when one is as old as I have become, the world looks different. You develop new understandings of what is important, of what has meaning. When I heard that Felix had died, I knew I had to come here."

The sun was fully up now, sending shafts of light through the front windows of Felix's house, and as the two women began to talk, the dirty dishes and soiled linen from the night before lay forgotten. They were weaving a tale of joy and sorrow, of comfort and pain, of good and evil, of truth and deceit, and the only thing that either of them could be sure of was that neither of their lives would have been the same without the presence of Felix H. Parker.

Chapter 2

Four a.m., September 15, and even the field hands on the Road's End plantation outside Red Clay, Alabama, were still sleeping. They had at least another hour before rising to work in the fields from "cain't see to cain't see"—from before sunrise until after sunset, when the vibrant hues of green-stemmed white cotton, rooted in red-brown dirt, faded to gray. Another day of scorching heat and salty sweat burning in the cracks of dry, calloused hands and bare feet. Another day of fearing the lash if they picked less than the quota, about two hundred pounds for a full-grown man.

But the inhabitants of the cabin where eight-year-old Felix lived with his parents—Elmira, the big-house cook, and Plessant, the master's valet—were already stirring in the dark. Although they enjoyed some privileges as enslaved house servants, they, like the field hands, were listed as property in the plantation's ledgers, along with the furniture, the house, the barn and the other outbuildings, the livestock, and the tools. And, like the field hands, they lived in terror of being sold away from each other at any moment. Elmira and Plessant had already lost their two older children, John, age fifteen, and Bessie, age thirteen—recently sold to a Mississippi planter, like a litter of hound dog pups.

One day, they had three children, and the next day they were left with one. The pain of the loss coursed through Elmira's soul. *What did I do to make God so mad? I didn't do nothin' to make Him do that to me*, she thought as she trudged toward the big-house kitchen, with Plessant walking beside her, carrying Felix. Tears welled up in her eyes, and a spasm shot through her gut as her mind replayed the image of her babies, chained together in the back of a wagon, disappearing down the long road away from home, away from her. Forever.

Plessant studied her in the pale predawn light. He knew what she was thinking, what she was feeling; his head hurt and his chest was tight from the stress of knowing there was nothing he could do.

"Gon' be a nasty mornin'," Elmira said. "Hope it don't rain." She could feel Plessant sliding into a dark, dangerous place, and she needed to pull him back. She ran her hand down his spine and felt his muscles twitch as he shifted the weight of Felix, asleep and draped over his left shoulder like a fifty-pound sack of flour.

"Ain't gon' rain, not today," Plessant replied.

"You just know it all, don't you?" she said.

Plessant winked at her and laughed quietly, and so did she.

They had reached the back door of the house, and from the chicken coop across the yard, a rooster crowed once and then a second time. "That old boy better shut up, or he gon' find hisself in my pot," Elmira whispered. "Massa been sayin' he want some chicken soup."

Barely 4:30, and it was time to go to work. Plessant began by laying out the master's clothes for the day, shining his boots, and stropping the straight razor in case he wanted a shave. He filled the master's engraved sterling silver pocket flask from the basement cask of applejack and set it on the bureau next to the master's pocketknife and his loaded derringer, pearl-handled with a bluesteel double barrel, imported from England before the war.

Plessant pulled a clean white linen handkerchief from a bureau drawer and placed it next to the freshly laundered socks. He took two cigars from the cedar-lined box and inserted them into a leather carrier, worn smooth and soft by daily use, and added it to the other objects already arranged on top of the bureau.

In the kitchen, Elmira awakened Felix and situated him on a short stool in a corner and began her daily tasks. There were fires to build; milk, butter, and eggs to retrieve from the springhouse; biscuits to roll out and bake; grits to boil; and ham to fry. Coffee was hard to come by in the wartime South, and the Parkers saved the little they had for company or special occasions. So, Elmira made a brew of roasted chicory. *At least it's brown*, she thought. She considered opening a jar of the good plum jam she'd put up last summer. At a quarter of six, Callie Mae, the maid, joined her in setting the table in the family's dining room. Breakfast was at 6:30 sharp, and they had no time to waste.

Felix sat on his stool, watching his mother move quickly and efficiently through the preparations for a big breakfast for the planter's family. There was the owner, John Robert Parker; the owner's wife, Marie Louise Beaulieu Parker; and their three children: Jean Louis, age eighteen; Claude, age fifteen; and Adelaide, called Addie. At nine years old, she was the closest in age to Felix.

When they were all assembled and seated in the dining room, the workday began for Felix. He picked up his stool, carried it into the dining room, and after saying a bright "Good morning" to the family, he set it behind Addie's chair and sat, waiting.

The aromas of breakfast filled the room—fried ham, a platter of steaming soft-scrambled eggs, and a bowl of hot grits with a dollop of yellow butter melting in its center. Elmira's plum jam in a crystal bowl lay next to a platter of golden-brown biscuits still warm from the oven.

For reasons known only to her, it pleased Addie to have Felix nearby at breakfast, like a beloved pet, and she fed him fragments of ham and egg and biscuit from her fingers. In return, he gave her grimaces that she interpreted as smiles of gratitude. The rest of the family had long since stopped trying to break Addie of her peculiar behavior, which she began when Felix was three years old and little more than a toddler.

"Maw, how come Miss Addie make me sit on that stool and eat out her hand like a dog?" Felix had asked. Elmira shook her head and replied, "They's somethin' odd 'bout that girl. Just let her do what she gon' do and let it go."

John Robert gave thanks for the meal in a brief prayer that reminded the family of their good fortune in living in an area that had escaped the worst fighting of the war and thus the hardships and privations that left many other Southern families' tables bare. Then, they dove in, eating with gusto, and John Robert declared yet again to his wife, "Marie Louise, that's the best cooking in Alabama. If I'd known you were going to bring Elmira with you from New Orleans, I'd have married you even sooner," and then they all laughed—as usual. And so the day began. The children headed off to their studies with the tutor John Robert had hired from Mobile to teach them history, mathematics, literature, Latin, and French, while Marie Louise picked up her needlepoint and reading. Later, she would direct Callie Mae on house-cleaning matters and discuss dinner and supper menus with Elmira. On most days John Robert disappeared into his study to review the plantation accounts. Some days he went into town to meet with his lawyers or his banker.

He had a lot to manage. Road's End was among the area's larger plantations, with 1,100 acres, about five hundred under cultivation, mostly cotton and corn as cash crops, and smaller plots set aside to grow collards, turnips, tomatoes, potatoes, yams, apples, plums, pears, pecans, and hickory nuts for household use. A few acres were reserved for pasture, but most of the remaining land was allowed to remain in its natural forested state. The Parkers hunted small game there and periodically harvested lumber. Buildings on the property included the main plantation house, a row of cabins where about fifty enslaved people lived, two barns for horses and cows, a chicken coop, a pigsty, a blacksmith shop, a carpentry shop, a smokehouse, and a springhouse.

After breakfast, Felix began his other duties, emptying the family's chamber pots from the night before, bringing fresh water and firewood into the kitchen, feeding the chickens, cleaning the coop, and gathering eggs when the hens were laying. This morning was different, however.

"Elmira," John Robert called into the kitchen.

"Yassuh?" Elmira responded, wiping her hands on a towel as she entered the dining room.

"I'm going into town this morning to take care of some business, and I'm taking Felix with me. You get him ready," he said.

Lightning struck the bridge of her nose. Cymbals clashed in her ears. Elmira's vision blurred, and for a moment it felt as though the floor had tilted at a crazy angle and she thought she might wet her drawers.

Her breath was coming quickly, her throat was dry, and her voice croaked when she spoke. "What you need him for, Massa? He too young to do anything for you. He just be in the way."

"Well now, that's none of your business, is it, Elmira?" he said. "You just get him ready. We'll be leaving as soon as Plessant brings the wagon around."

"Yassuh," she said, and went to find Felix to wash his face and hands.

Twenty minutes later, Elmira and Plessant stood by the side of the house watching the wagon disappear down the long road, their child in the back, away from home without them for the first time, not knowing if they would ever see him again. That old rooster crowed again, this time with the sun high in the sky. It was not a good sign.

Chapter 3

John Robert Parker had awakened that morning feeling as if the entire army of the Confederate States of America was marching through his brain, screaming rebel yells and firing muskets as drummer boys beat out the cadence every step of the way. His mouth was dry, and he could smell his own bad breath and the odor of sweat rising from his damp, wrinkled nightshirt. He sat up in bed and turned to watch Marie Louise lying next to him, still sleeping, her dark brown hair spread around her face on the pillow.

At thirty-seven, she was still the brunette beauty he had seen for the first time twenty years earlier, when she was studying at Hunt College, the women's college in Red Clay, and he was one of the county's most eligible young bachelors. Hunt drew students from prominent families throughout the South, and as a physician's daughter from New Orleans, Marie Louise Beaulieu had been a prime example. She was a tall, willowy Creole girl with hazel eyes that reflected her intelligence and did not hide her impatience with idiots and fools. Gazing at her now, he nearly lost his resolve to follow through on the decision that had kept him awake most of the night.

In his dressing room off the master bedroom, John Robert could hear Plessant quietly moving about. Plessant had been born on the plantation when John Robert was twelve, and his father had given Plessant to him as a birthday present.

"Thank you, Daddy, but what am I supposed to do with him?" John Robert had asked, staring down at the brown baby nursing in a corner of the kitchen.

"That's not the point, son," his father said, guiding John Robert out of the kitchen and into the parlor. He scanned the room to be sure they were alone and lowered his voice to a whisper. "The point is, that pickaninny, along with the ten-acre plot I deeded over to you last year, makes you a man of property," he said. "That's important, John Robert. A man without property is hardly better than a nigger. Truth be told, which they should never hear from you, the only thing that separates white trash from the niggers is the color of their skin, and what separates us from the white trash is that *we* are gentlemen, men of property."

"Yes sir," John Robert said. "Thank you, sir." He watched his father walk out of the room and then returned to the book he had been reading.

The fact was that he cared nothing about the enslaved workers or any of the rest of his father's property, except that their financial value would make it possible for him to go to Princeton University when he was older, like the scions of other Southern plantation families. But unlike so many of those other young men who returned to plantation society after graduation, John Robert planned to study the law and to open a practice in one of the big cities on the East Coast—New York, or maybe Boston—and never return to Red Clay, Alabama.

Yet here he was, heading a great plantation, the father of three, and a man with nearly godlike power over the lives of fifty men, women, and children whose black skin doomed them to lives of hard labor, interrupted by dark explosions of brutal pain and suffering made bearable only by faith. Some of them believed in the Christian God into whose arms they would be delivered after death, while others clung to legends that said when life became intolerable, Black people could gather together in a field, lift their arms into the air, rise into the sky, and fly home to Africa.

John Robert was here because the old man had died in an accident

two years into his time at Princeton. His father was being driven home
from town in his buggy when a possum fell from a tree and landed on
the horse's back. The horse spooked and ran off the road into the woods,
upsetting the buggy. The driver landed in a ditch, and the old man was
slammed into the trunk of a tree. The enslaved driver's right leg was
crushed and had to be amputated, but the old man's neck was broken
and he had died instantly.

John Robert was nineteen at the time, an only child, and he'd had
no other choice than to return home to assume his role as a man of
property and to care for his mother. It was his duty.

Now forty-three, John Robert reflected on the course his life had
taken as he drove down the long road from the house, the horse strutting and snorting in the cool mid-September morning air. Behind him
in the wagon, Felix was scared out of his wits but also strangely excited.
The plantation was all he knew, and except for church some Sunday
mornings, he didn't know what to expect of the wider world. Maw and
Paw hugged him before lifting him into the wagon, and he could see
that his mother had been crying.

They drove for about an hour. Felix saw stands of towering pines
and live oaks and chinaberry trees, and he listened to crows cawing and
robins calling out to each other and blue jays chattering. He wasn't afraid
any longer—he was entranced by the unfamiliar scenery—but he was
growing concerned about their destination.

They drove on for another hour before John Robert pulled the
wagon over to the side of the road, under the green canopy that covered the road fifty feet up.

"We'll take a little rest here," John Robert said. "You want some
water?" He handed the boy a tin cup into which he poured cool water
from a jug.

"Yassuh, thank you," Felix said as he accepted the cup.

For himself, John Robert reached into his pocket for the flask Plessant had filled that morning. He took a swig, recapped it, and leaned
against the seat, his head back and his eyes closed. A painter would
have been taken with the profile he presented: the dark hair swept back

past his ears, the finely sculpted nose and the high cheekbones, the jaw cleanly shaven that morning, and a droopy mustache with long ends that fell back into the same plane as the hair on his head.

"Felix, do you know there's a war going on between the folks up North and us down here?" John Robert asked.

"Yassuh, I heard they's fightin', but I don't know nothin' about it," he said.

"Well, there's a big war going on; it's been going on for half your life, and you know what? I think it's going to end soon and that we are going to lose, and that a lot will change if we do. Do you know what the biggest change will be?" said John Robert. "The slaves will be free. You won't have to work for us. You can come and go wherever you want."

Felix listened and thought carefully before speaking. "If the slaves be free, Maw don't have to cook for you?"

"That's right," John Robert replied.

"And Paw don't have to take care of you?" he asked.

"Yes, that's true," John Robert said.

"And I don't have to eat out Miss Addie's hand?" Felix asked.

John Robert threw his head back and laughed before answering. "Yes," he said. "You wouldn't have to let her feed you." John Robert shifted in his seat, and the expression on his face turned serious. "I want you to know something, Felix," he said. "I feel badly that I had to sell your brother and sister, and I want you to tell your folks that."

"Yassuh," Felix said, not knowing what to make of the master's comments.

They sat for a while before John Robert spoke again. "I'm going to tell you a story," he said, "and you must promise to remember every word. It's very important that you remember everything I say to you, every word. Can you do that?"

"Yassuh," Felix said, terrified now by the uncertainty of what was happening.

Midday sunlight filtered down through the green canopy as John Robert talked. His voice was controlled, and he stopped often to confirm that Felix had understood and could recall what had been said to him. This went on for nearly an hour, and when he was finished, there was great sadness in his eyes, the flask was empty, and the breeze that had cooled the morning air was still blowing. "This is a good day," John Robert said and lifted his face toward the sky as a flight of geese passed overhead.

———

The Parker household had retired for the evening when the wagon trundled down the road to the big house at Road's End Plantation. John Robert's big black stallion had pulled the wagon into the yard in front of the big house with a barely conscious eight-year-old Felix in the back and the master up front, slumped over dead with a bullet hole in his chest. There was so much blood. It stained the front of John Robert's white shirt, pooled on the floorboards beneath him, and had splattered across the front of Felix's shirt and on his face.

The racket from the horse's hooves and the creaking of the buggy awakened Callie Mae, who was still tying the belt of her robe as she burst onto the front porch and was confronted by the grisly scene. "Oh, my Lawd!" she shrieked, and she kept repeating it until Marie Louise came up behind her and collapsed when she saw her husband's body.

The children arrived on the porch. "*Maman, Maman*, what's wrong with Papa? Why is he all bloody?" Addie whimpered. Claude grabbed her and dragged her back into the house. Jean Louis knelt beside their mother and pulled her head onto his lap. He was pale, and his eyes were glazed. He said nothing, but he rocked backward and forward as he stroked Marie Louise's hair. She was mumbling, but all he could make out was his father's name, over and over: "John Robert, John Robert, John Robert."

Danny, the stable boy, appeared around the corner of the house. "Go get Elmira and Plessant," Callie Mae yelled, and he set off running toward the slave quarters.

Felix was vaguely aware of the raised voices around him and of the flickering lantern light. He felt himself being scooped up and held tightly by his father, and he could hear his mother crying.

Marie Louise was regaining her composure and was leaning on her son's shoulder as she stood shakily. Through the parlor window, she could see Claude and Addie huddled together on one end of the settee. She was nauseous, her head ached, and the light breeze felt like sandpaper against her skin. Through her shock, Marie Louise heard herself giving orders:

"Elmira, take your boy home, and you bring him up here as soon as he wakes up in the morning. Don't worry about cooking; you just get him up here so he can talk.

"Plessant, you help me get my husband's body into the house and upstairs.

"Danny, you put the horse and the buggy away.

"Jean Louis, you take the other children upstairs and see to it that they get to bed. Then, you take a horse and ride to the sheriff's house. Wake him up if you have to, and tell him I expect to see him here first thing."

———

The sun rose the next day in an uncertain sky, at turns overcast and brilliant when the winds pushed the gray, low-hanging clouds off to the east. It was a Tuesday, and the business of the plantation proceeded as if nothing had happened. Cotton was being picked, livestock were being tended, and iron was being hammered in the blacksmith shop. Fences were being mended, and a hundred other tasks were being performed by an army of slaves for whom life was a railroad line with just two stops: the one where you got on and the one where you got off. In between, for most enslaved people, there was just waiting, waiting for relief in the arms of sweet death and the embrace of those who had already made the journey.

And yet it was not really like any other day. At Road's End, nothing would ever be the same again.

Felix had been bathed, and he was wearing clean clothes as he walked up to the house between Elmira and Plessant. Callie Mae met them in the kitchen. "Y'all s'posed to go in the parlor. They waitin' for you," she said, and she squeezed Elmira's arm as she passed by.

They were all there—Marie Louise, Addie, Jean Louis, and Claude, and three men Felix did not recognize. One, he would learn, was the sheriff, the second was his deputy, and the third was a deacon from the church.

"Callie Mae," Marie Louise called out. "Bring that stool from the kitchen in here."

Callie Mae came into the room with Felix's stool, the one on which he sat each morning as Miss Addie's breakfast pet. "Set it down here," Marie Louise said, indicating a space in the center of the room that faced the sofa and easy chairs on which she and the others were sitting. "Elmira, you go back in the kitchen and prepare some refreshments for these gentlemen, and Plessant, you go out and make yourself useful. I'm sure you can find something to do."

Felix's parents had been standing against the wall, trying to disappear, hoping that no one would pay attention to them, but now they had no choice; they had to go, and Elmira shot what she hoped was a smile of reassurance to Felix before they left the room.

For the next hour, Felix repeated the story John Robert had drilled into him before he turned his back, pulled the pearl-handled derringer from his coat, and shot himself through the heart, killing himself and sending Felix into shock.

"Tell it to us again, boy," the sheriff said, and Felix obliged, concentrating hard to make sure he got it right.

"We was just ridin' down the road. I ain't exactly sure where we was, but there was lots of trees on the side of the road, and there was a big ol' pond near to the roadside. Massa say he hot and he pull the wagon over under a big tree. He give me some water in a tin cup and he take a drink out the silver bottle he carry in his pocket.

"He say this a mighty fine day and that he wisht he was goin' fishin' 'stead of havin' to take care of business. Right then, these white mens come runnin' up out the trees and they jump up on the wagon and point they guns at Massa."

The sheriff interrupted. "What did they look like? What kind of clothes were they wearing?"

"It's like I tol' you before," Felix said. "They was just reg'lar lookin' white mens, not too old, younger than him." He pointed at the deacon, a man of about forty. "One of them had brown hair, and other one had yellow hair like Massa Claude, and he had a beard," Felix continued. "They was kinda dirty, and they didn't smell too good.

"They made Massa give them his money, and when they was gettin' ready to jump off the wagon, Massa pull out his gun and shot at them, but he missed. Then them mens turned 'round and took Massa's gun and shot him with it. That one with the yellow hair, he put it right on Massa's chest and shot him.

"Then they look at me, and one of them say, 'We got to shoot him too,' and the other one say he ain't gon' do it. He say he cain't shoot no child, not even a nigger. Then they left."

"Sheriff, you don't reckon the boy done it himself?" the deputy whispered. "He coulda caught Mr. Parker unawares and got the gun somehow."

The sheriff stared at the small, trembling boy in front of him. "No, it don't seem likely," he replied after a long pause.

"But Sheriff—" the deputy protested.

"Deputy, you got a way to prove what you're saying?" the sheriff asked. "There ain't no weapon, there ain't no witnesses, and we ain't exactly sure of where it happened. Maybe this little nigger got ahold of Mr. Parker's gun and killed him, but it doesn't seem likely to me."

The deputy was silent.

"Well," the sheriff said, raising his voice to address everyone in the room. "I guess that's it. We've had the boy tell us what happened five times, and I don't see any inconsistencies in his story, and in the absence of any other witnesses I think we have to take his word. Besides, we've been getting reports about army deserters in the area, and my guess is that these two fellows are probably on the run."

The deacon stood up to go. "I think you know, Mrs. Parker, that the church will do all it can for you and your family in this terrible time," he said, and then he left with the sheriff and the deputy.

Marie Louise watched them go before turning her attention to her children. The boys were stone-faced, and she couldn't imagine what they were thinking or feeling. Addie's face was a mystery too, and Marie Louise couldn't tell if she was going to laugh or cry. "I think you should all go to your rooms and rest, and when it's time for dinner, I'll call you," she said to them. "We have some difficult days ahead of us, and it will be better if you are rested."

They got up to leave, the boys first and then Addie, who paused at the door and turned to Felix, still sitting on his stool. She gave him a long, questioning gaze, scrutinizing his face, which betrayed nothing, and then she pivoted and went out the door.

Marie Louise realized at that moment that Felix was still there. "Thank you," she said. "You can go now and find your mama."

"Yassum," Felix said and stood up. "But I got to tell you somethin' first."

Marie Louise nodded and told him to sit down again.

"Before he died, Massa told me to tell you somethin' that wasn't for nobody else to hear."

"Yes, what is it?" Marie Louise said.

"He was layin' there, and his chest was goin' up and down, like he couldn't breathe, and he say, 'You tell my wife she s'posed to go in my study and look for Sis Arrow.' He say it real important and don't tell nobody else but you, and then he died," Felix said.

"Sis Arrow," she repeated. "Is that all he said? What is Sis Arrow?"

Later that day, in the gathering shadows of dusk, Marie Louise forced herself to go into John Robert's study. He had loved this room, the walls lined with books—history, philosophy, astronomy, biology, literature, and the law—some in their original languages, Greek, Latin, and French. He had been a scholar at heart, and she knew that the plans he'd had for his life had not included returning from Princeton to be a planter. But she also knew that he was a man of honor, and that under the circumstances he could not have taken any other course.

She sat in the big leather chair at his desk, a massive thing crafted from solid mahogany imported from the Caribbean, and ran her fingers across its smooth surface. Lying on the blotter in the center of the desk was the last book he had been reading, a collection of works by Cicero. A bell rang in the back of her mind: not Sis Arrow, but *Cicero*. She picked it up, riffled the pages, and an envelope addressed to her fell onto the desk.

She regarded it for several long minutes, summoning the courage to open it. When she did, she found a letter inside and some official-looking documents. She put the documents aside, unfolded the letter, and started to read:

> *My Sweet Marie Louise,*
>
> *You are reading this because I am dead, and my dearest hopes are that you will know how much I have loved you and that you will understand and appreciate the circumstances of my demise . . .*

Marie Louise trembled, and her breath came in short gasps as tears rolled down her cheeks. She felt herself swept away to a place neither hot nor cold, dark nor light, wet nor dry, and where all she knew and understood about the world dissolved into a gray whirlwind that swirled about her. Good and evil lived side by side in this place, bound together in an eternal struggle that neither could ever win.

Down in the slave quarters, Plessant and Elmira had already fallen asleep. In the darkness, Felix, too excited by the events of the past two days to sleep, crawled out of bed and tiptoed across the room to the fireplace, removed a loose stone from the hearth, and reached into the space to retrieve his newest possession. Then he crept outside to examine it in the light of the waning moon. It was a pearl-handled derringer with a bluesteel double barrel, imported from England before the start of the war.

Chapter 4

Marie Louise, still alone in the big leather chair behind the desk in her late husband's study, reeled from the opening lines of John Robert's letter. The sun had set, and a velvety warm early-fall darkness shrouded the land, seeped through the windows, and wrapped itself around her heart. She seemed to hear everything—the shuffling of feet on the stairs, the sounds of her children's voices, the clatter of dishes, and the clanging of pots and pans being washed, dried, and put away in the kitchen. She could hear the horses neighing in the stables and the cows lowing in the barn. In the creek, fish rose to suck down insects that touched the surface of the water, chased there by whirling, darting bats whose silent, leathery wings roiled the air and made invisible waves that Marie Louise felt as whispers in her ears.

She opened the desk drawer, found matches, and lit the kerosene lamp on the corner of the desk. Then, in its dim light, she walked across the room to John Robert's liquor cabinet and poured a snifter of cognac from a crystal decanter. She took it back to the desk and sat down to resume reading the letter she had found tucked between the pages of Cicero's collected writings:

If all has gone as I have planned, you will already have heard a story from Felix about my death. It is not the way it actually happened, but rather the way I wanted the story to be told for reasons that will be apparent as you continue reading. I am not proud of this, but it is what I had to do to protect you and the children from the storm I fear is coming.

As you know, I had hoped as a young man to pursue the law and to set up practice in one of the big cities in the North. But alas, the necessity of my return to Red Clay to attend to my late father's affairs interrupted that plan. I cannot complain, however, as returning to Red Clay brought you into my life, and I shall be forever grateful to God for the warmth and affection you have showered upon me and the divine gift of our beautiful children.

Through the years I have been content, made all the more so by my poor attempts at scholarship. I have spent so many happy evenings in my study, surrounded by history's great philosophers. Oh, the debates I have had with Plato, Aristotle, and Empedocles! I have wrestled and argued with them, sometimes late into the evening when sensible men, especially those blessed with wives such as yourself, have long since taken happily to their beds.

In my correspondence with my mentor at Princeton, Professor Meredith, I shared my essays and other writings, and he, in turn, unbeknownst to me, shared them with his colleagues. I was surprised and delighted when I received a letter inviting me to join the faculty there to teach literature and philosophy should I ever decide to give up plantation life. Marie Louise, you cannot imagine the joy this gave me. It was as if the rapture had come, and I was being swept up into heaven.

But then I was brought back down to Earth. How could I walk away from all my responsibilities here? How would you and the children feel about moving up North, and would you miss the plantation life? And even if you agreed to go, how would we live comfortably on the compensation the university would settle on me? I set my mind to solving these puzzles, and the conclusion I reached was that I would have to first remove any financial obstacles. I believed that if we had no concerns about money, we might discuss the other matters more freely.

This was the beginning of my undoing. I focused all my attention on how to enhance our financial situation. It will come as no surprise to you that our greatest assets are the land and the slaves, and so I determined that if we had more of both, we could increase our wealth. When the time came, we could sell those assets, invest the proceeds, and live quite comfortably on the income, or so I thought. You will recall that I began to buy more land, purchase more slaves, and put more acreage under cultivation. The plan seemed flawless. There was plenty of land for sale, and new slaves were easy to acquire. All one needed was cash, but I solved that problem easily by borrowing against our existing assets.

For the first two years the plan worked splendidly. We had good crops, prices were high, and I was able to support our expenses, make payments toward the debt, and even save considerable sums. All was perfect—until it all went wrong. We had two years of poor crop production, and cotton prices started to slip when buyers grew anxious about the possibility of war.

Then, of course, the war began, the economy was devastated, and Confederate money of dubious value began to circulate in place of American currency. We kept up appearances, but it became increasingly difficult to meet all our expenses. By last year, we were in desperate circumstances, even though I have done my best to shield you—and others—from that disturbing knowledge. I began to sell slaves and borrowed more money. Before long, my position had become untenable. I was on the verge of ruin, and I did not know where to turn.

Marie Louise put down the letter, leaned back into the soft leather of the chair, and closed her eyes. *Such pain*, she thought. *Such desperation and fear.* She could feel it all rising from the words on the page, and her grief deepened, compounded by anger that he had not told her, had not allowed her to stand with him against the tide that threatened to topple them and drag them into the depths.

Just then she thought she heard something outside the door. She listened, but she didn't hear another sound. *It's probably Callie Mae shutting down the house for the night,* she thought, and resumed her reading of John Robert's letter.

So many nights I lay awake next to you, my mind skipping from one idea to another about how to retrieve our fortunes from the hole into which I had allowed them to fall. And then I had it. The way out was clear but fraught, and with a single misstep all would be lost. Yet I saw no other way, and I was determined to pursue the course that opened before me.

I had concluded long ago that the war was lost, that the South would go down in defeat, and that, in the end, boys like our Jean Louis and Claude would be sacrificed to no avail in a last desperate effort to repel the Union. It was obvious to me that the way of life here would end and that an economy built on slave labor could not be sustained. I feared that Confederate currency would be worthless and that plantations such as ours would go to ruin and us along with them.

Thus, I took what gold we still had, and through an old school friend up North, was able to purchase life insurance worth nearly $200,000 in Union money from the Beneficial Life Insurance Company of Newark, New Jersey. It is one of the finest such companies, and you can rest assured that when you present the policy, along with the facts that have been given to you and to the authorities, the proceeds shall come to you without delay. The policy is one of the documents accompanying this letter.

Perhaps you have now surmised that there were no villains who attacked me on the side of the road and that I have taken my own life, a fact known only to you and to Felix, a fact that both of you must take to your graves. You can understand now why it was so important for the story of my death to be told to the

authorities by a child whose word would be difficult to dispute
in the absence of other witnesses. To meet the requirements of the
policy and to protect our family's name and honor, it must never
be known that I have shamed myself in suicide. If God is truly
forgiving, I pray He will understand that what I have done was
out of love and that His arms will be open to me in merciful
embrace.

Marie Louise drained the rest of the cognac from the snifter. She did
not know what to feel or what to think. Indeed, it was all she could do
to retain her balance and to remain sitting in the chair. She rotated the
empty glass between her palms, once, twice, and on the third turn she
lifted it above her head and hurled it against the wall across the room.
She wanted to be angry with John Robert, to curse his name for leaving her this way, and yet she could feel only sorrow—deep, agonizing
wretchedness that she knew would remain with her forever.

She was committed now, an unwilling co-conspirator in a scheme
not of her making, and she could see that there was no way out but to
go forward. She began to read again.

My dear Marie Louise, there are other steps you must also take,
and you must take them quickly, as I believe the war is drawing
to an end, and with its conclusion everything will change. You
must have our attorneys contact Mr. George Flowers of Starkville,
Mississippi, immediately. He is a planter there, and you might
remember him as the man who bought a number of slaves
from us, including most recently Elmira's two children. He has
repeatedly expressed his interest in acquiring Road's End and has
a standing offer on file with the attorneys. The proceeds from
the sale would cover our debts with a considerable sum left over.
Those monies, added to the proceeds from the insurance policy,
carefully invested once the war is over, will leave you and the
children in fine condition to live as you are accustomed, though
absent the responsibilities of a plantation. My will, deeds, and

*the other documents you will need are in the envelope along with
this letter and the aforementioned insurance policy.*

*Some final things, my dear Marie Louise. We owe Felix
a great debt. He is only eight years old, but I have asked him
to shoulder a great responsibility, and I am assuming that he
has performed as required. I have also inflicted great pain on
his family by selling their children. Can you imagine, Marie
Louise, if our Jean Louis, or Claude or Addie, were suddenly
taken away? Some say these Africans have no souls and that the
Almighty intended for them to be at our service. Now, as I face
my own mortality, I must say that I cannot be sure. I know only
that they surely feel pain, and that I do not wish to cause them
more. Therefore, I ask one more thing of you. When you visit the
attorneys regarding the sale of Road's End, please also arrange for
the ten-acre plot given to me as a boy to be deeded to Plessant,
Elmira, and Felix when the war ends and if the slaves are freed.
I desperately wish for this to happen, and I trust that you will
honor my request.*

*That is all I can think of to say, Marie Louise, except to tell
you again that I love you and to ask for your forgiveness.*

*Your loving husband,
John Robert Parker
14th September 1864*

Marie Louise sat for a long time, not moving and barely breathing.
Then she folded the papers, reinserted them into the envelope, slid them
into the desk drawer, and closed it.

When Callie Mae found her the next morning, Marie Louise was
asleep in the chair, her head resting on her arms folded across the desk. The
lamp was still burning, drawing the last drops of kerosene into the wick.

Chapter 5

Adelaide Parker was an unusual child. She had walked at ten months old, and not with the tipsy stagger of other toddlers. Rather, she strode across the room from her mother to her father with the steadiness and confidence of a three-year-old. She had learned to read at age four, and by age six she was at ease sitting with her mother and the ladies from the church who visited for afternoon tea, chatting comfortably about local affairs and listening discreetly when the conversation turned to gossip, even the racy bits. "I've given up on trying to control what she hears," Marie Louise would say with a sigh. "Sometimes I think an eighty-year-old woman hides behind that child's face."

Addie loved walking across the plantation with her father. He would tell her the names of trees, flowers, birds, and other small animals, and he would tell her stories about the Choctaw tribe, who lived there before her grandfather acquired the land and built Road's End. John Robert even knew the Choctaw names for the arrowheads, pottery shards, and other artifacts they found and taught them to Addie.

Sometimes, John Robert would allow Addie to sit with him in his study in the evening before bed to read Peter Parley books for children while he worked on his essays or made notes based on his studies of philosophy and literature. They would sit that way happily until Marie

Louise came to take the child away to bed, and even after she was tucked in for the night, Addie would lie awake to listen for the sound of her father coming up the stairs and to catch the scent of his cigars and cognac as he peeked inside her room before continuing down the hall. Then she would fall asleep, wrapped in the soft darkness of the Alabama night.

Addie also had traits that others found unsettling. She had a way of appearing suddenly in a room, as if she had materialized without walking through the door, and the intensity of her eye contact disturbed adults when she engaged them in conversation. Addie would often become fascinated by something or someone for a period of time and could not be distracted from the object of her obsession.

Once, when she was six years old, she decided that the breakfast sausage had to be cooked before the breakfast bacon and never the other way around, and so for a month she would slip into the kitchen to watch Elmira cook, just to be sure she never deviated from that pattern. On one of her morning missions, Addie noticed a small Black boy sitting on a stool in the corner. "Who is that?" she asked Elmira, pointing in the direction of the boy.

"That my boy Felix, Miss Addie," Elmira replied. "Massa John Robert say it all right I bring him with me. He just be quiet in the corner and don't be in the way."

For the next week Addie observed Felix and peppered Elmira with questions: "Can he talk? How old is he? What does he eat? What can he do?" For the moment, the breakfast meat schedule had been forgotten.

The next Monday morning, when the family arrived for breakfast, they found Addie already in her seat at the table and five-year-old Felix sitting on his stool behind her chair. "This is Felix, Elmira's boy, and he is going to sit here while I have breakfast," she announced. Marie Louise opened her mouth to object and thought better of it, assuming that, like all of Addie's fancies, this one would end in due time. Three years later, however, Felix was still reporting for duty each morning to be fed scraps from the table by Addie, and the family had long since stopped questioning it, if only because they had learned there was no satisfying answer. It was just something Addie did, and there would be no telling her not to.

For his part, Felix had learned to recede into the background, and because no one could see him, he heard things, though there was not much an eight-year-old could do with the information he acquired, even those parts he understood.

"What they talk about in there?" Plessant once asked his son. It was the Sunday afternoon before John Robert's death, a pause in the otherwise unrelenting drudgery, when the Road's End enslaved people were allowed to rest. A few received passes to attend services at First Baptist Church in Red Clay, where balcony seats above the sanctuary were available to them, accessed by a stairway on the outside of the building to preclude them from entering the building through the front door with the white worshippers. On this particular Sunday, Plessant had taken Felix down to the creek that ran through the plantation, where they used homemade tackle to angle for catfish and bream to fry for supper.

"This mornin' they was talkin' 'bout the war," Felix said in reply to his father's question. "Massa say they's gon' be Yankees marchin' through town and won't nobody be able to stop 'em."

"When he say it gon' happen?" Plessant asked.

"He don't know; he just say he think it gon' happen soon," Felix said.

Just then Plessant's pole bent over, and he yanked a fat catfish out of the water and onto the bank. "That's a good 'un, Paw," Felix yelled.

"Yeah, we gon' eat good tonight," Plessant said, a smile on his face, already imagining the way Elmira would fry that big fish and make hot water cornbread, collard greens, and sweet potatoes from her little garden in back of their cabin to go with it. Plessant removed the hook and strung the catfish on a line with a mess of bream they'd already caught and lowered it back into the creek to keep the fish alive until they were ready to head for home. He threaded another worm onto his hook and dropped it into the water. He jiggled it a few times, and then his mood turned serious. "Felix, they's one thing you got to remember," he said. "Don't never tell nobody what you hear the white folks talkin' about 'cept me and your maw. Nobody. You got that, boy? Nobody. You tell anybody, an' it ain't no tellin' what happen to us."

"Yassuh, Paw, yassuh," Felix replied. "I know what to do."

Plessant looked at his boy and saw something he'd never seen before: a man's eyes looking back at him. He smiled and stroked his son's cheek. "Yeah, boy, I believe you do," Plessant said, the pride he felt twisted by anger that his son's youth had already been stolen.

—————

Relaxing on the bank of the creek on that September Sunday afternoon, a breeze blowing through the leaves of the live oak trees high above them, carrying only the faintest hint that summer was poised to give way to fall, neither Plessant nor Felix could imagine the ways in which their lives would soon be irrevocably changed.

Neither could imagine that the next day the master of the plantation would be dead and that Felix would be burdened with a secret so powerful that revealing it would bring one of Alabama's most prominent families to ruin. Indeed, if the secret of John Robert's suicide was ever disclosed, the lives of Felix, Plessant, and Elmira could also be in jeopardy.

Felix had managed to carry out his part of the plot on Tuesday morning. The mistress, the sheriff, and the deacon had believed his telling of the story, just as Massa John Robert had made him learn it. But now he was lying in his bed, a straw-filled pallet on the floor, listening to night sounds: an owl hooting, field mice scurrying across the roof, and, from somewhere down the row of cabins, a home-brew-fueled argument between two men over a woman they both wanted. In the next room of the two-room cabin, Elmira and Plessant were sleeping, and he could hear his father snoring lightly, punctuated by an occasional snort.

The shock of what Felix had witnessed on the wagon beside the road had worn off, but he remained anxious and frightened and unable to sleep. "I ain't gon' ask you what happened," Plessant had said to him, "but you remember what I told you when we was fishin'; don't never tell nobody about white folks' business. You decide you want to tell somebody, you tell me or you tell your maw. Nobody else."

Felix crawled out of bed and padded across the rough, unpolished wood floor to the fireplace that dominated the room. Elmira cooked in it, and in winter it provided the cabin's only heat. He listened again to be sure his parents were still sleeping, and when he heard their heavy breathing, he pried the loose stone from the raised hearth, reached into the space, and pulled out the pistol John Robert had used to shoot himself. The pearl handle reflected the light of the near-full moon that filtered through gaps between the window shutters, and Felix was surprised again by how heavy the little derringer felt in his hands. So small, and yet so deadly.

"You take this gun when I am gone, and you hide it where no one can find it," John Robert had said before turning his back and pulling the trigger.

The report had not been loud, more of a crack than a boom. The birds in the canopy above the road had hardly stirred. The gun was still dangling from John Robert's right hand, and Felix was afraid to touch the body, afraid that by touching John Robert's dead hand he would be marked for a ghostly visitation. He had heard plenty of stories from the old folks about the strange ways of "haints," and he didn't want to take any chances. He jumped down from the wagon, found a stick, and used it to pry the tiny gun loose before picking it up and stuffing it into his pocket. The matter of the gun settled, Felix snapped John Robert's buggy whip over the horse's head to start it moving before a wave of nausea swept over him and everything went dark.

The memory was still fresh in Felix's mind as he walked out of the cabin onto the porch and sat down on the top step. Then, staring into the darkness, he cried like the eight-year-old boy he was. What would happen to him, and could his life ever be the same again? The answer came on the wind that blew through the treetops. No, the breeze whispered, no, and Felix cried some more.

———

Up at the big house, Addie had awakened in the darkness of her second-floor bedroom, confused about why she felt so ill at ease until she remembered that her father had died, and that despite the story Felix had told, something seemed off, like a jigsaw puzzle piece that appears to fit in an empty space even though it's not the right one. Her mind raced through questions for which she had no answers: Where had her father been going that morning? Who was he going to meet? Had he been in pain? Had Papa thought of her as he lay dying?

And there was one more question: Why had he taken Felix with him? The sheriff had asked the question, too, and Felix's reply, over and over, was, "I don't know. Massa just take me in the wagon and go."

It was quiet throughout the house. Her brothers were in their rooms, and the maid Callie Mae was in hers, just off the kitchen downstairs, but Addie couldn't be sure if her mother had come to bed. She had watched her go into her father's study, and through a crack in the door she had seen Marie Louise looking at some papers she found in a book on Papa's desk. She had been about to enter when Callie Mae came up behind her and whisked her away to bed.

Addie thought about all of these things as she tossed and turned in her bed, the blessings of sleep continuing to elude her until the first pink streaks of morning light began to push through the darkness, and as her eyes finally closed, she determined to force Felix to give up the secret she knew he must be hiding.

Chapter 6

Breakfast was over, and Felix had returned his stool from behind Addie's chair to the kitchen before beginning his other daily chores. He had not slept well, and his head hurt as the stress from the events of the past two days continued to drain slowly from his body. Most of the time he felt fine, but then an unexpected wave of memories of John Robert's terrifying end would sweep over him and suck him down into a black pool that threatened to drown him in its murky depths. Feeling angry and off-balance, he moved as if in a daze to the backyard well to draw water for the kitchen. The fresh air and the sound of doves cooing from their perches in the eaves of the house calmed him, and he began to regain his emotional footing as he pulled up the full bucket from the well. But when he turned to walk back to the house, he found his way blocked by Addie, her feet planted and arms folded, her face frozen into a look of rigid resolve.

"How did my papa die?" she asked.

"I done already tol' y'all yesterday," Felix replied. "Them mens come up out the woods and take Massa's money and shoot him with his gun, and—"

Addie cut him off angrily. "I don't believe you. That's not all that happened. I know it. You tell me right now, Felix. You tell me, or I'll make something bad happen to you, and you know I can do it."

She was shaking, with her hands clenched into fists at her side, and Felix thought she might strike him.

"I swear, Miss Addie. Ain't nothin' else happened. I don't know nothin' else; ain't nothin' else for me to tell you," Felix said, and he could feel tears welling up in his eyes.

Addie was only a year older than Felix, and she was a head shorter, but as she advanced on him, forcing Felix to retreat until his shoulders were against the well, she might just as well have been twice her age and six feet tall. Her voice lowered to a whisper, and she hissed into Felix's ear, "You know what happened, Felix, and you're going to tell me, or you will be in more trouble than you can imagine."

Addie spun away, and, watching her stomp back to the house, Felix felt his chest tighten and scalding hot tears run down his cheeks. It had all been too much, and without thinking, feeling only the anger and the fear, he heard the words rushing from his mouth, "Ain't gon' tell you nothin', Miss Addie. You cain't make me tell you nothin'. Massa John Robert, he say the slaves gon' be free, and my paw don't have to work for him, and my maw don't have to cook for y'all, and I don't have to sit and let you feed me in the mornin', 'cause we gon' be free and won't nobody be able to make us do nothin'."

Felix's heart was in his throat, and the tears had stopped. Addie marched back to Felix, her face contorted with rage, and when she was standing directly in front of him, she looked him in the eye and slapped his face. She slapped him again, and then a third time. Still staring into Felix's face, she said quietly, "Do not tell me what I cannot do." And then she strode away and did not stop until she disappeared into the house.

Felix spent the rest of the day in terror. He did his chores, but when the day was over and he lay down on his pallet in the cabin, he passed out, unable to respond in any other way to the overwhelming panic he felt. No one could help him, not even his father, and he knew he had learned something a child should never have to know: He had learned what it means to be alone.

When Felix arrived in the big-house kitchen the next morning, his stool was missing. "Look in the dining room," Elmira said, already busy with preparations for breakfast. "Maybe Callie Mae moved it out there when she was cleaning."

Felix opened the door to the dining room, and sitting in the half darkness, with the curtains still drawn against the rays of the early morning sun, was Addie, her hands folded on the table in front of her. "Are you looking for your stool?" she asked, her voice flat, her eyes focused toward the head of the table where until three days ago her father had always sat. "Don't bother," she continued. "You no longer need it."

"What you talkin' 'bout, Miss Addie?" Felix replied.

"You said you didn't want me to feed you, didn't you?" Addie snapped. "Well, you shall have your wish. You will find out more when my mother comes downstairs," she continued, "and when breakfast is served, you can just sit on the floor where your stool used to be until you are told otherwise."

Felix was confused and afraid, and when the rest of the family arrived for breakfast, his mind raced through scenarios that could be unfolding ahead of him, and none of them were good.

In the kitchen, Elmira could barely contain herself when Callie Mae came in from the dining room and reported that Felix was sitting on the floor behind Miss Addie's chair and that "she ain't give him nary bit of food."

"Lawd have mercy," Elmira replied. "What gon' happen now?"

Addie never once looked in Felix's direction nor even acknowledged his presence throughout the meal, but a smug smile played at the corners of her mouth as she remembered the conversation she'd had with her mother the night before. She had found Marie Louise in the parlor after dinner, looking over the plans for John Robert's funeral, to be held on Friday.

"*Maman*," she'd said, using her mother's native French to address her before continuing in English, "everything is so different now that Papa is gone."

"*Oui, mon petite ange*," Marie Louise replied, "everything is different now, and who knows? It may become even more different in the days ahead. Your father would want us to be strong, and so we must continue, no matter what it takes."

"I think I have to change too," Addie said, "so I am going to do something different. I think I will not have Felix at table for breakfast anymore. I don't know why I have done that all these years, and now I don't see any reason to continue. Can we have him do something else? Can we send him to work in the fields?"

Marie Louise looked at her daughter, searching her eyes for some explanation for the sudden change, and finding nothing, she replied, "I think we can find something else for him." She paused. "And now that I am thinking of it, we must find something new for Plessant as well. He is no longer needed as a valet."

The clink of dishes being removed from the table halted Addie's reverie, and she heard her mother speaking to Felix, who had stood up to help with clearing the table. "Felix, go find your father and bring him into the parlor. I need to speak with you both," she said.

Felix found Plessant in back of their cabin, pulling weeds in Elmira's garden and chopping wood for the fireplace. Since John Robert's death, Plessant had thought it best to stay out of sight and found projects to stay busy away from the big house.

"What she want?" he asked Felix as they walked up to the house.

"I don't know," Felix replied. "She just say find you and come to the parlor."

Plessant exchanged an anxious glance with Elmira as he and their son entered through the kitchen and headed to the parlor, where they found Marie Louise on the sofa with her knitting. She let them stand there in silence for a minute before looking up to speak.

"Plessant," she began, "you have been part of this plantation longer than I. You were born here, and you served Master John Robert for most of your life, and I know that he thought well of you. But as you know, my husband is dead, and therefore your services as a valet are no longer required."

Plessant felt as though his intestines were being looped into knots and pulled tight, and he began to sweat at the thought of what he was sure would be coming next—that he was being sent to the fields to pick cotton. He had spent his entire life working in the big house, taking care of Massa John Robert, looking after his things, and (though he had never told anyone else, not even Elmira) being John Robert's eyes and ears around the plantation. His relationship to John Robert had not saved his own children from the auction block, but it had made life better than it might otherwise have been. And so he forced himself to listen as Marie Louise continued to speak.

"I have two sons, Plessant, but only the younger one has any real interest in the plantation, and he will want to step in to run things now that his father is gone. I am proud of that, but Claude is almost sixteen, and though he knows a lot, he does not know enough to take on the full responsibility of the plantation. So you are going to work for Claude, not as his valet, but as a helper who can keep him from making serious mistakes. He knows you were close to his father, and I believe he will listen to you when it is important."

Plessant felt his whole body relax, and the skin on his face felt warm, as if the sun had broken through for a moment on an overcast day, brightening the colors and lifting the spirits in all of the places and in all of the hearts of creatures touched by its golden rays.

"You will have other duties too," Marie Louise continued. "I will need you to drive the wagon for me when I go into town, and I will need you to do other jobs as I require you to do them."

"Yassum," Plessant said.

"One more thing," Marie Louise said. "I am not unaware that my husband relied on you to keep him informed, discreetly of course, about everything that goes on at Road's End. I will expect the same from you. Do you understand?"

"Yassum, you can count on me," Plessant replied.

"Good," she said. "I will let you know when I have spoken with Claude and when you can begin your new duties. Now leave me with Felix. I need to speak with him too."

Felix watched his father leave the room and then turned to face Marie Louise, waiting for her to speak.

Marie Louise set her knitting on the sofa next to her and took a deep breath before asking Felix a question he didn't expect to hear: "Felix, do you know why it's so hard to keep a secret?"

Felix kept his eyes focused on a space that had opened between two of the hardwood floorboards between his feet.

"The reason it's so hard to keep a secret," Marie Louise continued, "is because it makes you feel alone, and the bigger the secret, the more alone you feel. Don't you think that's true?"

"I don't know," he mumbled, still staring at the floor.

"I think you know what it feels like to keep a secret, Felix, because I think you are keeping a secret. I think you are keeping a very big secret, and I think you are feeling very alone," she said.

"No, ma'am, I ain't keepin' no secret," Felix whispered. He wanted to run away, but where would he go? They would find him, and even boys as young as Felix knew what happened when the slave catchers got you—mutilations, beatings, or even death if the planter wanted to make an example.

"It's a terrible feeling, isn't it, Felix, carrying that burden all alone?" Marie Louise said.

In his mind, Felix was reliving the entire scene in the wagon by the side of the road and remembering that Massa John Robert made him swear to keep his secret. His heart was pounding, he was sweating, and then he couldn't bear it any longer, and tears started to stream down his cheeks.

"It's all right, Felix," Marie Louise was saying. "I know the secret you are carrying, and I had to be sure you could keep it, and I see that you can do it as well as a grown man. Master John Robert would be proud of you. But we have a problem; my daughter suspects that something isn't right. You know how she is, and she is not likely to let it go. We have to get you out of her way, so I am going to give you a new job outside of the house."

Felix was so relieved he could barely focus on what Marie Louise was saying now, but he got the basics. He was going to the fields, not to pick cotton, but to be a water boy, carrying buckets of water and dippers up and down the rows to the field hands. He didn't know what it would be like, but at least now he could breathe, and he wouldn't have to deal with Miss Addie every day.

"You can go now," Marie Louise told him, but then she spoke to him again. "Felix, you and I are the only two people in the world who know my husband's secret. It is a great weight on our shoulders, but now each of us knows that the secret is held by someone else as well, and neither of us has to carry it alone. You remember that, Felix, and I promise you will not feel so alone."

"Yassum," he said, and he walked out of the parlor, through the kitchen door, into the backyard. Overhead, a red-shouldered hawk wheeled and soared high in the sky, and Felix felt his untethered spirit go with it, feeling for the first time what it is to be free.

Chapter 7

Claude Parker was the middle child, trapped between the elegance and sophistication of Jean Louis, his older brother, and the mysterious, searing intelligence of Adelaide, his younger sister. At nearly sixteen, he was average—average at his studies; average in height, about five feet, seven inches tall; and average in weight, about one hundred forty pounds. He had sandy hair that curled around his ears and open blue eyes and a pleasant face uninterrupted by either a beard or a mustache. When he spoke, his voice was clear, in the middle register, and when he sang in church, his voice was in tune but indistinct from all the others around him at Red Clay's First Baptist Church, which he attended with his family on Sunday mornings.

He had a special gift, however. He had a savant's understanding of agriculture—an innate sense of the changing of the seasons, the receptivity of the soil to one kind of crop versus another, and how to provide for the needs of healthy, productive livestock. Claude also understood people. He was respectful to the poor white men who worked as overseers at Road's End, using the honorific "Mister" when he spoke to them, and he did not share his grandfather's contempt for both the poor whites and the enslaved Blacks nor his father's indifference toward them. He was neither an egalitarian nor an abolitionist, but he saw no reason to be disrespectful or unpleasant to anyone.

Claude hunted and fished, and his love of the outdoors was one of the things he had shared with his late father. In the first days after John Robert's death, that was how Claude remembered him: walking together through the woods with their shotguns in the predawn hours, making their way to the creekside blind, where they would wait with the dogs for the arrival of migrating ducks and geese. He had loved those brisk mornings when he had his father to himself to talk about the crops, the workings of the plantation, and the financial management of the enterprise. His brother Jean Louis cared for none of that, preferring instead to engage with their father in academic pursuits, and he saw Addie as John Robert's favorite, a privileged status Claude did not begrudge her.

On the Sunday afternoon before his father's death, Claude had been walking along the creek, going nowhere in particular, just walking and thinking. He was worried that the plantation's operations were out of balance, that two bad harvests in a row had left them vulnerable to what might happen if a third season disappointed. He thought that they might have too many enslaved workers and not enough diversity in the crops they were raising. And then there was the war. Who knew how that might affect things? He had resolved to speak with his father the next day about his concerns.

Deep into his thoughts, he stumbled onto Plessant and Felix fishing. "How y'all doing; catching anything?" he asked.

"Yassuh, Massa Claude," Plessant replied and hauled up the full stringer from the water to display their catch.

"That's mighty fine," Claude said admiringly. "I guess Elmira will fix those up for you tonight just right."

"Yassuh, she sho nuff know what to do with a skillet," Plessant said.

"All right, y'all enjoy yourselves," Claude said and continued his walk.

When Claude was out of earshot, Felix asked his father, "Paw, you like Massa Claude?"

"Well," Plessant said, "he better'n most."

Marie Louise was coming to the end of a hard day. The conversation she'd had with Felix had been exhausting. How had she arrived here, plunged into a conspiracy with *un petit garçon noir*, a little Black boy, to conceal the circumstances surrounding her husband's death, with the financial and social future of her family hanging in the balance? It was outrageous! And yet here she was, and there was nothing for her but to make it work.

Later that day she stood on the big front porch of the house, watching evening shadows begin to close like thick gray drapes across the long driveway on which John Robert had driven away on Monday morning and on which he had returned that night, reduced to a bloody corpse slumped in the seat of the wagon, delivered by the horse that found its way home in the dark. Marie Louise had spent the last twenty years of her life at Road's End, and she had assumed that she would die here and be buried with her husband and all the other Parkers. But that was not to be. John Robert's letter had laid out the path she would have to follow, and she was already taking the first steps.

"Callie Mae," she called into the house, "find Master Claude and send him to me here on the porch." She slipped back into her reverie, gliding across a sea of memory, tacking into winds of regret and pushing forward on waves of joy. She remembered the reception at Hunt College where she had seen John Robert for the first time, so handsome, so confident, and how witless she had felt when they were introduced. She had known immediately that he would be the man she would marry, that he would be the father of her children and the north star of her existence for the rest of her days on this Earth. She could not imagine an existence without him, and yet here she was, alone but determined to sail on, with his hand reaching across time and space to hold hers steady on the tiller.

She heard steps behind her and turned to see Claude coming out of the house onto the porch.

"Mama, are you all right?" he asked.

Marie Louise gazed at her son, practically grown, and through him she could see clearly the course ahead. "I'm fine, Claude. I'm fine," she replied. "Sit down, I need to speak with you."

By the time they finished talking, night had overtaken the plantation, and the enslaved men and women had returned to their cabins. The scent of wood fires to cook evening meals wafted through the air, and the voices of children floated over the low rumble of men and women talking and arguing, laughing and crying. They did not know, could not know, that their world was about to change and that a vision of simple human dignity in all its awesome, terrifying, exhilarating glory would soon dance before their eyes. And for the fearless few, those with strong hearts, clear eyes, and a fierce desire to be free, the coming exodus would be worth everything. There would also be change for the Southern pharaohs, and whether they received it as a blessing or as a curse would make all the difference.

Marie Louise had long been impressed by Claude's knowledge of plantation operations, and the more they talked, the more confident she became in her plans for turning her late husband's plot into reality. "One more thing," she said, as she stood and took Claude's arm to go in for supper, "you know Plessant worked for your father his whole life, and he knows about as much as anyone about what goes on at Road's End. I want him to work for you now, not as a valet, but as a helper. You are going to be the boss, and you will be pulled in many directions, and there will be men who will seek to take advantage of you, and even though he is *un homme noir*, he will be someone you can trust. *Tu comprends?*"

"*Oui, Maman. Je comprends,*" Claude replied. "I understand."

Chapter 8

On the Sunday morning after John Robert's funeral, a guest preacher from Centreville stood in the pulpit at Red Clay's First Baptist Church and delivered a ferocious Old Testament sermon, reminding congregants of the day when God would exact a terrible price from doubters and evildoers. He was a great slab of a man whose collar barely contained the roll of fat around his neck and whose nose featured a network of broken blood vessels, a roadmap to every tavern between Centreville and Red Clay.

"For behold the Lord will come with fire, and with his chariots like a whirlwind, to render his anger with fury, and his rebuke with flames of fire," the Reverend D. T. Schmidt thundered, quoting Isaiah 66:15, and without drawing a fresh breath he continued to the next verse, "For by fire and by his sword will the Lord plead with all flesh: and the slain of the Lord shall be many." The words shot through the sanctuary and slammed against the back wall, a fusillade from the pulpit, startling those whose minds had wandered and waking those who had fallen asleep in the warm, still air. Children squeezed closer to their mothers for protection, and babies began to cry. The preacher gazed down at the reactions of the flock, his forehead glistening with sweat, his eyes shining with the intensity of the moment. A self-satisfied smirk began to form at the corners of his mouth, and the skin around his eyes crinkled to match, until he pulled it all back into a pursed-lip, well-rehearsed glare.

Quel idiot! Cet homme est un imbécile! thought Marie Louise as she sat with her children in the pews that morning. Raised a Roman Catholic in New Orleans, she had never really grown accustomed to the fire and brimstone of her husband's Baptist faith. She had accepted it, and she had embraced the idea of regular Bible readings. But she considered this Centreville preacher beyond the pale and made a mental note to ask the pastor not to invite him again. As the Reverend Schmidt plunged ahead, Marie Louise found herself thinking instead of a more soothing passage from Isaiah, chapter 65, verse 17: "For behold, I create new heavens and a new earth: and the former shall not be remembered, or come into mind."

She thought of new beginnings, for her, for her children, for Plessant and Elmira and Felix, and for everyone and everything else on Road's End Plantation. Summer was already turning into fall, and so too had the season arrived for looking to "new heavens" and leaving "former" lives behind. Nothing would ever again be the same, and she could not—would not—look back.

The next morning, however, she struggled to maintain the serenity that Bible verse had brought her as Plessant drove her into Red Clay to meet with John Robert's lawyers. Sitting in the back of the open carriage, Marie Louise watched the scenery go by—long stretches of forest land, interrupted occasionally by the end of a road leading into a plantation or by fields of cotton or corn that grew to the edge of the road. So different from the French Quarter of New Orleans, where she had grown up. Suddenly she missed it with an intensity that surprised her. She would have to examine this new thought later, however, because the carriage was pulling onto Main Street, where the courthouse was in view, and she knew that John Robert's lawyers' offices were on the other side of the square.

"Plessant, I want you to take the carriage over to the general store

and give the clerk that list I gave you for things we need at Road's End,"
Marie Louise said. "You load it into the carriage and come back here to
wait for me. Do you have that pass I gave you? You know you will be
in big trouble if you can't show that you have permission to be off the
plantation," she said.

"Yassum," he replied and guided the carriage to the curb. He opened
the door and pulled down the steps for Marie Louise.

The law offices of Campbell, Stewart & MacPherson were cool and
dark and smelled faintly of fine tobacco. Oil paintings of scenes along
the Cahaba River and local woodland landscapes hung in carved wood
frames on the walls of the anteroom, accompanied by framed certifi-
cates and other marks of distinction. Marie Louise settled into the soft
leather chair to which she had been shown and sipped tea from a fine
china cup brought to her by a young clerk.

"Please make yourself comfortable, Mrs. Parker," the young man
said. "Mr. Stewart will be ready for you shortly."

Marie Louise didn't mind waiting. Events were moving quickly, and
she welcomed a moment to reflect. Barely a week had passed since John
Robert's death, and here she was sitting in the lawyers' offices to take
the next steps in John Robert's plan to protect his family's future. He
had charted it well, but Marie Louise was already realizing that there
were blanks she would have to fill in, and she was terrified by the consequences if she made a mistake.

The clerk reappeared after a few minutes, and as he escorted her
into the firm's law library, she could appreciate that John Robert must
have felt at home here. The walls were lined with leatherbound books,
much like his study at Road's End, and the room was dominated by a
twelve-foot-long table of polished mahogany. At its head sat Andrew
Stewart, John Robert's personal attorney. He stood as she entered the
room. He was unexpectedly short—shorter than Marie Louise—but he
seemed taller, perhaps due to the great shock of white hair swept back
from his clean-shaven face, his athletic build, and his dignified posture.
He was of an indeterminate age, but Marie Louise guessed that he was
about fifty-five years old.

"It is a pleasure to meet you, Mrs. Parker," the attorney said, gesturing to a seat next to his. "I wish it could have been under other circumstances. You and your family have my deepest condolences."

"Thank you, Mr. Stewart," she said. "I know that my husband had great respect for you and your firm and that he relied upon your expertise."

"I am gratified to hear that, and I hope we can continue to be of service to the Parker family." He gestured to neat piles of paper on the table in front of them. "I have assembled the relevant documents and other information in anticipation of this meeting."

For the next hour and a half, Stewart walked Marie Louise through the will, which left everything to her, and then through the other documents and information that conformed to arrangements John Robert had described in his letter to Marie Louise, including contact with George Flowers of Starkville, Mississippi, to confirm his interest in purchasing the plantation.

"Your husband was quite thorough, Mrs. Parker," Stewart said, "but it is regrettable that we are executing these plans so soon."

"Yes, John Robert always paid attention to detail," Marie Louise said, anxious to leave now that she could see the conspiracy starting to be implemented, but she forced herself to remain calm. "This all seems in order, Mr. Stewart. I think it conforms to plans he discussed with me." She paused. "There are some additional matters, however, that I wish to discuss with you and for which I must have your promise of confidentiality."

"Of course, Mrs. Parker," Stewart said. "You may rely upon my discretion."

"Thank you," she said. "I am sure that I can, so I will be open, *candide*. My husband did not believe the South will prevail in this war, and he believed it would come to an end soon. Thus, he had discussed with me the need to convert our resources to gold and to US dollars, as much as possible, and to establish accounts in the North. He had planned to do this very soon, and had he not been interrupted . . ." She took a deep breath. "Therefore, I would like to ask your firm to establish those accounts and to see that the funds from the insurance policy are deposited into them," she continued. "Also, we would require the proceeds from the sale of the plantation to be paid in gold or in US dollars and deposited to those accounts. Is that something you can do?"

Stewart hesitated before replying, studying Marie Louise's face as if trying to read the thoughts behind her eyes. "Now I must rely upon *your* discretion, Mrs. Parker," he said finally. "We do not often discuss it, but Campbell, Stewart & MacPherson has two offices; one of them is headed by Mr. MacPherson, a native and resident of Philadelphia. Mr. MacPherson is younger than myself and Mr. Campbell. In fact, he is your husband's age, and the two were fast friends at Princeton and had remained so." Stewart paused before continuing. "It is through their relationship that Mr. Parker brought his business to our firm. I tell you this by way of assuring you that we are situated to handle your business as you have requested—and with the greatest discretion." He stopped speaking and kept his eyes locked on those of Marie Louise.

In that moment Marie Louise felt a great weight lifted from her shoulders, and she began to relax for the first time in days. "*Merci*," she said. "Thank you."

Stewart walked to the door of the library and asked the clerk to bring his client a fresh cup of tea.

"There are just two more things," Marie Louise said after taking a sip of her tea. "In talking about how he believed the war would end, my husband contemplated that the slaves would be freed. If that happened and if something happened to him, I was to make sure that a ten-acre plot along the creek at Road's End should be transferred to Plessant, his valet. The reason is not germane to our conversation here, but suffice it to say that John Robert felt he owed a special debt to Plessant and his wife and child, and that the plot, which had been given to him by his father, should be theirs.

"The other matter," she continued, "is that I would like to ask George Flowers to consider hiring my son Claude to run Road's End for him after the sale is complete. I believe that Mr. Flowers has similar arrangements on other properties he owns, and I think that Claude would be well suited. I have already asked him to assume that position in the absence of his father."

The lawyer listened and made a few notes. "I cannot speak for Mr.
Flowers, of course, but I believe he will be amenable to speaking with
your son, and likely with good results. As for the land transfer to your
slave, allow us to hold the matter close for now and to revisit it should
circumstances change."

"I am grateful to you, sir," Marie Louise said and rose to leave the room.

———

ROAD'S END PLANTATION

AUTUMN 1864

Felix had a new beginning that day too. It was his first day as a water
boy in the cotton fields, and it did not go well.

He arrived with the other Black men, women, and children as the
sun rose, trudging through dew-drenched grass and listening to the calls
of night birds retreating from the encroaching light. The cornbread and
fried fatback Elmira had handed to him through the back door of the
big-house kitchen sat uneasily in his stomach. "You eat this now," she
had said, "'cause you gon' need your strength. Today you gon' work
like a man; ain't no mo' little boy." And then she fled back to the stove,
where grits bubbled in a pot and biscuits browned in the oven. Felix
only glimpsed the tears running down her cheeks, and he used his sleeve
to wipe away his own.

He ate his breakfast quickly, sitting on the steps, and then rose to
walk away to the fields, pausing at the edge of the yard to look back once
more. He saw a figure standing in the doorway to the kitchen. In the
early morning light, he thought at first that it was his mother, and he
started to raise his arm to wave. Then almost immediately he realized that
it was someone else—shorter, thinner . . . and white. It was Addie, and
she was staring at him, her face fixed in a tight, grim smile. She waited
until she was sure he had seen her before disappearing into the house.

Felix made his way to the fields and found the overseer, a grizzled,
rough-looking white man who greeted him with a sneer.

"So, you the little house nigger I'm supposed to put to work out here," he said. "Well, you see that yoke over there with them buckets hanging on it? That's for you. Ain't nothin' to do but fill the buckets with water and walk up and down the rows so the field hands can get a drink when they need it. When the buckets are empty, you go back to the well and fill 'em up again. Got it?"

"Yassuh," Felix said, relieved because it didn't sound too hard.

The overseer looked over Felix's shoulder to speak with someone coming up behind him. "Jimmy, you come over here," the overseer said. "This is Felix. You show him what to do, and if any of my niggers fall out 'cause they don't get enough water, I'll whup both your little black asses."

When the overseer walked away, Felix turned to his new fellow laborer. Jimmy was a boy like himself, a little older, maybe eleven or twelve, taller, and more muscular.

"That all we s'posed to do, just fill up these buckets and carry 'em around the field?" Felix asked.

"Yeah, that's all, but it's hard," Jimmy said. "When it get hot, them field hands be callin' for more water, and they gets mad you don't come fast enough, and it hard to run when yo' buckets full."

They filled their buckets, and Jimmy showed Felix how to situate the yoke on his shoulders. Felix was surprised at how heavy they were, but he found that if he looked straight ahead, he could keep his balance as he walked.

"How come you out here?" Jimmy asked. "Ain't yo' mama Elmira, the cook, and you the errand boy at the big house?"

"Yeah," Felix replied, "but since Massa John Robert got kilt, everything changed up there. Massa Claude, he the big boss now, and my paw gon' work for him, and Miss Marie Louise say she want me to do somethin' else, so she send me out here."

"Well, here we go. You start down yonder," Jimmy said, pointing to the other end of the field, "and I'll start here."

By eleven o'clock Felix had already lost count of how many times he had refilled his buckets. His shoulders were rubbed raw under the heavy yoke, and his thigh muscles and calves felt as if they were on fire.

"You was right, this is hard," he said to Jimmy when they happened to arrive at the well at the same time.

"Yeah, but you got to keep movin'," Jimmy said, "'cause if you don't, that overseer sho nuff gon' whup you, and if he don't catch you, some of them big field hands might do the same thing."

Felix pushed on until they got a midday break, and then he collapsed under a tree at the edge of the field with Jimmy. He was sitting there, half asleep, watching a spider dangling from a long silk line a few feet from his face.

"Uh-oh, this ain't good," he heard Jimmy say. He looked up and followed Jimmy's gaze toward a group of five older boys headed their way, teenagers who looked like they were in search of trouble.

The gang stopped in front of Felix. "Look what we got here," said the boy out front. "Ain't this that little house nigger Felix? What you doin' out here with us field hands; ain't you s'posed to be up in the big house havin' tea with Miss Addie?" His gang laughed.

"Don't say nothin'," Jimmy hissed to Felix out of the side of his mouth. "Just let it go."

"You know my name?" the group leader asked. "They call me Big Joe, and you know what else? I better be the first one to get water every day, and if I ain't, this here is what you get." He bent over, grabbed Felix by the collar of his shirt, and yanked him to his feet, then spun him around and kicked him hard in the butt, knocking him to the ground.

Felix gasped, shocked more than hurt, as Big Joe and his gang sauntered away.

"You okay, Felix?" Jimmy asked as he reached down and helped Felix to his feet. "What you gon' do?"

Felix said nothing, but the look in his eyes said everything: *I don't know now, but when I do, you and everyone else will know too.*

Chapter 9

Big Joe was aptly named. At sixteen years old, he was over six feet tall and weighed more than two hundred and fifty pounds, making him substantially taller and heavier than most grown men anyone had ever seen, and he used his size to intimidate others. He had scars on his back from the lash on the Louisiana plantation from which John Robert had bought him, and his flat, broad-featured face was marked from fights—over gambling, over food, over young women, and over general cantankerousness, often fueled by homemade liquor. Big Joe had the animal cunning of a wolf but none of the self-control. Worse, he had surrounded himself with a gang of four other unattached teenaged boys, and they lived together in a cabin at the end of the row. Men steered clear of them, and women warned their daughters not to speak to them.

Now, Felix had caught Big Joe's attention, and that meant big trouble unless he could think of a way to shift Big Joe's focus elsewhere. Easier said than done. When Felix arrived for his second day in the field, Big Joe was waiting for him.

"You got my water, house nigger?" he asked with his gang standing behind him, snickering over Felix's discomfort.

Felix handed him the long-handled dipper and turned so that Big Joe could take water from the bucket on his left side.

Big Joe filled the dipper and drank, exaggerating the pleasure the water gave him by smacking his lips after each sip, patting his belly, and pronouncing the water to be "as sweet as honey."

And when the show no longer amused him, Big Joe gave the dipper back to Felix and told him to leave. Felix had barely taken a step when Big Joe kicked him, sending him tumbling to the ground and spilling all the water from both buckets.

"How come you done that?" Felix shouted as tears rushed to his eyes and his cheeks burned. "You got your water first."

"Just a reminder today so you don't forget tomorrow," Big Joe said and laughed as he and his gang swaggered away.

———

Plessant, sitting in a wagon with Claude at the edge of the field, watched Felix's encounter with Big Joe, his fists clenched at his sides in silent rage.

"That's your boy Felix on the ground, isn't it?" Claude asked. "You want to go help him?"

"Yassuh, that my boy all right, but he got to learn to take care of hisself, and it ain't gon' help nothin' if his daddy step in," Plessant replied. "I go over there, and them big boys gon' be all over him soon's I leave."

Claude regarded Plessant with an expression that might have been either admiration or surprise. "It's sad to say so, Plessant, but I expect that you are right, and that your interference would not obtain the desired results," he said. "Now, we have work to do to get this plantation in shape, and we are going to begin by covering every foot of this property to decide what works and what does not. I trust that I can rely on you to tell me what you think, as you would have told my father were he here today."

"Yassuh, Massa Claude, you can count on me," Plessant replied, then clicked his tongue and loosened the reins to start the horse moving.

Plessant and Claude spent the day driving around Road's End, trying to look at it as if they had never seen it before, questioning everything. Too much cotton, not enough corn? Too many workers in one field versus the number deployed in another? Did the blacksmith and carpenter have enough work from the plantation, or could they be hired out to other farms? Could uncultivated land be cleared and leased to other operations? Should the vegetable gardens be enlarged? The questions seemed endless, but Claude was determined to examine them all and to seek answers.

Dusk was coming fast when Plessant drove the wagon up to the front of the big house with Claude by his side. The cool evening breeze blowing in from across the creek and through the woods felt good after a day in the hot sun. Plessant could smell Elmira's cooking wafting through the air from the kitchen door in the back of the house, and he hoped that some purloined servings would make it to the table in their own cabin.

As if he could read Plessant's mind, Claude slapped him on the back and said that after he had put the horse and wagon away, he should tell Elmira to take home some of what she was making for their supper that night. "You tell her I said it's all right," Claude said.

"Yassuh, thank you, suh. That's mighty fine," Plessant said with a grin, careful not to let his face give away his knowledge that Elmira would likely have brought some food home anyhow, with or without the master's permission, and that she did so whenever she could get away with it. Amused by the thought, Plessant almost failed to notice that Claude had begun speaking again.

"I want you to think about what we saw today," he was saying, "and we will talk about it in the morning. What we're trying to do here is reduce our costs for running this plantation."

"Yassuh, I'll be thinkin' on it," Plessant said, "and thank you for lettin' Elmira take some food."

"That's all right, Plessant. You're a good man; I'll see you in the morning. You pick me up here with the wagon after breakfast, and we'll have a talk." Claude hopped down to the ground and headed into the house.

The fact was that Plessant didn't really need to think about the plantation's situation; he had been listening to John Robert talk about it for months before his death. He knew the late planter had been worried and that he had been taking small steps to try to fix the problems, tinkering around the margins, but that he had never stepped back to focus on the larger issues. For example, he knew he had too many enslaved workers, but he hadn't thought through how to deal with the problem. So he'd sold a few, including two of Plessant's three children, which brought in some cash but didn't tackle the overall labor efficiencies that were needed. Plessant could barely read and write—dangerous skills he kept to himself—but he understood that John Robert had been running around with buckets during a rainstorm instead of fixing the roof while the sun was shining.

With the horse fed, watered, and secured for the night in his stall, Plessant rested on a hay bale in the thick darkness that seemed to swallow all the light around it, a black hole from which nothing escaped, not even the yellow glow of the kerosene lantern hanging from a nail above his head.

He could see the faces of his missing children, John and Bessie, floating in the darkness just beyond his reach, and he could hear their voices calling out to him and to their mother as they were driven away in the back of a wagon. Plessant recalled the feel of Elmira's tears soaking his shirt as they clung to each other when the wagon vanished at the end of the road. "It ain't right, it ain't right," she had whimpered, again and again, as he tried to soothe her.

"Hush," he had told her. "They gone, and they ain't never comin' back, but I tell you what, Elmira, I'm gon' get Massa John Robert for this. I'm gon' get him, and cain't nobody stop me."

And he had believed it—until that day when another wagon brought home John Robert's bloody corpse and Plessant's own horrified little boy. John Robert was gone, but at times like this, the need for vengeance still swelled up in Plessant's heart, and he knew the day would come when he would not be able to hold it in check. He could feel it lurking in the darkness, a beast stalking him at a distance, waiting for the moment to lunge and kill.

Until that day came, he would continue as he had, for the sake of Elmira and Felix. He had to be sure they would be safe when he took his revenge. It didn't matter that John Robert was dead, he thought. The Parkers would pay for what they had done to his family. One way or another, they would pay.

Chapter 10

Elmira moved closer to her husband in the bed they shared in the cabin at Road's End Plantation. Plessant was already asleep, breathing deeply, and he hardly stirred when she pressed against him, flattening her breasts against his back and molding her body to the contours of his. She tried to match her breathing to his so that they moved together, two souls occupying a single space. She loved Plessant, and she knew that without him she would have lost all hold on reality when their son and daughter were taken from them. Felix and Plessant were all she had in the world, and she lived in terror that they, too, would be taken from her.

Earlier, they'd had a party, a quiet one to be sure, so as not to draw unwanted attention while they feasted on roast beef, mashed potatoes and gravy, and green beans that Elmira had brought home from the big-house kitchen. Elmira often smuggled out a few treats—a bit of meat, a slice of cake, or some freshly baked bread—but a complete meal such as the one they had enjoyed tonight was a rarity, and they had enjoyed every bite.

"Now you don't tell nobody about this," Elmira warned Felix. "This here was special, and folks get jealous when they think you got somethin' they ain't got and ain't likely to get."

"Don't be gettin' too used to it neither," Plessant warned. "Massa

Claude was just in a good mood today. Now I just got to make sure he stay in a good mood every day," he said with a laugh.

Elmira smiled in the dark as she remembered the big smile on Felix's face as she unpacked the food and the gusto with which he had eaten it. He needed good food now that he was working in the fields. She wanted to know how he was coping, but he had been closed-lipped so far, and Elmira had been reluctant to press him on it.

"How you doin' out there?" she'd asked as the last scraps of beef and gravy disappeared from Felix's plate.

"Okay," he'd replied.

"I heard you and that boy Jimmy gettin' to be good friends," Elmira said.

"Yeah, he all right," Felix replied.

"That's good. A man need to have good friends," she said.

Felix fidgeted but said nothing.

"I heard that Big Joe give you some trouble," she ventured.

"Yeah, but I can handle it," Felix replied.

"Well, you just take care of yourself," she said and let the matter drop. It didn't stop her from continuing to worry, however. It was dangerous in the fields—snakes and poisonous spiders hiding among the plants, arbitrary overseers with unchecked power to exact punishments, and other slaves for whom survival was paramount and whose instincts sometimes led them to terrible places with grave consequences for others. They all knew men who had been whipped for lies told about them, and women who suffered in silence from unwanted sex. It wasn't right, but there was little they could do.

Some escaped and were never heard from again, but no one knew if they had made it to freedom or died on the way. Others were caught and brought back to Road's End, where they told grisly stories of days and nights on the run before being caught by relentless packs of men and dogs and maimed as a warning to others of the fate that might befall them if they, too, chose to escape.

Elmira shivered as she thought about all the horrible things that could happen to her son, and she prayed to the Lord to protect him. Her prayers streamed up through the roof of the cabin and spread like stars in the heavens, messages in bottles drifting on a cosmic sea, each one an expression of hope that she and her little family did not stand alone in the universe.

———

Out in the cabin's main room, Felix lay awake on his pallet in the corner near the fireplace. His belly was full, his parents were asleep in the next room, allowing him to relax and surrender to sleep. His last conscious thoughts were of what his father had said to him after supper when Elmira left the cabin to go to the outhouse. "Listen, boy, I know Big Joe been after you, but you need to know somethin'. He ain't gon' stop 'til you stop him. Won't do no good if I do somethin'. That just make him go after you more if I get in it, and it gon' get worse if you don't do somethin', but you got to be smart. He too big for you to fight head-on, but he got to know that whatever you do, you the one that done it."

"I know, Paw, and I been thinkin' about it, and I'm fixin' to do it," Felix said. And though he knew he would face another round of abuse from Big Joe in the morning, he knew that it would end soon because he had a plan. It was like that preacher said in church last Sunday: "For behold the Lord will come with fire, and with his chariots like a whirlwind, to render his anger with fury, and his rebuke with flames of fire." To deal with Big Joe, Felix would be like the Lord Himself, come to *render his anger with fury, and his rebuke with flames of fire.* He couldn't wait to tell Jimmy about his plans.

Chapter 11

A gray fox on the hunt for field mice in the underbrush behind the slave cabins stopped its snuffling and froze in place as it watched the two boys make their way through the midnight darkness, creeping through the shadows and shushing each other whenever either of them stepped on a twig or made some other noise that might give them away. Equipped with a box of matches Felix had taken when he visited his mother in the big-house kitchen and a small jar of kerosene Jimmy had poured from a lamp while his mother was out, they were inching toward the cabin Big Joe and his crew occupied at the end of the row. It was Sunday night, and most of the enslaved workers were sleeping deeply, resting for another week in the fields. Nevertheless, Felix and Jimmy were being careful, fearful of what would happen to them if they were caught.

"You crazy!" Jimmy had said two days earlier when Felix told him about his plan to deal with Big Joe, whispering so as not to be overheard while they ate their midday meal in the field.

"I ain't crazy, and I'm gon' do it. Thing is, you gon' help me?" Felix replied.

After staring at his bare feet for what seemed like an eternity, Jimmy said, "Okay. I'll help you, but it's still crazy."

When they reached the back of the cabin, they paused and listened for any signs that their presence had been detected. All they heard was someone snoring in the cabin, and from the creek they heard the deep baritone croaks of frogs. In the underbrush behind them, they heard the furtive rustling of small furry creatures searching for food and hoping not to draw attention to themselves.

The easy part of their mission was over. Both boys had lain awake and waited for their parents to fall asleep before slipping out of their cabins and meeting by the big live oak tree at the upper end of the row of slave cabins.

"What took you so long?" Felix asked when Jimmy arrived.

"I had to wait for my maw to go to sleep first. Every time I thought she was asleep, I got up, and she start whisperin' across the room, wantin' to know what I'm doin', where I'm goin'. Finally I got up and she stay asleep, so I got out of there."

Having reached the back of Big Joe's cabin, Felix turned to Jimmy and whispered, "We here now; you ready to do it?"

Jimmy nodded. "Let's go."

Jimmy headed into the underbrush while Felix crept into the dirt-floored one-room cabin. Big Joe and his friends lay under quilts on straw pallets around the edge of the room. The only furniture was a table and two chairs. Above each pallet the boys' clothes—a shirt and one pair of pants—hung from a nail driven into the wall. Their shoes were on the dirt floor at the end of each pallet. Felix knew that on Sunday afternoons, the boys washed their underwear—he had watched them do it down by the creek—and he was happy to see it as he had hoped, draped across the table and chairs to dry. Under their quilts, Big Joe and his gang were as naked as the day they were born.

Moving quickly, Felix gathered the boys' clothing, underwear, and shoes and hurried outside, where Jimmy had laid a big pile of brush and small logs for a fire. He dropped the clothes and shoes on top and doused it all with the kerosene they had brought with them.

"Ready?" Felix asked.

"Ready," Jimmy replied.

Felix struck a match and dropped it onto the kerosene-soaked pile, which instantly erupted in flame. Jimmy ran to the back of the cabin and shouted through the window, "Fire!" Then he ran for home. Felix stood in front of the blaze and waited for Big Joe and his gang to emerge, and when they did, wrapped in their quilts, he looked them in the eye, turned, and walked away.

Standing in the shadows, Plessant smiled and rushed home, his chest swollen with pride. He climbed into bed next to Elmira and closed his eyes, the sight of his boy facing down the bullies burned into his memory forever.

———

By morning all of the workers knew what had happened, but no one said a word when the overseer asked about the absence of Big Joe and his cohorts, so he sent one of the young men to find them.

"They say they cain't come 'cause they clothes got all burnt up and they ain't got nothin' to wear," the young man reported.

"We'll see about that. Y'all get to work right now," the overseer said, and rode off on his horse in the direction of the slave quarters. Twenty minutes later he was back, driving Big Joe and the other four boys in front of his horse. The young men were wrapped in their quilts, tied at the waist with a piece of rope.

"Now y'all get to work," the overseer ordered loudly. "I don't care nothing about your clothes, or lack of them. I do care about whether you make your quota today, and if you don't, there will be consequences."

"Yassuh," they mumbled and headed into the field, dragging their cotton collection bags over their shoulders. Barely suppressed snickers from the other field hands followed them all the way down the row.

At the midday break, Big Joe found Felix and confronted him. "You think I'm through with you, house nigger? I ain't even started," he snarled, and took a step in Felix's direction.

"Yeah, I think you through," came a man's voice from behind Big Joe. "You and your boys through."

Big Joe turned around to see a male field hand and five others standing there. "This here boy coulda burnt your whole house down, with you in it, but he didn't," the man said. "That don't mean somebody else wouldn't do it. Now we think it time for you to move on, or you gon' have to deal with all of us."

By Tuesday morning Big Joe and his gang were gone—run away. By Wednesday morning they had been caught and brought back to Road's End, still wrapped in their quilts, and flogged in front of the enslaved workers who were assembled and made to watch. Big Joe lost his left eye when the lash wrapped around his head. The crowd had seen this kind of spectacle before, but this time no one lamented the fate of the five young men, and as they returned to the field to work, no one said a word.

Chapter 12

In the dimming evening light, Marie Louise gazed at her children around the dinner table, their faces illuminated by candelabras, laughing at each other's jokes and making verbal jabs. She smiled, happy to see them so relaxed, a rarity since their father's death a month earlier.

Addie, after her initial sadness, had resumed her position as the family's in-house critic, delivering sharp assessments of her brothers' behavior and opining on subjects ranging from household management to the course of the war. At nine years old, she was still small and would likely never grow even as tall as her petite mother. Nevertheless, she was already becoming a doll-like beauty, with softly curling blond hair, crystal blue eyes, and facial features Michelangelo might have carved from fine Carrara marble.

Claude was growing swiftly into his role as the manager of the plantation, and Marie Louise was especially pleased to see that he had embraced Plessant as a sounding board for his ideas on how to run Road's End. Perhaps because she had grown up in New Orleans, where she had seen the success of that city's small community of free men of color as artisans and small business owners, it did not seem odd to her that a Black man like Plessant might have ideas worth considering. In her view, and that of her son, Black people were not whites' equals, but neither did she think of them as subhuman creatures. As for their condition of servitude, well, that was simply how things were and not a situation she was inclined to question.

If there was concern in Marie Louise's mind about the future of any of her children, it was for that of her older son, Jean Louis. Named for her beloved physician father in New Orleans, Jean Louis was nearly nineteen, tall and dark, bookish like his father, and though he had accompanied his father on inspections of the plantation and to business meetings in town, it was clear to Marie Louise that life in Red Clay, Alabama, held little appeal for him. He yearned for the war to end so he might go to Princeton like his father and make his fortune in one of the great cities of the North, or perhaps abroad. He still spoke excitedly of the business trip he had made with his father in 1860 to New York, Philadelphia, and Washington.

"You cannot talk about those things now," Marie Louise had warned, back when the war began. "People here will not take it well, and it could go badly for you and for all of us."

"But why not, Maman?" the boy had whined. "It's just talk, and I do want the war to be over so I can go there again."

"I understand, *mon cher fils*, but you must keep it to yourself for now," Marie Louise had said.

Jean Louis had heeded her warning, but he was a man now, and Marie Louise knew that her influence with him was waning. He was unpredictable, and that made completion of the sale of Road's End more urgent; she did not know how he, or either of her other two children, would react. Marie Louise worried, too, that Jean Louis was old enough to be drafted into the Confederate army and that Claude would become eligible soon. The thought of her boys being pulled into this hellish war filled her with dread.

At the other end of the table, Jean Louis was going through the motions of having fun with his siblings for his mother's benefit. He understood the impact of his father's death on her, but he also was sick of waiting for the war to end, and he wanted to get on with his life. Now that he was eighteen, he especially feared that he might be drafted into the army with defeat a near certainty. General Lee was a great man, Jean Louis thought, but even Lee could not overcome the lack of supplies, mounting battlefield losses, and shattered morale within the ranks. Hadn't Jean Louis's own father been killed by men the sheriff thought were likely deserters? He would surely go mad, he thought, if he didn't find a way out soon.

As if reading Jean Louis's mind, Marie Louise interrupted the siblings' chatter. "I know these have been difficult times for all of you," she said, "with the loss of your father and how the war has made everything seem uncertain. But you should know that your father made certain arrangements for your futures, and I think the time has come for you to be aware of them."

———

Marie Louise had not been inside John Robert's study since the night she found his suicide note tucked inside a collection of Cicero's writings. But she had instructed Callie Mae to keep the room free of dust and to keep logs and kindling stacked in the fireplace. Now, as she walked inside, followed by her children, it seemed vaguely alien, the way one's hometown feels simultaneously familiar and unfamiliar after a long absence.

She stood behind John Robert's desk, gripping the top of the big leather chair where she had read the shocking letter. "Claude," she said, "please light the fire, and Jean Louis, please pour cognac for yourself, your brother, and for me, and a small sherry for your sister. This evening we will need the *courage liquide* of the drinks, even Addie." She smiled at her daughter. Addie beamed, obviously thrilled to be included in grownup conversation and feeling recognized by the small sip of sherry poured for her. The fire had caught quickly, and the warmth it generated was already easing the chill in the room.

Marie Louise moved from behind the chair and sat as Jean Louis passed around the drinks, and when they were all settled, she raised her snifter and nodded for her children to do the same. "To John Robert Parker, a magnificent husband, a fine father, and a friend to all who knew him," she said. They sipped their drinks and sat listening to the crackle of the fire.

Outside, bats swooped and dipped in the night sky to snatch the few remaining flying insects before winter settled in. Trees dropped their leaves as the winds blew ahead of an incoming storm. Down in the quarters, Black men, women, and children ate their meager meals and huddled around fireplaces to keep warm before going to bed. There would still be plenty of work to keep the plantation going when the fall harvest was done, but everyone at Road's End could feel the coming change in the air. On battlefields north and south, soldiers blue and gray fought on, dreading yet another winter of war seemingly without end, haunted by the prospect of death from the muzzle of a musket, a blast from a cannon, or the stab of a bayonet. Survivors struggled on, stalked by hunger, sickness, and exposure. The world was closing in on itself, shriveling into frosty darkness.

Marie Louise had dreaded this moment, but now it was here, and no other course was open to her than to go forward. She sipped her cognac, placed the glass on the desk, and began. "Your father was a man driven by duty. He so wanted a career as a lawyer and scholar," she said, her eyes focused above her children's heads, on the hands of the clock on the mantel. "But when his father was killed in an accident, he returned home from Princeton to take over the plantation. And when we were married and were blessed with you children, he accepted his responsibility and resigned himself to a lifetime as an Alabama planter."

She could feel Jean Louis's dread boring into her when she spoke of duty and life on the plantation, and she dropped her gaze to look at him directly. They held each other's eyes for seconds that felt like hours, and she knew then that what she was about to say next was the right thing—even though a lie was at the core of it. She took another sip of the cognac before she continued. "Your grandfather's untimely death haunted your father, and sometimes late at night he would speak with me about his fears that he, too, would die unexpectedly and how he did not want you to be forced to sacrifice your dreams as he had sacrificed his."

Jean Louis leaned forward, suddenly paying more attention to what his mother was saying. Addie's face was screwed into rapt attention, and Claude was leaning back in his chair as if studying the ceiling, his emotions impossible to read.

"Your father made extensive arrangements to ensure our financial well-being in the event of the untimely death he feared," Marie Louise said. "We will be well taken care of, but our lives will have to change."

"What do you mean, Maman?" Addie asked. "How will our lives change? What did Papa do?"

"Perhaps you will remember a Mr. George Flowers of Starkville, Mississippi?" Marie Louise said. "He is the one to whom your father sold some slaves last year." Jean Louis, Claude, and Addie nodded in unison as Marie Louise continued. "Mr. Flowers owns several plantations, and he admired Road's End, so much so that he sought to buy it. Your father declined, but they corresponded regularly, and they agreed that if Road's End ever came up for sale, Mr. Flowers would have the right of first refusal."

"What's that mean, Maman, right of first refusal?" Addie asked.

"It means," Claude said, jumping in uncharacteristically, "that Road's End has to be offered to Mr. Flowers before any other potential buyer." Then, glaring at his mother, he asked, "Are you selling the plantation?"

"*We* are selling it," she replied, "but not unless we all agree that it is the right thing to do. Before you make a decision, however, let me tell you what your father and I envisioned in the event of such a sale." Marie Louise felt nervous now; her palms were sweating. So much depended on what she said next. "Jean Louis, your father and I knew that you could never be happy living out your life here, so the sale would make it possible for you to leave for Europe right away to study and to remain there after the war if you choose to, or to return to America when the war is over to make your life in the North or wherever you might decide to settle.

"Claude, I know how much you have invested in Road's End. In fact, I have encouraged it, because Mr. Flowers, who lives in Mississippi, will need someone to manage the plantation. Through your father's attorneys, you have been suggested to Mr. Flowers as that person. He will be here next week to inspect the property, and he is inclined to offer you the position if he likes what he sees and hears during his visit. You must have your plans ready to share with him during his stay," she said.

"Addie, you would move to New Orleans with me to live in my father's home. You would go to school, and you would have friends among the other children there, and I think you will find them to be more sophisticated than the little girls here, more to your liking. I think you would have real friends and teachers at school who appreciate a smart girl like you."

There was silence in the room, and they all jumped in their seats at a knock on the door. They laughed nervously when Callie Mae entered the room. "Elmira gettin' ready to go. Y'all need anything 'fore she leave?" she asked.

"Thank you, Callie Mae. You can tell her we are fine," Marie Louise replied.

"Yassum," Callie Mae said, eyeing the Parkers closely before leaving.

Behind the closed door of the study, the four Parkers continued to sit, all of them contemplating futures none of them would have imagined a month earlier. Marie Louise broke the silence. "I'm very tired," she said. "We can talk again in the morning."

"Good night, Maman," Addie, Claude, and Jean Louis said in unison. "*Bonne nuit.*"

Chapter 13

In the weeks since Felix's encounter with the bully Big Joe, his stature in the fields had risen. He wasn't merely the water boy; he was someone to be addressed by name and engaged in conversation as he moved up and down the rows with his buckets. He and his friend Jimmy had become what passed for celebrities in the fields, and during the midday breaks, the other boys sought out their company. Little girls giggled behind their hands when they walked by. Big Joe and his gang had become objects of scorn.

"I guess you think you somebody now," Elmira said over her shoulder to Felix as she bustled about the kitchen of the big house in the early morning hours. He had walked up to the big house with his mother, as he often did while it was still dark outside. Plessant rose later now that he had new duties in the wake of John Robert's death, and so Felix accompanied Elmira. No one had asked him to do it. He just did.

No one else was awake in the big house at that hour but the two of them and Callie Mae, who was busy with other tasks upstairs.

"I heard about how you and Jimmy been struttin' around like you done somethin' important," Elmira said, her back still turned to her son.

"I ain't done nothin', Maw," Felix replied, feeling the heat of blood rushing up his neck to his face, and he nearly choked on a big bite of the fresh hot biscuit his mother had given him from the batch she'd made for the Parker family's breakfast table.

"That's right," she snapped, "you *ain't* done nothin'—leastwise nothin' to be struttin' around about like that old rooster used to crow so loud in the mornin'. You ain't heard him in a while, has you?" Not waiting for an answer, she continued, "You ain't heard him 'cause Miss Marie Louise got tired of hearin' him, and he wound up in my pot with some potatoes and carrots and celery and onions. Miss Marie Louise and Massa Claude say he tasted real good."

"I ain't no rooster—" Felix protested.

Elmira cut him off. "No, you ain't no rooster, Felix, but I'll tell you this. Folks happy now that you got the best of Big Joe and them, but 'fore long they gon' change and be wantin' to bring you down to where they is. Folks don't like to see nobody better off than them. Why you think your paw and me don't never talk about little extras we get? Why you think he don't talk about ridin' around in that wagon all day with Massa Claude, talkin' 'bout how to run this place? Folks get jealous, Felix, white folks *and* Black folks, and when they get jealous, they get mean." She stopped and looked her son in the eye. "You understand what I'm sayin' to you?"

"Yassum," he said, "I understand."

"Well, get out of here, then," she said, and hugged him tightly before shoving him toward the door. Felix skipped out of the back door and ran across the wet grass toward the fields.

Dawn was breaking, and the landscape, shrouded in shades of gray, was emerging into the golds, reds, browns, and greens of the Alabama countryside in autumn. The air was cool, and the smell of smoke from his mother's cooking fire and the aromas of bacon frying and biscuits baking mingled with earthy farm scents. In the underbrush and in the woods, the animals of the night were scurrying back to their dens, and creatures of the day were venturing out for their time on nature's stage. Felix ran fast, as fast as he had ever run, and when the first field hands appeared in the rows, he was already there, with his buckets full and a smile on his face.

By the time the sun had risen, Plessant was dressed and ready for work. He made his way to the stable and hitched the horse to the wagon. The sunshine felt good on his face, and the cool air invigorated him as he pulled deep draughts into his lungs. He liked his new job, and he enjoyed the time he spent with Claude. It seemed to Plessant that Claude was like his mother when it came to Black people; she didn't treat them like livestock, too stupid to do anything without somebody standing over them with a whip. Claude listened to him when they talked about how to run the plantation, but the boy was smart and had good ideas of his own.

He ain't nothin' like that brother of his, Plessant thought. *That Jean Louis ain't worth nothin'. He might be good with his books and stuff, but he don't understand nothin' about running this farm. Miss Marie Louise was right to put Massa Claude in charge.* Also, he knew that when the slave catchers captured Big Joe and his gang, it was Jean Louis—in Claude's absence—who had acquiesced to the overseer's recommendation that they be whipped to within an inch of their lives. Now that he thought of it, Jean Louis reminded him of the late John Robert, and the mere thought of the man who had sold his children stirred the deep anger in him that never really went away.

By the time he led the horse and wagon around to the front of the big house to meet Claude, Plessant had regained his composure, and he was looking forward to the business of the day.

———

Each of the three Parker siblings had reacted differently to their mother's announcement of her plans for their future. Claude had awakened the next morning after a night of fitful sleep. He had always assumed that he would join his father in running Road's End and that one day it would be his, and he felt a flash of anger that it was not so. Still, the deal with Mr. Flowers offered a chance. *I can do this*, he thought. *I can make Road's End profitable, and maybe I can make it mine someday.*

Addie had slept soundly. She had been to New Orleans once, when she was three years old, practically a baby, and she remembered very little of it, though she recalled her grandfather who spoke French and sang funny songs to her while he bounced her on his knee. In the years since, he had always sent gifts for her birthday and letters about things he had seen and done. She would be happy to see him again. Also, the thought of going to a real school with other girls like herself was intriguing. It would be different from having a tutor come to the house, and Maman had said the teachers would be nuns. Addie had never seen a nun, but her mother had told her about the stern black-and-white-clad women who had been her own teachers—brilliant, powerful women who terrorized you one moment and comforted you the next, and Addie was eager to see them and talk to them.

Of the three siblings, none was more excited about the prospect of selling Road's End than Jean Louis. He had long felt as if he had been born into the wrong family and that no one else could see it. It wasn't that he didn't love his family. But they were in the South and they lived on a plantation and liked it. Jean Louis loved the big cities, the faster pace and the sophistication of people who had traveled, were educated, went to the theater, and dined in fine restaurants. He knew he was like his father—everyone said so—but John Robert had settled for plantation life, and Jean Louis had no intention of doing the same. Now he'd been offered a way out, and he was going to take it.

Although the Parker siblings had accepted the sale of Road's End, none of them were more enthusiastic than Marie Louise, which surprised her. She had long ago settled into her life in Red Clay, focused on her family and friends and the household, controlled by the rhythms of the seasons that governed the pace of plantation life. So when her children told her over breakfast, one by one, that they supported her plans, she was caught off guard by the leap her heart made.

The sights, sounds, and smells of New Orleans came back to her in a rush, all so colorful when compared with Red Clay. She longed to speak French every day, to eat food prepared with a French sensibility, but influenced by ingredients and spices from Spain, Africa, and the Caribbean, and to reembrace her Catholic faith. Most of all she wanted to spend time with her father. He was in his sixties, and though he still practiced medicine and went to Mass daily, letters from friends suggested that he missed his late wife, taken in the yellow fever epidemic that ravaged New Orleans in 1853. Marie Louise believed that her presence, and especially that of Addie, would help to revitalize his spirits.

"So, it is agreed?" she asked as they finished the morning meal. She smiled as the three siblings nodded in assent. "Good."

In the kitchen, Callie Mae whispered to Elmira, "They's somethin' goin' on with them. They stop talking when I go in, and they all got this look on they faces like they got a big secret."

"Only thing I know is that they got company coming next week. It's that man from Mississippi what bought my son and daughter and some others from Massa John Robert last year, and I got to tell you it got me worried," Elmira said. "Miss Marie Louise say I'm supposed to cook like Sunday dinner every day while he here."

———

Claude stepped out onto the front porch just as Plessant brought the wagon around the corner of the house. "Good mornin', Massa Claude. What you gon' do today? Where you want to go?" Plessant said.

"Good morning, Plessant," he replied. "I want to take another look at that wooded land by the creek, and then you and I need to talk over some plans."

They drove in silence for a few minutes before Plessant screwed up his courage to ask the question that had been burning in his brain for a day and a half, since Elmira had come home with news that made her nervous and on the verge of tears.

"Massa Claude, I hope it's all right, but I got to ask you somethin'," he said. "You ain't gettin' ready to sell my boy Felix, is you?"

Lost in his own thoughts, Claude didn't respond immediately. "What's that? What did you ask me, Plessant?" he said, dragging himself back from his reverie about his possible future at Road's End. "Did you ask me something?"

"Yassuh, I asked if you was planning to sell my boy Felix."

"What makes you think that?" Claude replied.

"Well, suh, I wouldn't ask 'cept I heard that man from Mississippi what bought my other two children is comin' here, and I want to know if you plannin' to sell Felix?"

Claude regarded Plessant for a long moment before responding. "Do you trust me, Plessant?" he asked.

Plessant met the young white man's eyes, a simple act that could get a Black man killed, and said nothing. The silence was complete, broken only by the *clip-clop* of the horse's hooves on the packed dirt road.

"Stop the horse, Plessant," Claude said finally. Plessant pulled the reins and the wagon came to a halt. "The fact is that you don't have any reason to trust me, do you?" Claude said. "My grandfather hated the Coloreds and gave you to my father soon after you were born. Later, my father sold your other two children, and you have seen others sold off this plantation. You have seen the harsh punishments inflicted on servants for slight transgressions. You know the hypocrisy that overrides all manner of relationships between Black folks and white folks.

"In your place, I wouldn't trust me either. But I think I have given you reason to believe that I am a fair man who appreciates you and what you have contributed to Road's End. I cannot be specific about things that are going to happen here, but I can tell you that there will be many changes, and I can tell you that selling your boy is not one of them. You can choose to believe me or not, but that will be up to you."

Plessant regarded Claude for another long moment before picking up the reins and clucking to the horse to start moving again. "Yassuh," he said, "I reckon you is telling the truth."

By the time they had inspected the woodlands and spent a couple of hours reviewing observations they had made in recent weeks about ways to run the plantation efficiently and profitably, the sun was low in the sky, lighting up low-hanging clouds in shades of red and purple. Down at the creek, bream were starting to rise for bugs floating on the surface, even as they were themselves stalked by largemouth bass lurking below. Overhead, a V-shaped formation of migrating Canada geese had begun its descent to the three-acre pond down the road to rest for the night before the next leg of their journey the following morning. In the pasture, workers were herding their bovine charges back to the barn, and the first wave of field hands were on their way to the scales to have their harvest weighed. The day was drawing to a close at Road's End Plantation.

Claude and Plessant rode back to the big house in silence, their eyes fixed on the horse's rear end as it pulled them toward home. "Tomorrow," Claude said, "get the buggy ready to drive my mother and me into Red Clay. She has to meet with the lawyers, and I have business with some other planters. We'll leave right after breakfast."

"Yassuh," Plessant said. "I'll have it ready."

That night Elmira lay in Plessant's arms, wide awake as Plessant was drifting off to sleep. "You really think he tellin' the truth about not sellin' Felix?" she asked.

"I think so," he said, "and I think he was tellin' the truth about big changes coming around here, but I don't know what it got to do with that man from Mississippi coming to visit. All I know is things about to change; I just hope it don't mess up nothin' for us."

"I'm prayin'," Elmira said. "I'm prayin'."

Chapter 14

Plessant was relieved when, just after noon, he turned the buggy onto the drive up to the big house on Road's End Plantation. The morning in Red Clay had been long, while Claude met with other planters and Marie Louise sat with the lawyers, and he was tired. But something was wrong. The maid Callie Mae was standing on the front porch, wringing her hands and whimpering, "Lawd, Lawd, Lawd. This sho nuff is a mess." She was peering in the direction of the fields. Next to her, Addie stood with her arms folded, also craning her neck toward the fields from which the sound of raised voices could be faintly heard.

"What is this? What's going on?" Claude demanded as the buggy rolled to a halt in front of the house.

"First, one of the women from the field came running up to the back of the house, and you could hear them all shouting down there," Addie reported. "Then Elmira and the other woman ran back to the field." Jean Louis came out of the house while Addie was speaking, and Claude turned to him.

"Do you know what this is about?" Claude asked.

"Not really," he said. "One of the overseers came up here just now and said there was trouble with one of the young boys and his mama out there. I told him to handle it and not to bother me again about some pickaninny and his mammy."

Claude and Plessant, who had leaped from the buggy to help Marie Louise climb down, exchanged a look, and without speaking they ran toward the fields. When they arrived, they pushed through a crowd of workers and found a scene that stopped them in their tracks.

Felix was standing behind Elmira, backed against a tree at the end of a row of dried-out cornstalks ready to be plowed under to make way for planting the next year's crop. He was gaping at the overseer in terror from behind his mother's skirts. Elmira's eyes blazed in defiance, locked onto the hard gaze of the overseer. Neither blinked, and the overseer, whip in hand, was advancing slowly toward the mother and son.

"Stop," Claude said and stepped into the space between the overseer and Elmira. "What's the problem here, Mr. Wilson?"

"It's nothing you should be concerned about, sir. It's just the usual nigger trouble; I'll take care of it," the overseer said. Jacob Wilson was an older man, perhaps twice Claude's age, taller and half again the younger man's weight. His dingy white shirt was sweat-stained in the armpits, and his stale breath smelled of onions, tobacco, and whiskey.

"Well, Mr. Wilson, I believe that I shall reserve the right to decide what is worthy of my time at Road's End," Claude said. "So I will ask again: What is the problem here?"

Plessant had moved to stand next to Elmira and Felix. He still didn't know what had happened, but any time there was trouble between two white men with a Black boy at the center of it, the situation could become lethal at any moment.

Jacob Wilson considered the young man in front of him. He didn't know what to make of the soft-looking young man, but the determined set of his mouth and his unflinching gaze suggested that there might be more to him than met the eye. Wilson had liked the boy's father and had been sad when he heard about John Robert's death. He had figured that the older boy, Jean Louis, would take over, but the word around was that this younger one would end up as the boss, and Wilson needed his job. So, he answered carefully. "I give 'em their break at noontime, and when it's time to go back to work, the little nigger there was takin' his time gettin' back on the job. I say, 'Break is over. Get your black ass back to work.' He didn't move and looked at me like he didn't hear nothin' I said.

"So I tell the boy to come over here to me because I'm goin' to whip him to teach him a lesson. That's when the rest of 'em started gatherin' around. Then the boy's mama comes runnin' out here. She rips a switch off one of the bushes and says if her boy is goin' to be whipped that she will do it, and starts draggin' him off. That's when you showed up."

Claude listened until the overseer finished speaking. The enslaved workers were crowded around, hanging on every word. The children among them were terrified, and one of them, an older girl named Lucille, barely in her teens, buried her face in her mother's bosom. Not two days earlier, she had barely escaped Wilson's sexual advances when the overseer was distracted by a fight between two field hands and she ran into the woods.

Off to the side, Plessant, Elmira, and Felix were huddled together, their eyes moving back and forth from Claude to the overseer. Claude took Wilson's arm and guided him into the shade of a fifty-foot hickory tree, out of earshot of the workers.

"Mr. Wilson, did you ever hear of John Brown?" he asked. He continued when the overseer shook his head. "John Brown was a Yankee abolitionist who believed in the violent overthrow of the institution of slavery, an institution that benefits both of us. It is not in our interest to see it end, which is why we have been fighting this war against the Union for more than four years. Now, there are many abolitionists," Claude continued, "but Brown was especially dangerous, because he wanted to arm the slaves for insurrection.

"You are a smart man, Mr. Wilson, and I can see that you understand what would happen if the slaves got it into their heads to move against us, with or without weapons. All across the South, there are more of them than there are of us. Even the Yankees understood the problem, so when they caught Brown in a raid on a military arsenal in West Virginia five years ago, they took him over to Virginia and hanged him straightaway. Robert E. Lee himself, who was then in the Yankee military, led the raid at Harpers Ferry." Claude paused to let the impact of his words sink in with the overseer.

"So, Mr. Wilson, you can see how many of them there are in this field right now and that there are just two of us. I am sure you can imagine what they might do, even without weapons and already agitated as they are, if you put the whip to an eight-year-old boy in front of his mama and daddy." Claude was working to keep his voice calm and reasonable, striving to communicate with Wilson, another white man, albeit one who would never be invited to the Parker supper table.

"Here is what I propose, Mr. Wilson. That woman, Elmira, who is our cook and a favorite of my mother, said she would whip the boy herself. Is that right?" Claude said.

Wilson nodded.

"I say we can allow her to keep her word," Claude said. "You hold all the slaves here to watch while she whips him good with that switch of hers. That way, the boy gets punished and the rest of them get the lesson, and you hold on to your authority to keep them in line. And we don't have a rebellion on our hands. If you wish, you can say you persuaded me that this was the best option."

The overseer nodded as if assessing Claude with a new perspective. Then he squared his shoulders and said, "Yes sir, I think you, that is, *we*, have a plan."

"Thank you, Mr. Wilson," Claude said. "I can see why my father was glad to have you at Road's End."

———

Felix was sobbing by the time Elmira finished the punishment in front of the other field hands, and so was she. She had lost count of how many times she had struck her son on his buttocks, whipping him through his pants, but at least, she thought, he had been spared the overseer's lash on his bare back. His flogging might well have killed Felix, and her along with him.

"Now I got to finish fixin' y'all's supper," she said to Claude. She dropped the switch and marched back to the big house, leaving Felix with Plessant. He hugged the boy and then noticed Claude watching them. They did not speak, but a look passed between them that carried a message they both understood.

"I got to put the horse and buggy away," Plessant said to Felix. "You go on home now, and I'll be there directly."

"Yassuh," Felix replied and moved gingerly toward the cabin, his rear end burning with every step.

"I guess you ain't so high and mighty now, is you?" a familiar voice shouted out to him.

Felix whipped around to see Big Joe staring at him with a grin on his one-eyed face. He was going to say something back, but it was just too much trouble, so he trudged on toward home.

When Elmira returned to the cabin that evening, she took one look at Felix and burst into tears again. "I'm so ashamed," she sobbed, "but I didn't know what else to do to keep that man from beating you with that whip." Plessant, his own eyes brimming with tears, grabbed Felix by the hand and dragged him over to his mother, and the three of them held each other until the crying stopped.

"Felix, I have to ask," Plessant said. "Why was you actin' like that today, and why didn't you go back to work when the man told you to?"

Felix squirmed in his chair before answering. "I don't know. I had to pee, so I went in the woods by the field, and when I came out, that old overseer was yellin' at me. Everybody was lookin', and I guess I got mad and took my time. Old Wilson ain't nobody special. You better than him, Paw. You work for Mr. Claude and ride around in the wagon with him."

Plessant felt tears rising in his eyes, and he struggled to keep them from overflowing onto his cheeks. "Come here, boy," he said. He lifted Felix onto his lap and held him tightly. "It's a sad thing, son, but here it is. White folks think we ain't no better than animals, like the pigs and the cows, 'cept we can talk and know how to behave in the house.

"They forget we build they houses, cook they food, raise they crops, and do a whole bunch of other things they couldn't live without. It suits them to think they can treat us like animals—sell off our children, whip us, anything else—just 'cause they skin is white and ours is black. It ain't right, it ain't true, and it hurts me to have to tell you this, but you got to understand it if you want to stay alive. You understand what I'm sayin'?"

Felix nodded.

"All right, time to go to bed now," Plessant said. He blew out the kerosene lamp, and he and Elmira went into the other room.

Lying on his pallet in the darkness, his backside still smarting from the whipping, Felix thought about his father's words. He understood what he had said, and in the darkness he cried again. This time, however, it was because of the pain in his heart.

Chapter 15

The visit to Road's End by George Flowers of Starkville, Mississippi, was expected to be brief—less than a week—but everyone on the plantation seemed to understand that he was not making an ordinary social call.

In the days before his arrival, Elmira and Callie Mae had been beside themselves as Marie Louise bustled about, making new menus for Elmira and scrutinizing Callie Mae's cleaning in minute detail. She had even brought a couple of women in from the fields to help with cleaning floors, dusting, and washing and ironing.

"She ain't even do all this when the preacher comin' to visit," Callie Mae said. "What you think goin' on?" she asked Elmira during a quiet moment.

"I don't know," Elmira replied. "All I know is this the same man what bought my babies from Massa John Robert, so cain't nothin' good be comin' from it. Plessant say him and Massa Claude been talkin' a lot about how many slaves is on this plantation and the work they be doin'. I don't like this none at all."

Callie Mae reached out to hug her friend but pulled back when she saw the look in Elmira's eyes. Both women knew that if they surrendered to the moment, inconsolable sobbing would follow like a mighty wave of hurt and sorrow no seawall could stop, and they both knew there was no time for that. George Flowers was coming, and there was work to do.

———

In the wooded land on the far end of the plantation, bordered by the creek where catfish lurked in deep holes and largemouth bass cruised for minnows and frogs in the weeds, Plessant and Claude sat on the seat of the parked wagon and gazed upward through gaps in the treetop canopy. Menacing storm clouds spread across the sky, hiding the sun and causing insects and animals to prepare for the night even though it was just three o'clock. A light breeze rustled through the high branches of the trees, but on the ground, the air was still and humid. Perspiration clung to their skin and did not evaporate.

"I reckon it gon' rain, Massa Claude," Plessant said.

"I think you are right, Plessant," Claude replied. "We'll head back soon, but I wanted to stop here to talk to you."

"Yassuh?" he replied.

"I wanted to thank you for all the work you've been doing as I've tried to assess what the plantation needs. I have appreciated it. Good work has been done here, and I think we have a plan for going forward that will ensure success," Claude said.

Plessant nodded.

"There's one part of the plan that I think will be especially profit-able, and it's really your idea," Claude said. "You pointed out that the blacksmith shop and the carpentry shop have two problems in common: One, the blacksmith and the carpenter are getting old, and neither of them has a helper, an apprentice if you will, who can learn the trade and take over for them someday; and two, neither of them has enough work to keep them busy all the time."

Plessant nodded again, wondering where this was going.

"Here's what I'm going to do. I'm going to rent out the services of the blacksmith and the carpenter to other plantations when they can be spared here, and I'm going to give them each a young apprentice to help with the work and to learn the trade," Claude said. He turned to look at Plessant directly and waited for a response.

Plessant didn't know what to say. He had suggested this plan, but he was unprepared to hear his suggestion being taken seriously. "Yassuh," he said, "I think that will be just fine."

"I'm glad you agree, Plessant, because I want to know what you think about the next part of it," Claude said. "We need to pick a couple of young fellows to be those apprentices. I'm thinking about that water boy, Jimmy, to put with the blacksmith. He seems a likely boy, and he's a friend of your son Felix, isn't he?"

"Yassuh," Plessant said. "He's a good boy, and he been a good friend to Felix."

"That's what I thought," Claude said. He paused before continuing. "I guess Felix would miss having his friend in the field with him, so I was thinking that maybe Felix should have a new job too. What do you think about having him go to work for the carpenter?"

Plessant's eyes grew wide. Chances like that didn't come along often, and he didn't know what to say. Finally, he managed to squeeze out some words. "Thank you, Massa Claude," he said. "Thank you. I can't wait to tell his maw. She been so worried about him out there in the fields."

It had begun to rain, though neither of them had noticed until now. Plessant snapped the reins to start the horse toward home, and as the raindrops soaked his shirt and washed dust from his face, he smiled. It was, he thought, a good day.

———

George Flowers arrived on Tuesday, accompanied by a lawyer and an enslaved man who drove his carriage and saw to his personal needs. Marie Louise and her children greeted him at the front steps of the big house, squinting into the late morning sun as Flowers lowered himself onto the ground. Except for Addie, Flowers had to look up to smile into the faces of each of the Parkers. He removed his hat, revealing thinning, mostly gray hair, and bowed slightly, causing his waistcoat buttons to strain against his ample belly. "I regret that the death of your husband is the occasion of our meeting again, madam, but I am hopeful that our business will result in a measure of comfort for you and your family," he said.

That evening at supper, he praised Marie Louise for her hospitality, and especially for the spread of roast pork and gravy, mashed potatoes, and green beans, served with a fine old claret from John Robert's cellar, followed by blackberry cobbler and coffee. Pushing back from the table, he declared it to be "the most delicious repast I have enjoyed in many a year."

On Wednesday, he spent most of his time with Claude, accompanied by the lawyer, in John Robert's study, going over financials and listening to Claude's plans for how the plantation should be operated. On Thursday, Plessant drove Flowers and Claude around the plantation, as the prospective buyer inspected the property and questioned Claude on fine points about how his plans for land use and labor management matched the financial plans they had discussed the day before. On Friday, Plessant drove Claude and his mother into town to meet with Flowers, his lawyer, and the Parker family's lawyers.

Plessant waited outside with the horse and buggy, parked under a tree, next to Flowers's carriage. It was the first time he'd had a chance to talk to Flowers's driver, a rangy young man with dark brown skin and startlingly light-hazel-colored eyes that gave away nothing when he spoke. He said his name was Ben.

"They been treatin' you all right?" Plessant asked.

"Yeah, I been all right," Ben replied. "I been sleepin' on a pallet in the barn, and they been feedin' me good. The woman brought the food this mornin' say the cook is your wife. I ain't never had better than that."

Plessant laughed. "I got me a good one, all right," he said. "Say, let me ask you somethin'. How is it where y'all come from? They treat us all right there?"

"Depend on where you is," Ben said. "I was a boy on Massa George's plantation in Louisiana, and it was hard. Overseers like to use the whip, and the food and the cabins wasn't too good. Worked us hard. Two years ago Massa George bring me and some other mens up to his farm in Mississippi, and it was better there. I think it's 'cause that's where he live, and the overseers know they got to answer to him on the spot."

"You like him?" Plessant asked.

"Well, there's some a lot worse'n him," Ben said. "He always treat me all right since he pulled me out the field to look after him."

They stood in silence, each man considering the world and their place in it.

"I'm gon' get up on the buggy and rest," Plessant said. "Ain't no tellin' how long they gon' be in there. 'Fore I do, can I ask you one more thing?"

Ben nodded.

"You ever meet a young boy and his sister on your place, boy named John, about fifteen, and the girl named Bessie, about thirteen?" Plessant asked.

"No, I don't think so," Ben said. "Why you ask?"

"I know they mama been wondering 'bout them, and they daddy too. Just thought I'd ask," Plessant said.

Ben seemed confused, until he grasped the nature of Plessant's question. "I ain't seen them," he said, "but if I meet 'em when I get home, I'll let 'em know they is missed."

Chapter 16

On Friday, November 11, Marie Louise sat in the parlor of the home that was no longer hers. Road's End had been sold the day before to Flowers. *And not a moment too soon*, she thought. She was staring through the front window at a bleak afternoon landscape of trees stripped of their leaves and a lawn more brown than green under a slate-colored sky crowded with low-hanging clouds. Burning logs crackled and hissed in the fireplace, and she sipped cognac from one of her late husband's snifters. Her knitting lay untouched in a bag on the floor beside her chair.

Thanksgiving was fourteen days away, and the Parker family, like most of their neighbors, did not observe what they considered a "Yankee holiday." This year, however, Marie Louise had decided that they would celebrate at Road's End, because in spite of everything that had happened, she was grateful that John Robert's high-stakes gamble seemed to be playing out as he had hoped. "I do not know if the Church is right when it says suicides go to hell," she whispered to her husband, as if he could still hear her, "but surely God will understand that you did what you did to protect us and to make a future for our children. I pray that it is true and that I shall see you again in heaven."

The war was going badly for the South, and there was widespread

speculation that Lee would be forced to surrender by spring if no mira-
cle occurred to save the Confederates from defeat. The area around Red
Clay had been spared the worst ravages of the war, but no one knew
what would happen in the wake of hostilities. Marie Louise knew only
that her husband's fraud had saved the family from potential financial
ruin and that her sons would be spared the risk of death on the field
of battle. Jean Louis would be leaving the country to study in Europe
in a few weeks, and Claude, through the lawyers' connections, had acquired a minor civil service position similar to one his late father had
held. The position existed mainly on paper and required only a few
hours per week, but it provided an exemption from conscription into
the army of the Confederacy.

More importantly, the minimal duties also allowed Claude to accept
the position he had pursued as the manager of Road's End. He would
continue to live in the big house, and his mother and sister could remain
there as his guests until arrangements were completed for their move to
New Orleans, including settlement of the life insurance policy and investment of the proceeds from the sale of the plantation in banks and
brokerages up North. A suite of rooms would be maintained for George
Flowers's use whenever he visited the property.

"Your plan is working, my dear husband, but what a price we have
paid," Marie Louise said softly. "What a price we have paid."

———

On that same evening, Plessant and Elmira were sitting on the steps
of their cabin after supper. Felix had been sent to bed, and they were
luxuriating in the peace of the nighttime darkness, their faces illuminated by the glow of a nearly full moon. Shivering in the cool evening
breeze, Elmira moved closer to Plessant, felt the warmth of his body,
and rested her head on his shoulder. "Things ain't never gon' be the
same, is they?" she asked.

"No, baby, they ain't," Plessant replied, "but I think we gon' be all
right long as Massa Claude in charge. Didn't he already take Felix out

the field and put him in the carpenter shop? And he say he gon' talk to me tomorrow about what I'm gon' be doin'."

He hadn't felt so sure that morning when the enslaved Black workers had all been gathered in front of the big house to be told about the sale of Road's End and to meet George Flowers, the man who now owned them, along with the livestock, the house, the barn, the fields, the tools, and everything else within the confines of the plantation. The meeting was short, just long enough for them to get a look at Flowers's face and for him to announce that Claude would be in charge after his departure. He thanked them for their "faithful service" to the late John Robert and said he hoped they would continue to work hard for him.

Callie Mae stood off to the side with a woman she had known in the fields before she came to work in the big house. "What you think?" Callie Mae asked.

"Don't mean nothin' to me," the woman said. "Don't matter who in charge. Me and mine still be sweatin' in the fields."

For Plessant, Elmira, and Felix, however, Claude's position was critical, and Plessant was anxious to meet with him in the morning to learn what lay in store for him and for his family. In the early morning hours, before Elmira left for the big house, Plessant hugged his wife and whispered to her: "It's gon' be all right, Elmira."

"How you know?" she replied.

"I just know, that's all. I just know."

The next morning, Plessant drove Claude into town for his meetings and to check in at his ostensible courthouse job. They didn't speak for the first few minutes, listening instead to the rhythmic beat of the horse's hooves on the hard dirt country road and observing migrating birds flying low, a sign that a storm was on the way.

"You think we gon' be back 'fore it rain, Massa Claude?" Plessant asked.

"I think so, Plessant. Anyway, if it rains, we'll just get wet. It won't be the first time, will it?" Claude threw his head back and laughed. "Listen," he said, "I wanted to talk to you about what's going on at Road's End. There'll be a lot of changes. We're going to send about a dozen of the field hands over to Mississippi to work on Mr. Flowers's other plantation, and you already know that we're going to be renting out some others, and not just the carpenter and the blacksmith. This winter we're going to rent out some field hands to the county for building maintenance and other work too. And we're going to raise more cotton and turn some of that wooded land into fields for more produce."

"That all sound pretty good," Plessant said, worried now that he hadn't yet heard anything about himself and his family.

"How's Felix doing in the carpenter's shop?" Claude asked.

"I think he gon' do fine. He just been over there a few days, but he say he like it. Say the old man start teachin' him about all the different kinds of wood and what you do with it, and he say he like usin' the tools."

"That's good, but I guess you're wondering about you and Elmira," Claude said.

"I reckon so," Plessant replied.

"Well," Claude said, "I don't mind telling you that I had to fight with Mr. Flowers over her. He got a taste of her cooking on his last visit, and he wanted to take her with him."

Plessant's blood ran cold. *First my children and now my wife*, he thought. *I ain't havin' it. I ain't havin' it.*

Claude could see that he was growing agitated. "Don't worry," he said. "I was able to persuade him to leave her here."

The words were reassuring, but the whole exchange left Plessant with an uneasy feeling, and he could sense the anger that he managed to keep in check most of the time starting to boil up, threatening to over-flow in an uncontrolled torrent. He liked Claude, and he appreciated all that he had done for his family—unlike his siblings, especially that good-for-nothing older brother of his. *But if anything happen to Elmira or Felix, I won't stop before I get my satisfaction*, he thought.

"As for you," Claude continued, "I hope you'll be glad to hear that you'll be staying on with me, doing just what you're doing now. I'll prob-ably ask you to take on some other jobs too, but mainly I need you to be around the way you have been."

He waited for Plessant's reaction, but it was slow in coming as Plessant wound himself down from his agitated state. "Yassuh," he said to the man who was little more than half his age, "I'll be proud to work for you."

———

In the big-house kitchen, Elmira was preparing the midday meal when Callie Mae walked in, looking confused and dejected. "Where you been all day, Callie Mae? I ain't seen you since this mornin'," Elmira asked over her shoulder as she mixed batter for a fresh pan of cornbread. When Callie Mae didn't answer, she turned around to see the house-maid burst into tears.

"What's wrong with you, girl?" Elmira asked, alarmed to see her friend in distress.

Through her tears Callie Mae managed to say she had been with Marie Louise and learned that she had not been sold with the planta-tion. Instead, the mistress was taking her to New Orleans to work for Addie and her when they moved in with Marie Louise's father. "I'm so scared, Elmira. I ain't never been nowhere off this plantation 'cept to go to church now and then," she said. "I don't know nothin' about no New Orleans. I don't know nobody there. I been here all my life, and the only friends I got is here, and you my best friend, Elmira. I don't want to go," she sobbed.

Elmira hugged Callie Mae and let her cry until she stopped. As the tears subsided, Elmira pushed Callie Mae back and held her at arm's length. "You listen to me," she said. "First of all, ain't nothin' you or nobody else can do about this. You goin' to New Orleans whether you wants to or not. But the next thing is, it coulda been worse. You better be glad you goin' with Miss Marie Louise and Miss Addie. You coulda been goin' to that Mississippi plantation, and you don't know nobody there neither. This way, at least you know who you gon' be working for, and you know they's plenty worse than them two."

"But you my friend, Elmira," Callie Mae said. "I don't want to leave you, and I worry 'bout you. What if—"

Elmira cut her off quickly. "You ain't got to worry about me," she said. "Massa Claude done told Plessant that him and me gon' stay right here and keep doin' what we do. Felix workin' in the carpenter shop, and it look like he gon' do fine there." Elmira gripped the younger woman's shoulders tightly and looked into her eyes. "I'll miss you too, baby, but it seem like you gon' be all right." Then, with a twinkle in her eye, she added, "You know, I come from New Orleans with Miss Marie Louise all them years ago when she married Massa John Robert, and best I remember they was some fine lookin' mens there for a good-lookin' young woman like you to choose from."

Callie Mae wiped the tears from her eyes with the bottom of her apron, and they both started laughing, and they didn't stop until Addie showed up in the doorway. "What's going on in here?" she demanded.

"Nothin', Miss Addie," Elmira said. "We just actin' a fool. Supper be ready in a few minutes, and you and your mama and your brothers can come eat. Can I get you anything now?"

"No," Addie replied and flounced away. She had hardly disappeared from the doorway when Callie Mae and Elmira began to laugh again.

In the next room, Addie stood silently sulking, listening to the laughter in the kitchen and wondering what she had missed.

Chapter 17

Thanksgiving Day, 1864, arrived gray and cold with news that Confederate forces were in desperate straits, especially in Georgia, where General Sherman's "march to the sea" from Atlanta to Savannah was destroying everything in its path, depriving the South of material resources and weakening the combatants' resolve. Earlier in the year the fighting had come close to Red Clay, when General Polk retreated to Demopolis, Alabama, from the Confederate stronghold in Meridian, Mississippi, in the face of Sherman's relentless onslaught. The tide was turning against the Confederacy, and all but the willfully ignorant knew it. Change was coming, and no one could predict what it would bring.

The bounty of Marie Louise's personal Thanksgiving dinner at Road's End did not reflect the hardship and turmoil that afflicted the rest of the region. A golden-roasted wild turkey shot by Claude dominated the table, scenting the air with the aromas of herbs, spices, nuts, and fruit when he sliced into the bird's breast, releasing a puff of steam from the cavity in which cornbread stuffing had been baked. Green beans canned at the end of summer, mashed potatoes and gravy, roasted carrots, and fresh yeast rolls rounded out the feast. "This is a fine meal you have prepared for us, Elmira," Marie Louise said when the cook brought the last of the dishes to the table. "I want you to take some home to your family when you are done here."

"Yassum, thank you," Elmira said and rushed back to the kitchen.

The Parker family sat in their accustomed places around the table, leaving John Robert's chair empty. "Jean Louis, I would normally ask you as the eldest to give thanks for the abundance we are about to share, but as this could be the last time we will all be together around a table like this, I shall reserve that honor for myself," Marie Louise said and bowed her head. She continued, "Father, we thank you for the food on this table, and we ask that you help us to appreciate our good fortune, as so many others have so much less. We also beg you to help us keep the memory of my husband, the father of my children, in our hearts. Help us to appreciate the value of sacrifice and to find strength during the dark days that may be coming as this terrible war draws to a close. Protect this family, especially my son Jean Louis, as he departs in four days to find his place in the world. For these and other blessings, we pray. Amen."

Jean Louis echoed his mother's "Amen" along with his siblings, happy that he had not been asked to give the prayer. It wasn't that he was a nonbeliever; he simply didn't think about religion in any vein, and as his mother spoke, he felt himself already an ocean away. *Soon I shall be far from all this, a student at University College, London*, he thought.

Everything he had read about London, every image he had seen of the city's streets, cathedrals, palaces, and shops, danced through his mind. Even the famously rainy weather sounded romantic. He'd had his fill of the hot, humid summers and the dull, bleak winters at Road's End, of the mindless social lives of his peers, of the de rigueur attendance at Sunday services at First Baptist Church, of the war, and of everything else that had defined his life.

Knowing it would be futile to try to persuade him to wait, Marie Louise had agreed to his swift departure. Plans had been made for Jean Louis to leave on November 28, the Monday after Thanksgiving, to travel by train and stagecoach to New Orleans. After a few days at his grandfather's French Quarter home, he would take a boat to Jamaica, where he would get passage on a British ship bound for London.

In some ways, the journey from Red Clay to New Orleans could be more perilous than the voyage across the winter Atlantic to England. There were still Union troops in the area, as well as Confederate deserters who could be just as deadly to a hapless traveler.

The sun was low in the sky as Plessant guided the carriage onto Road's End's long driveway after an afternoon spent driving the Parker family to the train station to see Jean Louis off on his journey. Laughing and chattering away on the ride to the station, Marie Louise, Claude, and Addie were quiet and withdrawn on the ride home.

"He is gone; my baby is gone," Marie Louise said, dabbing at tears that streamed down her cheeks as they drove away from the station. Claude and Addie sat on either side of her and murmured comforting words, but Marie Louise had already retreated into herself and did not respond.

Serves them right, Plessant thought. *At least that boy gon' come home one day, but I ain't likely ever to see my John and Bessie again.* The bitterness of his thoughts washed through his brain, leaving a nasty residue that colored his mood for the rest of the trip. He was still stewing when they reached the plantation and didn't immediately hear Claude speak to him.

"Plessant? Do you hear me?"

"Yassuh," Plessant replied, with his back still to his passengers.

"Tomorrow morning we have surveyors coming to lay out the boundaries for the new fields we're going to carve out of that wooded land. I want you to stay with them to get whatever they need, and I want you to come get me before they finish for the day and bring me down there to take a look at it," Claude said.

"Yassuh, Massa Claude," Plessant said.

"Are you all right, Plessant?" Claude asked. "You don't look right."

"Yassuh, I'm fine," he said. "I guess I was just thinkin' about y'all havin' to see your brother off. It's sad when you lose family."

Claude stared at Plessant's back from his seat in the carriage for a long moment before answering. "Yes," he said. "Losing family is a sad thing, but one way or another, we all go through it, don't we?"

"Yassuh," Plessant said. "We sho nuff do."

———

Two weeks later Marie Louise was hanging decorations in the big house at Road's End for what would likely be her last Christmas there before moving to New Orleans. It was a rare sunny December day, and the pine trees seemed to strain toward the blue sky, soaking in the last warmth before winter arrived. Their dense coats of green needles quivered in each gust of wind. Marie Louise was staring absently through the window when she spotted the sheriff and one of the deacons from the church riding up the driveway toward the house. "Elmira," she called out to the kitchen, "it looks like we are about to have company."

When she had her guests settled in the parlor with tea and shortbread cookies, Marie Louise met their eyes and said, "I'm sure you gentlemen didn't ride out here just for cookies and small talk with a widow. How may I help you?"

Both men shifted uncomfortably before the sheriff straightened in his seat. "Miz Parker, I guess there ain't no way to say this but to come out with it straight," he said. "We got word yesterday from the authorities in New Orleans that the boat your son was on to Jamaica was lost at sea and that there were no survivors."

The world stopped turning on its axis. Birds in flight fell to the Earth. The oxygen in the planet's atmosphere was sucked into space, and God was no longer in His heaven. Everything went dark, and as Marie Louise fell to the floor from her chair, she was barely cognizant of the activity around her as the sheriff shouted for help. She was hardly aware that Elmira and Callie Mae were lifting her and carrying her to her room, or that Addie was at her side, sobbing "Maman! Maman!"

"Somebody get Massa Claude," Elmira ordered, "and tell Plessant to go for the doctor."

Only after Plessant was a mile down the road, driving the wagon to Red Clay to get the doctor, did he remember he was off the plantation without a pass, and who knew what would happen to him if he was stopped and challenged. Suddenly the absurdity of the situation struck him, and he began to laugh uncontrollably as he urged the horse forward, faster and faster, as fast as the horse could go.

———

That night Plessant and Elmira lay awake, too tense from the day's events to fall asleep. "I swear, Elmira, I thought I was losin' my mind when it come to me that I didn't have no pass and here I was tryin' to get a doctor for that woman, and if I got stopped I'd be lucky if they just decided to kill me," Plessant said.

In the dark, Elmira nodded and murmured, "Uh-huh."

"You know I hate to say it, but I ain't sad that boy died. He wasn't good for nothin', and don't forget he was gon' let Felix get whipped and didn't think nothin' about it," Plessant continued. "I do feel bad for Massa Claude and Miss Marie Louise and Miss Addie, but maybe it's God paying them back for what they done to our family, sellin' our children and all. What that preacher say the other Sunday, 'As ye sow, so shall ye reap'?"

In the morning Plessant came around to speak with Claude before going off to meet the surveyors on the wooded parcel, and what he saw shocked him. Marie Louise was sitting alone on the porch with a shawl draped around her shoulders and a blanket covering her legs. She had a faraway look in her eyes, and she appeared to have aged ten years overnight. He was about to walk away when Claude came through the door onto the porch.

He looked at his mother and then at Plessant. "Maman has not taken the news about my brother well," he said.

"Yassuh," Plessant replied.

"We'll talk while we walk to the barn to get the wagon and horse," Claude said. Just at that moment, Marie Louise began to shriek rough animal noises, and then she began to cry. "The doctor is coming to see her today," Claude added.

Plessant looked more closely at Claude, and he could see the strain on his face too. First his father's death, then his brother's, and now his mother appeared to be on the edge of madness. *Massa Claude don't deserve that,* he thought, *but me and Elmira don't neither. Don't nobody deserve the hurt the world can put on you.* And then he felt all the anger and all the pain draining from his soul, and he felt something new and different taking their place. A beat passed, and then he recognized the new feeling, and he realized that it was something special, something to be cherished, something he knew would be his forever. What Plessant recognized was the sure knowledge that in his heart and in his soul, he had become, and always would be, a free man.

Part Two

REVELATIONS

Chapter 18

Addie came awake with a start. She had fallen asleep during a pause in the conversation while Eileen went to the kitchen to make tea. The women had been talking nonstop, sharing stories, filling gaps in what each of them knew of Felix's life. Her heart was pounding. Her breathing was ragged and rough, and her blouse clung to her skin, damp with perspiration. Her eyelids snapped open, and she scanned her surroundings, looking left and right without moving her head. Where was she? What was this place? A moment of panic set in before she realized that it was the middle of the afternoon and that she had fallen asleep in a living room chair in the home of the late Felix H. Parker.

Addie pulled herself into a more upright position and looked up into the eyes of Eileen Epps, Felix's granddaughter, staring at her quizzically.

"Are you all right, Miss Parker?" Eileen asked.

"I keep forgetting that I am an old woman who can fall asleep at the most unexpected moments in the most unexpected places," Addie replied. Glancing down at the thick, intricately patterned quilt of burgundy, blue, and gold fabric remnants that covered her, she added, "Thank you for covering me with this beautiful quilt."

"Mama made it. She taught me to sew, but I'll never be able to match her fine needlework," Eileen said, nodding toward Maybelle, who, along with Luther, had come into the room while Eileen and Addie had been talking and had been listening quietly to their exchange. Introductions had been made, but the dialogue had continued.

"What happened? I hope I didn't fall asleep in the middle of a sentence," Addie said.

Eileen laughed, relaxed in the presence of the old white woman she'd known only for a few hours. "No, you didn't fall asleep while you were talking," she said. "I had just finished telling you about how much Grandpa had hated that you fed him under the table at breakfast when you were children, and I thought you looked tired. I offered you a cup of tea, but by the time I returned with it, you were sound asleep."

Addie winced at the memory of those breakfasts. "I never imagined that it hurt him so deeply," she said. She turned her face toward the ceiling. Her eyes glistened with tears that did not fall. "Do you think we might sit outside for a while?" Addie asked. "It's cool, but if I may take this quilt with me, I believe I shall be quite comfortable."

"Of course," Eileen said. "I'll get a sweater for myself and get you a fresh cup of tea."

On the front porch, Addie settled into a rocker, snug under the quilt, and enjoyed the warmth of the sun on her face. It was the way the sun had felt when she sat in Parisian cafés as a young woman. She had traveled throughout Europe, hearing performances by celebrated orchestras, viewing antiquities in the great museums, and dining in fine restaurants. But it was the coffee-fueled debates on the issues of the day with friends in the cafés that were among her most cherished memories. Her Parisian friends—one in particular—had changed her life forever.

Eileen joined Addie on the porch, carrying a tray with cups of steaming hot tea for herself, Addie, and Maybelle, and sank into the rocking chair next to Addie's. Maybelle followed and sat silently in the nearby porch swing, continuing to eye Addie suspiciously. Luther wandered into the yard to admire the car and to engage the driver in conversation about it.

"This has been fascinating," Eileen said, "but are you sure you want to continue?"

Addie wrapped her hands around the warm cup and looked pointedly at Eileen. "I most certainly do. I've appreciated all that you have been able to tell me about Felix, and I hope you have found what I've told you to be of interest."

"Oh, yes," Eileen exclaimed. "Grandpa told me a few stories, but you've told me more than I ever imagined. What I want to know, though, is why you're doing this. Why did you feel you had to come here to tell me these things?"

Addie didn't answer right away. She stared into the yard, watched a pair of squirrels chase each other up and down the chinaberry tree, and wondered if they would survive the winter. Small things were vulnerable in this big world, and the odds of survival were stacked against them. When she spoke, her voice seemed to come from far away, crossing an ocean and spanning time. "I don't suppose you have been to Europe, have you?" Addie asked.

"No, ma'am," Eileen said. "I've never been away from Alabama, but I'm going to visit my cousins in California this summer."

"I've been to Europe many times—before the war, that is," Addie said. "I think you would like it. The French do not treat Negroes as we do. Although I suppose that Negroes may not be welcome in some Parisian circles, you and I could have sat in a café, just as we are sitting here, and few would have thought anything of it. And before the war, the Negro entertainers were all the rage in Paris. Perhaps it will be that way again when it's over."

"Yes, ma'am, I've heard that," Eileen said, wondering where Addie was going with this line of thought.

"But we're here to talk about Felix," Addie said, closing her eyes to the day and sending her thoughts racing back across the decades. Memories flickered in her brain, a riot of images, sights and sounds taking her to another place and another time, when she was young and the world appeared to exist only for her. She took a sip of the tea, reached across to pat Eileen's hand, and the two women resumed their exchange.

Chapter 19

Elmira shivered as she slipped silently out of bed into the early January morning darkness to get ready for another day in the kitchen of the big house. She hardly needed a light after so many years. She moved efficiently to dress and walk out of the bedroom into the only other room, grateful that the cabin she shared with Plessant and Felix was one of the few with a rough plank floor over the dirt. Plessant remained asleep, and for a moment she envied him for not having to awaken before sunrise. But she knew he worked hard and that she and Felix would be all right as long as he could hold his position with Massa Claude—at least as all right as it ever got to be for the enslaved. "I got to stop thinkin' on that," she said to herself, because she knew where it would lead. "I cain't be thinkin' on that," she said again to herself.

"You all right, Maw?" came a high voice from the corner of the room. At age ten, Felix might be working as a grown man, apprenticed to the carpenter, but he still sounded like her little boy.

"I'm okay," she replied. "You gon' walk with me this mornin'?"

"Yassum," he replied.

They walked in silence on the moonlit path. When they were nearly at the back door that led into the kitchen, Felix hung back.

"Maw, has you ever seen a haint?" he asked.

"How come you askin' 'bout haints?" In the dim light, she could see fear in his eyes.

"Well, has you ever seen one?"

"No," she said, "I ain't never seen no dead spirits walkin' 'round, but the old peoples say dead folks can come back if they still got bizness to 'tend to. Say they can be real mean and do bad things to livin' folks that done them wrong when they was livin'. But I ain't never seen one; don't want to, neither. How come you askin'?"

"You know that boy Danny what clean out the stables and take care of the horses?" Felix asked.

"Yes," Elmira replied.

"Well, he say at night the haints come 'round the plantation 'cause they was whupped when they was alive or got kilt, and he say if they cain't find the ones what did it to them they go lookin' for anybody they can find," Felix said, his expression grave. "He say they steal children and don't nobody never hear 'bout them again."

Elmira stopped walking to pull him in close to her. "Felix," she said, "ain't no haints here, and if they is, they got to get past me and your paw to get you."

They walked the rest of the way in silence, and Elmira never took her arm from around Felix's shoulders. She could see that he was terrified, and truth be told, she thought he knew more about the way Massa John Robert had died than he had let on, and that he had seen things a little boy ought not to have seen. It was better, though, to let such thoughts remain buried along with John Robert.

At the kitchen door of the big house, Elmira turned Felix around to face her. "You go to the well and get me a bucket of fresh water while I go in here and get the fire goin'. Then I'll give you somethin' good to eat 'fore you go off to the carpenter shop." When he looked off into the darkness and didn't move right away, she added, "Go on! They ain't no haints out there."

It was still dark outside when Felix reached the shop, a small out-building near the stable. He opened the door and savored the smell of freshly cut wood and paints and solvents before lighting a lantern to il-luminate the shop's interior. Then he began his apprentice chores, laying out the tools and making sure the chisels and knives were sharp and ready for use. He dusted the worktables and swept the floor, even though he had done all those things the night before. John, the old master carpen-ter, always said that nothing good could come out of a dirty shop, and Felix wanted to be good. He was learning about the different tools and how to use them. He listened carefully when John explained about the various kinds of wood and the best use of each. Today, John had prom-ised to start teaching him about finishes.

"You doin' good, boy. You got a lot more to learn, but you doin' good," John had said, and Felix's chest had swollen with pride.

He was thinking about all of that when he heard a voice from out-side, moaning under the window. "Ooooooh, oooooooh, ooooooh." Such agony, such anguish. Startled, Felix froze and listened for it to come again. There it was: "Ooooooooooh, ooooooooooh, ooooooooh." Felix couldn't run. He couldn't shout. It must be one of those haints, come to get him because it couldn't find the one who'd tormented it in life. "Oooooooooh," came the sound again, this time from two places at once—from outside the window and from just outside the door. *There must be two of 'em*, Felix thought. All avenues of escape were cut off.

Just when Felix thought he couldn't stand it any longer, the door burst open and in came John with a small struggling boy gripped in each of his massive hands. One was Danny from the stables, and the other was Felix's pal, Jimmy. They stopped struggling at the sight of Felix, wide-eyed and trembling, and broke into laughter.

"Ooooooooh," Danny yelled. "I is a haint, and me and all the other haints gon' get you!"

"That's enough. Y'all get out of here right now," John said as he began dragging the boys to the door.

"I'm sorry, Felix, but you was so scared. It was funny," Jimmy said as he disappeared through the door, cackling as he went.

John closed the door behind the boys and turned toward Felix, who was still trembling with tears streaming down his cheeks. "Come over here, boy. Let me ask you somethin'," the old man said. "Why you think them boys makin' fun of you?"

"I don't know. I ain't done nothin' to them," Felix replied.

"Yes, you have done somethin' to them; you just don't know it," John said. "You done somethin' that made them mad, and they couldn't do nothin' 'bout it but try to hurt you."

"But what did I do?" Felix pleaded.

"Every day you get up and you come here to learn how to be a carpenter, and you ain't worried about nothin' but learnin' this trade, and I got to tell you, you learnin' it good," John said. "Then, at the end of the day, you go home to your maw and paw, and everybody know y'all be eatin' good and the white folks don't mess with y'all too much. The thing is, you ain't never got nothin' to be scared 'bout.

"Now, you take that boy Danny. He all by hisself. He ain't got nothin' nor nobody. He live in the stable with the hosses, and he eat whatever he can get his hands on. He good with the hosses, but he scared all the time. He don't know what gon' happen to him day after day."

John stopped to look at Felix. The boy was no longer trembling, but he still had questions in his eyes.

"Then there's your friend Jimmy," John said. "He a good boy, but he had it hard 'fore you knowed him in the field and 'fore he got apprenticed to the blacksmith. 'Fore he come to Road's End, him and his big brother was on another plantation pickin' cotton with they maw and paw. Now you seen Jimmy's maw; she a fine woman, and the overseer on that other plantation decide he got to have her for hisself. So one day he just drag her off in the woods next to the fields." Innocence died young on plantations, and Felix, barely ten years old, understood exactly what John was saying about what had happened to Jimmy's mother.

"Jimmy's big brother and paw, they seen what was goin' on, and they run into the woods to stop that overseer, and when they caught him, they beat him half to death," John continued. "Well, all hell broke loose when the massa found out what happened. Jimmy's paw and brother had to run, but they got caught and brought back to the plantation. They got beat 'til they was near dead, then they got strung up from a tree 'til they died, and the massa let 'em hang there for days so everybody could see 'em. Then Jimmy and his maw was sold to Massa John Robert, and they come here."

Felix didn't know what to say, and his eyes remained downcast as the horror of what John was saying washed over him. He wanted to vomit.

"Thing is," John said, "them boys is scared all the time, but here you is with everything goin' good. So even your friend Jimmy, he ready to go along when Danny start talkin' to him 'bout doin' somethin' to make you scared too."

"But that ain't right," Felix protested. "It ain't my fault what happened to them."

"It don't matter," said John. "When peoples is scared, they don't think straight. Thing is, Jimmy ain't mad at you. He still your friend, but he got caught up in somethin'. You talk to him, and you'll find out. That Danny ain't bad neither. Maybe all y'all can be friends, and on a plantation, a friend is a mighty fine thing to have."

Chapter 20

RED CLAY, ALABAMA

WINTER 1865

Zeus, the big black stallion that had belonged to John Robert Parker, was in good spirits, exhaling twin jets of hot vapor into the crisp February air and tossing his head this way and that with each prancing step. He would surely have galloped all the way to Red Clay if Claude hadn't reined him in, heedless of the young man's weight on his back or of the need to conserve energy for the return trip later that day. The Parkers had held back some personal items in the sale of the plantation, including Zeus. The stallion belonged to Claude now, and he rode him whenever he could.

Claude was feeling good too. He had welcomed the chance to get away from the plantation for a few hours, even if it meant spending most of the time in the law offices of Campbell, Stewart & MacPherson. He didn't know why he had been summoned, only that the meeting had been arranged at his mother's request and that it concerned his late father's estate.

Upon his arrival, he was quickly escorted into the firm's conference room, where Andrew Stewart sat at the end of the twelve-foot-long table that dominated the space, surrounded by book-lined walls that rose from dark-stained wood floors enhanced by rich Oriental rugs. As Marie Louise had done before him, Claude immediately recognized the chamber as one in which his father, the scholarly gentleman farmer, would have felt completely at ease.

But rather than feeling comforted by the surroundings, he found himself irritated. He felt a dawning awareness of how much he was enjoying being his own man with responsibilities, separate from his late father. It was a new sensation, and it unsettled him. Stewart rose to greet him. "Come in, Mr. Parker. Please take a seat."

Claude shook the man's proffered hand and settled into a chair at the table.

"I regret that we are meeting this way for the first time, but it is a pleasure nonetheless," Stewart said. "As you know, my firm represented your father, and I always enjoyed our times together. It is a great shame that he has left us while still in his prime. I, of course, was also acquainted with your older brother, and his untimely death was also deeply regrettable, such a—"

Claude, still bothered by his conflicting thoughts about his father, raised a hand to interrupt Stewart. "Thank you for the condolences, Mr. Stewart, but I must ask that we move on to the business at hand, beginning with why I am here."

"Of course, Mr. Parker. It was rude of me to leave you in the dark," Stewart replied. If he was annoyed by the younger man's impatience, it did not show in either his manner or the expression on his face. "When the plantation was sold to Mr. Flowers, there was one piece of property that was not conveyed to him, and which remained in your mother's hands," Stewart said. "You are no doubt familiar with the ten-acre plot along the creek at the edge of Road's End, part of the wooded, uncultivated land?"

"Yes," Claude said. "We hunted and fished there. I thought it was sold along with the rest of the plantation. You're telling me that it was not, that we still own it?"

"That is correct," said Stewart, "or more precisely, your mother owns it."

Claude's mind was racing, trying to understand the significance of what he had just been told. "What does this have to do with me?" he asked.

A beat passed, and Claude heard the grandfather clock in the hallway outside the conference room ticking and then the soft chimes marking eleven a.m. He was aware of footsteps passing in the hallway and of muted voices in energetic debate.

The old attorney regarded Claude for a long while before speaking, perhaps wondering if he was correctly reading the character of the younger man. "Your father was a good man," he said. "I thought of him as more than a client; I thought of him as a friend. He was imperfect, as all men are, but he had a core of decency that I admired, and so I respected a decision he made before his death, which your mother has conveyed to me."

Claude's eyes narrowed, and his grip on the arms of his chair tightened.

"John Robert had been convinced for some time that the South would not win the war," Stewart said, "and judging from what we have been hearing, he was right. He had already begun to think about what that might mean for planters like himself and for his family. So, many months before his passing, he came to us for help to make certain financial arrangements that would secure his family's fortunes if the South loses—"

"Yes, yes, and we are grateful—" Claude said brusquely.

This time the older man interrupted. "There was one more thing, however, and that is the reason for your being here today," Stewart said. "Your father had also begun to question the institution of slavery, and he was racked with guilt, especially about the impact it had on his valet, Plessant, and his family."

Claude sat with his eyes glued to a spot on the ceiling, his hands still clenching the arms of the chair. He had seen how his father behaved around the slaves and heard the way he spoke about them in private, but he had never imagined that John Robert's misgivings about slavery had been so intense. If anything, he had seemed indifferent to the Blacks. Returning his attention to the lawyer, Claude asked, "What was he going to do? Free them?"

"No," Stewart said, "but he felt especially aggrieved about Plessant, and he instructed his wife to keep those ten acres, which had been a gift to John Robert from his father, out of the sale, and in the event that the South were to lose the war and if the slaves were freed, she was to arrange through our firm for the land to be deeded to Plessant."

"There was nothing about this in the will," Claude said.

"No, there was not, but it was John Robert's wish, which he communicated to us and to your mother."

"Still," Claude responded, "what does this have to do with me? If the war is lost and the slaves get their freedom, my mother can do with the land whatever she wants."

Stewart nodded before speaking. "Absolutely she can do that," he said. "However, I think you should read the letter she enclosed for you with her instructions to me to invite you to this meeting." He slid an envelope with Claude's name on it across the table.

The younger man recognized Marie Louise's handwriting, but he eyed the envelope warily, as if it might burn him if he touched it, as if the knowledge it contained might force him to go in a new direction, toward a place he might not want to go. He reached out slowly to pick up the envelope and withdrew the single page:

My Dear Son,

The news you will have received from Mr. Stewart is no doubt unsettling, but I urge you to accept his word that it accurately reflects your father's wish to give the land to Plessant in the event that the slaves are freed. He was very clear to me about this, and I am determined to fulfill his request. However, my health is failing, and I fear that I may be unable to discharge this responsibility when the time comes.

My dear Claude, you have always been the most sensible of my children, and I believe I can rely upon you to meet this obligation in my stead. Therefore, I have instructed Mr. Stewart to transfer ownership of the property to you with my expectation that you will hold it until the appropriate time to assign it to Plessant.

I regret that I must place this burden on your shoulders, but I

am confident that you will understand and appreciate your father's
wishes and that you will see that the matter is properly handled.

With all my love, your mother,
Marie Louise Parker
18th January 1865

Claude looked up at Stewart and said nothing. A moment passed, then Stewart stood up and left the room. Shortly thereafter he returned with a young clerk, who placed a stack of papers and a pen and inkwell on the table in front of Claude.

"These are the papers that will transfer ownership of the property from your mother to you," Stewart said. "Mr. Scott will show you where to sign, and he will witness your signature. When the paperwork has been filed at the courthouse, the new deed will be delivered to you at Road's End. As always, it has been a pleasure to be of service to the Parker family." He did not extend his hand before leaving the room.

⸺

By the time Claude and the big black stallion were on the road again, the gray morning clouds had given way to a dazzling blue sky, and the rays of the afternoon sun on his skin made the day feel warmer than it actually was. Yet, Claude was troubled. He had been given a great responsibility by the mother he loved to carry out the wishes of the father he had admired. Why didn't he feel happy and proud? Why did he feel annoyed and angry instead?

Without Claude's noticing it, Zeus had slowed to a walk, then to a halt and was nibbling grass on the side of the road. Claude dismounted, took the reins, and began walking toward home with the horse behind him. The plantation was still two miles away, but he needed time to think.

What was that story John Robert had told him, the one about his father giving him the land and the baby Plessant as birthday presents? Having the land and ownership of the child had made young John Robert a "man of property," Claude's grandfather had said, and being a man of property, a gentleman, set him apart from the poor whites and the Blacks.

How was it that he was not himself a man of property, and yet he was expected to be the instrument for making Plessant one if the slaves were freed after the war? *It doesn't make sense; it's wrong*, he thought. The vehemence with which he felt the need to protect his superior position shocked him. After all, he liked Plessant and enjoyed being around him, but he'd be damned if he would ever see him as his equal, and damned if he would ever help him to achieve that status.

Road's End was coming into view, and a gusty wind blew in from the southwest, kicking up red dust from the dirt road and making the pine needles shiver in the branches above his head. He felt the chill of winter, the cold, dark time when animals huddle in their dens, when seeds lie underground waiting for a signal to send shoots upward into the spring sunshine, and when men and women curse the gloom and hope for better, brighter days ahead.

Chapter 21

ROAD'S END PLANTATION
SPRING 1865

Claude placed another oak log on the fire in his late father's study as remnants of fatwood kindling snapped and popped, releasing a comforting aroma of burning wood that blended with the scent of tobacco smoke rising from the cigars that he and George Flowers held between their fingers. The fire's heat was soothing on the evening of March 20, the first day of spring, and as dusk shrouded Road's End Plantation, the flames cast flickering shadows on long shelves of leatherbound books. The two men sipped cognac from cut-crystal snifters, cupping the bowls in their hands and savoring the bouquet before drinking. John Robert had loved fine cigars and good cognac, passions he had passed on to his son Claude. And though he had been dead for seven months, John Robert's presence was still palpable and perhaps always would be.

"That was a mighty fine dinner, Claude," Flowers said. "You know, I still think I made a mistake by letting you keep that cook when I bought the plantation."

"I'm glad you enjoyed it, Mr. Flowers, but you know Road's End wouldn't be Road's End without Elmira in the kitchen," Claude said, and the two men smiled and resumed their silence.

Moments later, however, Flowers broke the quiet again. "With or without Elmira," he said, "we both know that things are going to change dramatically in the days ahead, and we have to be ready. I think that I shall retire now, but we'll begin making our plans early tomorrow."

"You're right, sir, and thank you for traveling here. We have much to discuss, and I'm glad to be able to meet with you face-to-face," Claude said. "I'll see you at breakfast, and we'll get down to work."

Flowers nodded, pushed open the heavy door, and made his way to the stairs.

Claude remained in his seat, staring into the fire, slowly rolling his cigar between his thumb and forefinger. It had gone out, but an inch-long ash clung firmly to the end, a testament to the quality John Robert had insisted upon for his cigars. In the warm semidarkness, the effects of the heavy meal, served with good red wine, followed by the cognac, were making Claude drowsy. And yet he knew that sleep would not come easily. Too much had happened, and too much was at stake.

John Robert's death in September 1864 had been the start of an unsettling series of events that disrupted life as the Parker family had known it. The war continued, but throughout the South, few believed the war was not lost. President Lincoln had long since issued his Emancipation Proclamation, in 1863, and the planters knew it was merely a matter of time before the slaves might have to be freed. That could spell disaster for the plantation economy, beyond the price the South had already paid for the war in both blood and capital.

Claude walked over to the fireplace and tossed his cigar into the coals before going upstairs to bed. In the elaborately carved and gilded wood-framed mirror above the mantel, he was struck by what he saw: The boyish countenance he knew so well had been transformed into the face of a man with obligations. His eyes had become those of a man who understood that fortune flies on butterfly wings, beautiful and fragile, but resilient when strong winds blow.

Later that night, Claude slept fitfully as clouds sped across the face of the moon and as the wind murmured dark warnings of things to come. In a wakeful moment in the final hours before sunrise, it occurred to him that his restless slumber might be the best sleep he would have for a very long time.

Chapter 22

Three days after George Flowers's departure, Claude sat at a table on the front porch of the big house at Road's End, ignoring the remnants of his breakfast and contemplating all that had happened in recent days. The path ahead was tricky, and he had to plan his next steps carefully. He watched as a pair of red-winged blackbirds fought off a determined Cooper's hawk that showed too much interest in their nest. The blackbirds were nasty, ill-tempered creatures, he thought, but he sympathized with their resolve to fight for what was theirs.

Claude and Flowers had engaged in hours of hard talks about the plantation that left him anxious and exhausted. The day before his departure, Flowers had announced that he was unwilling to risk the uncertainty that surrounded the operation of Road's End in a post–Civil War economy, one in which the virtually free labor of slaves might not be available. Thus, he planned to sell the plantation.

The two men had been strolling across the lawn after Elmira's supper of baked chicken, roasted sweet potatoes, collard greens, butter beans garnished with rings of white onion, and fresh-baked cornbread. For dessert she had served hot fried pies, filled with apples from the cellar, and glasses of thick, cold buttermilk from the springhouse. "These are strange times," Flowers had said to Claude, "and a smart businessman has to know when to minimize his exposure to risk. I have two other plantations, and this one is just too far away from home and too costly to operate from a distance. I have no other choice than to sell."

Flowers's words hit Claude like a cannon blast, and all the good feeling generated by that feast was lost. Claude stopped walking and turned to face Flowers. Blood rushed to his head, and the Earth seemed to tilt under his feet. He looked into the older man's eyes and saw the truth he'd hoped not to find: Flowers had never intended to save Road's End.

"Why?" Claude asked. "Why did you come all the way up here from Mississippi, and why did we spend all this time talking about how to protect Road's End when you never planned to save it?" he demanded. "What right do you have to sell Road's End? Maybe you bought it, but this is Parker land, and it always will be."

Flowers reached out to grasp the younger man's shoulder. "I had to be sure that I was making the right decision, and the only way was to come here and talk to you," he said. "I'm sorry, Claude, but my decision is final. I'll be leaving in the morning. The lawyers will conduct the rest of the business."

Claude had been staring at his feet while Flowers spoke, but as the Mississippi planter walked away toward the big house, Claude looked up and blurted out a proposal that stopped Flowers. "I will buy it. I will buy Road's End," Claude had said, startled to hear the words tumbling from his mouth.

Flowers turned to face him before speaking. "If you are serious, I will consider your proposal," he said. "You will have my answer before I leave in the morning."

"Thank you, sir," Claude said and walked away toward the trees. Night was falling, and he was soon swallowed by the dark.

Claude arose the next morning feeling discomfited by his outburst of the night before and resolved to apologize to Flowers over breakfast. To his surprise, however, when he came downstairs, he found that Flowers had already departed. Elmira entered the dining room with hot biscuits, butter, plum jam, and a cup of the chicory brew, which she set in front of him at the dining table. Then she handed him a sealed envelope.

"'Fore he left, Massa George say give you this letter when you come down this mornin' and that he sorry to leave so early."

Claude ate his breakfast without tasting it, tucked the still-unopened envelope into his jacket pocket, and headed out to the stable, where he asked Danny to saddle Zeus. When the boy returned with the horse, Claude took the reins and walked the black stallion out into the sunlight. Both the horse and the man seemed to relish the way the sun felt, cutting through the last of winter's grip. The time for new things was coming, and the time for the old was slipping away. Claude mounted the horse, made a *click-click* noise with his mouth, and they flew down the driveway and out onto the main road at a gallop, leaving a red dust cloud behind them.

"Where Massa Claude goin' in such a hurry?" Plessant asked Elmira as he came through the back door into the big-house kitchen.

"I don't know," she said, "but he got a look on his face like a man with big troubles on his mind and no way to get no comfort."

A quarter mile away from the entrance to the plantation, Claude slowed Zeus to a walk and rode aimlessly. Thus, he was surprised when he found himself in the outskirts of Red Clay, approaching the Ridge Inn, a roadhouse known locally for good beer, liquor that hadn't been watered down, and passable food. But it also had a seamier side. For a price, access could be had to upstairs rooms, where a running poker game and women of easy virtue could be found. Men with reputations to protect were careful about being seen coming and going from the Ridge Inn. Today, however, Claude didn't care. He tied the stallion to a hitching post and went inside.

It was semidark inside the Ridge Inn. The only light filtered in through windows that hadn't been washed in years. A long bar ran down one side of the room, and five tables with four chairs each filled the rest of the space. A man whose face he recognized from town sat at the bar with a shot glass and a half-empty bottle of rye whiskey in front of him. Claude took a seat at the table in the corner farthest from the door and ordered a beer. When his drink arrived, he took a sip, pulled the letter from his pocket, and settled in to read:

Dear Claude,

I regret having taken you by surprise with my decision to sell Road's End, but as I explained last evening, retaining the property under the current circumstances is not viable for my business. Allow me to say, however, that you have been an excellent manager during these months of our association, and because of that, and also because of the respect and friendship I had for your late father, I am willing to entertain your offer to purchase the property with certain conditions. They are as follows:

I would make a portion of the property available for sale to you, approximately 250 acres, including cultivated land for cash crops, the household gardens, the pastures, and some wooded acreage to be defined should we come to terms. The sale would also include the main house and the outbuildings such as the barns, stables, workshops, sheds, and the slave quarters. The sale would also include the livestock not already owned by you, as well as the slaves if they have not been emancipated at the time of the sale. I would retain the remaining 850 acres, most of it unimproved, possibly for sale at some future date.

However, I must have an answer about your intentions as soon as possible, as I cannot keep the parcel off the market indefinitely. You can make your intentions known by having your attorneys inform mine. I wish you the best, and I am hopeful that we shall reach an agreement.

> *Sincerely,*
> *George Flowers*
> *21st March 1865*

Claude looked up from the letter, carefully refolded it, and returned it to the envelope, which he placed in his jacket pocket. *I can do this*, he thought. *I will own Road's End.*

Chapter 23

When the commotion in the yard began, Felix was in the carpentry shop cutting two-by-fours to measure for a barn Claude had hired John out to repair on a nearby farm. He had been busy all day. He relished the responsibility that the old carpenter had given him, and he was proud of the boards of varying lengths that he had produced and stacked against the wall. Felix tried to ignore the noise at first, but the sound of raised voices pierced the walls of the shop, so he headed outside. He was astonished by what he saw. Soldiers astride massive red-coated horses, as big as Massa Claude's black stallion, filled the yard, snorting and dancing nervously back and forth, as men and women he knew from the fields gathered around them. *They must be Yankees, 'cause they got them blue coats on*, Felix thought.

He heard steps and turned to see Jimmy and Danny coming up behind him.

"What's happenin'?" Jimmy asked. "Why them soldiers here?"

"I don't know," Felix replied. "I just come out the shop and they here."

"Maybe your paw know," Danny said and pointed toward the soldiers.

Felix's eyes followed Danny's outstretched arm to the center of the crowd and came to rest on his father's back. The soldier who appeared to be in charge was leaning down to speak with Plessant. "Is that all of them?" the soldier asked.

"Yassuh, all 'cept John. He hired out to work on another plantation today," Plessant said.

Claude had been in town on business all morning. He appeared tired as he rode up on Zeus, and annoyed by the disorder he found on his return. "What's the meaning of this? Who is in charge here?" he demanded.

"Captain William Allen, First Regiment, Alabama Cavalry, US Army, at your service, sir," said the soldier who had been speaking with Plessant.

Claude drew himself upright. "Well, Captain, I am Claude Parker. I am in charge here at Road's End Plantation, and I demand to know your intentions."

"Sir, I am acting under Regimental orders, and I am obliged to inform you that with the surrenders of Confederate Lieutenant Generals Richard Taylor and Nathan Bedford Forrest to Union forces, the war in Alabama is over and that the Emancipation Proclamation signed by the late president of the United States, Abraham Lincoln, will be enforced," he said. "The men and women and children assembled here are now free and no longer your property."

"Captain," Claude said, "I am the manager here, but the plantation belongs to Mr. George Flowers of Mississippi, and I am not authorized to dispose of his property—"

"Mr. Parker, these people are neither the property of Mr. Flowers nor of anyone else," the captain said, cutting Claude off. "They are free people, and they do not require permission from you or Mr. Flowers to take whatever actions they might choose."

A gasp, and then confused babble erupted from the crowd.

Captain Allen moved his horse alongside Claude's stallion and leaned close before speaking in a quiet voice. "Mr. Parker, you know as well as I that this was inevitable. General Lee surrendered his forces last month at Appomattox, and it's just a matter of time before the rest of the generals surrender their commands. I appreciate the position in which you find yourself, but if I may make a suggestion, contact your employer immediately to discuss the situation. Left unmanaged, things can go badly."

All afternoon, winds had been rushing ahead of a front, and now the first drops of rain were beginning to fall as the sun began to set.

Claude told the overseers to let the field hands go for the day. Raising his voice to be heard over the nervous chatter, he called, "This was big news today. Come back here tomorrow morning, and we'll talk about what's next. I'm sure everything will be fine." But in his heart and in his head, he was not so sure. Who could know what lay ahead for Road's End and for all who called it home?

———

Before sunrise the next morning, Claude was already awake and dressed. He could hear Elmira working in the kitchen downstairs, and he could smell breakfast aromas. He was hungry, but the thought of eating left him feeling queasy. Nevertheless, he knew he would need to be strong for the coming day, so he headed downstairs for breakfast.

In the kitchen Elmira was going through the motions, as if the momentous events of the previous day had never happened. "Elmira, what do you think about the news the Yankees brought?" Claude asked as she served him black tea, biscuits and jam, and grits.

"I don't know, Massa Claude. Me and Plessant, we just waitin' to hear what you gon' tell everybody today," she replied. Claude nodded and did not press her to answer more fully. The truth was that she and Plessant had lain awake for much of the night, talking about what they would do with their freedom. There were many questions: Where would they go? How would they make a living? What dangers would they face? Could they protect Felix, and what would freedom mean for their son? They were excited, but they were also frightened. Their world had suddenly grown larger, and they felt small in it and more vulnerable than they had ever felt before. Enslavement had been nearly unbearable, but the unknown was terrifying.

Claude finished eating and walked outside, where he found Plessant waiting for him with the wagon.

"Thank you, Plessant," he said, "but today I need you to go down to the fields and find the overseers and tell them I said to bring all the field hands up here. On the way, tell your boy Felix to get the rest of them. I need to talk to everybody."

"Yassuh," Plessant replied and drove away.

The previous night's rain had freshened the air, and Claude opened himself to all the familiar sights, smells, and sounds of spring—flower buds starting to open, manure worked into freshly turned soil in the fields, birds chirping, and new green tree leaves rustling in moist breezes coming up from the Gulf, swooping across 160 miles of South Alabama towns, forests, and farmland to get there. When he thought of Road's End, this was what he saw in his mind's eye and felt in his spirit. It made him calm. He couldn't imagine himself disconnected from the plantation, and he feared that it might be slipping from his grasp.

The workers had begun to assemble in front of the big house, waiting to hear what he had to say. For the enslaved, there was none of Claude's nostalgia; there was only uncertainty and fear, and for a moment, Claude sensed their anxiety like the fleeting green flash at sunset on the coast the moment the sun disappears into the sea.

"Yesterday, you heard what that Yankee cavalry captain said about y'all being free, and I guess he was right," Claude said, raising his voice to be heard over the murmurs in the crowd. "The South has been losing the war for a long time now, and we all knew this day might come. My father knew it, even if he didn't talk about it, and I knew it too, as did other planters, but none of us talked about it. We didn't talk about it because we didn't know what we would do if it really happened. Well, now it has happened, and we still do not know what we will do. And we most certainly do not know what you will do."

Elmira had come out to the porch and was standing off to the side with Felix and his two friends, Jimmy and Danny. Claude glanced at her and saw something different in her demeanor. Anger? Fear? No, it was something else, something deeper. Then he had it; it was defiance, and the recognition of it was disquieting. He faced the crowd and began to speak again. "The thing is, I no longer own Road's End; it belongs to Mr. George Flowers, and therefore I am not in a position to tell you what to do. I reckon you could all leave if you want to. It's up to you. You can stay if you want to for now, but that could change, depending on what Mr. Flowers decides to do. Now, to the overseers, you still have a job here, as do I, until we hear otherwise from Mr. Flowers, but I cannot promise you anything until I have spoken with him. So I guess we are all in the same situation for now.

"The reason I wanted to get together here this morning is to tell you that I am leaving tomorrow to see Mr. Flowers in Mississippi, and maybe when I return, we will have some answers. In the meantime, I would urge you to go back to work, and we will see what happens."

Claude was not sure of how the formerly enslaved might react to his remarks, but he knew he had to keep the plantation going if his plan to buy part of it was to succeed. He needed time, and time was in short supply.

The Black workers were beginning to disperse and return to the fields, though not without some grumbling. Claude walked down onto the yard and over to the wagon, where Plessant sat stone-faced and where the two overseers still sat astride their horses. "You can go ahead and put the wagon away, Plessant," he said. "I won't be needing it today."

Claude waited for the wagon to move out of earshot before speaking to the two overseers, Jacob Wilson and Benjamin Tyler. "I hope I can count on you gentlemen to stay with me until I know what all of our situations will be," he said. "Mr. Flowers is a fair man, and I think I can assure you that your wages will continue if you keep things together here while I am away to meet with him. Mr. Wilson, you will be in charge, but I need your word on something."

"What's that?" Wilson said.

"I'll need you to keep in mind that under the law the field hands are no longer property that you can whip or otherwise assault without consequence. These are new circumstances, and we do not know yet how the law will view such things," Claude said. "If you injure one of them, there could be consequences for you as well as for Mr. Flowers or me. One more thing," he added. "You can use Plessant to drive you around and do other chores for you. I think you'll find him useful."

"I don't know if I like the sound of all this, but I'll do as you say," Wilson said.

"Thank you, Mr. Wilson. That is all I can ask," Claude replied.

Claude went looking for Plessant and found him handing off the wagon and horse to the stable boy. "Plessant, I am not going to ask you what you think about all that is going on, but I have something to say to you," Claude said. "Let's walk out in the yard where we can talk."

The two men crossed the yard to the long driveway that led to the main road and turned to walk along it.

"You don't care for Mr. Wilson, do you?" Claude asked.

"Nosuh, I do not," Plessant replied, failing to exercise his usual caution. "But they ain't nothin' I can do about that, is they?" When Claude did not respond, Plessant added, "You remember he the one was gon' whip my boy?"

"I remember," Claude said. "Now that you are a free man, what will you do about it?"

This time it was Plessant's turn to be silent. He continued to walk and did not look in Claude's direction. In the silence the squishing of their shoes in the red-brown mud from the previous night's rain was loud and disagreeable. They stepped off the road into the grass and turned to walk back toward the big house.

"The thing is, Plessant," said Claude, "I'm going to be away for two weeks, and while I am away, Mr. Wilson will be in charge. I need to know that there will be no trouble."

"Ain't that up to him?" said Plessant.

"Yes, in many ways," Claude said, "but I need you to help him stay out of trouble by standing back, even if he does some things that are wrong. You see, Plessant, I have some big plans, and I can't have anything bad happen right now."

Plessant looked directly into Claude's eyes, something he had rarely done before. There was something there, something that made Plessant put up his guard, but he couldn't get a fix on it, and he decided to let it go. "Okay, Massa Claude, I'll stay out his way," he said.

"Thank you, Plessant. I'll let him know that he should use you to do whatever work he needs done, and I'll get back as soon as I can," Claude said.

Back at the big house, Claude turned before going inside. "Plessant, I'll need you to drive me to the train station tomorrow morning."

"Yassuh," Plessant replied. "I'll be here."

Chapter 24

The morning after Claude departed for his meetings with George Flowers in Mississippi, Elmira arrived for work as usual, even though Claude was away and there was no one to cook for. She had planned to help Lucille, the new maid, give the house a good cleaning and then recruit her for help in digging a new kitchen garden for vegetables, herbs, and flowers.

She didn't know fifteen-year-old Lucille well, but Callie Mae had vouched for her with Marie Louise before they departed for New Orleans, and she had proven to be a hard worker and good company. Working together on a quiet day would be a chance to get to know her better.

Elmira lit the kerosene lamp and spread some butter on one of yesterday's biscuits to give to Felix when he arrived with a bucket of well water. While she waited, she sat at the table in the yellow glow of the lamp and tried to comprehend what it might mean to be free.

The floor creaked behind her, and she whirled around, expecting to see Lucille. Instead, there was Wilson, the overseer, leaving Lucille's room, buttoning his trousers and grinning when he saw the look on the cook's face.

"What you doin' here? What you done to that girl?" Elmira demanded, knocking over her chair as she stood.

Wilson laughed and moved to block her way when Elmira tried to rush past him to get to Lucille's room. "Ain't nothing in there that's any of your business," he snarled.

"You better not have hurt that girl," she shouted.

"Or what?" Wilson replied. "Mr. Parker ain't here to get in the way like he did when I was gon' whip your boy that time, and he left me in charge, so what I say goes."

A sudden crash made both of them turn to the doorway, where Felix stood with his mouth open and his eyes wide. His bucket lay on the floor with water pooling around it.

"Run, Felix. Get your paw!" Elmira shouted. Felix disappeared through the door into the first hint of dawn, running as he had never run before, running as if the devil himself was at his heels.

"Now you done it," Wilson hissed. "I got to deal with you and deal with you good." He slapped her, knocking Elmira to the floor.

He was bending over to grab Elmira to pull her to her feet to hit her again when Lucille burst into the room, wearing the faded blue night-gown Callie Mae had left behind for her, and launched herself through the air onto Wilson's back. He twisted and bucked like a wild horse, but Lucille clung to him, biting into his shoulder and drawing blood that stained his old dingy white shirt. Wilson opened his mouth to scream, and when he did, Elmira, who had made it onto her feet, smashed his face with the backside of a cast iron skillet before a sound could escape from his lips.

Wilson went down backward, taking Lucille with him. She clawed her way from under his inert body, and before Elmira could stop her, Lucille grabbed the skillet and struck Wilson's face again. His nose went flat and a great gash opened up across his forehead. His body trembled once and then went still. His dead eyes stared at the ceiling, and a circle of blood expanded around his head on the kitchen floor.

Elmira and Lucille were standing in the middle of the room, holding each other, when Plessant and Felix rushed into the kitchen. "Oh, Lawd!" Plessant exclaimed, and Felix wrapped his arms around his mother's waist.

Hysterical, Lucille began stammering an explanation, but Plessant shushed her. "We can talk later," he said. "Right now we got to take care of this here mess. Felix, look outside and see if anybody out there. If there ain't, you go 'round the side of the house and open up the root cellar and come back here. Elmira, when Felix get back, me and him gon' move Wilson's body down there 'til we can figger out what to do next. Lucille, put some clothes on; then you got to clean up this blood. Elmira can help you; cain't nobody see what happened here."

By the time the sun was fully up, Felix was at work with John, making overdue repairs to the barn, the stable, and other outbuildings; Elmira and Lucille had cleaned all traces of the struggle from the kitchen; and Plessant was on the sunny side of the house, turning earth for the new kitchen garden.

"Hey, you, Plessant. You seen Wilson today?" said a voice from over Plessant's shoulder. It was Benjamin Tyler, the other overseer.

"Nosuh, I ain't seen him," Plessant said. "I was s'posed to drive him to town for somethin' today, but he didn't never show up, so I started diggin' this here garden for the kitchen. Elmira, my wife—you know, she the cook—say she tol' Massa Claude she was gon' try to get one done 'fore he come back. So I figgered I'd help her since Massa Wilson didn't come 'round today."

"Okay, you go ahead and work on that, but you come let me know if you hear anything about Wilson," Tyler said.

"Yassuh, I sho nuff will," Plessant said.

At midday Plessant went around to the kitchen door and sat on the steps with Elmira. She gave him a glass of cool buttermilk, a piece of warm cornbread, and a strip of fried fatback.

"That garden is lookin' good," she said. "Look like I can start planting in it tomorrow."

"Yeah, but it gon' be better after Felix and me work on it tonight," he replied, and she nodded her head knowingly. "Did Lucille tell you any more 'bout what was goin' on with that overseer?" he asked.

"She was so 'shamed she didn't want to tell me, but then she let it all out," Elmira said. "Seem like Wilson been after her a long time in the field, and she thought he'd let her alone when she come to work in the big house. And he did at first, but when Massa Claude went away, he seen his chance, so he come to her room last night and say if she don' give him what he want, he gon' take it out on her maw. Say he'll make like she run away and that he caught her and had to whip her. He tol' Lucille that if she didn't do it, he might be too mad to stop when he whip her maw and she might get killed."

"Well, we free now," Plessant said. "Cain't be no more of that whippin' goin on."

"Yeah, but she just a girl; she don't know no better, and truth is, the grown folks ain't sho neither. Plessant, you know you and me ain't even sho 'bout what's happenin'," Elmira said.

"That's true," he admitted, "but one thing we know: Wilson ain't gon' be whippin' nobody no more."

"How you think Felix is doin'?" she asked.

"I think he okay," Plessant said. "You know that boy is young, but sometimes I look at him, and I see a grown man lookin' back at me. I'm proud of that boy, Elmira. I'm proud of him."

"Me too," she said.

Later that night, when everyone else at Road's End was asleep, Felix and Plessant slipped out of the cabin and made their way back to the big house to put "finishing touches" on the garden. "It got to be ready for plantin' in the mornin'," Plessant whispered.

"Yassuh, Paw," Felix replied.

"You understand cain't nobody know what we workin' on out here tonight," Plessant said. "Cain't nobody never know. You understand that? You and me, even we ain't gon' talk about it to each other after tonight."

"Yassuh," Felix said.

By sunrise, Road's End's formerly enslaved workers were in the fields, the new kitchen garden was properly tilled and ready for planting, and when Elmira went into the cellar to retrieve her bags of seeds, there was nothing on the floor to block her way.

Chapter 25

STARKVILLE, MISSISSIPPI

LATE SPRING 1865

"That was an excellent meal, sir. Thank you for your hospitality," Claude told his host. He had arrived in Starkville in the late afternoon and was met by a buggy sent for him by the old planter, just in time for dinner. He swirled an excellent cognac in a snifter as formerly enslaved servants removed remnants of baked ham, collard greens, yams, and black-eyed peas from the table.

"I'm sure it is not up to the standards of the Road's End kitchen," George Flowers replied. "But we do our best out here." He paused before speaking again. "You know, you and I have been fortunate during this war. So many have lost so much, but through God's grace and good luck, we have prospered. I do not take this to be our due, but rather that we were well-positioned to meet problems as they confronted us. Do you mind if we take our drinks out to the porch?" Without waiting for a reply, Flowers stood up and took his snifter and the decanter with him.

Claude followed him, and as they passed through the parlor on their way to the door that led outside, he was reminded of his first impression of the house earlier that day. It was small: a kitchen, dining room, front parlor, and two bedrooms—a master bedroom and a guest room to which Claude's luggage had been taken. A few regional landscape paintings of little distinction hung on the parlor walls, and a large portrait of a couple that Claude took to be Flowers's parents surveyed the dining room.

"Not so grand as Road's End, is it?" Flowers said.

"It seems like a fine home, Mr. Flowers," Claude replied.

"Indeed it is," said the older man with a firm nod. "And though it is small and undistinguished, it is the house in which I was born and raised, and it serves to remind me of where I started and of how important it is to be thankful for all I have achieved."

"Yes, sir," Claude said. "I admire that, and though the scale of your house and of the one in which I was born and raised are quite different, it does not escape me that you are now the owner of my house and that my future depends in large measure on the decisions you make during my visit here."

Sitting in rocking chairs on the front porch and sipping their cognac, the two men gazed out into inky blackness that concealed evergreens swaying in warm, moist, floral breezes, marauding owls on the wing, and the nighttime ramblings of small furry creatures in the underbrush. The chairs creaked as they rocked on the painted-wood porch floor.

"Let me answer a question for you, Claude," Flowers said. "Yes, the deal we discussed for you to buy part of Road's End is still available. However, the status of the slaves will have an impact on the value of the property and very likely your ability to purchase it. I think we have a solution, but I'd rather show it to you tomorrow than tell you about it tonight. Right now, let's finish these drinks, and we'll get a fresh start in the morning."

The morning sun drove powerful shafts of light past open bedroom curtains, boring through Claude's closed eyelids to wake him from the proverbial sleep of the dead. *Oh, no*, he thought. *Mr. Flowers will think I'm lazy, oversleeping like this.* He hurriedly dressed and was still tucking his shirt into his trousers as he walked out through the parlor and into the dining room. Flowers was already at the table and had finished his breakfast.

"Take your time, Claude," he said. "We have a lot to do today, but it can wait."

"Yes, sir," Claude replied, "but I wouldn't want you to think that I sleep late every day. At Road's End, I'm always up and at work early."

"I understand; you had a long day yesterday, and you obviously needed the rest. Eat, and I'll tell you what we will be doing today." Flowers gestured to an empty chair. The cook had laid out a simple breakfast of boiled eggs, slices of the ham from the previous night's dinner, and hot biscuits. Claude tore into it as if he hadn't eaten in weeks.

Flowers watched as Claude attacked the food. He liked this boy, the son of a man he had respected, who had done a fine job of managing the Alabama property. Flowers had never married and had no heirs, but as he watched Claude, he wondered what it would have been like to be a father and to have had a son such as this young man.

Claude felt Flowers's eyes on him and looked up from his plate, embarrassed that he had eaten so voraciously and without engaging in polite conversation. "My mother would be ashamed of me, Mr. Flowers, for the poor manners I have displayed this morning," he said. "First I slept too long and kept my host waiting, and then I failed to show proper appreciation of this fine meal."

"All is forgiven," Flowers said with a laugh. Then he turned serious. "We should leave now," he said, "and we'll talk on the way."

Flowers drove the buggy himself. "More privacy for our discussions," he noted as miles of pine trees rooted in rich loamy soil rolled by. "How did the Coloreds at Road's End react when they heard about being free?"

"Quietly," Claude said, "as if they didn't know what to make of it. Fortunately, I was there when the Yankee soldiers arrived with the news, and I was able to speak to them right away. I believe I was able to buy some time to keep things going until I return. But I don't know how long it will stay that way. Even Elmira and her man, Plessant—you know them—were closemouthed when I tried to draw them out."

"It's that way here too," Flowers said, "and I know that a bunch of them have run off from some of the farms around here since they got the word that they are free. That's why I wanted you to see what I'm about to show you." He turned the buggy off the main road onto a narrow dirt lane with cultivated fields on either side. Blackberry bushes already showing small red fruit grew along the fences that separated rows of cotton, corn, sweet potatoes, and peanuts from the road.

"This looks like a nice place, Mr. Flowers. Is it one of yours?" Claude asked.

"It is," Flowers said. "It's not big, just fifty acres, but it does well—and without a single slave." He turned to look at Claude to see if his words had sunk in, but before Claude could react, Flowers stopped the buggy in front of a barn and raised an arm in greeting to a man coming through the open door. "Hey, Isaiah," Flowers said.

"Mr. Flowers," the man replied as he walked to the side of the buggy and extended his hand. A broad smile split his sun-darkened face. He used his other hand to remove his floppy hat, revealing a full head of graying blond hair that flowed down his cheeks into a full beard, which in turn spilled over the bib of his worn denim overalls. He was not wearing a shirt, and his arms and shoulders were as dark as his face.

"Isaiah Watkins, this is Claude Parker. He runs my plantation over in Red Clay, Alabama," Flowers said. "Claude, Isaiah used to be one of my overseers, but now he runs this farm with his wife and son, and I think he feels that he has a good life here. My arrangement with Isaiah is different from the one I have with you, Claude, but I think there's something important that you can learn from it."

The three men spent the rest of the afternoon walking around the property while Flowers detailed the arrangement he had with Watkins. The former overseer and his family were tenants. That is, they paid rent to Flowers for the use of the property, which he collected annually after the harvest. Flowers also served as their banker by providing loans to cover upfront costs for seeds, livestock feed, and the occasional hired man. The loans were repaid with interest each year after the harvest.

"What happens if Watkins has a bad harvest and can't meet his obligations?" Claude asked as they rode back toward Flowers's home.

"I take a portion of the crop, and the rest of his debt carries over with interest to be paid from the proceeds of the next year's harvest, along with the new debt. It's a fair arrangement," Flowers said. Claude nodded but did not reply. The deal Flowers had described sounded attractive for the landowner, but risky for the tenant.

"Why did you think it was important for me to see that operation today, Mr. Flowers?" he asked.

"You want to buy that two hundred and fifty acres at Road's End, and I want you to buy it, but the uncertainty we are facing worries me. I am concerned about the effect it might have on your ability to secure the funds to complete the transaction. So here is what I propose," Flowers said. "You take over that two hundred and fifty acres at Road's End in an arrangement like the one I have with Watkins while you continue to put together the funds to buy the place outright; let's say over five years.

"You keep one hundred acres under your direct control while you parcel out the other hundred and fifty acres to sharecroppers," he continued. "The land under your direct control will give you a good living, and the shares will provide you with funds you can apply toward the purchase."

The end of the lane to Flowers's house had come into view, and the sun was low in the western sky at their backs. Claude realized suddenly that he had stopped breathing while Flowers spoke, and he gasped as he sucked in air through his nose and open mouth. "I don't know what to say, sir," he sputtered.

"Don't say anything yet," Flowers replied. "Take the next few days to visit Watkins again and think about it, then go home and speak with your lawyers. If it still feels right, we'll have a deal." He extended his hand, and Claude shook it heartily as the sun slipped below the horizon. The night sky stretched out above them, a stygian expanse relieved by billions of pinpricks of starlight, each one a beacon of possibility in a universe of endless opportunities. Claude slept well again that night, and he rose the next morning exhilarated. When Flowers sat down for breakfast, Claude was already gone, off to look at Watkins's place with fresh eyes and new purpose.

Claude's return trip from Mississippi was uneventful but disturbing. Everywhere he looked, it seemed there were young men—some barely in their teens—with old men's eyes and scarecrow bodies draped in tattered uniforms of Confederate gray. Some were missing limbs, and they hobbled awkwardly on crutches to which they had not yet grown accustomed. They struggled to light cigars or pipes with only one arm.

Those men—most of whom would never benefit from the cruel institution of slavery, for which they had risked their lives—had received wages of war in the form of physical and emotional disfigurement. And, as in the wake of all wars, they were already becoming ghosts on the periphery of civilians' minds. Claude had escaped military service, and as the train hurtled eastward into the darkness of night, he was rocked into a restless sleep with bayonets of shame and regret piercing his heart.

As the train drew closer to Red Clay, he reflected on the time he had spent with George Flowers, and despite his initial fears, he now saw his way clear to buy back Road's End, at least the part of it that had meaning for him.

Plessant was at the train station with the wagon when Claude returned from his two-week trip to Mississippi.

"It's good to be back," Claude said as they drove along the familiar road on the way to the plantation. "What happened while I was away?"

Plessant filled him in with all the minutia of the day-to-day operations, and then he added, "The big thing is Massa Wilson just disappeared. The day after you left, I was s'posed to drive him to town, but he didn't never show up, and didn't nobody never see him no more. The other overseer, he sent for the sheriff, and they looked for days, but they didn't never find nothin'. His house at Road's End look like he just walked away and didn't take nothin' with him."

Claude asked questions all the way back to Road's End, but there were no more satisfying answers about Wilson's disappearance. "I guess we'll never know," he said.

"Yassuh, I guess we won't," Plessant replied.

As the wagon slowed to a halt in front of the big house, Claude turned to Plessant and asked if there had been any good news.

"You know that new kitchen garden Elmira tol' you she was gon' make? She made it. I helped her dig it, and she got it all planted. A few little shoots already comin' up."

"Well, that is good news," Claude said. "How big is it?"

"It's 'bout long as a man is tall, and 'bout this wide." Plessant stretched both arms out to their full length. "It ain't too big, but it big enough to do the job."

Chapter 26

RED CLAY, ALABAMA

AUTUMN 1943

Maybelle hardly knew what to think about the old white woman who had settled so comfortably on her front porch, wrapped in the quilt Maybelle had made with her own hands, chatting away with her daughter, telling stories about Maybelle's father. She had heard some of the stories from Felix himself, and she was fascinated to see the woman who had made him sit behind her at breakfast to be fed like a dog when they were both children.

Of all the stories Felix had told her about slavery times, the one about sitting on that stool to be fed by a child hardly older than himself was the one that most embittered him. "She acted like I was some kind of animal begging for scraps from the table," he would say, and Maybelle could see the hurt in his eyes, swirling just beneath the surface. "I wasn't nothing but a dog to her, and maybe not even that," Felix would say.

Now Felix was in his grave, and here was the selfsame Addie of his youth, sipping tea and telling tales, and for what: Forgiveness? Redemption? She would get none of that from Maybelle—at least not today.

In the driveway, Maybelle's son, Luther, was peppering the chauffeur with questions about Addie's car. The hood was up, and Luther's head was down in the engine compartment, from which he emitted murmurs of appreciation for the elegance of the mechanical design. Maybelle smiled, enjoying Luther's enthusiasm for the car and hoping a mother's hope that his interest in mechanics would secure him a position away from the front line when he returned to duty with his army unit the following week.

"Mama?" It was Eileen trying to get her attention. "Mama, do you know anything about what Grandpa did after slavery ended, before he met Grandma?"

"I would be most grateful, Mrs. Epps," Addie said. "I learned some things about my brother's relationship with your family after the war, but I suspect that what I know is incomplete. It would mean so much to me to hear about it from you."

Maybelle scrutinized Addie's face for a sign of sincerity. It had not been lost on her that Addie had addressed her as *Mrs. Epps*. It was an act of respect that was rare among white people in 1940s Alabama, especially among those old enough to remember the slavery times.

Addie leaned forward when Maybelle didn't respond immediately, so that she could look directly into her eyes. "You must be wondering why I am here, why I would come all this way to talk to you. I wish I had a simple answer for you, but I do not," she said. "What I can tell you is that as a child I was mean to Felix, perhaps even cruel, out of ignorance and spite, but years later when we met again as young adults, at a time when my life had become complicated, at a time when my ties to everyone and everything I had ever known were in jeopardy, Felix gave me something I needed to move forward.

"As I said this morning, he and I had not been in touch for many years, but I have continued to think of him as a friend, and I have hoped that he thought of me in the same way. If I have regretted anything in this long life of mine, it is that I did not make a greater effort to maintain our friendship. So, when I learned of his passing, I thought, presumptuously perhaps, that the best way I could honor him would be to share my memories with his family. And I hoped that you would be willing to share yours with me. I am already more grateful than you might imagine."

Maybelle studied Addie's face long and hard before speaking. "I know just little bits and pieces," she said. "Daddy didn't like to talk about that period, but I'll tell you what I know."

———

ROAD'S END PLANTATION

SUMMER 1865

Claude rarely visited the slave quarters at night, and he felt anxious and self-conscious as he made his way to the cabin where Plessant and Elmira lived with their boy Felix. He had been home from Mississippi for six weeks, and it was nearly summer. The season was a feast for the senses in South Alabama. The earthy aromas of the fecund soil of the fields and all the living things in the stables, the barn, and the forests that made up Road's End surrounded him. He could feel the future unfolding ahead of him, drawing him forward on a tightwire, and he dared not stop for fear of falling off.

Plessant answered his knock and stepped outside when he saw Claude standing there in the dark. "Massa Claude? What can I do for you?" he asked.

"I need to talk to you, Plessant. Let's walk while we talk." He started to walk away before Plessant could respond. "You've been a big help to me, Plessant, especially since so much has happened in this last year," he said once they were some distance from the cabin.

"Yassuh," Plessant said. Their walk had taken them to the edge of the woods that separated the creek from the cultivated land and the grounds around the big house and the outbuildings.

"This is a good spot, Plessant," Claude said. "It was one of my father's favorite places at Road's End. There's ten acres here that his father gave to him as a present back around the time you were born. And I'll tell you something else that very few other people know. These ten acres were not included in the sale of Road's End to Mr. Flowers, and they still remain in the hands of my family." A cloud passed in front of the moon, darkening the landscape for a moment.

"Yassuh," Plessant said and waited to hear what Claude had on his mind.

"Here's something else, Plessant," Claude continued. "My father thought the South would lose the war and that the slaves would be freed. He also thought that if it happened, your family deserved something for the way you have served ours and for the loss of your other two children."

Plessant remained silent.

"In the morning, I'm going to tell everybody that the Yankee cavalry officer who came here the other week was right. You're all free, and you can go wherever you want, but if you want to stay here, it will be under a new arrangement," Claude said. "You see, Plessant, I am buying Road's End back from Mr. Flowers, at least part of it, and the only way I can operate it is to have people working on shares. What do you think about that?"

"I don't know what to think, Massa Claude," Plessant said. "What is 'working on shares'?"

Claude explained the sharecropping system he had learned in Mississippi—the way each farmer would be allotted a share of land and advanced an amount of cash to buy seed and other farming necessities in return for a share of the proceeds from the farmer's crops after the harvest. If the income from the crops was inadequate to pay the landowner, the remainder would be carried over to the next year, with interest.

"It sound good, Massa Claude. Matter of fact, it sound too good. Sound like a man could be in trouble if he have a couple of bad years in a row. But I guess a man got to take his chances," Plessant replied. "Why you tellin' me this tonight, 'stead of in the morning with everybody else?"

"It's because of what I was saying earlier," Claude replied, "about how my father wanted to do something good for you and your family. Instead of working a share, I want you and Elmira to work for me. I'll pay wages; it won't be much, but you can count on it, and I'll need Elmira to do house cleaning, too, since there's just me living there, and I don't need a cook *and* a housekeeper. As for you, I'll need you to help keep an eye on things the way you always have and also to be a general handyman around the place."

Plessant nodded thoughtfully.

"There's something else too," Claude continued. "I intend to make arrangements with the blacksmith and the carpenter to allow them to use the shops and tools for their own businesses in exchange for a share of their earnings and also in return for work at Road's End. That means that Felix can remain apprenticed to the carpenter and learn the trade. Now, what do you think?"

"I think it's good, Massa Claude. Elmira will be glad to hear it, and Felix too. He like workin' for the carpenter, and John say he good at it."

"All right, then it's settled," Claude said, and they started walking back toward the quarters. "Two more things. After we get all these shares settled, I'm going to need y'all to move out of that cabin. It looks like Mr. Wilson isn't coming back, and I think you should move into his house. I think you'll be more comfortable there, and I'm going to need your cabin for a sharecropper family.

"Also, as the first job in your new role, I'll need you to build a fence around that ten acres I showed you. With things the way they are, I want it to be clear that it's *my* land. You understand?"

"Yassuh, first thing, and thank you," Plessant said.

Claude smiled broadly. "You're welcome, Plessant, you're very welcome."

They were nearing the quarters, and in the underbrush along the path, a feral cat lay on its belly, ready to pounce on a hapless field mouse that was coming into range with every step it took. It was the way of things, and change was nowhere in sight.

Chapter 27

ABOARD A NORTHBOUND TRAIN

AUTUMN 1868

The train chugged resolutely into Richmond, Virginia, slowing as it pulled into the station, drawn by a massive black steam locomotive. Escaping steam from the engine hissed, and a long, thick black cloud flowed from the engine's smokestack while the fireman, his sweat-drenched shirt plastered to his back, leaned hard on his coal shovel, his job done for the moment. On the platform outside, passengers handed over luggage to porters before boarding, and arriving passengers rushed into the embrace of friends and family who had come to greet them.

Behind a sooty window of the first-class car, thirteen-year-old Addie sat next to Colette Deville, her aunt, mildly interested in what she saw. She had expected to be more excited about being in Richmond. The war had raged through a third of her life, and the city had loomed large in her imagination as the former capital of the Confederacy. Although she was young, she was aware of the white southerners' sense of loss in a cause they had persuaded themselves was just.

They told themselves that "Northern aggressors" didn't understand their way of life. In their view, Yankees couldn't see the natural order of things that guided life in the South, where Black slaves toiled for their masters as God had intended. The Bible, they insisted, proved they were right, and they cited Colossians 3:22: *Slaves, obey in all things your masters according to the flesh; not with eyeservice, as menpleasers; but in singleness of heart, fearing God.* Was the Bible wrong? Was God wrong? Was it not manifestly clear, they contended, that God created white men as superior and had blessed them to grow wealthy on the labor of the Blacks and the horses and the cows and the pigs and all the other animals He placed at their disposal? It was simple, they said. Why couldn't the Yankees see it?

Still, the war was already receding into the thirteen-year-old's historical memory, rather than occupying a central space in her mind as a lived experience, and she did not share the intensity of her elders' feelings. "Will we be here long, Tante Colette?" she asked.

"No," Colette replied, "just long enough for some new passengers to board and for the train to take on water and more fuel."

"Good," Addie said, already focused on what might lie ahead.

Two middle-aged men entered the car, dressed in modern sack coats and carrying brown leather satchels that appeared to be conveyances for important documents. They had copious facial hair, one red, the other brown; the scents of tobacco and whiskey trailed behind them as they passed Addie and Colette on their way to seats in the rear of the car.

"Damned Rebs don't know a good deal when they see one," Red Beard said to his companion.

"Yeah, they don't understand that they lost the war, and deals like ours don't come along every day," Brown Beard agreed.

Addie strained to hear the rest of their conversation, but her eavesdropping was halted by a rap on the knuckles from Colette. "Curiosity killed the cat," she said and shot Addie a disapproving look.

———

Colette, the younger sister of Marie Louise, was not happy to be there, and the sooner she could be rid of this odd child, the happier she would be. Marie Louise had died a few months earlier, having never fully regained either her physical or emotional health in the wake of her son's death so soon after the loss of her husband. Initially, she had seemed glad to return to her father's home, but New Orleans had chafed under Union occupation through most of the war, and it did not seem the sunny place of her childhood. Then, the year after the war ended, her father was killed in a terrible mishap during a Republican Party convention in New Orleans to address implementation of the so-called Black Codes. A deadly riot broke out, and the old man was caught in a clash between factions as he walked to his Dauphine Street medical office.

With Addie's grandparents and parents dead, one of her brothers lost at sea, and the other one living hundreds of miles away in Red Clay, Alabama, Addie was essentially alone. At Marie Louise's funeral, she had sat dry-eyed in the pew as relatives and family friends—most of whom she had never met—shed decorous tears. Her lack of apparent grief didn't go unnoticed by her aunt. "Something is wrong with that child," Colette whispered to an older cousin. "She hasn't shed a tear, and her mother is lying in her coffin right in front of her."

"I know," the cousin said. "I've always thought she was peculiar. By the way, who's going to take care of her?"

Colette sighed. "I guess that falls to me. We'll let her finish the term here, but after that—I've already spoken with my husband about it—we'll send her to that boarding school in Connecticut, Miss Porter's. I would never send a child of mine up there, but I suspect that being among all those Yankee girls will suit Addie just fine." And within weeks, Addie found herself on the train on the way to Miss Porter's, accompanied by Tante Colette.

———

NEW ORLEANS

SPRING 1872

Her motives notwithstanding, Colette's speculation that Addie would thrive at Miss Porter's was accurate, and by the time Addie returned to New Orleans four years later, in 1872, she had matured into a confident young woman of formidable social and intellectual power. That she was also beautiful and financially well-to-do made her the object of numerous suitors. Even Tante Colette was impressed and sought to persuade Addie to allow herself to be presented during the upcoming debutante season.

"You really must, *chérie*," she implored. "It is a grand thing, and you will undoubtedly be the envy of all the other girls. You can have your pick of the young men, and you will be a leader in New Orleans society."

"That all sounds lovely, Tante Colette, really," Addie replied, "but I intend to see more of the world before I settle down. You can understand that, can't you? I've never been to Europe like my friends at Miss Porter's, and except for my time at school, I've hardly been anywhere outside of the South. I want to travel, I *need* to travel, and then, perhaps, I can think about suitors. You are my guardian and you can stop me, but I beg of you, let me go. Just one year, and I'll return to New Orleans. The debutante balls and the rest of it will still be here."

They were sitting in the grand parlor of the French Quarter house in which Marie Louise and Colette had grown up, and which would belong to Addie when she came of age. Summer was coming, and a warm breeze blew through vents in shutters that covered open windows, carrying the sounds of birds singing, the *clip-clop* of horses' hooves, the babble of commerce in the streets, and the aromatic hint of feasts being prepared in nearby restaurant kitchens. With the end of spring, the most prominent families would soon decamp for the country until cooler weather and the start of the social season drew them back in the fall.

Colette closed her eyes and shifted in her chair. "You have never been easy, Addie, and I am not persuaded that what you seek is the right thing. But I think I know what Marie Louise would have done," she said. "So this is what we shall do. I will travel to Europe with you for the summer, and if things are going well at the end of August, I will return alone and you can go ahead on your own for the rest of the year. If they are not, however—and it shall be my decision—we will both come home together in the fall. Is that satisfactory?"

"Oh, thank you, Tante Colette. *Merci, merci, merci!*" Addie exclaimed and rushed across the room to embrace her aunt. "We shall have such a wonderful time. I just know it."

Chapter 28

On a crisp late fall morning, with the sunlight breaking through naked tree branches to cast jagged shadows on the ground, Felix pushed open the door to his shop. Technically, it wasn't *his* shop, but John, the old carpenter from whom Felix had learned his trade, came to work less and less frequently as age, arthritis, and failing eyesight took a greater toll on his energy and health. Customers had begun to think of it as Felix's shop, and they expected to deal with him when they placed orders for new work.

"I guess you got yourself a business now," John said on one of his recent days in the shop. He had been sitting on a bench in the corner when a customer, a white man who wanted new horse stalls built in his barn, walked in and greeted him, but turned to Felix to discuss the order. John smiled ruefully when the man left. "You knows everything I know," he said, "so it's up to you to make a livin'."

"Yassuh, you taught me good, but you ain't done yet," Felix replied. "I expect you still gon' be around a long time, and I'm grateful to you."

John shrugged. "It's like the preacher say: 'To everything there is a season,' and I reckon winter is comin' on soon for me, and you gon' be on your own. I know you can handle it, though, and I'm proud of you."

Felix opened the shutters to allow the sun to brighten the shop's interior, and he began loading his carrier with tools he would need to work on the shed he was building at a nearby plantation. His grapefruit-sized biceps bulged, and his shirt pulled tight across his flat belly as he worked.

"This where the top carpenter 'round here work?" The voice came from the open door, and Felix turned to see his mother, Elmira, standing in the doorway with a lunch pail in her hand and a smile on her face.

"Hey, Maw," he replied and crossed the room to embrace her and to take the pail. "Thank you for this. I'm gon' be workin' all day on that shed, and I'll need this to keep goin'."

"You ain't even looked inside. Might be just some old nasty stuff like what buzzards eat," Elmira said, her eyes alive with pride in her son's accomplishments.

"Don't have to look. I got a nose like a old hound dog." Felix made a great show of sniffing the top of the lunch pail. "Let's see," he said. "Fried chicken, cornbread, and apple pie. Did I get it right?"

"Wait and see when you open it up," she said, and they laughed.

Felix loved his mother. He loved her for the gentle warmth in which she had always enveloped him, and he loved her for her fierce protection, like the time she had put herself between him and the overseer's lash and for the tears she shed when she was forced to whip him herself. The emotion of the memory encircled Felix's heart and squeezed it until his eyes filled with water that spilled onto his cheeks.

Elmira hugged him and then pushed him away. "Go'n now. Grown man like you cain't be late for work."

Elmira stepped out into the sun and watched her boy walk away. He was tall and strong like his father, and he had a good heart. He would be all right, but on this beautiful day she was glad she had not burdened him with the news that had arrived with the boy who had delivered Claude's new boots from the cobbler in town: Danny, the former stable boy and Felix's childhood friend, was dead. Murdered. His broken, mutilated body had been found in the underbrush along the road heading north out of Red Clay on Saturday morning.

Elmira hung her head as she walked to the big house to begin her cooking and cleaning duties. She had been afraid that it might end that way for Danny, and she said a quiet prayer for the safety of her own son. *Danny never had a chance*, she thought. She had tried to help him; the Lord knew she had tried.

———

On the night after Claude returned from Mississippi and outlined the new situation for Plessant and his family, Elmira and Plessant had lain awake, trying to work out what they would do next. "I think we gon' be all right," Plessant said. "We gon' get a new house and Felix can keep on learnin' the carpentry trade, and to tell the truth, I'm glad we ain't got to sharecrop. Somethin' about that don't sound right to me. I think a man could get hisself in a lot of trouble if he don't watch it."

Elmira turned on her side to face Plessant. "I think you right," she said, "but either way, we still don't own nothin', and Massa Claude get to decide everything."

"Yeah, but the way I see it, we got a chance to save some money and maybe buy some land of our own. I been around here long enough to know somethin' about how to raise crops and make money on it," Plessant replied. "The main thing, though, is we got to make sure Felix is set, and the best way to do that is stay here 'til he ready to be on his own."

Awake in the dark, lying quietly and listening to the night sounds outside, they held each other close as the realization of what it could mean to be free settled around them. The sea had parted, and they were racing across the dry land, hearing hoofbeats behind them, terrified to look back for fear that they might stumble and be overtaken by Pharaoh's chariots. Plessant tightened his arm around Elmira. Faith had to prevail; going forward was the only choice.

Plessant had nearly fallen asleep when Elmira spoke again. "Plessant, you know Felix's friend Danny?"

"Yeah, the stable boy," he mumbled.

"I been thinkin', what gon' happen to him? He cain't take no share; he too young, and he ain't got nobody and nowhere to go."

"Well, what you want me to do about it?" Plessant asked.

"I was thinkin' maybe we could take him in. Him and Felix already friends, and we gon' have more room when we move out this cabin into that house . . ."

Plessant was awake now and not happy with the direction of this conversation. "Look," he said, "I like Danny, and I'm sorry about his troubles, but I don't think we ought to be taking him in. We got our own son to look after, and that boy could put some bad ideas in Felix's head. And where you gon' get the extra money to feed him?"

In the other room, young Felix had strained to hear the debate between his parents. He hoped his mother would win. He liked the idea of having a "big brother," and he was happy when his mother's argument won out. Even Plessant came around as Danny blended into the family, and Elmira never seemed more pleased than when Felix, Danny, and Felix's longtime friend Jimmy were together at the house.

———

Although Jimmy now lived with his mother in town, where she worked as a cook and maid for another white family, he was at work in the blacksmith's shop at Road's End every day. Notwithstanding the social turmoil of the time and limited financial resources, the boys seemed headed in the right direction. Felix's carpentry skills were improving with each passing day, Jimmy's proficiency as an apprentice blacksmith was rising as well, and Claude had begun paying wages to Danny to take care of the horses and other livestock at Road's End.

Danny was eighteen when his behavior began to change, sneaking into the house late at night and being evasive when asked about where he had been. His clothes reeked of tobacco, whiskey, and cheap perfume, and when Plessant confronted him about it, he snapped back, "You ain't my paw."

"That's right," Plessant replied. "I ain't your paw, but you livin' in my house, and I cain't have no disrespect, and I cain't have my son around that stuff."

That night Danny slept in the loft above the horse stalls, as he had when he was a slave boy, and the next morning he averted his eyes and tried to leave when he met Elmira at the water pump. She moved to block his path and grabbed his chin with her left hand so that he couldn't look away.

"Now you listen to me, boy. You might think you a man, but you ain't no man yet, and 'til you is, you better listen to what grown folks got to tell you," she said. "And what this grown woman got to tell you is that you actin' a fool, and you gon' find yourself in big trouble if you don't straighten up."

Danny tried to walk away, but Elmira had a firm grip on his chin. "Maybe you think don't nobody know what you up to, but word get around," she said. "I know you been carryin' on with that Colored girl Pearlie what work upstairs at the Ridge Inn. I know what she do for the white mens that come in and lay their money down. You do too."

Danny started to speak, and Elmira talked right over his stammering protests. "It's bad enough you messin' around with a woman that make her living that way—I don't blame her; she got to eat and have somewhere to stay—but you can do better. And besides, it's dangerous, more dangerous than you know."

"What you talkin' 'bout, Miss Elmira?" Danny asked. "I know all 'bout what Pearlie do, but she don't care about them. She love me, and I love her. Ain't nothin' dangerous about that."

"It's dangerous because the white mens picked her out for theyselves, and they don't expect to share her with some young Colored boy," Elmira said. "I'm telling you the same thing I'm gon' be telling my boy Felix." She relinquished her grip on Danny's chin and gently stroked his cheek with the palm of her hand. "We might be free," she said, "but the rules for them and the rules for us is different. It ain't fair, but that's the way it is, and you got to watch out or get hurt bad."

Tears were forming in Danny's eyes, and Elmira swept him into her arms and hugged him. "You know what you got to do," she said. "You go up there tonight and tell Pearlie you cain't be comin' 'round to call on her no more. Then you come back here to the house and sleep in your own bed."

"Thank you, Miss Elmira," he whispered.

"Mr. Claude is goin' out this morning, so you go get his horse ready, and when he's gone, come up to the kitchen, and I'll get you something to eat," Elmira said.

Elmira stood watching as Danny walked away to attend to the animals. *Maybe it's not too late*, she thought as she turned to head back to the big house. A cold gust of wind, a harbinger of the season to come, blew across the yard, and Elmira felt it through her shawl as she climbed the steps to the back door that led to the big house's kitchen. *Lord God*, she prayed silently, *please don't let it be too late.*

—————

Danny was buried a week after his body was found. It was seasonably cold and overcast. A light wind blew, carrying the sound of crows cawing in a nearby tree and the scent of leaves being burned in the backyard of a house down the street. Mourners had been few—Plessant, Elmira, and Felix; Jimmy and his mother; and a handful of others from Red Clay's Black community. Pearlie stood back from the others at the graveside, acutely aware of the low regard in which she was held generally and of the contempt that flowed from the older women especially. "I feel bad for her, Plessant," Elmira said. "In a way, she just like Danny; no family, just tryin' to make her way in the world with nobody to show her the way."

That afternoon, the loft above the stables where Danny had slept as a young enslaved boy was warm and filled with piles of soft hay that smelled of the earth. Cobwebs stretched from beam to beam, illuminated by sunlight through cracks in the wall. At night, mice traveled around the perimeter in their never-ending search for food. A pitchfork Danny had used to toss hay down to the horses stood in the corner as the only reminder that he had worked there, or that it had once been his home.

"You think it hurt to die?" Felix wondered and shifted his position in the hayloft. As children, they had used it as a hideout after Danny moved in with Felix's family. It was where they had escaped to laugh and talk about things they didn't want to share with family or anyone else. It had been their special place, and though they hadn't used it for years, it seemed to Felix and Jimmy that it was where they needed to be that afternoon.

"I don't think it hurt," Jimmy replied, "but what they done to him before he died sho nuff must have hurt real bad."

"You think he cried?" Felix asked.

"I don't know, but I know I woulda been yellin' like anything if somebody was takin' a knife to me between my legs," Jimmy said.

The young men were quiet for a while, contemplating the awfulness of what had happened to their friend.

"Say, Jimmy," Felix said, breaking the silence. "Did you ever do it?"

"Do what?" he replied.

"You know, did you ever do *it* with a girl?"

"Man, that ain't none of your business. 'Sides, you too young to know 'bout that stuff. Leave that to us grown folks," Jimmy said, laughing and poking Felix in the ribs.

"I'm eighteen, and you just twenty-one. I'm grown enough," Felix protested. "I bet you ain't never done it anyhow."

"Well, if you got to know, I did do it," Jimmy said.

"No, you didn't," Felix said, his eyes growing wide.

"Yeah, I did," Jimmy said, "but like I said, it ain't none of your business."

"Come on, man, who you do it with?" Felix demanded. "Somebody I know?"

"I ain't tellin' you, so quit askin'," Jimmy said and stood up to leave.

"Who was it?" Felix asked again. "I bet you didn't even do it for real."

"Felix! Jimmy! I know y'all up there." The voice came from below. It was Plessant. "Elmira got food on the table, so y'all come on down here and eat before it get cold."

When they didn't acknowledge his call or move right away, Plessant spoke once more before leaving. "Y'all think I don't know you up there? That's where you always go, so get down here 'fore I come up and throw y'all down. I ain't too old to do it, neither."

"Damn," Felix said.

"Damn," Jimmy echoed.

"I guess we better go."

"Yeah," Jimmy said. "I guess we better."

Chapter 29

Freedom brought changes, big and small. Almost without thinking about it, *Massa* Claude had become *Mr.* Claude in the minds of Plessant and Elmira. Claude seemed not to notice when they altered the way they addressed him, and he made no change in the way he spoke to them. For Claude, Plessant and Elmira still had only their first names. And though they no longer needed to carry a pass when they left Road's End, a knot still formed in their bellies when they were away from the plantation and passed a white man on the road.

For a brief time after the war, when federal authorities enforced the law, it seemed that rights equal to those of whites might be at hand. Black men had served in state legislatures all over the South, and Hiram Revels from Mississippi had even served in the US Senate. But, day by day, rights for Black men and women were slipping away.

It all added urgency to Plessant and Elmira's determination to secure their own financial future and that of their son. They worked hard, and they were saving their money. Plessant had even opened a savings account at the bank downtown. For the first time in his life, he had needed a last name. "I been with the Parkers, Mr. Claude and his daddy before him, near 'bout all my life, so just put down Parker," he told the clerk.

"Here you are, Plessant," said the young clerk, barely half Plessant's age, as he handed over the new passbook. "You just bring that book in with you whenever you make a deposit, and we'll write down the amount. You understand?"

"Yassuh, I understand," Plessant said, showing deference to the younger man, a courtesy that would never be returned. It didn't matter, he told himself. Yet it did matter, and it infuriated him. Still, by the time he arrived at home, Plessant had shaken off his dark mood, and he rushed through the door to show Elmira the little book that represented their future. Their reading and writing skills were limited, but they could make out the name and the numbers representing their funds, entered by the clerk. And as 1874 drew to a close, they had saved nearly enough to buy a small piece of land, and they had begun to dream of leaving Road's End behind.

"You think we can really do it?" Elmira asked. "You think we can really have our own place?"

"Why not?" Plessant said. "We near 'bout got the money to buy it, and I know how to run it. We can build a house—Felix will help—and put in crops we ain't got to share with nobody."

They were sitting on an old quilt on the ground beneath the spreading branches of a live oak tree next to the creek at Road's End. It was Sunday afternoon, and Felix had stayed in town with his friends after church. Plessant was fishing, and Elmira was sitting with him, enjoying the last fall days before winter set in and made it too cool to relax outside.

"I used to bring Felix to this spot right here to go fishing when he was little," Plessant said. "One time—it was a Sunday just like this, the day before Massa John Robert got kilt—we was fishing and caught a big mess of bream and catfish. Massa Claude come walkin' by and asked was we havin' any luck. I told him yes we was and pulled up the stringer to show him. When he left, Felix asked me, 'Paw, you like Massa Claude?'"

"What you say?" Elmira asked.

"I said he better'n most," Plessant replied.

"What you think now?" Elmira asked.

"Oh, I still think he better'n most," Plessant said, "but I ain't sure that still mean the same thing."

The postwar years had also been good to Claude. His sharecropping enterprise had been successful, and he had been able to buy back most of Road's End as planned. His relationship with George Flowers had evolved into an agricultural investment partnership on two other properties in the Mississippi Delta, where Black labor was cheap.

"Congratulations, Claude. I'd say you're in good shape," said his banker, Roger Tyler, as they concluded a meeting to review Claude's finances.

"I've been lucky, Roger. You know as well as I that many others around here haven't been so fortunate. The war took a toll, and having all these Yankees around here with this Reconstruction nonsense hasn't helped. Besides," Claude added, "I have to keep the money coming in now that I'm getting married."

"That's right!" Tyler exclaimed. "I heard that you and a young woman over at the courthouse were engaged. It's that stenographer, Carrie Anderson, isn't it? She's beautiful, and smart too, I hear. Congratulations!"

He rose from his desk and shook Claude's hand. "Come on, I'll walk you out." Claude beamed as they made their way through the busy bank lobby, a short journey that took a long time, because he was stopped every few feet by men who wanted to shake his hand and have a quick word. Due to the success of Road's End and leadership roles he had taken in civic affairs, Claude's star had risen dramatically, socially as well as financially, and he had become someone with whom the rich and powerful sought to be associated.

Claude shook each man's hand in turn, looked him in the eye and appeared to listen to what he had to say. A smile here, a slap on the back there, a sympathetic wrinkling of the brow when they shared bad news.

Claude knew the names of their wives and children, and he never failed to ask about them. In return, they showered him with flattery and even some genuine respect, and Claude wolfed it down as if his plate might never be full again.

Tyler stopped and lowered his voice as they approached the door. "Say, Claude, I've heard something else about you too. Is it true you're thinking of running for mayor?"

Claude smiled. "Let's just say that some people have talked to me about it."

"Well, whatever happens, you know you can count on me," Tyler replied.

Claude stepped out of the bank onto the sidewalk, where the sun seemed to shine just a bit brighter than it had when he went inside.

———

Plessant was crossing the yard to start his day the next morning when Claude called to him from the front porch of the big house. "Plessant, I need you to get the wagon and drive me into town again today," he said. "I have a meeting with the lawyers and some other business, and I'll need you to pick up some supplies at the hardware store and the dry goods store."

Plessant waved to acknowledge that he had heard Claude and headed for the barn, glad to have escaped the way he would have spent his afternoon: digging sweet potatoes in Elmira's garden, repairing a broken shutter at their house, and attaching a new rope to the bucket at the well. *I guess them chores can wait another day*, he thought. He stopped by the kitchen on the way to the barn to tell Elmira about the change in plans. He was rewarded with a hard look, but she also wrapped up a lunch of biscuits and some bacon left over from what she had cooked that morning for Claude.

They drove mostly in silence, punctuated by the beat of the horse's hooves on the hard-packed dirt, enjoying the cool, sunny morning. The hardwood trees—oak, hickory, and black walnut—had already dropped their leaves ahead of the coming winter, in stark contrast to the ever-greens along the road. Chipmunks scurried among the leaves on the forest floor, gathering acorns and other food for their winter stores, all the while keeping a wary eye out for circling hawks in the air and for foxes and feral cats on the ground.

"It looks like we're going to have a good year," Claude said. "Most of the sharecroppers have had good harvests."

"Yassuh," Plessant replied, "but you know the Smiths and that Hawkins family still ain't caught up from two years ago. What you gon' do 'bout them? I don't know if they bad farmers or they just have bad luck."

"I don't know either, but I can't keep carrying them. I'd hate to throw them out, especially with them owing me money, but I'm beginning to feel that I have no other choice," Claude said. "I'll think about it, but I have to make a decision soon."

After dropping Claude at the law offices, Plessant headed to the hardware store to pick up a new saw, an axe handle, nails, screws, rope, and sundry other items before going on to the dry goods store to purchase household cooking and cleaning items Elmira had ordered for the big house. He was loading the last of it into the wagon when he was approached by a young man about twenty-five years old, tall, lean, and with a distinguished bearing. With his olive skin and softly curling black hair, he might have been perceived as a Greek or a southern Italian in a big northern city.

"You are Plessant Parker? Mr. Claude Parker is your employer?" the man asked.

"I am," Plessant replied. "Who askin'?"

"My name is David Allen. I am the steward at the law firm that handles the Parker affairs."

They eyed each other momentarily before Plessant broke the silence. "Well, now we know who each other is. What you want with me?"

"I was sent to find you to tell you that Mr. Parker and the partners will be having lunch and that you need not come to pick him up for at least two hours," the steward said.

"That's good," Plessant answered. "I was gettin' hungry myself, so I reckon I can just find me a good spot to eat and take a rest."

"Would you mind if I come with you?"

"You can come if you want," Plessant said, surprised. "My Elmira didn't pack no extra in my bag, but you welcome to share what I got."

"Thank you, but I have already eaten. I just need to talk to you, and what I have to say is better said in private."

They drove about two miles out of town to a wooded area Plessant knew. "Say, Mr. Allen, where you from?" Plessant asked. "You talk like a white man, and I know most of the Colored families around here, including the light-skinned ones like you."

"I'm from Washington, DC, Plessant. By the way, can we just call each other by our first names? As for speaking 'like a white man,' I suppose that is due to my having had the privilege of being educated at some very good schools, paid for by my white father. I think he believed tuition payments would make up to my Colored mother for the way he dropped her after I was born. In any event, I came south to be a teacher at a church-affiliated school in northern Alabama that folded soon after I arrived. Then my mother died, and I found that I had nothing to draw me back to Washington, so I started looking for work, and here I am."

"That's a great story, David, but it still don't explain why you wanted to talk to me," Plessant said.

David didn't reply immediately. He stepped down from the wagon and walked around to Plessant's side before speaking: "I was never a slave, Plessant, and neither was my mother, but she was a maid in a wealthy white household, and one of the things she would tell you if she were here is that we Colored people have a magical power—we can disappear."

"What you mean?" Plessant asked. "Cain't nobody just disappear 'less he a haint."

David smiled and continued. "When we are out in public—on the street, in a store, or on a public conveyance—we are quite visible, and white people go to great lengths to keep us at a distance. On the other hand, when we work in their homes—cooking their food, washing their clothes, cleaning their houses, caring for their children—we become invisible. Perhaps not so much invisible as ordinary, unnoticed, like a table or a chair that has rested in the same place for twenty years. After a while no one pays attention to it. It's as if it isn't there at all."

Plessant was chewing a biscuit and bacon and listening to this educated Colored man. He had never heard such words from one of his own, not even from the preacher at Third Baptist Church, and he was fascinated. "I think I know what you gettin' at," he said. "When my boy Felix was little in slavery times, the mistress's daughter used to make him sit by her chair when the family ate breakfast, and she would feed him out her hand like givin' scraps to a dog. He hated that, but they used to forget he was there, and they talked 'bout things they didn't want us to know. I would ask Felix what they talked about, and I would get it all from him. Same thing with my wife, the cook, and Callie Mae, the maid."

"Precisely," David said. "I have no illusions about why the lawyers hired me. My physical appearance is, as *they* would say, 'presentable.' I am well-spoken, and I read and write with facility. I am not a disturbing presence when I serve refreshments to clients or when I enter a room to tidy things, and they trust me to handle tasks that require a modicum of education. Over time I have become as invisible as the conference table, the paintings on the wall, or the drapes at the windows. Thus, I have heard and seen many things."

"So I guess you sayin' you seen somethin' you want to tell me about?" Plessant said.

David nodded. "Am I correct to assume that you believe you and Mr. Parker have a good relationship, and that he has treated you well?"

"You could say that," Plessant replied. "I cain't say much good 'bout his daddy, or his daddy before him, but Mr. Claude and his mama, Miss Marie Louise, been good to me and mine."

David looked at Plessant with sadness in his gray eyes. "Then I regret that I must be the messenger who brings news that might change the way you feel, and thus I must apologize in advance."

As winter approached, dusk arrived earlier each day, and by the time Elmira finished her work in the big-house kitchen, night had fallen, and the glow of the moon and the twinkling of stars lit her way back to her cabin. Plessant was sitting in the dark at the kitchen table, with the dirty dishes and the remnants of a cold supper he and Felix had eaten still on the table.

"What's the matter with you? How come you ain't lit a lamp?" she asked. "Where is Felix?"

"Felix left after we ate; said he was goin' somewhere with Jimmy. He'll be back before too late 'cause he got to be up early tomorrow to start a new job." Plessant's voice was flat, distant, and Elmira decided not to light a lamp and instead sat beside him in the dark.

"What's the matter?" she asked. "I know somethin' wrong."

Plessant reached out and took Elmira's hand. "You remember how we was talkin' about Mr. Claude, and how I said he was better'n most, but that I didn't know what that mean nowadays?"

"I remember," Elmira said.

"Well, now I know what it mean. It mean he a snake like all the rest of 'em, but he don't kill when he bite; he just hurt you real bad and make you sick and then don't think nothin' 'bout it," Plessant said. Without letting go of Elmira's hand, Plessant told her about his encounter with the light-skinned steward from the law firm.

David had told Plessant: "I was dusting the furniture in the hallway outside the conference room where the partners were meeting with Mr. Parker when their discussion became heated. I heard Mr. Parker yell, 'I don't care. The land is mine, and unless you have some legal objection, I intend to keep it.' That was when they decided to continue their conversation over lunch, and they called me in to ask me to find you.

"Before they left, Mr. Stewart, the senior partner, asked me to clear the conference table and to put the papers back in their files. As I told you, they had become accustomed to me and relaxed about what was said in my presence or about documents I was asked to handle. That's how I happened to see a certain old letter to Mr. Parker from his mother. It advised him that her late husband's wish had been for a ten-acre parcel at the plantation to be deeded to you if the slaves were freed. I realized then that Mr. Parker's agitation was due to the partners' encouragement to fulfill his parents' wishes—and that he was resisting."

Plessant gripped Elmira's hand more tightly and said, "You know what land he talkin' 'bout, don't you? It's that piece by the creek that he so particular 'bout, the one he had me fence in soon as slavery was over. That s'posed to be our land, Elmira—yours and mine, and he just sittin' on it and actin' like he don't know it s'posed to come to us."

"Oh, Lawd," Elmira sighed. "What we gon' do?"

"Ain't really nothin' we can do," Plessant replied. "David say he looked at all the papers 'fore he put 'em away, and he say the land belong to Mr. Claude, and we ain't got no claim on it 'less he decide to honor what his mama and daddy wanted."

They sat together in the darkness, listening to the wind whistling through the trees and to the deep rumble that emanated from bare branches when they rubbed against each other, a somber prelude to a night of fitful sleep, eased only by the warmth they shared as they lay in each other's arms. And as the first pink hints of a new day appeared on the horizon, they knew they had to set a new course from which there would be no turning back.

Chapter 30

SPRING 1875

Felix was in his shop, cutting pieces of fine-grained walnut for a custom chiffonier he had been commissioned to design and build for one of the town's prominent white physicians. It was to be a wedding present from the doctor to his daughter and her new husband, and it would be the focal point of the master bedroom in their new two-story house, which Felix had also helped to build.

But his mind wasn't really on his work that Monday morning. Instead, he was thinking about the girl he sat behind every Sunday at Third Baptist Church and about how he might work up the courage to speak to her. He recalled every feature of her appearance: smooth caramel skin, sparkling deep-brown eyes behind rimless glasses that rested on a delicate nose, shiny black hair that fell from beneath her hat and cascaded over her shoulders, and white teeth that seemed to glow with their own internal light when she opened her mouth to sing. Felix had called on a number of young women, but none of them had captured his attention the way she did.

At church, Elmira caught him staring at the young woman. "You look any harder, your eyeballs gon' fall out your head and roll across the floor. Then what you gon' do?" she had whispered, and though she hid her grin behind a handkerchief as Felix's head whipped around in embarrassment, she couldn't stop her shoulders from shaking with suppressed laughter.

Felix was standing at his workbench, staring into space, when his friend Jimmy came in. "Man, if you was acting like that around the forge in my blacksmith shop, you'd be all burnt up by now," he said. "What you thinkin' 'bout so hard anyhow?" He filled the doorway, his bare, heavily muscled arms dangling from broad shoulders, his chest covered by a sweat-stained neck-to-knees leather apron.

"What I'm thinkin' about ain't got nothin' to do with you," Felix replied.

"I bet you thinkin' about that girl at church you been starin' at like some old hound dog droolin' over a pork chop bone," Jimmy shot back with a glint in his eye. "You know, her daddy got some money, and I reckon he ain't about to let the likes of you come courtin' his daughter."

"Jimmy, you think you know everything just 'cause you three years older than me, but you don't know everything," Felix replied.

"I know one thing," Jimmy said. "I'm hungry. You think maybe Miss Elmira will give me somethin' if I go up to the big house?"

"I reckon it is time to eat. Let's go see what she got," Felix said.

As a free journeyman, Jimmy worked in the same shop on the Road's End plantation where he had learned his trade as an enslaved apprentice, and, like Felix, he was gradually taking over the business from his old mentor. Also like Felix, Jimmy was earning a reputation for quality work. They were like brothers, and Elmira was never surprised to see the two of them show up together at the kitchen door, hoping for something good to eat. That day she obliged them with tin plates filled with cornbread, chopped yellow squash fried with onions, and a sweet potato roasted in the coals of the kitchen fire.

The grateful young men took their plates out to the shady side of the blacksmith shop and plopped down on the cool grass with their backs against the wall. "Man, how you stand it over that hot fire in your shop?" Felix asked, pulling his own sweat-dampened shirt away from his skin.

Jimmy laughed. "Ain't nothin' a real man cain't handle." A hard-shelled, iridescent green June bug buzzed about as they ate hungrily, washing the food down with cups of cold water from the well.

"So, you been courtin' Lucille?" Felix asked. The former maid at Road's End had taken a similar job at a nearby plantation after Claude let her go.

"What you know about that?" Jimmy replied.

"I don't know nothin' 'cept I heard you and her was sweet on each other and that you been comin' 'round to see her after church on Sunday," said Felix.

"So what?" Jimmy said. "Ain't nobody's business."

"I didn't say it was. Just what I heard."

They were quiet for a while, watching the June bug and appreciating the delicate scents of the earth as a light breeze kicked up and caressed the grass around them.

"I guess we better get back to work," Jimmy said.

"I guess so," said Felix as he stacked their dishes to return them to the kitchen. "So, you in love with Lucille?"

"I don't know," Jimmy said, stretching before heading back to his forge. Then he grinned. "But if I was, it still wouldn't be none of your business."

———

PARIS, FRANCE

SPRING 1874

After nearly two years of traveling through Europe, almost a year longer than the agreement she had made with Tante Colette, Addie's wanderlust was waning. She had returned to Paris, her favorite city, where she felt at home, and where she had learned to navigate the streets, the shops, and the cafés like a native. Addie had been charmed by Paris and its people from the first day. But now, somewhere deep in her inner being, she was beginning to feel that it was time to go home.

"Isabelle, do you miss New Orleans?" she asked Isabelle Buard, a young woman Addie's aunt had engaged to accompany them to Europe to serve as their maid and traveling companion. She had remained with Addie when Colette returned to New Orleans. They were sitting in a sidewalk café on the Left Bank, one of Addie's favorites, near the Pont Marie. Students from the Latin Quarter were strolling and beginning to fill tables in cafés along the Seine as the sun set. Artists, having lost the light for the day, had put away their brushes and turned their attention to selling their paintings.

"I suppose I miss my family," Isabelle said. "I should very much like to see Mama and Papa and my brothers, but, no, I do not miss being in New Orleans as I expect you do."

Addie regarded Isabelle in the fading light, the softly chiseled facial features similar to her own, the dark brown eyes and the lustrous, softly curling brown hair that framed the creamy olive-toned skin of her face. She realized that over the course of two years she had come to think of Isabelle as a friend, rather than as a mere employee. More importantly, she had stopped thinking of her in the explicit racial terms that would have defined their relationship in New Orleans. Isabelle was a Creole of color, *une Créole de couleur*, and though French-speaking mixed-race families like hers had long occupied a privileged social position between whites and Blacks in New Orleans, their status had eroded dramatically since the Civil War, and they had become subject to many of the same degradations as Black freedmen in the postwar South.

The two young women were of similar age—at twenty-two, Isabelle was slightly older—and thinking about their different situations, Addie understood why Isabelle might not be as enthusiastic about returning to New Orleans as she.

"Why did you ask?" Isabelle wanted to know, and seeing the expression on Addie's face, she knew the answer. "When are we to return?" she asked.

Before Addie could reply, however, they were interrupted by a shadow that fell across their table. They looked up into the face of a strikingly handsome young man, his hat in his hand and a smile that revealed even white teeth. He was tall and lean, brown-eyed and olive-skinned, and his gaze was intense but without malice. "My apologies if I have startled you," he said in French with an accent Addie could not place. He bowed slightly. "I wish only to introduce myself to two such charming ladies. I am Étienne Dupuis, and I hope you will do me the honor of allowing me to join you over a glass of wine."

"Well, sir, you are quite forward," Addie said, "but since you have presented yourself in such an intriguing manner, please join us. I am Adelaide Parker, and this is my companion, Isabelle Buard."

Étienne flashed his smile again, pulled a chair from another table, and signaled to the waiter to bring wine and another glass. This glass of wine led to dinner, and before the evening was over, Addie and Isabelle had been won over by their new acquaintance, the son of a fisherman from Sainte-Maxime on the Côte d'Azur, who had come to Paris to study and who had remained as a junior member of the faculty at his university. When they ordered, Étienne opined that "the fish in this restaurant is wonderful, but I ate so much seafood as a child that I have vowed never to touch it again," and chose the *steak au poivre saignant*.

He kept both of the women laughing and talking throughout the evening, but after he left them, having escorted them to their hotel, Isabelle remarked on what would have been obvious to anyone seated at their table. "Mademoiselle Addie, you have a new admirer."

Addie blushed. "Perhaps," she ventured, "we shall remain in Paris just a bit longer."

Chapter 31

SPRING 1875

The moment Felix had been waiting for had finally come. The woman he admired—he'd learned her name was Zilpha—was standing alone beside her family's buggy after the Sunday service while her parents and her brothers were still at the church entrance, chatting with the preacher and some of the other leaders of the congregation. This was his chance to speak to her, and he was going to do it. Really.

If he could get his muscles to move.

If he didn't trip over his own feet.

If his mouth didn't go dry.

If he could concentrate hard enough to put two sentences together.

If he didn't turn out to be a cowardly idiot and miss his chance.

If . . .

"What you waitin' for, Felix? Her folks gon' be over there any minute to put her in the buggy and take her home." Felix whipped his head around to see his old pal Jimmy, standing behind him grinning. "Course you got to make sure you don't drool on her when you talk to her," Jimmy added.

"Get outta here, Jimmy," Felix muttered under his breath.

"I don't know about that," Jimmy said. "I think you need somebody to hold your hand while you go over there."

If it had been anyone else, Felix would have punched him, but it was Jimmy, the best friend he'd ever had. Besides, Jimmy was right. He *was* scared, and it was all he could do to keep his knees from buckling as he started to walk toward Zilpha.

But it was too late. Zilpha's family was already saying their goodbyes to the pastor and the others and walking toward their buggy.

"Guess you outta luck," Jimmy said and walked away to join his girlfriend Lucille, who was waiting at the edge of the churchyard.

Later that night, after his parents had gone to bed, Felix sat on the front steps of their house, mentally replaying his failed effort to talk to Zilpha. In the darkness, he thought about what he should have said and how he should have said it. He would have been charming, and she would have been dazzled by his wit and confidence. But none of that had happened, and there he was, sitting alone in the dark, listening to the chirping of peepers and catching the scent of honeysuckle blossoms on the breeze—sweet, but not sweet enough to overcome the stench of shame and self-pity that enveloped him.

A floorboard creaked behind him as Elmira approached from inside the cabin. She was wearing a faded green robe over her nightgown and carrying a brown, white, and orange blanket that had been Felix's since he was a little boy. Plucked from a pile of discards at the Road's End big house, it had covered him practically every night of his life. Elmira draped it around his shoulders and sat beside him on the steps. They were quiet together, watching the stars and listening to the songs of nightbirds.

"You need to get some sleep, Felix," Elmira said.

"I ain't sleepy," he replied.

"Still, you need to get some rest if you gon' get up early tomorrow."

"I don't have to get up no earlier than usual."

"You do if you gon' ride into town with your paw."

"But I ain't goin' into town."

"I would if I was you," Elmira said. "Your paw is goin' in to pick up some supplies and drop off some papers at the lawyer for Mr. Claude."

"He don't need me for that," said Felix.

"No, he don't, but he goin' right by the Moore Funeral Home." Elmira stopped talking and watched Felix's face as he tried to understand what his mother was really saying.

Then he got it, and a smile spread across his face. Zilpha was Zilpha *Moore*, and she worked for her father, the owner of Moore Funeral Home, an important Black-owned local business.

"After church today, I heard Mr. Moore talkin' 'bout how he was tired of having to spend so much money to get fancy wood coffins shipped in and how he wished he could get the same quality workmanship around here," Elmira said. "Seem to me like a first-class carpenter ought to be talkin' to the Moores, especially the daughter what runs the office."

"You know what, Maw? Maybe I will go in with Paw tomorrow," Felix said.

"You a right smart young man, Felix," Elmira said before standing up and going inside to bed, leaving her son staring up at the sky, watching clouds race past the moon.

Felix and Plessant didn't talk much at the start of their trip into Red Clay the next morning. Each was lost in his own thoughts as they passed forests on both sides of the packed dirt road. Although it was a Monday, Felix was wearing his Sunday clothes, including a freshly laundered white shirt with the top button closed. His shoes were shined, and he had shaved the light stubble from his eighteen-year-old face.

"I guess you just about a grown man now, huh son?" Plessant said and laughed at Felix's unintelligible grunt of embarrassment. "The thing is," he continued, "a grown man got to know what he want and what he got to do to get it. You know what you want?"

Felix said nothing and continued to watch the horse's tail switch and the puffs of dust that rose from each strike of the horse's hooves.

"Let me ask you a question," Plessant said. "Why you goin' to the Moore Funeral Home today?"

"I'm goin' to talk to Mr. Moore about makin' coffins and sellin' them to him," Felix said.

"You sho that's the reason?" Plessant asked. "That the only reason you got for goin' in there?"

"Why else would I be goin'?" Felix snapped.

"I think you goin' 'cause you want to court Mr. Moore's daughter, and you think that's how you can talk to her," Plessant said.

"Oh, Paw . . ."

"Don't 'Oh, Paw' me," Plessant shot back. "I learned some things along the way, more than Mr. Claude or his daddy thought I knew. I had to so they would keep me workin' for them and not out in the field, and so your maw and you could have it a little easier. Tell the truth, I probably know more about how to run Road's End than Mr. Claude, but that ain't what this is about. This here is about you and your future. Now, you off to a good start. Everybody say you a good carpenter, and you makin' some money, but you got to do more than that. You got to make a business, not just go from job to job. That's how you get what you want."

Plessant was on a roll, and Felix sat back and listened.

"The thing is, it's all about taking the right steps," Plessant said. "You take one step, then you take another step, then you take another one. Pretty soon, you get where you want to go. See, you think you in love with Zilpha, but you ain't even talked to her. Maybe she ain't nothin' like you think she is. She pretty and all that, but what if she one of them mean women don't never give a man a minute of peace? I ain't sayin' that the way she is, but you don't know 'cause you still ain't even talked to her, let alone spent no time with her."

Plessant stopped talking and reached down for a jar of water he'd put in the wagon before they left Road's End. He took a drink and passed it over to Felix. "Here's somethin' else," Plessant said. "The Moores ain't like us. They educated and talk proper, and right or wrong, they think they better than people like us. They might not say it, but that's what they think. Now, you cain't take nothin' away from Mr. Moore. He worked hard to build up his business and make his family comfortable, and that's what he respect in other folks, and that's what he gon' be lookin' for in any young man that want to court his daughter. So," Plessant said, "the one you got to impress is Mr. Moore. Then maybe you'll get a chance to impress his daughter."

"But how do I do that, Paw?" Felix asked, now more nervous than before.

"Remember what I said; take everything step by step. Today you just have to introduce yourself. Don't worry about meeting Zilpha or tryin' to sell them somethin'. Just make sure Mr. Moore know you and what you do. Talk about the furniture you built and how you know about workin' with good wood and fine finishes. Talk about how you build anything made of wood, and—this here is important—talk about how Colored *and* white come to you when they want the best carpentry.

"This is important too: Tell Mr. Moore you respect him and admire the way he built his business and that you honored to have a chance to talk with him. Be sure to say thank you for his time when you leave and that you hope to see him and his family at church on Sunday."

They had entered the outskirts of town, and Plessant stopped the wagon so that Felix could get down and walk into the Colored business section. "You come on over to the feedstore when you done. That's where I'll be."

———

The Moore Funeral Home was a large two-story, white-painted house with four columns supporting the roof over a broad front porch, two blocks into the Colored business section. The Moore family lived upstairs, and the first floor was given over to the business. A horseshoe driveway bounded by a manicured lawn and meticulously trimmed hedges swooped up to and past the front door, and crape myrtle trees, festooned with electric fuchsia blossoms, swept along the inside curve of the driveway. A spotless black hearse was parked behind the doors of a carriage house next to a stable for a team of two shiny ebony-coated horses. The elegant property was a source of pride in the Black community and a target of resentment among some local whites.

Albert Moore, the family patriarch, was the unacknowledged son of a white planter and an enslaved Black domestic on a plantation near Memphis, Tennessee. He had been raised as an enslaved house servant, indulged by his owner/father, and against law and custom, he had been allowed to learn to read and write. When the planter died, the first act of his widow, who had long known and resented Albert's parentage, was to sell the young man out of the state to a plantation near Red Clay, Alabama. The widow's spite became Albert's good fortune, because he met and jumped the broom with the housemaid, Esther, like him the offspring of a plantation owner's liaison with an enslaved woman. They had three children, Samuel, Walter, and Zilpha.

Felix was standing on the porch, screwing up his courage to enter, when the door swung open and he came face-to-face with Zilpha. For Felix, lightning flashed, thunder roared, and his heart beat so fast that he thought it would fly right through his throat and out of his mouth. For a moment, the absurd image of his throbbing heart lying on the porch in front of his feet amused him, and he let out a nervous giggle.

Great, he thought, *now she'll think I'm a crazy man.* Then he realized that she was speaking to him.

"May I help you?" she was asking. "Are you all right?"

"Yes, ma'am," he managed to reply. "My name is Felix Parker, and I come to see your father. Is he in?"

"Come in," she said. "I was just going out, but I'll get him for you. You can wait in there," and she pointed toward a parlor off the foyer. "Have a seat. He'll be with you directly," she said before disappearing down the hallway.

Alone in the parlor, Felix calmed his nerves. The room was as he had guessed it might be: the walls painted a soothing shade of light green, heavy burgundy-and-green drapes on the windows, pulled back to let in the sun. Over the sofa was a painting of the Moore family with Mr. Moore standing behind his wife and children, formal, like an English lord.

Felix heard someone entering the room behind him, and he turned to see Albert Moore. Zilpha was behind her father, and she smiled at

Felix before she dashed out the door. No matter what happened now, the memory of that smile would make the trip worthwhile. It was still fresh in his mind an hour later when he climbed into the wagon with his father.

"Well, how did it go?" Plessant asked.

"I did like you said, Paw. We talked about how Colored people have to make their way in the world and have their own businesses, and he wanted to know about my work and about my plans for the future. He said he knew who you and Maw was and that y'all was known to be respectable people."

Plessant smiled and nodded his head. "Did you say the part about workin' for Colored *and* white customers?"

"Yassuh. He was real interested in that," Felix replied. "He wanted to know who they was and what kind of work I did for them."

Plessant nodded again. "I thought he would be interested in that," he said. "Some men put a lot of store by what the white folks think. Well, the big thing is, did you meet Zilpha?"

"Yassuh, I did, and she's nice as she is pretty," Felix replied.

"Well, son. I'd say you took your first step," Plessant said. "I'd say you on your way."

Chapter 32

SPRING 1875

Claude awakened in the dark on Friday, April 9, 1875, ten years to the day since Robert E. Lee's surrender of the Army of Northern Virginia to Ulysses S. Grant at Appomattox Courthouse. He sat up in bed, considering getting dressed and starting his day early, but there was a chill in the room, the bedclothes were warm, and he had no plans for anything that couldn't wait for daylight. *Enjoy it while you can,* he thought, *before marriage and children change everything.*

Not that he had any regrets. He had been elated when Carrie Anderson, the woman he had courted for months, accepted his proposal of marriage, and he was looking forward to their wedding the following spring. But when he tried to envision himself as a husband and father, sometimes the images in his head dissolved into gray mist and anxiety roiled his gut. He wished he could talk to his late father about it, and he imagined introducing his late mother to his bride-to-be. He was sure she would have loved her, and he fell asleep again with dreams of the imagined meeting playing in his head.

When he awakened again, the sun was fully up, and he dressed slowly, thinking about the business that lay ahead of him that day.

Plessant would drive him around to meet with his sharecroppers to discuss the crops they would soon be planting and to talk about their respective financial situations. Most were in passable condition, good news for them and for Claude, but at least two of the families were in trouble, and Claude would have to remind them that they owed him money and that this season could be their last at Road's End.

Then he would ride Zeus over to the next plantation, where Seth Riordan, the owner, wanted to discuss breeding the black stallion with Riordan's mare. That would be the interesting part of the day, not only because of the horses, but also because Riordan had invited him to stay for supper to discuss some other important business and to meet some men who would be joining them later. Riordan had been vague about the business he wanted to discuss and about the identities of the others. Claude was intrigued, but he was also uneasy. *Why is Riordan being so mysterious?*

The answer came after supper that evening. Having said goodnight to Riordan's wife and daughters, thanking them profusely for their hospitality, Claude followed his host outside for cigars on the front porch, and, when they were seated with their cigars lit, Riordan produced a jug of applejack distilled on the plantation and two glasses.

"I'll give you this, Seth, you know how to persuade a fellow. That was an excellent meal, the company of your family was delightful, and this applejack and the cigar are as fine as any to be had in the county. How could I disagree with your terms for breeding your mare with my stallion?" Claude said.

"Thank you, Claude. I'm glad you enjoyed it, and I hope it won't be the last time, especially with you about to become a married man," Riordan said. "My wife Rebecca is already talking about entertaining you and Carrie after the wedding."

"And I'm sure Carrie and I will look forward to hosting you at Road's End as well. In the meantime, we can work out the details and get the paperwork done for the breeding this week," Claude said. "Right now, however, I am curious about your other reasons for having me out here this evening. You'll have to admit that you have been secretive."

Riordan laughed and blew out a stream of cigar smoke into the gathering darkness. "You're right, I have been a bit cagey, but I think you'll see why shortly," he said.

Claude looked down from the porch to see Zeus and another saddled horse being led around the corner of the house by Riordan's stable hand.

"Come with me," Riordan said. "We're going for a short ride, and I think all your questions will be answered at the end of it." The two men set out across Riordan's property at a leisurely pace, headed for the edge of the plantation, bordered by the same creek that wrapped around Road's End. Above the sounds of the rushing water, the horses' hooves, and the wind blowing through the leaves overhead, Claude could hear men's voices, growing louder as they drew closer. As they emerged from the woods into a clearing, he could see a cluster of about thirty shadowy figures surrounding a pile of wood as tall as a man. The smell of kerosene and smoke from handrolls and cigars permeated the air. One of the men rushed forward carrying a torch, touched its flame to the pile, and jumped back when it exploded into a red and orange blaze that lit up the nighttime sky. Claude could hear them intoning what sounded like an oath, though he couldn't make out the specific words.

"What is this?" Claude turned to look at Riordan, whose eyes were glazed and whose lips were moving without making a sound, mouthing the words of the oath. The bonfire raged, and its light cast eerie shadows across the faces of the men surrounding it. When the fire flared, Claude was surprised by how many of the faces he recognized—small-farmers, shopkeepers, tradesmen, and even a few prominent businessmen and professionals. Former Confederate Captain Ralph Greene, owner of the Pinewoods Plantation, was among them. Claude admired Greene for the way he had rebuilt his plantation after it slipped into decline during the war.

"I don't understand," Claude said to Riordan. "This looks like the Klan, but I thought it was gone, disbanded three years ago."

"It was, officially, but that doesn't mean all of us have forsaken what we believe or the mission with which we, as white Christian men, are charged," Riordan said. "We might not use the name anymore, but our sacred mission remains the same."

Claude was silent as he thought about what Riordan was saying. He had heard about attacks on the freedmen, but he had no idea that it was so organized. "Another thing," Claude said. "I understand the white trash running around terrorizing the Colored folks. They don't have much themselves, and it rubs them the wrong way for the Coloreds to look like they're getting ahead. But men like you, Greene, and the other gentlemen here, why are you doing it? There's no threat to you."

"That's where you're wrong, Claude," Riordan said, with his eyes still focused on the bonfire. "I used to think the same way, but then I stepped back to look at what's been happening since the war ended, and I changed my mind. Look, you and I both know the difference between niggers and white trash isn't worth a plugged nickel; let them fight over the scraps. But the stakes are higher for men like you and me. We might have lost the war, and one might even debate the morality of slavery, but one thing is for certain: Niggers can never be the white man's social or economic equal, and this damned Reconstruction is trying to make them just that. It's going too far when they're serving in the state legislature and even in the Congress, making laws for white people. It's wrong." Riordan turned his horse to face Claude directly. "Someone has to stop it, and that's why I and the other gentlemen here are involved, and that's why we want you to join us," he said. "No one would expect you to go along with those yahoos when they go nightriding, but there are other ways for men like us to make a difference."

"I don't know, Seth. I understand what you're saying. It's a problem, but I don't know if this is the right way to address it," Claude said. "I'll have to think about it. All I can promise is that I will give it serious consideration."

———

RED CLAY, ALABAMA
SPRING 1875
The following Sunday, Plessant, Elmira, and Felix mingled with the other worshippers outside the Third Baptist Church, chatting about

the sermon and simply enjoying the pleasure of each other's company. The women in particular also exchanged the latest gossip, including their takes on what Edna Mae Daniels had worn to church that day. The young girls admired her fancy outfits with matching gloves and parasols, and the older married ladies kept their distance and whispered about the men—white and Black—who purportedly paid Edna Mae's expenses and kept her purse full of cash.

With her gray-green eyes, rouged thick lips, broad nose, and skin the color of fresh-churned butter, Edna Mae was not a conventional beauty. She was plump and was likely to become heavier in her later years. But for now, in her twenties, her full figure, her suggestive walk, and her way of seeming to be always available, made her an object of desire among most of the men she met.

For Felix, however, the churchyard was where he could speak with Zilpha, albeit under the vigilant gaze of her parents and brothers. Since his first meeting with Albert Moore, Felix had produced a coffin for the funeral director's inspection. It was a work of art, a solidly built pine box with a veneer of fine-grained walnut, stained a dark-chocolate color and polished to a lustrous furniture finish. It was trimmed with shiny brass hardware, and the padded interior was lined with scarlet silk. Moore bought it on the spot and promised to order more. Felix had been happy to make the sale, but he was elated to have more chances to be near Zilpha. He had been emboldened to speak with her whenever he saw her at church, and, best of all, she seemed to like him too.

He was about to walk over to her when Plessant grabbed his arm and whispered, "You can talk to Zilpha another time, Felix. We got to go. Your maw and me got somethin' to show you." When they were all aboard the wagon, Plessant clicked his tongue and the horse pulled them onto Main Street, heading north.

"Where we goin', Paw?" Felix asked. "This ain't the way home."

"You just wait," Plessant replied, and a grin split his face. They drove on in silence, up Main Street, then a right onto Oak Lane, and finally another right onto Jefferson Street, a rutted dirt road. They were out of town now. Houses were few in number, interspersed among stands of pine trees and cultivated fields. Plessant slowed the wagon as they came to an open expanse of red clay on their right, which rose gently from the road up a slight hill. The land on the other side of the road climbed more sharply to about ten feet above the roadbed. From the wagon, Felix could see that the elevated land was lightly wooded, in sharp contrast to the bare red hill on the other side of the road.

"All right, we here," Plessant said and climbed off the wagon to help Elmira down. Once on the ground, she reached back into the wagon and produced a picnic basket from under an old quilt.

"What we doin' here? A picnic?" Felix asked.

"You just come along," Elmira said and started walking with Plessant up a dirt driveway cut into the hillside. When they reached the top, Elmira walked over to a chinaberry tree, spread the quilt on the ground, and began to set out a picnic dinner of fried chicken, biscuits, baked sweet potatoes, and apple pie in the shelter of the tree's low-hanging branches.

Felix was mystified. *What is going on?* he wondered. Before he could say anything, however, Plessant tapped his shoulder. "Look around, Felix. What you see?" he said.

Felix rotated his head to view the landscape. "Trees, grass, some fields over yonder," he said, pointing away from the road.

"That's all you see?" Plessant asked.

"Yassuh, that's all I see, and I still don't know what we doin' here," Felix replied.

"It's a whole lot more than what you say, but let's go eat, and we'll talk about it," Plessant said.

By the time they were settling back with wedges of Elmira's apple pie, Plessant had told Felix the story of how he had learned of Claude's duplicity regarding the ten-acre plot. "I couldn't trust Mr. Claude no more," Plessant said. "He been good to us in a lot of ways, but knowin' he goin' against his folks' wishes and keepin' that land from us, it just ain't the same. I don't know what other dirt he might do us."

"Well, what you gon' do?" Felix asked.

"Remember what I told you about how you got to know what you want and then work at it one step at a time?" Plessant said.

"Yassuh," Felix replied. "So what *you* want?"

"What I want?" Plessant picked up one of the tiny, marble-hard chinaberries and rolled it between his thumb and forefinger before tossing it away. "What I want," he said, "is what any man want: to make sure his family is safe and that his children is free. It ain't enough to be free from bein' owned like a horse or a cow. We got that. But Felix, you got to be free in your head and free in your heart too, and we got that. Still, long as somebody got control over you, like Mr. Claude got over us with our wages and the house we live in, we still ain't completely out of bondage."

"How you gon' fix that, Paw?" Felix asked.

"I guess it ain't fair to keep you guessin'," Plessant said with a laugh. "You say all you see 'round here is trees, grass, and some fields. Well, what you really lookin' at is our freedom. All this land you see, where we sittin' and them fields back there, fifteen acres, it's all ours. That's the first step."

Felix turned to Elmira, saw the smile on her face, and felt the warmth that radiated from it permeate his body and give it strength. He was ready for the journey that lay ahead, whatever it might be.

Chapter 33

Miss Estelle Watson's Boarding House for Young Ladies had rules, and the first one was that gentlemen were not allowed on the upper floors where the residents lived. So Claude waited in the main parlor while the maid went upstairs to inform Carrie Anderson that he was there to escort her to church. The maid, an attractive young Black woman in a simple forest green dress covered by a starched white apron, returned a minute later to tell Claude that "Miss Carrie say she be with you shortly and to see if you would like a cup of tea while you wait."

"Yes, thank you," Claude said, and then added, "Don't I know you? Aren't you Lucille who took over for Callie Mae at Road's End when she left to go with my mother to New Orleans?"

"Yassuh, Mr. Claude," she replied. "I been workin' for another family, but I come over here to work for Miss Estelle just last week. You still like your tea with a little milk and no sugar?"

"I do, and thank you," he replied.

Lucille returned shortly with the tea and set it on an end table next to the settee where Claude was perched. "I heard your mama passed on a little while ago, Mr. Claude. I was sorry to hear that. She was a good woman," she said.

"Thank you, Lucille. I'm sure she would have appreciated knowing that you thought of her that way."

Claude had barely finished his tea when Carrie swept into the room. Dark hair framed her ivory face, her clear hazel eyes glittered, and her lips curved in a way that made it seem as if she was always on the verge of a smile. "Good morning, Claude. I'm sorry to have made you wait, but I trust that Lucille looked after you," she said in French. She had learned the language at school, and she enjoyed speaking it with Claude.

Now, they were strolling past the courthouse, a block from the church, enjoying the warm weather and chatting about an upcoming social event. When they reached the corner at Main Street, Claude switched the conversation to a more serious topic.

"What do you think about these night riders?" he asked.

Carrie stared at him. "Why do you ask? Are you planning to join them?"

"I just wondered what you think," he said.

She regarded him for a long while before responding. Speaking deliberately, she said, "I think those robes are ridiculous and that hiding their faces under hoods is cowardly. I also think the lynchings and the house burnings are barbaric. It's just gratuitous cruelty and un-Christian. But I also think they might have a point about the Colored people trying to take over everything. At best, the Coloreds are like children, and as the old saying goes, 'Children should be seen and not heard.'"

"If I did decide to join," Claude said, "what would you think?"

Carrie's face went blank, and then she said in a flat voice, "I would think that it was none of my business."

———

Plessant and his family had arrived at their church at about the same time as Claude and Carrie arrived at theirs, and the pastors of both churches, just two blocks apart, had taken their sermons from the same text, John 20:19–29, traditional for the Sunday after Easter, marking the moment when the risen Christ appeared to his disciples and charged them with continuing to spread the Gospel: *Then said Jesus to them again, Peace be unto you: as my Father hath sent me, even so send I you.*

Plessant fidgeted as the service dragged to a close, and he was on his feet while the last words of the benediction still hung in the air. By the time Elmira and Felix made it out of the church, he was already bringing the horse and wagon around for the drive out to the newly acquired land. He was ready to start outlining his plans for the family's eventual departure from Road's End.

Claude was squirming, too, and when the service ended, he took Carrie by the arm to escape the sanctuary before Riordan, seated with his family two rows ahead, could corner him for a response to his invitation to join the night riders. Claude shared the opinions of many of his peers that Reconstruction had gone too far—he'd told Riordan as much—and he believed the freedmen were gaining too much ground too fast. White supremacy, he had concluded, was the natural order of things, even though violent terrorism offended him. Riordan's assurances that there were other roles for men like him to play seemed merely a fig leaf to enable hooligans to do their worst. He would be able to put off Riordan today, but he shivered at the thought of the dark nights of the soul that lay ahead before resolving his concerns.

———

On Jefferson Street, Felix helped his mother pack up the picnic things before he and his father set off on a walk around the property as Plessant outlined his plans, which included renting most of the land, twelve acres, to two Black farmers for three years. "They won't be on shares; they will pay a flat amount to use the land. That way we'll have some money comin' in," Plessant said.

"We got to keep this quiet for now, 'til we ready for folks to know what we doin', but you need to know all the details," he told Felix. "First, we bought this land with money your maw and me saved. It took 'most everything we got, so we got to keep our jobs and that house at Road's

End 'til we ready to make a move. You know how folks is—if they think you gettin' ahead, they'll do anything they can to keep you down. That goes for Colored and white. They might have different reasons, but it's the same if everything come down on you."

"But Paw, how you gon' keep it quiet?" Felix asked. "Folks is bound to find out."

"You know our friend David Allen, the steward at that law firm what takes care of the Parker family's business, the one who told me about Mr. Claude keepin' that land from us?" Plessant said. "We wouldn't never have knowed about it if not for him. Well, David is from Washington, DC, and he knows some Colored lawyers up there, and he arranged with them to fix it so the deed look like the property belong to one of their clients, which is us, but without our name bein' on it at the courthouse. So the rent money go to the lawyers in Washington, and we get it from them. David is a good man, and you need to get to know him better, Felix. You can learn a lot from him."

Felix nodded, and then he asked, "What about the rest of the land, the part up by the road where we had the picnic?"

"That's where you come in, son. You the carpenter. You think you can build us a house?"

Felix was taken aback. "I worked on houses, but I ain't never built one from the ground up by myself. But I reckon I could. I need materials, though, and that cost money."

"It don't have to be big and fancy," Elmira chimed in. "It could be somethin' like what we livin' in now at Road's End."

"I figure you can harvest a lot of the lumber from that stand of trees on the back side of the property and get it cut into planks at the mill," Plessant said. "It's got to be cleared for farming anyhow, and we might as well use the wood ourselves."

"It ain't as easy as it sounds, Paw, but I guess we could do it and say them Washington, DC, clients hired us to do it so they could rent out the land," Felix said. "The big thing is, though, I got to keep workin' to make money, just like you."

"We'll manage, boy. We'll manage," Plessant said.

As they talked, Felix could see his mother resting on the quilt under the tree where they had shared the picnic dinner. Her eyes were closed, and her face was turned toward the sun. She might have been asleep, and she didn't hear footsteps approaching her.

"Ain't every day a man find a beautiful woman under a tree, just like a ripe peach waitin' for somebody to pick it up and take a bite."

Elmira opened her eyes to see Plessant above her, with Felix standing behind him, silhouetted by the sun with his hands stretched out to her. She took them and was pulled to her feet and into his arms and squeezed in a hug that nearly took her breath away.

"What was you thinkin' about?" Plessant asked.

"I was thinkin' how blessed I am to have two strong men to take care of me and how good-lookin' one of them is."

Plessant released her from his hug and replied with a glint in his eyes, "I don't have to ask which one is good-lookin', 'cause I already know."

They laughed, and Plessant pulled her close to him again. "We gon' be all right, Elmira," he whispered. "Cain't nothin' stop us now."

Chapter 34

As did many freedmen, Felix's pal Jimmy and his mother had chosen the name of a former owner as their own surname; thus, Jimmy had become Jimmy Flowers, and it was the name he gave to Lucille when they were married, with Felix standing up as his best man.

Jimmy had made a good life as a blacksmith, working in the shop at Road's End, sleeping in the attached shed, and paying rent to Claude. He had saved his money, and when an older white blacksmith near town was ready to retire and put his property up for sale, Jimmy was ready to buy. The property included a well-equipped shop and a small, neat house in the back, to which he had taken his new bride after the wedding.

"I reckon Jimmy's got it made now," Felix said. He was holding Zilpha's hand while sitting next to her in the porch swing at her parents' home after the wedding. The moist air was warm and flower-scented, and he felt drowsy after the excitement of the day and a sumptuous dinner with the Moores, at whose table he had become a frequent guest as his relationship with Zilpha grew.

"They looked really happy," Zilpha said, glancing at him shyly. "Do you think you'll get married and be happy like that one day?"

"I don't know. I got to find the right girl, and they're hard to come by, but I guess I'll keep looking 'til I find her."

Zilpha reached over with her free hand and swatted him, and they both laughed. Just then the front door opened, and Zilpha's father stepped onto the porch. Felix leaped to his feet so quickly that the swing lurched and almost pitched Zilpha to the floor.

"Nice night, isn't it?" said Mr. Moore.

"Yes, sir," Felix replied. "I was just saying that to Zilpha."

"It's too bad that a man with business to attend to in the morning can't just sit around and enjoy it," he said.

"Yes, sir. It sure is, and I've got business to attend to, so I guess I should be going. Tell Mrs. Moore that dinner was delicious." Felix waited a beat, hoping Moore would go inside so he could say good night to Zilpha alone. Moore didn't move.

"Well, I guess I'll be going," he said.

"Have a good evening, son."

"Good night, Felix," Zilpha said. Her eyes twinkled, and her shoulders shook with barely contained laughter.

———

A week before Jimmy's and Lucille's nuptials, Claude had married Carrie in Huntsville, Alabama, where Carrie had grown up as the only child of Bartholomew Anderson, a prosperous banker, and his socialite wife, Mathilda. Like Claude's mother, Carrie was a graduate of Hunt College in Red Clay, where she remained after school and where she met Claude. Following a honeymoon trip to London, they returned to Red Clay to begin their lives as the masters of Road's End. As a welcome-home surprise, the Riordans hosted a reception in their honor, to which Red Clay's most prominent young couples had been invited.

"I don't know how to thank you for this, Rebecca," Carrie said to her hostess as the evening drew to a close and the guests began to depart. "Claude and I are looking forward to entertaining you and Seth soon at Road's End, and I know that we shall all be such good friends."

"That will be lovely. Besides, those two are already as thick as thieves." Rebecca nodded in the direction of Seth and Claude, who were having an animated conversation on the other side of the room. Both women suspected, but neither would acknowledge, that the activities of the night riders, which Claude had eventually agreed to join after much urging from Seth, was likely the subject of their discussion.

Claude had not reached his decision to join the group easily. He told himself he didn't hate Black people. He liked Plessant, Elmira, and their son Felix well enough; he had known them all his life. Plessant and Elmira were good employees, but they knew their place in Claude's view and appreciated the manifest truth that white people were superior and deserving of their position of power. Even that uppity Colored undertaker, Albert Moore, didn't try to put himself above white interests. *Let him have his fancy house and business, as long as he doesn't try to take more,* Claude thought. As far as Claude was concerned, they and others like them were the good ones, the Coloreds who could be counted on not to rock the boat. *The rest of them,* he thought, *well, that was a different story.* They needed a firm hand to keep them in their place.

Claude's attitude had crystallized on a recent Saturday morning while shopping in the hardware store. A middle-aged Black man was completing the purchase of a hammer, nails, and some other building supplies when a white man stepped up to the counter to inquire about some equipment he had ordered. The clerk turned his attention to the white customer, leaving the Black customer standing there while he attended to the white man's query.

"Hey," the Black man protested. "I was here first, buying these things. How come you walked away like that to 'tend to him?" The clerk ignored him and continued to deal with the white customer. "What's the matter with you? You deaf or something?" the Black customer protested.

The clerk, red-faced and grimacing, wheeled around to face the Black customer. "You know what's good for you, nigger, you'll stop interfering with white folks," he snarled.

"That ain't right," the Black man said, leaving the merchandise on the counter and walking away. Before he went through the door, however, he turned and said, "You crackers got to remember we ain't slaves no more. You cain't treat us like dirt no more."

The audacity of that boy, Claude thought. The idea of him speaking to a white man that way and not expecting to be punished was unacceptable. At that moment Claude's decision about joining the erstwhile Klan had been made, but he did not speak to Carrie about it. She had been clear that she did not wish to know.

A few weeks later, his decision became clear to someone else as well. While putting away clean laundry, Elmira came across Claude's robe and hood. She closed the drawer, walked downstairs to the kitchen, sat down at the table, and put her head in her hands.

"What's wrong, Elmira? Are you feeling all right?" It was Mr. Claude's new wife. Elmira hadn't heard her enter the kitchen.

"Yassum, Miss Carrie. My head was just swimmin', but I feel good now," she said. "I was just thinkin' about y'all's supper. You think Mr. Claude would like some pork chops?"

Chapter 35

Felix listened quietly while his mother told his father about finding the night riders get-up in Claude's drawer. "Well, that just settles it," Plessant said. "I thought maybe he was just greedy, but now we know it's more than that. He's greedy *and* he got it in for Colored people. Them night riders is dangerous, and he is the worst kind. He smiles, and maybe he even do you a favor, but give him a chance and he'll hurt you bad."

"What do we do, Paw?" Felix asked.

"We do like we always done," Plessant said. "We go on like we don't know nothin' different. Meantime, we just take care of our own business, the way we bought that land and the way we gon' build our house."

"Oh, that reminds me," Felix said. "I was at the lumber mill with a load of the trees we cut off the property, and I heard these men talking about that old one-room schoolhouse out from town. They said the government didn't want it no more since they built that new school, so they was just gon' tear it down. So I went over there and I said, 'Excuse me, sir, but I heard y'all talkin' about tearing down the school,' and did they know what the government was gon' do with the lumber from it? They say they don't know, but a Mr. Walker at the courthouse is in charge of it."

Plessant perked up as Felix spoke. "I know that old schoolhouse, and I think I know that Mr. Walker they talkin' about. I believe Mr. Claude had some business with him. If we can get that lumber, it would save us a lot of time and money. If they let us tear it down, we can rebuild it on our property and then just add on to it." Plessant was at the courthouse early the next morning, and by noon he had struck a deal for the lumber. By noon the next day, he was confronted by Claude, who wanted to know all about it.

"Ain't much to tell, Mr. Claude," Plessant said. "You know my boy Felix is a carpenter, and he heard about the schoolhouse when he was at the sawmill the other day, and that Mr. Walker at the courthouse was in charge of it. Well, he always looking for building material, so I thought couldn't be no harm in askin' about it. They was just gon' tear it down anyhow."

"I see," Claude said. "Next time, if you want to do something like that, you come to me first. I'll take care of it for you. You understand?"

"Yassuh," Plessant said, "I'll sho nuff do that."

RED CLAY, ALABAMA

SUMMER 1875

The biweekly meeting of the Third Baptist Church's deacons the following Wednesday night, Plessant Parker among them, convened in the parsonage parlor of the Reverend Ezekiel Jones. There had been prayer at the beginning, followed by a discussion of the budget and plans for repairs to the parsonage, as they sipped coffee and nibbled shortbread cookies baked by the minister's wife.

Third Baptist was the center of Black religious and social life in Red Clay, ironically built with the help of the white First Baptist Church, where they had been forced to enter through a side door and sit in the balcony prior to emancipation, never coming into contact with the white worshippers. Rather than face the unpleasantness that might have accompanied telling freed Black Christians that they were not welcome in the main sanctuary, the First Baptist Church fathers instead directed funds toward construction of a Black church a block away. Thus, Third Baptist Church was founded, and it had flourished.

"I think that concludes the church business," the pastor said, wrapping up more quickly than usual, "but we have other matters to address. Deacon Plessant Parker has brought a guest to our meeting to discuss an important issue. Deacon Parker, you have the floor."

"Thank you, Reverend Jones. I think some of you already know my friend David Allen. He is employed by Campbell, Stewart & MacPherson, an important law firm here in Red Clay. He has some thoughts he would like to share with us this evening."

"Thank you, Mr. Parker," David said as he rose from his chair in the corner. "Some of you gentlemen may not know me, but I know who all of you are. I respect you, and you command the respect of the whole Colored community. That is why I prevailed on my friend Plessant Parker to invite me to speak to you this evening." He paused and looked around the room at the men assembled there. In addition to Plessant and the pastor, there were Aaron Smith, owner of a popular candy store and bakery on Main Street, the only Black-owned business on the strip; Jesse Arnold, owner of the barbershop and other small businesses; Thomas Jackson, a farmer and the largest Black landowner in the area; Albert Moore, the undertaker; and William Jefferson, the only local Black physician.

"I am originally from Washington, DC," David continued, "and I was back there recently to attend to some business in connection with the disposition of my late mother's estate. While I was visiting, an old friend invited to me to go with him to hear that great orator, Frederick Douglass, the man who escaped from slavery himself and who spent the duration of the war fighting to abolish that evil institution. His is a powerful voice on behalf of our race.

"Gentlemen, I cannot tell you how inspiring it was to hear this great man. Each word was like a lightning strike, and they came one after the other with such power and eloquence that no one in the hall, Colored or white, was unmoved. Mr. Douglass spoke of many things, but he had

two overarching messages: one, that education is the key to our eventual success as a free people; and two, that we must exercise our right to
vote, as guaranteed by the Fifteenth Amendment to the Constitution,
despite all the obstacles in our path."

"So," Thomas Jackson said, "what would you have us do? We have
heard of Mr. Douglass, of course, and we admire him. But what exactly
are you proposing?"

David reached into his jacket pocket, pulled out a folded sheaf of
paper, and held it high above his head. "Years ago, before the war started,
Mr. Douglass gave this speech in which he anticipated a situation such
as the one we face now. He said: 'Find out just what any people will
quietly submit to and you have found out the exact measure of injustice
and wrong will be imposed . . .' In that same speech," David continued,
"he said two other important things: 'Power concedes nothing without
a demand,' and 'If there is no struggle, there is no progress.'"

"You will find no disagreement with those words," said Moore. "But
again, what can we do? We are just a handful of men with no illusions
about what we have to lose. The risk of acting out, or even speaking
out, is too great for us, too great for our families."

Plessant had been sitting quietly, listening to the exchange, but
now he stood to speak. "It's true that you gentlemen have a lot to lose,
maybe more than a man like me. You're educated, and people respect
you," he said. "It seems to me you got to be willing to be leaders, but
you also got to be smart about it. Now, David was able to help me with
a couple of things because of what he learned on his job, things white
folks might not have been happy about if they knew it.

"What that mean to me is we got to be willing to help each other. I
just found out my boss, Mr. Claude Parker, is one of them night riders.
I'm tellin' y'all about it because you might have to deal with him on
something, and it's better for you if you know. Don't you think they
pass around what they know about us? You do somethin' make one of
them mad, and then all a sudden you ain't got credit at the feedstore no
more. Your house burn down, or you lose your job. They keeps track
of us, so we got to keep track of them too."

"That's right," David interjected. "Plessant has it exactly right. Each one of us has dealings with white people, and so do our friends. I'm here to propose that we keep our eyes and ears open and share information. I will not lie to you; we have to be careful, even with our own community. As deacons, you will all appreciate the story of Judas and our Lord." He paused to let that thought sink in. "We cannot allow fear to stop us, however. We must move forward, and this group provides the core of what we can accomplish.

"No one needs to take unacceptable risks. You already meet every two weeks to discuss church business. Who's to know if you add something to the agenda that will benefit us all? If you'll allow me, I'll join you. I believe we can do this. What do you say?"

The men looked at each other, and one by one, they nodded their assent, some more enthusiastically than others.

When the meeting was over, David and Plessant stood on the front lawn of the parsonage and said goodnight to the deacons as they departed. "That was good," Plessant said.

"Yes," David replied. "As an ancient Chinese proverb I learned in school says, 'A journey of a thousand miles begins with a single step.' Plessant, we have a long way to go, but we have taken the first step."

Chapter 36

Addie stepped off the railroad platform onto Alabama soil for the first time since she was a child. She had been away for a decade, living in New Orleans until her mother's death, then Connecticut for school and in Europe for the past three years. Now, as a grown woman of twenty-two, Red Clay looked familiar to her, but the red dirt beneath her feet seemed unreal, and she was put off by the thick, cloying scents of magnolia and honeysuckle mingled with the smoke from the locomotive. The dense flora all around her felt claustrophobic. *I will not be here long*, she thought. A brief visit and then on to New Orleans.

"Miss Addie?" She strained to see the source of the voice until her eyes came to rest on a familiar face.

"Plessant, is that you?" she asked. The face was lined, and the hair was gray and thinning, but it was surely him, and a smile lit up her face. "How are you, and how are Elmira and Felix?" she asked.

"Yassum, it's me, and we all fine. Mr. Claude sent me to get you and . . ." His voice trailed off as he looked in the direction of an apprehensive-appearing young woman gripping the hand of a toddler standing beside her.

"Plessant, this is Isabelle, my traveling companion, and her little boy, Alexandre. I'm sure that Elmira can find suitable quarters for them during my stay?"

"Yassum, Miss Addie, she'll take care of it," and he bowed slightly in Isabelle's direction. "The carriage is right over here."

They had been traveling about ten minutes in silence when Addie spoke again. "Plessant, how is my brother, and how is his new wife? Her name is Carrie?"

"Mr. Claude doin' real good," Plessant replied over his shoulder. "I guess you know he bought Road's End back from Mr. Flowers; the crops been good, and it look like he makin' good money off the share-croppers, and he gettin' to be an important man around here. He got connections at the courthouse, and some folks say he might run for office. Elmira can tell you more about Miss Carrie, but it look to me like she good for Mr. Claude. Seem like he been real happy since they got married—'specially now that they got two little girls, twins that look a lot like you did when you was a child."

"I am looking forward to meeting them," Addie replied. "And how is Felix?"

Plessant's shoulders straightened, and the pride in his voice was unmistakable. "Felix doin' good too," he said. "He a carpenter now, and he got a good business workin' out of the old shop at Road's End. Folks come to him with all kinds of carpentry jobs—big things like building a house and fine work like furniture and cabinets, and he even got a deal with the undertaker to make fancy caskets."

"I'm happy to hear that. You know, I wasn't always kind to Felix, and I hope to see him while I am here," Addie said.

"I'll tell him you asked about him. I know he'll be glad to hear you said that," Plessant replied.

Addie peered at Isabelle and Alexandre. Isabelle had not spoken a word and had stared straight ahead, except to speak quietly with the boy in French to answer all his questions about what he was seeing. Her arm was wrapped around the boy protectively. That she loved him deeply would be evident to anyone who saw them. *How did we ever get here?*

Addie thought, and her mind raced back through the past two years—two years that had irrevocably changed the course of her life.

———

It had all begun with that chance encounter with Étienne Dupuis at a Paris café in the summer of 1874. Until that meeting, she had been ready to return to the United States after her two years in Europe, but she had been smitten with the young university professor who was so charming and whose circle of friends was so smart and so witty. Swept up in a whirlwind courtship, the idea of returning to New Orleans and to Tante Colette's plans for her social debut was unthinkable. Paris was where she belonged. The life she wanted to live was there, and she had decided to stay—at least for a while. She wrote to Colette, telling her of her plans to remain for a while longer and asking her to make arrangements for the New Orleans house to be maintained. *I cannot tell her that I might stay in Europe permanently, at least not yet*, she thought.

The moment Addie posted her letter to Colette she felt lighter, more relaxed and free to pursue her life as she saw fit, and she was still in a good mood when Étienne arrived to take her to dinner. "What is happening?" he asked. "Did you get some good news?"

"You might say so," she replied.

"Good," he said, "because I have what I hope you will also take as good news. I have told my parents about you, and they have invited you to come to Ste. Maxime for a visit. The term at university is nearly over, and we can leave as soon as classes end. Will you come?"

"Of course," she said.

Two weeks later they arrived in the fishing village in the South of France. "It is so beautiful," Addie exclaimed as they strolled along the beach, barefoot, feeling the sand between their toes and breathing in the salt air that swept in over the deep, cold, and spectacularly blue Mediterranean Sea.

"I must admit that sometimes in Paris I forget how stunning the view can be and how fresh and clean the air smells, but when I come home it all returns, and I wonder how I could ever have wanted to leave," Étienne said. "Then I remember all the wonders of Paris, and I am ready to be there again."

He put his arm around her waist, and they stared into the distance, across the waves, past the bay and St. Tropez on the other side, beyond the horizon and into the place where lovers go, where no one else can see what they see or feel what they feel. "Come, it is time to go meet the family," Étienne said.

She followed him through the winding streets up the hill, away from the water, until they came to a small cottage with whitewashed stucco walls, a red-orange tile roof, and lavender growing in the front yard. "This is it," Étienne said. "It is small, but it is my home, the place where I grew up."

"It is delightful," Addie said, and she meant it. "I can't wait to meet your family."

"Étienne!" came a booming voice from behind them. They turned to see a big man—six-foot-two, at least, and two hundred pounds—with a shock of black hair streaked with gray, a two-day-old beard, and skin deeply tanned from years of working under the sun on the water. He wore the clothes of a fisherman that smelled of salt, sweat, the day's catch, and strong pipe tobacco.

"Papa!" Étienne dropped the bags and ran into his father's embrace. The men laughed and hugged and slapped each other on the back.

"Manners, boy," the older man said. "I am Phillippe Dupuis, the father of this young man, and you must be Mademoiselle Adelaide Parker of America." He took her hands and turned them palms down before kissing them. "Welcome. Now let's go inside to meet Mama."

Addie was overwhelmed—and utterly charmed.

They had just stepped inside and entered the parlor, a sparsely furnished room that matched the elegant simplicity of the exterior, when a tall, slender Black woman carrying a carafe of wine and goblets on a tray came through the door.

"Maman," Étienne exclaimed, and the two embraced enthusiastically.

"Careful, son, or you'll make me drop the wine, and then what would we serve our guest?"

Addie fought to keep the shock from showing on her face, but not before Étienne's mother saw it, though she proceeded as if she hadn't noticed. "I am Madeleine Dupuis, and I am honored to have you as a guest in our home. Please sit and have some wine," she said.

The good Provençal rosé helped to steady Addie's nerves, and she was beginning to settle into small talk about the trip down from Paris when the door opened and the second shock of the day walked into the parlor. A young man as big as Phillippe, also dressed as a fisherman, walked in and tossed a bag of coins to the older man. "That pirate Hugo tried to cheat us as usual, Papa," he said, "but we got a good price for the catch."

"More likely you cheated Hugo," Étienne said, and embraced the young man as they both laughed. "This is my little brother, André," he told Addie. Standing side by side, they were clearly siblings, but unlike Étienne, André had light brown skin, their mother's full facial features, and more tightly curled hair—a true synthesis of Phillippe and Madeleine.

"I am pleased to meet you, Mademoiselle Addie, but I can't imagine why you would be interested in my brother," said André, and he ducked to avoid the punch coming his way from Étienne.

Dinner was a rich bourride of local shrimp and fish with good bread, salad, and more of the rosé. The conversation was lively, and at times Addie forgot her surprise over the discovery of Étienne's racial heritage. Still, when she was in the kitchen after dinner with Madeleine, while Phillippe, Étienne, and André went outside with pipes, she began to think about it again, and once more her face betrayed her.

"It is good to finally meet you, Addie," Madeleine said. "Étienne has told us so much about you, but clearly he did not tell you about me. I know that in much of your country, we would not have shared a meal and that your involvement with my son would be illegal. Indeed, there are many here in France who would find our family unacceptable, though they would be too polite to say so, and it is not illegal. So I know that this is all a shock for you. But it is who we are, and we are happy."

"I'm embarrassed to admit that all you say about my country and fellow citizens is true," Addie said. "Before the Civil War, I was a child on an Alabama plantation, where you would have been a slave. I have also lived in New Orleans, a French-influenced city where there are many mixed-race people. But they mostly marry within their group, and relationships where one of the partners is white are not acknowledged."

Madeleine fixed a hard, unflinching gaze on Addie before replying: "I like you, Addie, and I know my son is enamored with you, but I must say that I will not tolerate his being hurt by you or by anyone else. If it comes to it, I would welcome you as a daughter-in-law, but if you are merely toying with him, you should walk away and never see him again."

By the time the visit was over and Étienne and Addie had returned to Paris, Addie was sure of just one thing: She could not tell Étienne that she was two months pregnant.

Chapter 37

Elmira had arranged for Isabelle and Alexandre to stay in the room off the kitchen while Addie visited Road's End, but a week went by before the two women had a conversation. It happened when Elmira arrived early for work and found Isabelle feeding Alexandre at the kitchen table.

"I hope it's all right," Isabelle said. "He awakened early and was hungry, so I thought I would give him some breakfast."

"Certainly," Elmira said. "I remember when my boy Felix was his age. Seem like he was hungry all the time. Still is."

"When we were coming here from the train station, I heard your husband say your son is a carpenter and that he has a good business. You must be proud of him," Isabelle said.

"I am," Elmira replied. "He a good boy, and smart."

"Do you have other children?" Isabelle asked, and she realized immediately that her question must have been a mistake when she saw a shadow fall across Elmira's face. "I'm sorry," she said. "Perhaps I should not have asked that question."

"It's all right," Elmira said. "I had two other children, a daughter and another son older than Felix, but old Massa John Robert sold them off, and we ain't never been sure what happened to them, 'cept they was sent to a plantation somewhere in Mississippi. Ain't a day go by I don't think about them. I don't know if they livin' or dead, if they had children. I could be a grandma and not even know it."

Isabelle reached across the table where they were sitting to rest her hand on top of Elmira's. "I'm so sorry," she said. "My family was free in New Orleans, and even free people of color had limits on what we could do. Still, we didn't suffer having our children taken away like that. It must have been horrible."

Elmira shook her head and moved her hands to pat the backs of Isabelle's hands. "None of it was right, and some of it was just strange," she said. "You know when Felix just a little older than your boy, about three years old, Miss Addie got it in her head she wanted him to sit on a stool by her chair at breakfast, and she would feed him pieces off her plate. Felix would come in here and ask me, 'Why Miss Addie make me sit on that stool so she can feed me out her hand like a dog?' and I would say, 'Felix, just let her do what she gon' do.' It's funny now, but it was sho nuff peculiar, and she did it for years."

Isabelle threw her head back and laughed. It was the first time Elmira had seen Isabelle smile since her arrival. Then, perhaps because she had a new appreciation of the absurdity of what she had described, Elmira started to laugh too.

The two women were wiping tears from their eyes when Addie came into the room. "What did I miss?" she asked.

"Oh, mademoiselle, Elmira just told me a funny story, but it was nothing. How are you this morning? Can I get anything for you?" Isabelle said.

"Perhaps some coffee. How is Alexandre?" she asked.

Elmira got up to make the coffee, but she didn't miss the look that passed between Isabelle and Addie when Alexandre was mentioned.

"Elmira, where can I find Felix?" Addie asked.

"I reckon he in his shop," Elmira replied. "He said he was gon' be workin' all day on a dining table and chairs for a family over in Marion."

"Thank you. I'll go out to find him after breakfast. I have some things to talk about with him," Addie said.

Felix was taking a break when he looked up to see Addie Parker enter his shop, now a shapely grown woman, though still petite, her blond hair swept up in a sophisticated braided chignon. He had been work-ing since early morning, and his hair, face, and arms were covered with dust from sanding the top of a dining table that, when finished, would seat twelve comfortably. The ornately carved legs lay off to the side, al-ready sanded smooth and waiting to be cleaned before being stained and polished. When it was completed and installed in the customer's dining room, the set would be an object of admiration to all who saw it.

"This is handsome work, Felix," Addie said. "Who knew that you would grow up to be so talented?"

"Miss Addie. My folks told me you were here, but I didn't expect to see you," replied the startled Felix. "How do you do?"

"I am well, Felix."

Following an awkward silence, Addie spoke. "Felix, this will not be easy, but we need to talk. I know that the last time we saw each other, I was horrible to you. I was a child, a spoiled one, and I knew that I had power over you, because you were a slave and I was the daughter of the plantation owner. But that's no excuse for the way I acted, and as I have grown older and have experienced more of the world, I have wanted to apologize for what I said and did all those years ago."

Felix crossed the room to a bucket of water, plunged a towel into it, and used it to wipe wood dust from his face and hands. "I guess that was a long time ago, Miss Addie," he said. "But I still remember it, and to tell you the truth, I ain't had much reason to trust white folks since the war ended and we got our freedom. It means something to me, though, that you remember it and that you got enough respect for me to come here to say you were wrong. I appreciate that, and I won't forget it."

"Thank you, Felix," Addie said. "I want to ask you something, but

I don't want you to think that I apologized only to get an answer to my question."

Felix nodded but said nothing.

"Felix, I still need to know what happened to my papa, and I still think you know more than you told anybody back then," she said. "I loved him so much, and his death left a hole in my life that only the truth can fill. Can you help me . . . please?"

Felix remained silent. Addie sensed the conflict in Felix, and she needed a way to gain his trust. *What would it take for him to give in?*

They stood there, assessing each other, trying to guess what the other was thinking. Addie swallowed hard, then said, "I need you to trust me, Felix. I can't make you do it, but maybe if I tell you something just as powerful as what you know about my papa, something that no one else can know, maybe you can trust me."

"Maybe," he said. "I can't promise."

"I think you are an honorable man, Felix, and I don't believe you will let me tell you this secret if you don't believe you can reciprocate," she said. "Just promise me that you will stop me if what you are hearing is something you can't keep to yourself."

Felix nodded.

Addie sat down on a bench near the worktable, took a deep breath, and began. She told him about meeting Étienne in Paris and how they had become lovers and about how she discovered his parentage after she had learned that she was pregnant with his child. "I didn't know what to do," she said. "I loved him, and I knew that I would love the child, but what if it came out like Étienne's brother—a handsome man, sweet and charming, but obviously of mixed race? Maybe it would be all right in France, but I could never come home again. My family would disown me—something I never imagined would matter to me, and yet it did. I couldn't bear it.

"Finally, I came up with a plan. I would make an excuse to leave Paris and go somewhere else in Europe to have the child and give it up to the nuns for adoption. No one would know. But then I realized that I couldn't live with myself, never knowing what had happened to my child. I would be a monster that not even God could forgive. That was when Isabelle came up with a new plan."

Felix had been staring at his shoes the whole time that Addie had been speaking. He looked up, and Addie believed she saw sympathy and compassion in his eyes.

Addie was in her own world as the story came pouring out of her. She didn't hear the bees buzzing around the verbena in beds beneath the open window. She didn't feel the breeze blowing through or smell the farm scents it carried with it. "You have seen Isabelle, my traveling companion? She is from a mixed-race family in New Orleans, a Creole of color, and in families such as hers, there has been such blending that a range of skin colors and facial features is not uncommon. She offered to say the child was hers. We would say she became involved with a man in Europe and that he was killed in a tragic accident before Alexandre could be born. They would return to New Orleans with me, where Isabelle would remain in my employ as a housekeeper. She would raise the boy under my roof as her own, and I could see Alexandre grow up. She loves him as if he truly were her own, and he will be part of Isabelle's extended family. I will ensure that he and Isabelle never want for anything. It is a sad story, a tragic story, but it is the result of choices I have made, and with which I now must live." Addie closed her eyes. She was perspiring, and strands of hair stuck to her forehead. She was diminutive, but now she seemed even smaller and vulnerable.

"Now, Felix, you must tell your story," she said.

Felix took a deep breath and sat down on a bench facing Addie. He recited the whole story of John Robert's suicide and how he had forced Felix to memorize the narrative about being set upon by bandits. He told her about retrieving the derringer and whipping the horse to start it going back to Road's End before he passed out in the back of the wagon.

"And you have never told anyone?" Addie asked.

"No," he said. "No one."

"So no one else knew?" Addie asked.

"Well, your mama knew, but I didn't tell her," he said. "Before your daddy shot himself, he told me to wait 'til nobody else was around and

to tell Miss Marie Louise that she was to go into his study and look for
Sis Arrow. I did it, but I didn't know what it meant, and I still don't.
Somehow after that she knew, though, 'cause a few days later she called
me in the parlor and told me we had to keep the secret. She said she
was going to send me to the fields 'cause if she didn't you would figure
it out or get it out of me somehow. Going out there was near 'bout the
end of me when Big Joe and his gang went after me."

"Now it makes sense," Addie said. "I think Papa left her a message
in the study about what he was going to do. I was peeking through the
door that night when she was sitting at his desk, reading something she
found in a book and crying. I would have found out more, but Callie
Mae caught me and made me go to bed. Something else makes sense
too. I didn't think about it at the time—I was too young—but I realize
now that Papa must have invested his money in the North. Otherwise
we wouldn't have been so well fixed when the war ended." Addie stood
up and took a deep breath. "Thank you, Felix," she said. "Now we must
each keep the other's secret, and I will be glad to do it."

"Me too, Miss Addie," Felix said. "Me too."

Chapter 38

The morning sky over Road's End was thick with clouds, bulbous gray harbingers of a thunderstorm likely to roll in that afternoon. Perspiration clung to Addie's skin under her habit as she rode a chestnut mare next to Claude astride Zeus. The stallion was about fifteen years old now, but he was still lively, and his nostrils flared and his eyes widened as Claude held him to a walk. "This old boy would run himself to death if I let him," Claude said. "I have to save him from himself."

"Papa loved that horse. I'm glad you were able to keep him," Addie said. She was three weeks into her visit with her brother, and a week away from returning to her home in New Orleans after three years of living abroad. She had enjoyed her stay, getting to know Claude's new wife, Carrie, and on some levels, Claude himself. Except for their mother's funeral, they had not been together since she was a child and he was a teenager, barely old enough to take on his responsibilities at Road's End. If not for some shared childhood memories, they might have been strangers.

"I'm so proud of what you've accomplished here, and you know Papa would have been proud too," Addie said. "Saving the estate would have been more than enough, but I've heard that you have also become a man whom others look up to. I've heard that you might even run for office."

The lapels of Claude's jacket bowed slightly as his chest rose. "I have to admit that I'm gratified by what we've done and that people seem to recognize it," he said, struggling to maintain a modicum of modesty. "But I'm also humbled by the fact that none of it might have happened if Papa hadn't made financial arrangements that positioned us so well after he was killed. Addie, I can't tell you how many other families around here lost everything when the war ended."

They rode in silence for a few minutes, following the curve of the creek that marked the boundary of the Road's End property before encountering the fence Claude had ordered Plessant to build when he learned that the ten-acre plot had not been included in the estate sale to George Flowers.

"What is this? Why is this fence here?" Addie asked. "I used to walk here with Papa. We would bring food for a picnic, and he would teach me the names of trees while he fished."

Claude pulled up, dismounted, and held the reins of Addie's horse while she dropped to the ground. "He brought me here too," Claude said.

Addie waited, expecting to hear more, but Claude said nothing. "I still don't understand why you put up a fence, especially since you've bought Road's End back," she said. The humidity was becoming more oppressive, and she loosened the buttons of her habit to allow air to circulate.

Claude looked up at the treetops as if he expected to find some revelation there. What he saw instead were storm clouds streaking by overhead. The air stank of ozone, and from a distance came a faint clap of thunder.

"You don't know what it was like, Addie," he said finally. "The war was ending, the plantation had been sold, and although I had a job running the plantation and some independent income because of Papa's arrangements, I felt like a nobody. We come from landowners, and I didn't own a thing. I was just hired help, and I didn't like the way that made me feel.

"I was working for George Flowers and living in our house on our land, yet I couldn't claim anything as my own," Claude went on. "Then

I got a message from Papa's law firm in town, asking me to come in for a meeting. That's how I found out that these ten acres had not been sold with the rest of the plantation and that Mama owned them. They also said that Papa had spoken of his regrets about slavery and especially about the way he had treated Plessant and Elmira by selling off their two older children. To make up for it, he wanted this plot to be deeded over to Plessant if the South lost the war and the slaves were freed. They had a letter from Mama confirming it and directing that the land was to be deeded over to me to be held until Papa's wishes could be enacted."

"So," Addie said, "this land belongs to Plessant, and that's why there's a fence around it?"

Leaves were rustling in the trees as the wind picked up speed, and thunder rumbled louder and closer. Small animals in the woods fled to their dens. The horses danced and snorted nervously.

"Let's go," Claude said. "We don't want to get caught in this." They made it back to the stable just as the first heavy raindrops began to fall, and as lightning bolts flashed all around them.

"That was close," said Addie, laughing as they finished putting the horses away. "But we'll get soaked if we try to make it to the house in this storm."

"No need," Claude said. He opened a cabinet on the other side of the stable and removed a bottle of whiskey and a couple of tin cups. Gesturing to a bale of hay, he said, "I think we can wait it out here."

Ensconced on the hay bale with two fingers of good whiskey in her tin cup, Addie said, "You didn't answer my question. Is that land fenced because it belongs to Plessant?"

Claude let her question hang in the air while he pondered how to respond. "Did Papa ever talk to you about our grandfather?" he asked.

"Not much," Addie said.

"He talked to me about him a lot," Claude said. "I think he saw something of Grandpa in me. I didn't think about it then, but as time has passed, I think he might have been right. I remember one story in particular, about how Grandpa gave him the land and the baby Plessant to make him a man of property.

"I was just a boy myself when Papa told me that story, and I didn't think much about it. But that morning in the lawyers' offices, I found that I couldn't think of anything else. Until that ten acres of land was deeded over to me, I didn't own a thing, and if Plessant was to get it, he would be a man of property, and I would be no better than the Coloreds and the white trash. I couldn't stand the thought of it."

"You kept it? You didn't turn the land over to Plessant? What about Papa's wishes?" Addie didn't try to hide her disappointment.

"I said you didn't know what it was like back then," Claude snapped. He told her about all the uncertainty and the deal he struck with Flowers to buy back Road's End, financed by proceeds from parceling out plots to sharecroppers. "I had Plessant put up that fence to make sure there would be no confusion about who owned that parcel."

"But you were going to own the plantation again, and you couldn't spare the ten acres to fulfill Papa's wishes?" Addie asked, her voice low and hoarse.

"At first I was determined to keep it just until I got Road's End back," Claude said. "Besides, I took care of Plessant and Elmira by giving them jobs and letting them live in a better house. I even set it up so their boy Felix could apprentice with the carpenter and learn the trade.

"Then time passed, and the Yankees started coming in here with Coloreds from up North, trying to change everything with that Reconstruction. You've been in Europe, Addie. You didn't see all these Colored boys walking around like they were as good as white folks. It was disgusting. We had to do something about it."

"Who is 'we,' Claude?" Addie asked. Claude just stared through the door into the downpour that was slowing to a drizzle. Addie narrowed her eyes at him, waiting. When he didn't respond, she continued. "Even in Europe we heard about the vigilantes that came in after the Ku Klux Klan was shut down. Have you joined that bunch?"

Claude remained silent.

"I see," Addie said and emptied her tin cup.

"No, you don't see," Claude retorted. "We're all that's standing up for civility and honor and all that white people have accomplished.

Maybe you don't care if the whole country gets mongrelized like that maid of yours and her bastard child. Maybe that's all right in Europe or New Orleans, but not here."

Addie rose and set down her cup. "I see all too clearly, Claude, and I don't like what I see—not in you, and maybe not in myself, either," she said. "In any case, I think my 'mongrelized' maid, her 'bastard child,' and I will leave. We won't trouble you with our presence for another week."

Outside, the rain had stopped, but the sky was still gray. The heat and humidity were already moving back in behind the storm. It would not be a good night for sleeping.

Chapter 39

Alexandre was sitting on the stool in the corner of the kitchen at Road's End. His light-tan face, under softly curling brown hair, contained alert gray eyes that followed Elmira's every move as she prepared supper for the household. He was also chatty, but most of his babbling was in French, and Elmira didn't understand a word. Still, she enjoyed having the toddler around, and she tried to imagine what it might be like when Felix married and had children of his own.

Alexandre was with Elmira because Isabelle was having a walk around Road's End with David Allen, and Elmira had agreed to watch the boy while they had their stroll, nearly a daily occurrence since they had met a week earlier.

David had come to deliver rent checks from the farmers on the land Plessant and Elmira secretly owned. "I didn't see Plessant anywhere around," he had said, "so I thought I'd bring these to you, Elmira." His eyes locked onto Isabelle, and they never left her, even as he continued to speak to Elmira. "I'm sorry not to have gotten these here sooner, but they had me busy at the firm all day yesterday and the day before," he said.

"Thank you," said Elmira, but when she took the envelope from David's hand, she could see that his attention was still focused on Isabelle.

"David, this is Miss Isabelle Buard, the traveling companion of Miss

Addie, Mr. Claude's sister, who is visiting Road's End," Elmira said. "Isabelle, this is Mr. David Allen, a good friend to Plessant and me. He works for a law firm in town."

"I am pleased to meet you, Mr. Allen," Isabelle said and extended her hand.

"And I, you," David replied. "Is that a French accent I hear?"

"I am from New Orleans, Mr. Allen, and my family is Creole. We speak French as our first language. Also, I have been in Europe with Mademoiselle for the last four years, speaking French most of the time, so I suppose my accent is more pronounced now," she replied.

"*Charmante*," David said.

"*Parlez-vous français, monsieur?*" Isabelle replied.

"Only a little that I learned at school, but it is lovely to hear it spoken."

Aware that her presence had become irrelevant, Elmira returned to her work, pleased to see Isabelle in a happier mood.

———

Finding Isabelle feeding Alexandre in the kitchen before the rest of the household was awake had become a pleasurable ritual for Elmira. The two women would talk quietly as Elmira bustled about. Elmira especially enjoyed hearing Isabelle talk about New Orleans, a place she had not seen since her youth, when Marie Louise brought her to Red Clay to cook at Road's End.

"I was old enough to remember leaving my maw," she told Isabelle. "She cooked and cleaned for the old doctor, Miss Marie Louise's daddy. Oh, I cried like a baby when they told me I was goin' away with Miss Marie Louise, and my maw, she said, 'Girl, you just shut up 'cause ain't nothin' nobody can do about it. Folks like us, we just got to go where they say go, and do what they say do.' Then she hugged me, and that was the last time I ever seen her. I heard through Miss Marie Louise that she died some time back."

A tear escaped from each of Elmira's eyes, leaving a glistening trail down each of her cheeks. She did not expect the mixed-race Creole whose family had never been enslaved to understand her pain, but she sensed Isabelle's sympathy, and for that she was grateful.

This morning, however, Elmira arrived to find Addie in the kitchen with Isabelle and Alexandre. The two women had been feeding the boy and playing with him, and his delighted giggles filled the room. They looked up when Elmira came through the door, and suddenly she knew with absolute certainty what had been gnawing at her about the way Isabelle and Addie acted when they were together with the baby. Her eyes met Isabelle's, and something passed between them, a sharing of knowledge that did not require words to be spoken.

"Well," Addie said, "I have some news. We will be cutting our visit short and will be returning to New Orleans sooner than planned. I told Isabelle last night, and I wanted to tell you first thing this morning, Elmira. We will be leaving early tomorrow, and I wanted to say my goodbye now. Isabelle, will you come and help me pack later?"

"Yes, of course, Mademoiselle. I will be with you presently," she said. Her eyes never left Elmira's.

"I'm gon' miss you, Isabelle," Elmira said when Addie left the room.

"I will miss you too." Isabelle crossed the room to embrace Elmira.

The women held each other for a long while, and before they parted, Isabelle whispered into Elmira's ear, "Alexandre is *my* son."

"That's right, baby," Elmira whispered in return. "He *your* boy, and ain't nobody gon' say nothin' different."

———

When Plessant brought the carriage around the next morning to drive Addie, Isabelle, and Alexandre to the train station, they were alone on the front porch with their bags. Neither Claude nor Carrie was there to say farewell. While Plessant loaded their luggage, Elmira joined them and handed Isabelle a basket. "Alexandre might get hungry, and I know what that boy like to eat," she said.

Isabelle took the basket and hugged Elmira tightly. "I do not think that I shall ever again have a friend such as you," she said.

They were about to drive away when Felix came running around the corner of the house.

"Oh, Felix, I am so glad you are here. I have something for you," Addie said. "I was going to give it to your father for you, but now I can give it to you directly." She reached into her purse and pulled out a sealed envelope with Felix's name written on it. She leaned down from the buggy, handed the envelope to him, and said quietly, "Open it when you can do so in private."

"Thank you," Felix said. "I have something for you too." He reached into his coat pocket and pulled out a small wooden box, polished to a soft sheen, fitted with leather hinges and fastened with a shiny brass latch.

"Did you make this, Felix?" she asked. "It's beautiful."

"Yes, ma'am, I did," he said, and added quietly, "It would be better if you open this when you are alone too."

Perhaps the person most saddened by the departure was at the railroad station when they arrived. David Allen was waiting with a bouquet for Isabelle. "I could not let you go without seeing you once more," he said. "*Au revoir.*"

"*En attendant de nous revoir,*" she said and kissed him on the cheek.

Addie took in the scene—the young man, the young woman, and the child; they looked like a family. She smiled and waved goodbye to Plessant before stepping onto the train, followed by Isabelle and Alexandre.

"I reckon you might be gettin' on that train sometime soon," Plessant said to David.

"You might be right," he replied. "You might be right."

Addie settled back in her seat in the white section aboard the train to New Orleans, stretched her legs, and hoped that she would be able to fall asleep. This was probably the last time she would ever be in Red Clay, she thought, and perhaps the last time she would ever see her brother. Their lives had taken such different paths, and it seemed unlikely that they would ever again intersect. She felt a tear roll down her cheek. She reached into her purse for her handkerchief and felt the box Felix had given her. There was no one in the seat next to her, and there was no one in the row across the aisle, so she pulled it out and opened it.

Inside, nestled in red velvet, was something she recognized immediately, even though she had never seen it before—a pearl-handled derringer with a bluesteel double barrel, imported from England before the war.

Addie's shoulders shook as she began to cry. She had lost everything: her father, her mother, her brothers, and now even her own son, and for what? What was to become of her? She closed the box and pushed it deep into her purse. When she reached her home in New Orleans she would take the box and bury it under the cobblestones in the courtyard where it belonged, in the ancient earth. Then the tears would be gone, and her heart would feel alive, ready to beat again in the sunshine of a new day.

———

That evening, sitting in the swing with Zilpha on the Moores' front porch, Felix pulled out the letter Addie had given him and handed it to Zilpha. "I want you to read this to me," he said.

"Why?" she asked. "You've been doing well with your reading lessons from that old schoolteacher. You can read it perfectly well yourself. And I'll tell you something else. Mama told me she's noticed how well-spoken you've become."

Felix nodded. "Miss Dixon is a good teacher, and she says I've been doing well too. But I think this is important, and I want to be sure I get it right. I'm supposed to read it when I'm alone, but I trust you, Zilpha. Whatever it is, I know I can trust you to keep it quiet."

"Well, okay," she said, and moved closer to him before beginning to read:

Dear Felix,

I want you to know how important it was to me that we were able to share our secrets. The information about my father

*ended the mystery of his death, and I feel better for having
learned the truth.*

*I am so impressed with the way you have grown up to be
a fine man with a good future. I hope it all turns out well,
including finding a wife who will stand by you and the family
you may have together. Your mother told me that there is a young
woman about whom you are apparently quite serious. I wish you
all the best in that relationship and that you will have a long and
happy life together.*

Zilpha stopped reading and looked into Felix's eyes. What she saw
there caused her heart to leap and tears to form in her own eyes. Felix
wrapped her shoulders in his arms as she continued to read.

*The main reason for this letter, however, is to tell you that I
have learned some things about my brother that have made me
uncomfortable and given me reason to think that there may
come a time when he might seek to do harm to you or your
parents. I do not know how, when, or in what form this might
occur, but you should be aware that he has changed and that
anything is possible.*

*I know something of his ambitions, and I believe that he
could be deterred from seeking to hurt you if he feared that his
reputation might be damaged. Therefore, if he tries to harm you
or your parents, you have my permission to let him know the
secret I have shared with you and to let him know that it will
become public if he tries to move against you. I truly hope it will
not come to that, but if it does, I believe this will be your best
defense against him.*

Thank you again for what you have given me.

*With sincerest best regards,
Adelaide Parker
18th September 1876.*

The sun was setting, and the bright green of the lawn and the vibrant pink of the crepe myrtle blossoms in the Moores' front yard were fading in the dim light. The hum of bees had gone quiet, and the first bats of the evening could be seen swooping for insects. One of the horses in the stable neighed as it settled for the evening.

Zilpha took Felix's hand. "What does it mean?" she asked. "Are you in trouble?"

"No, I'm not in trouble," he said. "What it means is that I have a friend I never expected to have, and, I think, a good one."

Part Three

REDEMPTION

Chapter 40

RED CLAY, ALABAMA

AUTUMN 1943

At sunset the day after Felix's funeral, the encroaching darkness arrived with a sudden drop in temperature, and Addie was trembling despite the handcrafted quilt around her shoulders. "I'm tired, and these near-ninety-year-old bones need a rest," she said to her hosts. "Would you allow me to come again tomorrow morning so we might finish our conversation?"

"Of course," Maybelle said. "We will look forward to it." In spite of her initial misgivings, she had warmed to this old woman who had been such an important part of her father's life.

Later, standing on the porch as Addie was being driven away in the big burgundy sedan, Eileen draped an arm around her mother's shoulders. "What do you think about her? Do you like her?" she asked.

"Well," Maybelle replied, "she's better than most."

Mother and daughter stood together for a long time, staring into the darkness, listening to voices that whispered sweet tidings over time and space, carried on a sudden gust that gently caressed their cheeks before slipping past them through the open front windows into the house and rushing out through the screened kitchen door into the backyard.

Eileen shivered. "Grandpa was just here, wasn't he?" she whispered.

"Yes, he was, and all the rest of them too," Maybelle replied. "They're always here. Your people will always be with you, whether they're living or passed on. It doesn't matter; they'll always be around to look after you when times are hard or when you're just feeling sad. Close your eyes and relax and call out to them in your mind, and they'll be right there to comfort you and to remind you that you're never alone. Your great-grandma Elmira knew all about that. I'll tell you a story she told me a long time ago."

———

ROAD'S END PLANTATION

AUTUMN 1876

Elmira was bustling about the kitchen of the big house, rushing because she had gotten a late start on the family's supper that day, and Claude had grown fussy about having the evening meal served on time. She was chopping carrots for a stew when Plessant burst into the kitchen with a big grin on his face and a white envelope in his hand.

"Look what come for you today," he said and dropped the envelope on the table. The old habits of a lifetime in slavery—when possessing a letter and having the ability to read it might have terrible consequences—were dying slowly. Elmira eyed it warily, as if by merely looking at it she might be turned into a pillar of salt.

"Who it from?" she whispered.

"I don't know. I reckon you got to open it to find out," Plessant replied.

"You take it home," Elmira said. "I got to finish makin' supper for Mr. Claude, Miss Carrie, and them children. I'll open it when I get there."

Plessant threw his head back and laughed. "You know you want to open it now," he said. "How you gon' wait?"

"Got to wait. That letter ain't gon' make this supper, so it got to wait. Now get out of here," she said. Still, as she watched Plessant go through the door, she couldn't get the letter out of her mind. *Who would be writing to me? What do they have to say?*

Later that evening, Elmira and Plessant sat at a table in their house, looking at the address on the unopened letter, illuminated by a kerosene lamp:

Mrs. Elmira Parker
c/o Road's End Plantation
Red Clay, Alabama

She used a knife to slit the envelope open, the way she had seen her old mistress Marie Louise do it with her fancy silver letter opener during slavery times, and though neither Elmira nor Plessant were proficient readers, they managed to get through the letter:

Dear Elmira,

This is your old friend Callie Mae. I am fine, and I hope you and your family are fine too. You know I never learned to read and write, but Miss Isabelle Buard, Miss Addie's housekeeper, is taking down what I say and making it proper. She told me she got to know you at Road's End and sends her regards. She says her boy Alexandre is fine too. She says you were good to them when they visited there, and she sends her thanks.

You know when I came to New Orleans to work for Miss Marie Louise I was scared because I had never been anywhere else except Road's End and Red Clay, and I didn't know anyone here. It was terrible at first, but then the war ended and we got our freedom, and it was easier to meet people. But then Miss Marie Louise passed, and I didn't know what was going to happen to me. Well, Miss Marie Louise's sister, Miss Colette, hired me to work in her house, so it turned out all right.

I've been lucky. I have this job and friends, and I rent a nice room in a boarding house for Colored women. It's clean, and the lady who runs it is nice, and she doesn't allow immoral behavior. I still remember that when I had to leave Road's End you told me there were some good-looking men in New Orleans. Well, I've seen a few, but they haven't seen me . . . yet. But there's still time.

You will be glad to know that your mama was beloved by the Colored people here, and when they found out that you were my friend back in Alabama, they welcomed me. And guess what? I even met some of your family. You got cousins here, Elmira, and they wanted to know all about you, and they wanted me to tell you that you would be welcome if you were to ever come back to New Orleans. I would be glad to see you too.

Well, that's all for now. I miss you.

Sincerely,
Callie Mae Claiborne
22nd October 1876

PS How do you like my last name? There's a pretty street near where I live called Claiborne Avenue. Maybe you remember it? I like the way it sounds, so I decided to take that name.

Elmira set the letter down and stared straight ahead. Plessant pulled his chair around to her side of the table and put his arm around her. She relaxed against him and allowed herself to cry. Outside, clouds rolled in, and rain began to fall in the darkness, a blessing for the earth.

They were still there when Felix came home to find his parents sitting at the table with the letter from Callie Mae in front of them. Elmira could barely contain her joy about its contents. "You got people, Felix!" she exclaimed. "Not just your paw and me. You got cousins, and who knows who else there might be."

"I guess that's all right," Felix said, "but I don't know if we'll ever go to New Orleans, and I don't think they'll ever come here."

Elmira's shoulders slumped in response to her son's lack of enthusiasm for her big news. "Maybe one day you'll understand," she said. "It's a big thing to know you ain't alone in the world, even if the rest of your family is far away. I pray every night that your brother and sister know that. I hope they know they ain't alone and that they got family that loves them and that one day we might all be together again.

Here," she said. "You take this letter and keep it. Maybe it'll help you remember that."

She pushed the papers across the table to him and waited until he picked them up. "Yes ma'am," Felix said. "I'll keep it."

———

RED CLAY, ALABAMA

AUTUMN 1943

Addie arrived early the next morning as Eileen, Maybelle, and Luther were putting away breakfast dishes. "Please come in, Miss Parker," Eileen said when she heard the knock at the door and saw Addie through the screen. "Would you care for something to eat? Coffee? It's fresh and still hot."

"Thank you, no," Addie said. "I've already had breakfast and plenty of coffee, more than my doctor would think wise, but I so enjoy it. Actually, I'm anxious to pick up where we left off yesterday. It seems so strange to be here in this house and learning about the life of someone I knew so long ago."

"It's been . . . what's the right word . . . revealing?" Maybelle said. "To sit with someone who played such an important role in Daddy's life. Until now you just seemed like somebody he made up."

"Revealing *is* the right word, Mrs. Epps—for both of us," Addie said.

Chapter 41

Plessant was waiting in the front yard when Claude returned to Road's End from a day of meetings with lawyers, bankers, and politicians in Red Clay. The Black man's eyes were downcast, his hands were stuffed in his pockets, and he shifted his weight from one foot to the other, like a child who needed to pee.

"Hey, Plessant. What's the matter?" Claude said as he dismounted from Zeus. "You look worried."

"Well, Mr. Claude. I need to talk to you about some things."

"Nothing too bad, I hope," Claude replied.

"Not the way I see it," Plessant said.

"All right, then. I'll tell you what. I'm worn out. I'm going to go inside, get a hot bath, have a shot of whiskey, and sit down with my family for some of your wife's good cooking. We'll talk in the morning. You meet me here after breakfast, and we'll talk about what's on your mind. Is that all right with you?"

"Yassuh, I'll be here in the morning."

Elmira rushed home to find Plessant after the Parkers had been served supper and after the kitchen had been cleaned and readied for the next morning's breakfast. "Did you tell him? What did he say?" she asked.

"Didn't get to say nothin'. He said he was tired and that we was to talk in the morning after breakfast."

"Guess we better try to get some sleep then," Elmira said. "Tomorrow gon' be a big day."

Sleep didn't come, and while it was still dark, long before Elmira rose to go to work, Plessant eased out of bed, dressed, and stepped outside to sit on the porch steps. Despite the moonlight and the glowing canopy of stars, the darkness was profound, and he could hear, rather than see, leaves rustling in the light breeze and small creatures scurrying in the weeds. In truth, he didn't need to see any of those things to know they were happening. He had spent his entire life at Road's End, and the rhythm of life there resonated throughout his body. Nevertheless, he was startled when Elmira touched his shoulder. He had not heard her come up behind him, and she laughed softly when he jumped.

"You better go back in there and try to get some sleep. Felix can wake you up when he get up. Plenty of time for you to come up to the big house to see Mr. Claude," she said.

"I'm all right. Maybe I'll just come up there and keep you company in the kitchen. Then I know I won't miss him when he get through eatin'." Plessant stood up, and they hugged—a lingering embrace before they walked to the big house as scarlet streaks encroached on the dark eastern sky.

Later that morning, Elmira rushed into the kitchen with a tray full of dirty breakfast dishes and whispered to Plessant, "They through eatin', and Mr. Claude say he goin' out to the front porch to finish his coffee."

Plessant slipped through the back door and arrived in the front yard as Claude stepped outside.

"Ah, Plessant, you had some things to discuss with me this morning," Claude said, as Plessant approached the porch steps.

Claude seemed delighted with the first part of Plessant's report: The tenants on Road's End property had successfully planted their cotton, and the land Claude controlled directly was prepared for planting. He

erupted in anger, however, when he heard Plessant's second announcement—that he was resigning and leaving Road's End.

"What the hell do you mean, you're quitting?" Claude slammed
his coffee cup onto a table and rushed down the steps into the yard to
confront Plessant, inches from his face.

Plessant took a step back, but his voice was firm when he replied, "I
said what I mean, Mr. Claude. Don't mean to upset you, but I been here
all my life, and it's time for me to go. I been glad to work for you and for
your daddy before you, but comes a time when a man got to move on."

"Look here," Claude exclaimed, "you can't go. Who'll look after
these 'croppers and all the other things you do?"

"That's why I waited 'til the crops was planted and everything was
in order. You can get somebody to take my place," Plessant said.

Claude's heated response morphed into unmitigated rage. "You un-
grateful black bastard. You look around. Not too many other Coloreds
have a situation like yours. I gave you a good job, a house to live in. I
even let your boy work out of my carpentry shop. And this is how you
repay my generosity?"

Plessant tried to interrupt, but Claude, his face reddening, his brow
shining with perspiration, and his voice rising, cut him off. "What are
you going to do, anyhow? Where the hell are you going?"

"Fact is, ain't none of your business where I'm goin'," Plessant said.
"But if you got to know, I been given a chance to work some land for
myself over across town, and that's what I intend to do. Seem like you
forgot we ain't slaves no more, much as you and your friends wish we was."

"Son of a bitch!" Claude bellowed. "You think you can talk to a
white man like that and get away with it?" Claude had been planning
to exercise his horse that morning, and he raised the riding crop he was
carrying to strike Plessant.

"That's enough, Mr. Claude!" It was Felix. He had heard the raised
voices from inside his shop and walked to the corner of the house where he
had been eavesdropping on the exchange between Claude and his father.

Moving quickly, he positioned himself between the two men and
stared directly into Claude's eyes, and when he spoke, his voice was

low and determined. "Like my paw said, we ain't slaves no more. We're grateful for what you did for us after we got our freedom, but my paw worked hard for you, and I paid you the rent for the shop on time every month. So if we want to leave, we can leave, and you ain't got nothing to say about it."

"We'll see about that," Claude replied. "You think you can work for yourself? Just wait until you try to get credit or buy supplies around here." Then he added darkly, "Besides, bad things have a way of happening to uppity niggers. Of course, I wouldn't wish a fire or any other disaster on anybody, but isn't it strange that things like that happen to Colored folks who don't know their place?" Claude turned to walk back to the house, but he found Felix standing in his way. "Get out of my way, nigger," he growled.

"Oh, I'll get out of your way, Mr. Claude, but I got to tell you some things first," said Felix.

Blocking Claude's path with his body, Felix laid out what he knew about John Robert's death, which enabled the fraud that saved his family financially, including the fact that he had invested his funds in ways that depended upon a Union victory.

"None of that is true. None of it!" Claude spluttered.

"Oh, yes sir, it is," Felix replied. Then he revealed what he knew about Addie's affair with a mixed-race man and that a son had resulted from the union. "Of course, you know all about that, Mr. Claude, seeing as how they visited you here," Felix said. "I think your nephew is right handsome."

"You can't—"

"Look here, Mr. Claude, everybody knows you've become a big man around here, rich and powerful, and you got pull at the courthouse. Ain't no secret that you expect to run for mayor, or maybe even something bigger. What do you think they would do if they knew your daddy put his money with the Yankees, or that your sweet little sister got herself pregnant by a half-Colored man, and not by rape?"

"Or," Plessant added, "what would the church elders think about a man who would ignore his father's dying wish to give a little piece of

land to the Colored man who served him so well? Most of them probably don't care one way or the other about Colored people, but ignorin'
your daddy's last request? That ain't decent."

"What do you know about that?" Claude snarled. He took a step
closer to Plessant. Spittle ran from the corner of his mouth.

"I know all I need to know," Plessant replied.

"I'll tell you what *I* know," Claude growled. "I want all of you out
of here by tomorrow morning—you, Felix, and Elmira. I want you out,
gone. You hear me?"

"Yassuh," Plessant said. "I hear you just fine." Turning to his son,
he said, "Felix, go get your maw. We got work to do."

"Yes sir, Paw," Felix replied and turned to walk toward the kitchen
door of the big house, releasing his grip on the razor-sharp woodcarv-
ing knife in his right pants pocket as he went.

Elmira had just finished cleaning up after breakfast and was preparing to move on to some light housekeeping when Felix arrived at the
kitchen door to tell her what had happened. Standing in the middle
of the kitchen, she said nothing. She slowly removed her apron and
folded it carefully before laying it across the back of a chair. Whatever
she was feeling was hers alone to know, and her face betrayed no emotion as she turned to meet her son's gaze. "It's time to go," she said, and
followed Felix through the door and across the yard. She didn't look
back, even once.

Plessant, Elmira, and Felix were gone by six o'clock that evening,
along with all of their furnishings from the house and Felix's tools from
the workshop, leaving behind those that had been owned by the plantation, with which he had learned his trade. Everything else was hauled
away in two wagonloads to the house Felix had built over the past year
and a half. Nothing of them remained at Road's End but the echoes of
their lives—all they had seen, all they had done. The past was finished,
and the future beckoned.

The farmers who had been renting the land from an anonymous
landlord had been notified that their leases would not be renewed, but
they had been paid to plant new crops of corn, sweet potatoes, collard

greens, turnips, tomatoes, and peanuts in anticipation of the arrival of a new resident tenant. A well had been dug, a pit for an outhouse had been excavated, and Felix had built a chicken coop, a hog pen, and a stable for the mule. A workshop for his carpentry business was still under construction. The future wasn't ahead of them anymore; it was all around them, and for the moment, at least, it seemed limitless.

Chapter 42

AUTUMN 1876

The Black Parkers' move to Jefferson Street in the wake of their hostile split from Claude and Road's End had been exhilarating, even joyous—until the night, two weeks later, when they were awakened from their sleep by loud voices, the clatter of horses' hooves, the smell of kerosene, and the flickering light of torches outside their bedroom window.

Robed and hooded figures, about a dozen of them, were laying a pile of kerosene-soaked logs in front of the house when Plessant burst onto the front porch, wearing pants he had hastily pulled on, suspenders stretched across his bare shoulders, clutching the shotgun he used to hunt small game. But before he could fire a shot, someone grabbed him and dragged him into the yard.

Felix started to leap from the porch to save his father, but stopped when Plessant shouted, "Go back. Protect your maw!" He managed to throw the shotgun to Felix before he was wrestled to the ground.

The logs burst into flame, shooting sparks into the dark heavens and pushing back the shadows in the yard. A doe and two fawns broke cover and fled past the house into the fields. Elmira had come to the front door. "Plessant! Plessant!" she screamed, as Felix held her back.

By the light from the bonfire, Felix saw that Plessant's feet had been tied to the end of a rope attached to a rider's horse. His hands were bound behind his back. The rider kicked the horse's flanks and the animal leaped forward, towing Plessant around the yard, again and again, with his head bumping every stone, every tree trunk they passed. And when the leader gave the signal, they rode away, dragging Plessant behind them, but not before the leader turned to look directly at Felix. He was hooded, but Felix would have recognized Zeus, the big black stallion, anywhere. The eyes glaring at him through holes in the hood belonged to Claude Parker. Still holding the shotgun, Felix raised it to aim at the mounted figure's heart. They stared at each other for a long moment before Claude spurred his horse and galloped into the night.

Plessant's corpse was found the next day, lying beside the road on the other side of town, his face bloody and mangled and his chest and back scraped raw. His neck was broken, and his left arm was connected to the rest of his body only by the rope that bound his wrists together.

To no one's surprise, an inquest produced insufficient evidence to charge anyone with Plessant's death, and the case was closed.

RED CLAY, ALABAMA

SPRING 1877

Felix had recreated the old Road's End carpentry shop on his own property. The building was about the same size, and it was configured similarly, with storage for his tools around the walls and a solid workbench in the center of the one-room structure. He loved the way it looked and the way it smelled, and he was meticulous about cleaning it up at the end of each workday. Old John, the enslaved carpenter who had taught him his trade, would have been proud. Felix was puttering around in his shop, thinking about how to deal with the contemptuous response of the local establishment to his father's murder. If there was to be justice, he would have to secure it himself.

He let his mind range through the possibilities, and then he had it. He felt his mind go numb and his heart grow cold, but there was no other solution: He would kill Claude and take down the rest of the Parker family too. He might be destroyed in the process, but so too would they. First, he had to write two letters—one to Addie, expressing his regret that he might have to use her secrets in a public way, and another to the Washington lawyers with instructions on how to use the information he would provide.

Thus, six months after Plessant's funeral, he found himself with his father's shotgun, pressed into the shadows in a corner of the stable at Road's End at sunset, waiting for Claude to make his nightly visit to the horses before retiring for the evening.

Predictably, Claude made his appearance as the plantation slipped into darkness, as bats that lived in the rafters dropped from their toe-holds, spread their wings, and disappeared into the night through cracks in the siding in the loft above where Felix stood. The horses—the black stallion, a chestnut mare, and a dapple-gray gelding—snorted and tossed their heads, nervous, as if they understood that something was wrong.

"What's the matter? What's the matter?" Claude said in a soothing voice as he moved from stall to stall, seeking to calm the animals.

"Maybe it's me." Felix stepped out of the corner, holding the shotgun at his hip with the barrel aimed directly at Claude's chest. "Animals know when there's danger, and tonight I'm just about the most dangerous thing around."

Claude whirled around, his body tense and his eyes bulging as he sought to locate the source of the voice. "Who's that? Who's in here?" he said in a hoarse whisper.

"It's just me, Mr. Claude," Felix said as he moved out of the shadows and kept the gun pointed at Claude's chest. "The last time I had a gun on you, I didn't pull the trigger, but maybe this time I will."

"What's going on here? What do you want?" Claude asked.

Felix ignored the question. "Yes sir, I think I might pull the trigger this time. You need to be shot after what you and your friends did to my paw."

"Now wait a minute," Claude said. "You think you can just come in here and kill me and get away with it?"

"Why not?" Felix replied. "You got away with killing my paw, you and your coward friends. You ain't in jail. You didn't hang. Nobody found your body in the dirt on the side of the road. Maybe I'll just shoot you here and leave your body for your wife to find."

"You know as well as I that it won't work for you. It's different for a white man," Claude said.

"And that's supposed to make it all right?"

Felix moved closer. Claude backed up, never taking his eyes off the shotgun, until his back was against the door of Zeus's stall. Felix put the muzzle of the shotgun against Claude's forehead and pressed hard enough to make a red horizontal figure-eight in the skin with the pressure of the double barrels.

"You don't have to do this, Felix. You can just walk away. I won't say anything about you being here. We can just act as if this never happened," Claude said. His shirt was drenched; his eyes were wild, darting about, as if he was seeking an escape route.

"You know, I just figured something out, Mr. Claude," Felix said. His eyes never left Claude's, and he did not relieve the pressure of the gun's barrels on Claude's forehead. "I could shoot you, and you would be dead, and it would just be over. You might be scared right now, and you might feel some pain when the buckshot hits your face, but then you would be gone, and it wouldn't matter. My paw wouldn't be here, and you would be gone, and everything would still be the same. Sit down, Mr. Claude. Sit down on the floor right where you at. I got to think about this a minute."

The muscles in Claude's legs were trembling so hard that he lost his balance when he tried to sit, and he crashed to the floor with his back still against the stall door. His bladder released a stream of urine down his leg. The stallion stomped and snorted in his stall, driven into a frenzy by the tension in the air around him and the stench of terror rising from Claude's skin.

Just then Felix heard a sound at the stable door. "Shush," he hissed. "Be quiet, Mr. Claude. Don't say nothing. I still got this gun on you." He melted back into the shadows and waited.

"Claude? Are you in here, Claude?" said a voice from the door. Claude's wife pushed the door open and thrust a lantern through the gap before coming in herself. She moved the lantern slowly from left to right, straining to see into the building's recesses until the light revealed Claude huddled on the floor. "Oh, my Lord!" she said and rushed to Claude. "Are you all right? Are you hurt?"

"He's all right, Miss Carrie," Felix said as he stepped into the light cast by the lantern. "You just sit down there beside him, and you'll be all right too."

Carrie gaped at Felix and the shotgun before she settled on the floor next to Claude. "What is this? What do you think you're doing?" she demanded. She gestured to Claude, who sat motionless in a near-catatonic state. "What have you done to my husband?"

"I ain't done nothing to him . . . yet," Felix said. "But that could change."

"I know you. You're Felix, Elmira's boy," Carrie said.

"Yes, ma'am, I'm Felix, Elmira's *son*," he replied. "I'm also *Plessant's* son. You remember him? He's dead now, and your husband and his friends killed him."

"Well, what do you want here? You know you're in a heap of trouble, coming here this way," Carrie said. "And if my husband doesn't recover, you know what will happen to you." She wrapped her arms around Claude and pulled him close to her.

"You know, Miss Carrie, until you came in here, I wasn't sure of what I was going to do," Felix responded, keeping the gun pointed at the couple on the stable floor. "Now I know. You just stay down there. I got a story to tell you. Don't worry about Mr. Claude; he already knows this story, and that's why I came. But now you need to know it too." He repeated the information he and Plessant had told Claude when he opposed their plans to leave Road's End and how they had planned to release it if any harm came to them.

"But that didn't stop Mr. Claude and his night rider friends from murdering my paw," Felix said. "And they got away with it too. I guess he figured from the beginning that a couple of Colored men couldn't hurt him, no matter what they had to say. So I came here tonight to kill him. But when I had the gun up against his head, I changed my mind. He ain't worth it. Just look at him, so scared he pissed in his pants. What kind of man is that?"

Carrie was glaring at Felix the way a cornered fox might defy a pack of baying hounds. No options left but to fight and hope for the best.

"The thing I figured out about Mr. Claude is that there are just two things he couldn't bear to lose," Felix continued. "One of them is Road's End, and the other one is being a big man, maybe the governor or a senator one day. Now the first thing, Road's End, he would die for that. There's nothing he wouldn't do to keep control of this plantation. The second thing, being a big man; he feels the same about that as he does about Road's End. But he was willing to risk it, because he figured that he could murder my paw and keep me quiet. Everything else, including you, Miss Carrie, comes after that."

Claude was stirring and hearing Felix through a haze. "Not true," he murmured, slurring his words like a drunk. "None of it's true. I love you, Carrie. Don't let this nigger tell you anything different."

"You know it *is* true, don't you, Miss Carrie?" Felix said. "And you know what would happen if all your fancy lady friends heard about your sister-in-law and her half-Colored baby and what she did to try to cover it up. You know what would happen if word got around that your husband's father saved his family's fortune by putting his money with the Yankees and how he killed himself to avoid the shame of losing everything. Maybe Mr. Claude don't care, but I'm guessing you do. I'm guessing you like being important around here as much as he does."

"I can't believe you have the audacity to come here and threaten us this way and to think you can get away with it," Carrie said.

"I don't care what you think," Felix said. "All you got to know is that what I told you won't die with me. I got it set up so if something happens to me, the newspapers in Huntsville, Montgomery, and New York City will get the story. They'll use it too. Don't think you can stop 'em. Newspapers love to bring down the high and mighty. And don't think that just because I'm a Colored man that it won't happen. White folks think all the time that Colored folks don't know how to do things."

The horses had settled down, and, outside, the wind had stopped blowing and the leaves on the trees hung straight and unmoving. The reflection of the moon on the creek was steady, as if the current had come to a halt. Predators in the woods withdrew, and the field mice, the rabbits, and other small prey escaped to see another day.

"What do you want?" Carrie whispered.

"I come here for one thing: to hurt Mr. Claude the way he hurt my maw and me, by taking away something that means everything to him. I thought it would be his life. But now I want to take away the one thing that will cut him like a knife, and that he won't forget," Felix said. "I want Mr. Claude to give up on being the big man, something he wants like other men want to breathe, and if he ever gets the chance to be mayor, or governor, or any other big thing, everything I told you tonight will come out. And if anything happens to me or my maw, or if you try to hurt my business, everything will come out. That's all I want. I want him to be this little man I see here on this stable floor and to know that it's all he can ever be."

In the flickering lantern light, Felix saw Carrie nod almost imperceptibly, stand, and then reach down to help Claude. By the time she had him on his feet and his arm over her shoulders, Felix was gone, and once again time resumed at Road's End.

Chapter 43

ROAD'S END PLANTATION

SPRING 1877

Standing by the upright liquor cabinet across from the heavy mahogany desk in the study that had been John Robert's retreat, Claude poured himself a cognac from the decanter that had also belonged to his father. A fire blazed in the massive fireplace. Although the house and everything in it had long been his, it annoyed him that he couldn't stop thinking of this one room and its furnishings as his father's. *I miss you, Papa,* he thought, *but it's mine now, and I wish you would let it go.*

He heard the wind blow outside and thought a step creaked on the stairway outside the study door, but he knew he was alone. The housekeeper had left for the day, and Carrie had taken the year-old twin girls to visit her aging mother in Huntsville. He reached into the cedar-lined box for a cigar and carried it with his cognac across the room, where he dropped into a big leather chair.

He pulled hard on his cigar, then released a stream of fragrant smoke, savoring the taste of leather and herbs on his tongue. He followed it with a sip of cognac, the way his friend and mentor George Flowers had shown him years earlier. "Take a small sip of the cognac, just a small one, and let it dissipate in your mouth. Don't swallow it; just let it disappear," Flowers had told him.

Each time he repeated the ritual, another layer of the day's frustrations peeled away. *This is good*, he thought. He needed to get rid of the stress more than usual because of his recent encounter in the stable with Felix and the decision he had been forced to make today as a consequence. His stomach churned, and blood pounded in his temples as he remembered the moment.

Some Democratic Party leaders had come up from Montgomery to once again urge Claude to run for an open seat in the state senate. "You have what it takes, and we need you," they had said. "And it doesn't stop in the state capital. You win the senate seat, then we run you for governor, and when you've served a couple of terms, you run for the US Senate, and you'll win. We have all the financial and political backing you'll need."

Claude desperately wanted what they were offering. He wanted it the way he had wanted Road's End when it seemed lost to him. Yet, when they had finished their pitch, he stood up, shook their hands, and said, "Thank you, gentlemen, for your time and for your wonderful encouragement, but as I have told you before, I cannot accept your offer. I regret that you had to travel all the way up here to hear it from me."

"But why not?" the lead delegate asked. "You're a bright young man with a lovely family. You're well-known and well-liked. You're a successful landowner and a leader in your church. Also," he said, lowering his voice to a whisper, "we know you have certain associations that confirm your commitments to states' rights and the Southern way of life, which are important to us."

"At the risk of appearing immodest," Claude replied, "what you say is true, but nevertheless I must decline your offer. Thank you again." He walked out of the room with his fists clenched at his side, down the hallway, and out of the offices of the law firm where the meeting had been held. *Damn that Felix. It's all his fault*, he thought. *Imagine being blackmailed by a nigger.* He poured himself another drink.

Under the same night sky, on the other side of town, Felix was drinking, too, huddled on Jimmy's back porch, passing a jug back and forth.

"You know you're my best friend, Jimmy," Felix said.

"That's 'cause everybody else got the good sense to keep you at a distance," Jimmy replied.

Felix glowered at him in mock resentment. "Why you want to treat me like that? I've been a good friend to you, and I just want you to know I think you've been a good friend to me."

"Well, since you put it like that, have another drink," Jimmy said and handed the jug back to him. "Say, Felix, you got somethin' on your mind?"

"What makes you think that?"

"Nothin', 'cept you had this stupid grin on your face since you got here."

"I can't just be happy?" Felix asked.

"Now, see? You come over here and drink my liquor and make me play some child's guessing game," Jimmy replied.

Felix could see that Jimmy was actually becoming annoyed, so he stood up, handed the jug back, and said, "Jimmy, I've got big news. She said 'Yes.'"

"What?"

"She said 'yes.' Zilpha said she would marry me."

Jimmy let out a whoop. "Lucille, get out here," he shouted. "Felix is getting married."

Even Lucille, usually a teetotaler, took a sip of her husband's whiskey to mark the occasion. "We're so happy for you, Felix," she said.

"Thank you, Lucille, but I have a favor to ask of Jimmy. I want you to stand up with me when the day comes. Will you do that for me?"

Jimmy embraced Felix in a bear hug. "You know I will. Congratulations."

Earlier in the day, when Felix broke the news to his mother that he was going to ask Albert Moore for his daughter's hand, she collapsed in tears. "Oh, Felix. I'm so happy. Zilpha is a wonderful girl, and I just know you gon' be happy," she said.

He had put on his best suit and waited on the funeral home's front porch for Zilpha to open the door for business. "Did your father have a good breakfast? Is he in a good mood?" he asked. His voice was shaky, and the armpits of his shirt were wet.

"Don't worry. I'll be right there with you," Zilpha said.

When it was all done, Felix went home to tell his mother, who hugged him and then pushed him back to arm's length. "I have some news too, Felix, and this is the perfect time to tell you. I'm leaving. I'm moving back to New Orleans. I'm going home."

Felix sat down hard in a chair behind him. "Why? When?"

"I can't stay here. Your paw's death just hit me too hard," Elmira said. "I can't stop thinking about him, and I'm just upset all the time. Everywhere I go, something make me think about him, and I'm tired of havin' to smile at these white folks, knowin' what they did to my husband. So I'm leavin'. You gettin' married, and you don't need me no more. Before long you gon' have a family of your own, and you can bring my grandchildren to visit me."

"Maw, you can't leave. I need you," Felix said, and the memories of all they had experienced together washed through him, then pushed up and out as tears that streamed down his cheeks. "What will you do there? How will you live?" he asked.

"I got it all worked out," she said. "You know my friend Callie Mae is there, and she say the rooming house where she live is about to have a room open up. And Isabelle Buard has a cousin with a catering business, and she told them about me, and they say they got a job for me if I want it. Plus, I want to get to know all those kinfolks down there.

"And you know what else?" she continued. "I'm givin' you this property for a wedding gift, so you and Zilpha can start out with a home of your own. You'll need it when you start a family."

"I don't know what to say, Maw," Felix said. "You won't go before the wedding, will you?"

"I have to leave in a couple of weeks, but I'll be back for the wedding. Maybe you don't know it, but David Allen is going too. He been courtin' Isabelle, and they gettin' married. So we gon' ride on the train together. Before he leave, though, he gon' set things up with the lawyers to make you the owner of this property," Elmira said.

"I guess you've got it all figured out," Felix said.

"Yes, I do," Elmira replied.

Then she grabbed him and squeezed him until he thought he might pass out.

Chapter 44

Breakfast was over, and Carrie remained at the table, sipping coffee and watching Claude sort through the previous day's mail across from her. They had argued the night before, said things that could not be taken back, and now they were sunk in a tar pit of anger from which neither knew how to escape. She was indulging in a violent revenge fantasy when Annabelle, the new housekeeper and cook, came into the dining room. "Mr. Claude," she said, "there's a Mr. Oliver Cummings here to see you. He say he sorry to break in on you so early but that it's important."

Claude did not look up or give any other indication that he had heard Annabelle. "Thank you, Annabelle," Carrie said. "Show him into the study, give him some coffee, and tell him that Mr. Claude will join him directly."

Carrie watched as Annabelle disappeared through the door into the foyer. "Well," she said. "Are you going to leave that man waiting? You could at least show some respect to a guest, even if you can't show any to your wife. Anyhow, you know why he's here, and you know you can't give him what he wants. Just go in there an act like a man and say that you have to decline his offer of the Democrats' backing to run for office. You still know how to be a man, don't you?"

"What an old shrew you've become," Claude snapped before getting up and heading off to the study.

Since the encounter with Felix that night in the Road's End barn, life with Claude had become unbearable for Carrie. He drank too much, he had grown surly, he had become indifferent to their daughters, and their romantic life had shriveled. Even now, the stench of Claude's flop sweat and his urine-soaked trousers filled her nostrils as she recalled Felix's audacity. The memory of him telling her that Claude cared more for his ambitions and the plantation than he did for her remained infuriating. Her heart pounded in her chest, and her face reddened as she struggled to purge the memory of herself agreeing to Felix's terms on her husband's behalf.

On her last visit with her parents in Huntsville, Carrie had confided in her mother, Mathilda. The older woman listened and then spoke words that at first humiliated Carrie, then angered her and finally left her feeling dead inside, a jack-o'-lantern whose twisted smile belies its hollow interior.

"I had so hoped this day would never come, sweetie, when you would have to learn that men are cruel, selfish beasts and that it is our fate to cater to them," her mother said. "They are weak and think only of themselves."

"Surely that's not true, Mother," Carrie protested. "Father isn't like that; he's good and kind, and look at the life he has given us. He loves you, he loves me, and he would never treat us as Claude treats the girls and me."

Mathilda shook her head. "You were always special to him, Carrie, a prized possession that he enjoyed showing off for the admiration of his friends and associates," she said. "So was I when I was young and we were first married, but as time passed, and as I grew older, I no longer held that appeal for him. It was miserable and humiliating, and I suffered alone to keep up appearances.

"I thought of leaving him and taking you with me, but what would that have accomplished? Women in our circle do not divorce, and our prospects on our own would have been limited. I had to think of you, and it would have been selfish to deprive you of a father and the comfort and advantages you enjoyed. So I stayed.

"Being forced into such impossible choices is wrong, but it is as things are, and a wise woman learns to make her own way. She must do what she must to survive."

Mathilda reached across the divan on which they were sitting in her sewing room to stroke the back of Carrie's hand. She stood up and walked toward the door, pausing briefly when Carrie said in a hoarse non-whisper, "But I don't know what to do, Mother. What should I do?" Mathilda did not answer and disappeared into the hallway.

Back at Road's End, Carrie winced as she reflected on the encounter with her mother, and a bitter snort escaped her lips.

"Miss Carrie, are you all right?" Annabelle had appeared at the end of the table. "Can I get you something?"

"I'm fine, Annabelle. I just had something on my mind."

———

RED CLAY, ALABAMA

AUTUMN 1881

Jim Bibb was a Black man who knew how to make money. In the Reconstruction years after the war, he had fingers in every pot of money in the county, legal and illegal, and when the fleeting freedoms that Blacks enjoyed were constricted in the Jim Crow era that followed, Jim Bibb had friends in high places and low, whose loyalty was guaranteed by the money he put into their pockets each week.

Among his enterprises were his Saturday night shindigs, big parties under a revival-style tent in the woods. He hired a band to play dance music, and there was a running craps game out back. He sat out front and collected a dollar from each customer for an evening of liquor, dancing, and food, including barbequed spareribs cooked slowly over an outdoor pit and served with sides of sweet potatoes and collard greens. He also sold fried whiting or catfish sandwiches on white bread with mustard, hot sauce, a slab of sweet onion, and dill pickle slices.

One Saturday night a month, Felix and Jimmy would leave Zilpha and Lucille at home and go to Jim Bibb's with promises that they would not stay out late, which they rarely kept. On those nights, Zilpha and Lucille would get together at one of their homes to eat supper and share the local gossip. Although they would never say so to Felix and Jimmy, they had come to appreciate the men's outings as an excuse to spend time with each other.

On one of those Saturday nights, a chilly fall evening in 1881, Lucille was putting on her coat to go home to wait for Jimmy when she looked Zilpha in the eye. "You've seemed far away all evening. Are you worried about something?" she asked.

Zilpha suddenly burst into tears and slumped down on the sofa behind her.

"Oh, honey, what's wrong?" Lucille peeled off her coat, sat down beside her friend, and draped her arm around her shoulder.

Zilpha's response was to cry harder. "I don't know," she said between sobs. "I just have this feeling that something bad is going to happen. I woke up with it, and I can't let it go. I begged Felix not to go out tonight, but he just laughed and said I was being silly."

Lucille held her friend and tried to soothe her. "It's all right, baby. It's all right," she said. "I'll stay here with you 'til Felix gets home."

At Jim Bibb's, Felix and Jimmy were having a grand time. They had eaten their fill of ribs and fish sandwiches and were playing "the dozens" with friends while knocking back round after round of whiskey. Felix was in the thick of it. He was doing well until one of the fellows lobbed a tough one his way: "Yo mama so fat, she leave grease spots on the chair every time she sit down."

Between the lateness of the hour and all the drinks he'd had, Felix was too slow with a good comeback, so the circle of spectators roared and declared his opponent the winner. "I guess you got me, man," Felix said and clapped the other fellow on the back.

"Listen, Felix. I got to take a piss," Jimmy said. "Then we need to go home. Lucille and Zilpha gon' skin us alive if we don't show up soon."

"Okay. Watch out while you're in the woods. I'll have one more little taste while I'm waiting for you here." Felix turned around to head for the bar and collided with a man who had been standing behind him. It wasn't just any man; it was Ray "Sharp" Stevens, known as Sharp because of the straight razor he carried in his pocket, honed to the finest edge he could attain. Sharp was so fast and deadly with his blade that it was said he could cut a man's throat and be a mile away before the head fell from the victim's neck. He was as vicious as a wolf, as agile as a hummingbird, and as unpredictable as a hornet. Worse, you never knew what might set Sharp off, and you didn't want to be within reach when he lost his temper.

Felix tried to head off trouble that might come his way. "Hey, Sharp, I'm sorry. I didn't mean to bump into you," he said.

"Sorry ain't good enough," Sharp snarled. "Look here at what you done to my brand-new shoes. First time I done wore 'em." He pointed to a scuff on the toe of his right shoe.

"That's not so bad. I'll tell you what. You take them over to the barbershop next week, and I'll pay for a shine," Felix said.

"Naw, man. You messed up my shoes, and you got to pay," Sharp replied and whipped out his razor. The crowd around them went quiet as Sharp started to circle Felix, swinging the blade back and forth as he moved.

"This is crazy, Sharp. I told you I'd pay for a shine," Felix said, rotating slowly to prevent Sharp from getting behind him. The crowd around them had grown, and every avenue of escape was blocked. *I could die here*, Felix thought. He pictured his body lying motionless on the floor, blood running from a gash in his neck. He saw Sharp coolly having another drink afterward while Jimmy took his body home to Zilpha.

Jim Bibb had pulled out his wooden club and was moving around the periphery of the crowd, looking for an opening to get in and stop things before they went too far. He had a good thing going with his Saturday night business, and a killing would scare customers, and worse, invite unwanted scrutiny by the law.

Felix was sweating, sober now, and remembering that Zilpha had begged him not to go out tonight. "You worry too much," he had told her. "Me and Jimmy are just lookin' to have a little fun. We'll be back early. You'll see," he had said.

Sharp was moving in closer. He could strike at any moment. Jim Bibb was pushing into the crowd, keeping his eyes on Sharp, not wanting to draw attention to himself before he was ready to swing. Out of the corner of his eye, he saw someone else advancing on a path parallel to his own. It was a big man, over six feet tall and weighing at least two hundred and fifty pounds, and he was a step ahead of Jim.

Suddenly the big man broke into the circle from behind Sharp and tapped him on the shoulder. Sharp, startled by the touch, pivoted to see who was behind him, but all he saw was a massive fist heading toward his face. The crowd heard the cartilage in Sharp's nose crumble, and they saw the blood spurt into the air. Then they heard his jawbone crack from the impact of a second blow. Sharp's head snapped back when a third punch, an uppercut, lifted him off the ground before he collapsed into a heap on the floor in front of the man who had hit him. Sharp's razor went flying, and Jim Bibb picked it up and stuck it in his pocket. No one saw him do it; they were too riveted by the display of force in front of them.

Felix was dumbfounded—and so relieved—that he might have collapsed if Jimmy hadn't rushed in to catch him. "What kind of mess you got yourself into, Felix?" Jimmy asked. "I got to get you home. Zilpha's gon' kill you—and me too. Then Lucille's gon' kill me again. I'm a dead man comin' and goin'."

Felix didn't reply. He was staring at the man who had likely saved his life, and though there was something familiar about him, he couldn't quite place him.

"How you doin', Felix?" the man said.

Felix studied the man even more.

"You don't remember me, do you?" the man said.

Felix stepped back for a better look. His rescuer had dark brown skin and was missing his left eye. A thick ropy scar ran from his forehead through his eyebrow, across the eyelid that covered the missing eye, and down onto his cheek.

"Damn!" Jimmy exclaimed. "It's Big Joe."

Felix felt as though the floor had dropped away from under his feet, and for him, the room went silent. No babble of voices, no twanging of guitars, no thumping of drums, and no thudding of dancing feet on the movable wooden dance floor Jim Bibb and his crew laid out under the tent every Saturday. Felix might have been a grown man in his twenties, but suddenly he felt like the ten-year-old boy who was facing his teenaged bully.

"It *is* you," Felix said in a raspy voice. He clenched his fists, ready for a fight.

Big Joe threw his head back and laughed. "Man, you look like you about to shit your pants. I ain't gon' do nothin' to you. Besides, you look like you growed up some since we was in them cotton fields at Road's End. And," he added, "I got older." He stuck out his hand.

The two old enemies shook hands, and Felix felt himself relax.

"Where you been all these years, Big Joe? What you been doing?" Felix asked. "Let's get us a drink and get caught up."

Big Joe, Felix, and Jimmy got whiskey refills and took them outside. By the light of the moon, Felix could see that there was a worn, tired-out look on Big Joe's face, and when he spoke, his voice seemed to echo as if emanating from deep inside a well.

"I hear y'all doin' real good," Big Joe said. "I heard both of y'all got married, got your own businesses. Folks look up to you."

"Yeah, I guess we're doing all right, but we've been here the whole time," Felix said. "When you left, didn't nobody know where you and your boys went. I bet you been all over. Did you go up North? Did you go to Chicago? Did you see New York City?"

"Yeah, I been all over," Big Joe said, "but I got to tell you, it ain't all you think it is up there."

Chapter 45

RED CLAY, ALABAMA

AUTUMN 1881

Zilpha was beside herself when Felix walked into the house at two a.m., drunk and accompanied by a big man with a hideously scarred face. She opened her mouth to shriek, but Jimmy, who had come in behind them, held up a finger to his lips to quiet her. "It's all right, Zilpha. This here is Big Joe," he said, gesturing to the big man. "Felix and me knew him back in slavery days at Road's End. He needs a place to stay tonight, and Felix said he could stay out in his shop."

Confused, Zilpha turned to Lucille, who was glaring at Jimmy. Without taking her eyes off her husband, Lucille said quietly, "I remember him from the plantation. He was mean as a snake, but you can let him stay if Jimmy says it's all right. You stay here. I know where you keep your bed things. I'll get him a blanket, and Jimmy can take him out to the shop."

"Thank you, ma'am. I'm sho nuff grateful," Big Joe said.

Zilpha acknowledged him with a nod.

Later, when Jimmy and Lucille had gone home, and Big Joe was ensconced in Felix's shop, Zilpha sat up in bed next to her sleeping husband and tried to understand what had happened. Felix had gone out against her wishes and returned drunk with a man she didn't know, offering vague assurances that he would explain everything in the morning. Zilpha was frightened—for herself, for her husband, and for the new life growing in her belly. She had planned to tell Felix about the baby on Sunday before church so they could give a prayer of thanks in the sanctuary, but that plan would have to be delayed. There were other things to discuss this Sunday morning in the daylight, when demons of darkness had flown, clearing the way for angels of light and, she hoped, the truth.

———

At Road's End, Carrie was restless too, alone in her separate bedroom that Claude rarely visited. In his estrangement, he hardly spent time with their daughters either. He had become a wraith in his own home, a spectral visitor who came and went without taking notice of the people who loved him. The couple kept up appearances, but invitations to social occasions had dwindled, and callers to the house were rare due to Claude's cranky demeanor.

"I don't know how much longer I can take it," Carrie had confided to her friend Rebecca after a recent dinner at the Riordans' home when their husbands had retired to Seth's study for cigars and cognac. "I don't know what to do, Rebecca. I could leave him, but where would I go? My parents wouldn't approve, and you and I both know that a woman with children, one who's left her husband, wouldn't have a chance getting an office job, even if I was once a stenographer, and a good one at that. And though it sounds high and mighty to say so, I'm not prepared to accept the kinds of jobs that might be offered. To tell the truth, it would be simpler if there was just some awful accident and he died."

"Well, I would be lying if I said Seth and I hadn't noticed a change," Rebecca said. "What's happening, Carrie?"

"I wish I knew. I can tell you this much, though. Claude craves the public eye. He had become quite prominent in politics before he dropped out, and not being in it is driving him crazy."

"Then why doesn't he run for office?" Rebecca asked. "He could still win if he ran."

"That's just it; he can't run. I can't tell you why, so don't ask. But he were to run, something awful would happen," Carrie said. "It would destroy him."

"It seems," Rebecca said, "that he is being destroyed anyhow and taking you down with him."

———

Seth Riordan's study was nothing like Claude's. There were no book-stuffed shelves, no elegant mahogany desk, and no richly colored and detailed Oriental rug on the floor. Instead, there were smooth white walls on which paintings of Riordan's ancestors and medieval armaments were mounted. Comfortable, well-used leather armchairs faced the fireplace, and handcrafted rag rugs defined areas on the polished wide-planked floor. A case with long guns behind glass doors above drawers that contained shooting paraphernalia dominated one end of the room, and a capacious liquor cabinet presided over the other.

Claude sat in one of the leather chairs and sipped the cognac between drags on his cigar.

"We're good friends, aren't we, Seth?" Claude asked as he watched the stream of tobacco smoke drift upward and then be pulled back down into the fire and up the chimney along with the smoke from the wood fire.

"Yes, of course."

"Then I can count on your discretion if I choose to bring up a difficult subject?"

"Of course," Seth answered. "What's on your mind?"

"This is serious, and you must promise to stop me if the discussion becomes too uncomfortable."

"Yes, yes, get on with it," Seth said. "I can't imagine anything you might say that could be so disturbing."

"All right, well here it is then," Claude said. "I'm going to kill a man."

Seth's face remained impassive. He poured Claude a fresh drink and one for himself. Then, in a voice that belied the queasiness in his gut, he asked, "Who are you going to kill?"

"Does it matter?" Claude asked. "If I do it, I'm going to hell. It's not like when those yahoos in the group do it and we stand by and watch. We go home and sleep because we know the cause is just and that we are doing God's will to protect His natural order by keeping white men in their rightful place of dominance over His creation. This is different. I have to kill this man because he stands between me and something I want."

"What's so important that you have to kill for it?" Seth asked.

"It's my life, Seth, my life. Surely you and Rebecca have seen that I'm not myself. I don't sleep. I ignore my wife and children. I'm quarrelsome with friends. I don't recognize the creature I've become."

"But what does this man have to do with all that?" Seth asked.

"Don't you see?" Claude said. "I was supposed to be somebody. I was supposed to have power and stature and not just be another backwoods planter. I was supposed to run for office and win."

Seth stiffened. "Do you think that's what I am, just 'another backwoods planter'?"

"No, no, it's not that being a planter is a bad life," Claude said. "You work hard, you're respected, and you enjoy your life. But I wanted something else. I wanted more. I'm ashamed to admit it, Seth, but I like the limelight. I wasn't always that way, but once I had a taste of it, you know, after I managed to regain Road's End, and after people started paying attention to my accomplishments—to me—I couldn't get enough.

"Then this man—he's a nigger, did I tell you that?—threatened to ruin me with something he knows if I run for office, and I can't let that happen. He's taken my dreams hostage. So you see, I have to kill him. It's the only way."

Seth took a long drink of his cognac and eyed Claude closely. His friend was perspiring, and his eyes were darting back and forth. The glass Seth had just filled for him was already empty, and he was fidgeting in his chair.

"Let me ask you again, Claude. Who do you want to kill?" Seth was speaking quietly, soothingly.

"Can't tell you," Claude murmured.

"Will you wait for me here just a moment?" Seth asked him before hurrying down the hall to the parlor, where his wife and Carrie were sitting. He was pale, and his forehead was slick and shiny with perspiration.

"What's wrong?" Rebecca asked.

Seth sat next to Carrie and took her hands in his. "Carrie, we have a problem. We have to get Claude home, and in the morning, we have to get a doctor in to see him. I believe he is in deep mental distress. He's talking crazy, about needing to kill somebody and going to hell for it. It is"—he paused, searching for the right word—"unsettling."

"I guess we won't be going to church this Sunday," Zilpha said. She was buttoning the front of her dress and preparing to go into the kitchen. "I suppose your friend will be joining us for breakfast?"

Felix was getting dressed on the other side of the bed and squinting in the bright morning sunshine streaming through the bedroom window. "You have to understand, Zilpha. Big Joe saved my life last night. I'll explain later."

Zilpha's expression was frozen. "Bring him in for breakfast," she said and left the room.

An hour later, Big Joe was looking longingly at the remains of pork sausage patties, grits, eggs scrambled with pork brains, and a platter of fresh-baked biscuits with butter and jam. "I ain't never ate better than that, Miss Zilpha," he said, pushing back from the table and patting his belly. "I'm grateful for that good food and for you lettin' me stay in Felix's shop last night."

Zilpha smiled her appreciation of the compliment.

"Look here," Felix said. "We didn't get to talk last night. Let's take some coffee out on the front porch. Zilpha, leave the dishes on the table and come out here with us. You need to know everything."

Zilpha and Felix sat together in the porch swing, facing Big Joe, who settled into a rocking chair, flanked by pots of begonias with their red and yellow blossoms glowing in the soft morning sun, swaying in the gentle breeze, infusing the air with their delicate scent.

"Back when we was still slaves, we didn't get along," Big Joe began. "The white folks had just put Felix out the big house to work in the fields. Him and Jimmy was water boys, and me and my boys didn't treat them too good."

"Didn't treat us too good?" Felix exclaimed. "They kicked my ass every day and threatened Jimmy. But we got them back. One night we slipped in their house while they were sleeping and dragged all their clothes out into the yard and burned them up. The next day the over-seer made them come to the fields and work anyhow, with blankets wrapped around them tied with a piece of rope. Everybody laughed at them, and Big Joe swore he was going to kill me."

Zilpha gasped. She had just made breakfast for a man who had threatened to kill her husband, and there he was sitting across from her with a grin on his face. Felix reached over to take her hand. "It's okay. I'm still here."

Big Joe picked up the narrative. "We ran away after that, but they caught us and beat us and dragged us back to the plantation and whipped us again. That's how I got this," he said, pointing to his scar and the empty eye socket. "I still wanted to kill Felix, and I was just waitin' for the right time."

"Obviously you didn't. What stopped you?" Zilpha asked.

"Felix wasn't but about eight years old, and his daddy and mama worked in the big house for the family, and they was protected. So I had to wait and pick my time. But somethin' happened 'fore I could do it. Somethin' made me change my mind." Big Joe paused.

"What was that? What made you change your mind?" Zilpha asked. She was on the edge of the swing seat, wringing her hands in her lap.

"One day that old overseer Massa Wilson got mad at Felix 'cause he didn't get back to work fast enough after the break. Well, a big ruckus started up, and Felix's mama come runnin' out the kitchen in the big house and got between old Wilson and Felix. Just then, Massa Claude come up there and got Wilson to back off, but they made Felix's mama whip Felix with a switch herself. She was cryin' somethin' awful, and you could tell it hurt her every time she brought that switch down on Felix."

Zilpha closed her eyes and tried to imagine Elmira facing off those two white men, risking her own life to protect her child. She laid one hand on her belly and took Felix's hand in the other, wondering, *Could I have done it? Will I love my baby like that?*

"The thing is, I ain't never had nobody stand up for me like she did for Felix," Big Joe said. "I never even knew my mama. I got took away from her when I was still a baby. I had to fight to live, and when I seen Miss Elmira fight for Felix, I couldn't think about doin' somethin' to hurt her. If I had killed Felix, it woulda killed her too."

"I remember that day as if it had been last week, and how my mother had cried. Thank you, Big Joe," Felix whispered. "Not for me, but for my maw. I guess I made my own trouble, but you're right; if anything had happened to me, it would have killed her for sure."

They sat quietly, lost in their thoughts with only the groan of the porch swing, where Felix and Zilpha sat holding hands, and the creak of Big Joe's rocking chair to break the silence.

"Say, Big Joe, you haven't told us why you came back." Felix said.

"Ain't much to tell. Like I said, up North ain't all folks think it is. Some things is better for us, but Colored folks still get the short end of the stick, and in the wintertime, it's just too cold for me. And lookin' for work, I get turned away lots of times 'cause of this." He pointed to his face. "So I figgered I'd come back down here. Sad thing is, a Colored man with scars ain't so rare around here."

Felix stood up from the porch swing and stared into the yard. "If you don't care too much about what kind of work you do, I might have an idea."

"I just need a job, Felix. I ain't partic'lar."

"I can't make a promise, but Jim Bibb, the man who owns that operation out there in the woods where we ran into you, was just telling me the other day that he might have to hire somebody to help him keep an eye on things and bust up fights and guard the money and so forth. I could talk to him if you want," Felix said.

"You would do that for me?"

"Why not? You probably saved my life last night, and I owe you."

Felix shot a look at Zilpha and said, "I know, I still have to tell you everything that happened last night," he said.

She gave a curt nod. "Well, I have something to tell you too."

"I believe I really should leave now," Big Joe said. "Thank you kindly for the place to sleep last night and that fine breakfast."

As Big Joe walked away toward the road, Felix called out to him. "Big Joe, I forgot to ask: What last name do you go by?"

Big Joe stopped and turned. "To tell the truth," he said, "I ain't had much use for one, but when I do, I use Miles 'cause I traveled so many of them, and I still got so many to go."

"See you later, Big Joe Miles," Felix called and waved as Big Joe continued down the road.

Zilpha turned to Felix. "I don't know why," she said, "but I like him."

"So do I," Felix said. "So do I."

———

Felix was thrilled by the news Zilpha shared with him. He sat down right away to write to his mother, and afterward, in his excitement, he went all around town telling anyone who would listen about his great fortune.

"Don't you think people are getting sick of hearing you talk about having a child?" Zilpha asked.

"Uh-uh," he replied, "because there's never been a child like the one we're going to have. I have to talk about it."

Elmira's reply to the announcement came in the form of two letters, one to Felix, in which she congratulated her son and sent her love, and the other to Zilpha, in which she told her daughter-in-law to remind Felix about the fate of a certain rooster at Road's End.

"What does she mean about a rooster, Felix?" she asked. And when he explained about the old rooster on the plantation that wouldn't stop crowing and ended up in the stewpot, she laughed.

"Your mama was right. You'd better watch out," Zilpha said.

"Nobody's going to put me in a pot," Felix declared. "Besides, I'm too tough—and too good-looking."

"All right, Mr. Good-Looking," she replied with a snicker. "Still, you'd better watch your mouth."

"Say, Zilpha, I was thinking about going out to Jim Bibb's place Saturday night with Jimmy. You wouldn't mind, would you?" Felix said.

The smile on Zilpha's face faded. "You remember what happened the last time you went out there? You nearly got killed, and now that we're going to have a family, you have to be careful."

"You worry too much, Zilpha. Jimmy and me can look out for each other, and Big Joe's working out there now. It's safe as a church picnic."

Chapter 46

RED CLAY, ALABAMA

AUTUMN 1881

Ray "Sharp" Stevens shoved his hands deep into the pockets of his overcoat and pulled his hat down to keep the wind from blowing it off. Although it was a late September evening, it felt like December, and ever since his jaw had been broken in that fight at Jim Bibb's place, Sharp felt the cold more intensely, like a dull toothache that wouldn't go away. *My jaw ain't never gon' be right again*, he thought. He watched his breath form a cloud in front of his face, and he strained to see through the trees at the end of the Road's End driveway, looking for a sign of the man he was supposed to meet.

That afternoon, Sharp had been shooting craps behind the feed-store when a small Black boy, about eight years old, came up to him and whispered that Claude Parker wanted to see him that evening and that he would be paid for his time. "He say come by yourself, and don't let nobody see you," the boy had said.

Sharp knew who Claude Parker was; few Red Clay residents didn't, Black or white. But Sharp had never met Parker, and he wondered why he had been summoned to the plantation. *What he want from me? I ain't got nothin' he needs.* He had almost decided to leave—*Don't no good ever come from gettin' too involved with white folks*—when he saw the light from a lantern moving down the driveway toward him, and he stiffened there until the man carrying the lantern was standing in front of him.

"I'm glad you decided to accept my invitation, Sharp. My name is Claude Parker, and I believe we can do some business together."

The two men faced each other warily. Sharp was still trying to decide whether this meeting had been a good idea. In the tree branches overhead, a black rat snake followed the movements of the men below while lying still and digesting a field mouse it had swallowed whole that afternoon.

"Well, I'm here, like you asked," Sharp said.

Claude started to move again, circling Sharp until he was again facing him. "Am I correct that there is no love lost between you and Felix Parker, and that you were going to kill him at Jim Bibb's tent party in the woods until that big fellow stepped in and broke your jaw?" Claude asked.

"What you know about that?" Sharp asked, growing more uneasy by the minute.

"I know lots of things," Claude replied, "but I want you to tell me if it is true."

"What if it is?" Sharp said.

"If it is, and if you think you can do what I need to have done, you stand to make some good money," Claude said. "If it's not, then we will go our separate ways. I will pay you something for your trouble this evening, and we will never speak of this again."

Sharp was silent, weighing Claude's words. He saw something disturbing in Claude's demeanor, and he sensed danger. "How much money we talkin' about?" he asked.

Claude reached into his pocket and pulled out a wad of cash. "Half now, and half when our venture has been completed." He fanned the bills out so Sharp could see how much he was holding.

"Shee-it," Sharp gasped at the sight of the cash, more than he had ever seen in one place. "What you said," he hissed, "it's true. It's all true."

"Good," Claude said. "Now let's talk about what needs to be done."

In the big house, Carrie sat at the dining table alone, staring straight ahead and seeing nothing. The children had already been put to bed after their supper earlier, and the table had been cleared of dishes from the meal she had shared in silence with Claude.

"Lawd, she is just about the saddest woman I ever did see," Annabelle, the housekeeper and cook, had said of Carrie while gossiping with a friend and fellow domestic worker after choir practice the previous night. "She got everything you could want, and she still mope around that house like it her last day on Earth. I don't think she got no friends except that Rebecca Riordan from the plantation down the way. Seem like all the others just fell away."

As Carrie sat at the table, the churning in her gut quieted, the storm in her mind subsided, and she felt peace envelop her for the first time in months. She had made a decision, and there was no turning back. *God help me*, she prayed, but in her heart she knew that the course on which she was about to embark placed her beyond all hope of redemption.

Chapter 47

RED CLAY, ALABAMA

AUTUMN 1881

A week had passed since Sharp agreed to kill Felix. He had taken Claude's money greedily, but he'd had some second thoughts. *One thing to kill a man that done you wrong, but to do it just for money, I don't know,* he thought. *I was mad at Felix when he stepped on my shoe, but I was just gon' cut him. Don't know about killin' him for money.* Still, he had taken the cash, and there was more to come if he did the deed.

"What if I don't do it?" Sharp had asked Claude.

"I will, of course, expect you to return the money you have taken," Claude had said.

"If I keep it?" Sharp had replied.

Claude stared hard at Sharp, and the craziness Sharp had sensed in Claude seemed to intensify. "Look how easily you agreed to kill Felix for money," Claude said. "I think I could just as easily pay someone else to do a different killing, don't you think?"

The implied threat was resonating in Sharp's head as he slouched in a chair pushed into a dark corner of Jim Bibb's Saturday night tent, sipping whiskey and barely nodding whenever anyone acknowledged his presence. It was the second Saturday night of the month. That was when Felix and his friend Jimmy usually came to Jim Bibb's place, and Sharp figured it to be the best time to get the job done. *I got to find a way to get Felix off by hisself, so won't nobody see me do it. Plus, I got to get clear of that big one-eyed ass-licker what broke my jaw. Damn Jim Bibb for puttin' him on the door.*

Soon enough, Felix and Jimmy arrived and began making their way through the crowd, stopping to greet friends on their way to get drinks, laughing and talking all the way. *What make them so special?* Sharp wondered, and his resentment of Felix's popularity began to overtake his misgivings.

A couple of hours into the evening, Felix started heading to the front of the tent. *Good*, Sharp thought. *Probably goin' to take a piss. This here's my chance.* Sharp began to move, mirroring Felix's movements, trying to avoid drawing any attention to himself. Just as Felix left the tent to head for the woods, Sharp felt someone grab his right arm and someone else grab his left one.

"Where you goin', Sharp?" a voice asked from over his right shoulder. "Look to me like you up to no good." It was Big Joe.

From over his left shoulder came the voice of Jimmy Flowers. "Yeah, look that way to me too."

"What's wrong with y'all? I ain't done nothin'," Sharp protested.

"That's right," Big Joe said." You ain't done nothin' yet, and I aim to keep it that way. I had my eye on you all night, and I seen how you was watchin' Felix. Funny the way you been drinkin' in one spot all night, then all of a sudden you start movin' when Felix start to move."

"That don't mean nothin'. I was just goin' to get one more drink and go home early," Sharp muttered.

"That sound like a good idea," Jimmy said and tightened his grip on Sharp's arm, using muscles strengthened by years of hammering hot metal at his forge. "Let's go get us another drink together, and then you can go home."

They were steering Sharp to the bar, three broad planks laid across sawhorses, when Felix arrived.

"Hey, what's going on?" he asked.

"Sharp was goin' to buy us a drink and then go home, 'cause he ain't feelin' too good. You want one too? Sharp is buyin'," Jimmy said.

Felix looked at Jimmy and then at Big Joe and a grin split his face. "Yeah, I'll have one," he said and clapped Sharp on the back. "Thanks, Sharp. That's mighty nice of you, especially since we had that misunderstanding a while back."

———

ROAD'S END PLANTATION

AUTUMN 1881

Carrie had fretted all morning about what she was committed to doing, but after another meal in which Claude kept mumbling about "getting free of that nigger," she knew there was no going back. It was hard because Claude had long stretches of lucidity in which he seemed normal, like the man with whom she had fallen in love and conceived two children. Ever since the night Felix had humiliated Claude and extracted that promise, however, something had broken in her husband. Now, the shards of that shattered vessel threatened to rip apart her life and those of her children as well.

Carrie was nothing if not methodical about the course she had chosen. She had arranged for her daughters to stay with her mother in Huntsville for a week and asked Annabelle to lay out a cold midday meal. She gave her the rest of the day off and mentioned that she was planning to go riding. The stage was set.

From across the table, Claude glanced up at Carrie, blinking as if seeing her for the first time that day. "You going somewhere?" he asked, having noticed that she was wearing her riding habit.

"Yes, don't you remember? I told you that I was going riding today."

"Oh, yeah," Claude replied, and his eyes clouded over again.

"You don't mind, do you? I planned to go today, because you said you would be here all day, and I thought it would be a good time for me to do it."

"That's fine," Claude muttered. "You go ahead and have a good time."

"Now I feel bad. I'll tell you what. Why don't you go out on the front porch and get comfortable in that chair you like, and I'll bring you a cigar and the cognac decanter. Who cares if it's still afternoon? You should enjoy yourself, and when I come home, I'll make a good supper for us. I don't cook often, and I'll enjoy it. We'll have a nice evening to ourselves."

"Sounds good," Claude said and headed for the front door.

Carrie went into the study and closed the door behind her before withdrawing a small bottle from her handbag. She retrieved Claude's pocket flask from the liquor cabinet and poured several drops of the clear liquid from the bottle into it. She topped off the flask with cognac from the decanter. Then she poured more of the clear liquid into a snifter and added a generous portion of the cognac. Carrie arranged the drink, the decanter, an empty snifter, the flask, an ashtray, and Claude's cigar box on a silver tray.

On the porch, Claude was settling into his favorite chair when Carrie returned with the tray. "I have an idea, Claude," she said. "Why don't you come for a ride with me? We'll have a drink here together and then go. Look, I've filled your pocket flask so you can take it with you."

"That's a wonderful idea, Carrie. Thank you for asking me," Claude said.

She poured a drink for herself, and they clinked their glasses before taking a sip.

They relaxed in the afternoon sun, watching bees buzz around late flowers while Claude puffed his cigar and downed his drink. "I guess this is one of the last warm afternoons we'll have before the season changes," he said. "I'm glad we're spending it this way."

"Yes, dear. Let's go for our ride now." Carrie could see that the sedative she had poured into his first drink was already working. Claude was slurring his words, and he was having trouble keeping his eyes open. "I'll go saddle the horses and bring them around front. You take it easy here," she said. "I'll be back in a few minutes."

By the time she returned, Claude was woozy, and Carrie had to help him mount Zeus. "I don't know if I should go with you, Carrie. I'm really tired," he mumbled after he was situated in the saddle.

"Nonsense," she replied. "The ride and the fresh air will do you good. We won't go far. We'll be back before you know it, and you can have a nap while I make supper. Have a sip from your flask. It'll perk you up."

They rode for about twenty minutes, keeping the horses at a walk as they left Road's End and headed down the road toward the Riordans' plantation, paralleling the creek that separated the two properties. They were approaching a bend where a narrow wooden bridge spanned a ravine with water twenty feet below. Claude was wobbling precariously in the saddle.

"Claude?" Carrie called out. "Claude, do you hear me?"

He swiveled his head to gape at her, slack-jawed, through glazed-over eyes. A trail of drool ran from the corner of his mouth.

Carrie kicked her horse's flanks, urging it to a gallop. As she hoped, Zeus, always eager to run, followed suit, pitching Claude head over heels to the ground, where he lay in a motionless heap. Zeus whinnied and returned to Claude, where he stood snorting and pawing the ground as Carrie reined in her horse and turned to rejoin them.

She dismounted, turned Claude over to feel for a pulse, and found none. Looking around to make sure she was alone, Carrie felt inside Claude's jacket for the flask, spilled some of the contents into his mouth and onto his shirt, and poured the rest out in the roadside weeds. Then she returned the flask to his pocket. Checking once more to be sure she was alone, she shoved his body over the side of the ravine and watched it crash through brush and bounce off rocks until it came to rest at the bottom, with his head and shoulders submerged in the water.

———

The Reverend Jason McHenry, pastor of First Baptist Church, was always fidgeting with his shirt cuffs, pulling them down to hide knobby wrists at the ends of his long arms. In this Alabama town, the pastor's thin, pale face, scraggly black hair, and short beard led his fellow southerners to derisively call him Abe behind his back. Indeed, he bore a striking physical resemblance to the late president, though he shared none of Lincoln's intellect or grace. When he arrived at Road's End the morning after Claude's death, a haggard, red-eyed Carrie greeted him at the front door.

She led him into the parlor, where Annabelle served them coffee and cookies, which the pastor devoured between noisy slurps of coffee.

When the plate was empty, he wiped his mouth with his napkin and gazed mournfully at the crumbs.

"Would you like to talk, Mrs. Parker? If you like, we might pray together," he offered. It was already after eleven a.m., and the ride out to Road's End had been hot and dusty. If he stayed a bit longer, he thought, she might ask him to stay for a meal. *A bit of ham, some fresh bread, and perhaps some more of those delicious cookies would be perfect. Maybe a glass of cold buttermilk to wash it down.*

He was imagining such a repast when Carrie spoke. "It was awful. As I told the sheriff last night, the children are away, and I gave Annabelle the afternoon off so that Claude and I might have some quiet time together. We decided to have a drink on the porch to enjoy the fine weather. We were sitting there, and Claude suddenly got the idea to go for a ride with me. I was reluctant because Claude had drunk quite a bit, but he was determined to go. So I finally agreed, and I saddled the horses while he sat on the porch and had another drink.

"It was all right at first. He was steady in the saddle, but he kept drinking from that flask of his. He was laughing and having a good time. I hadn't seen him that way in a long while, and I was enjoying it. I'm sure you've noticed that he hasn't been himself for some time."

The pastor started to object, but Carrie held up her hand. "It's fine," she said. "You don't have to pretend you haven't noticed. It's been obvious."

Reverend McHenry closed his mouth and dropped his eyes.

"We were riding along slowly," Carrie continued, "and I noticed that Claude wasn't so steady anymore. His voice was shaky, and his eyes seemed unfocused. I said, 'Let's go home; we've ridden far enough,' but he wasn't listening. I kept after him, though, and he finally agreed. He said, 'I'll race you to the bridge, and then we'll go back.'

"Before I could say anything, he took off, and I followed. We rounded the turn, and the bridge was coming up. Claude was far ahead, and it appeared that he was starting to slow down. But Zeus stopped suddenly—I don't know why—and Claude went flying into the ravine. I scrambled down there, but it was too late. He was gone."

"Oh, my dear," the pastor said. "This is surely so upsetting for you.

This is a tragic loss, but I hope you know that we at First Baptist will rally to your side. We will be there for anything you might need."

"Thank you, Reverend. It is a comfort to know that. Everyone has been so kind. I was especially grateful to the sheriff, who personally handled the investigation and had the death declared a tragic accident, which it so obviously was, to spare us further grief. However, I'm not worried for myself, I'm concerned for the girls," Carrie said. "I intend to join them in Huntsville and stay there with them and with my mother for a while. We'll come back for the funeral, but I think we need to be away from here for now."

"That sounds like a good plan, my dear," the pastor said. "I'll take my leave for now, but you must promise to send for me if I can help in any way." He stood up and hovered, but an invitation to stay for lunch did not come, so he began walking toward the door.

"Thank you again, Reverend," Carrie said.

Once they were outside, the pastor looked up and squinted into the sun. "I guess if I hurry, I can make it home in time to eat with Mrs. McHenry. Of course, she does like to eat early, and there's likely to be just some leftovers," he mused aloud. When Carrie said nothing, he climbed into his buggy. His shoulders seemed to sag a bit, and he glanced up as a kettle of vultures circled high overhead.

"Reverend," Carrie called out. The pastor looked back hopefully. "Do you think the Lord really is a forgiving God?"

He allowed a beat to pass before responding, as if trying to grasp something unsaid in her question. "I believe the Lord is all-knowing," the pastor said, "and that He appreciates the content of all His children's hearts. In the end, His judgments are always right."

Chapter 48

PARIS, FRANCE

AUTUMN 1881

Even Paris was quiet at four a.m., and dark despite the new electric streetlights installed along the major thoroughfares for the 1881 Exposition Internationale d'Électricité, which had opened two days earlier in the Palais de l'Industrie on the Champs-Élysées. Addie paced in the sitting room of her hotel suite, unable to sleep. A white silk dressing gown clung to her body, damp with perspiration, and the scent of sex still filled her nostrils. She could hear the steady breathing of Étienne Dupuis, asleep in her bed in the next room. She had been in Paris less than a week, the first time since her departure two years earlier, and the chemistry between them was as strong as it had been before she left.

Addie had written to Étienne before her arrival, promising to explain her mysterious exit and expressing her hope that he would see her. His reply had been noncommittal, but she had booked passage anyway and sought him out at the university as soon as she was settled in her hotel. Would he meet her the next evening for dinner at the restaurant that had been their favorite? "I shall be there at eight o'clock, and I hope I will have the pleasure of your company," she wrote in the note she left for him.

He was already seated at one of the tiny bistro's ten tables when Addie arrived, perusing the fine wine list and the menu, which changed daily depending upon the market and the mood of the *chef de cuisine*, a cranky fifty-year-old bag of bones who smelled of garlic, olive oil, and sweat. His wife, a portly woman with a big smile, gray hair that had once been blond, and sharp hazel eyes that missed nothing, showed Addie to the table.

Étienne stood when she came through the door and held her chair as she sat. He ordered their favorite house red wine, and they touched glasses before taking a sip. "Madame says the *poulet rôti* is excellent tonight," Étienne said.

"I'm sure the chicken will be fine," she murmured, and then there was silence again. "Oh, Étienne," she began. "I have so much to tell you, but it's hard, and I am afraid that you will send me away when I have told you my story."

He raised a finger to his lips to silence her. "There is nothing you could say that would make me send you away. It is more likely that you will wish me to leave when I tell you of my situation."

"Of course I won't—" Addie started to say, but she stopped when Étienne raised his finger again.

"Addie, I am married, and I have a daughter," he said.

Addie felt blood rush to her head and her skin turn hot. Dizzy, she slumped back in her chair and might have fallen to the floor if Madame, watching the couple with curiosity, had not rushed to her side. "I will bring a wet towel. Does Mademoiselle need to lie down?"

"*Merci beaucoup*, Madame, but I shall be all right. Thank you for your assistance," Addie said.

"I am so sorry, Addie. I should have realized that this news would be a shock," said Étienne.

Addie regained her composure, and after taking a sip of wine, she asked, "What is your wife's name, and how did you meet? And what about your daughter? What do you call her?"

"When you disappeared, I thought that I would never see you again," he said. "So one evening while I was in Ste. Maxime visiting my parents,

I happened to run into a girl I had known many years ago, a girl with whom I had gone to school. Well, one thing led to another, and Jeannette, that's her name, became pregnant. We were married, and then the baby came."

Addie saw his face light up when he mentioned his daughter. "Tell me about her," she said.

"She is a year old and the most wonderful thing in the world," he said. "She is so beautiful and so smart. She is everything to me." He paused, and then he added, nearly in a whisper, "Her name is Adélaïde. That is the name of my wife's mother, but it has a different meaning to me."

"Where are they tonight?" Addie asked.

"They are in Ste. Maxime with Jeannette's family for a month," Étienne said.

Addie was silent, thinking, wrestling with an idea. "Do you love Jeannette?" she asked.

"I care for her. She is my wife and the mother of Adélaïde, and I will always support her and protect her," he said.

"In New Orleans, where I live, many people believe in ghosts and other spirits," Addie said. "This is not always a frightening thing. Benevolent spirits can come to the living to comfort them in times of sorrow, or be present to share in happy occasions. Sometimes they intervene to protect loved ones from harm. I have always liked this idea." Addie smiled. "It is a pleasant notion to me. What do you think?"

"I think it could be very nice, I suppose." Étienne searched her face for clues to what she really had in mind.

"Do you think you could see me as a spirit, Étienne? Do you think you could see me as a presence who comes to you to share happiness and then goes away when the moment is over?"

"I'm not sure of what you mean," he replied.

At that moment the roasted chicken arrived, hot and fragrant, drizzled with pan juices and flanked on one side by *pommes frites*, salty and crisp on the outside and creamy inside. Sweet roasted carrots rested on the other side of the platter. Madame refilled the decanter with the good *maison vin rouge*. "Bon appétit," she said and smiled broadly as she left the table.

"I will be in Paris for three weeks, Étienne," Addie said softly. "If you wish to know what it is like to be visited by a spirit who goes away when the moment has passed, you will come to my rooms with me tonight after this wonderful dinner. By the time Jeannette and Adélaïde return from Ste. Maxime, the moment will have passed, and only you and the spirit will know what they have shared."

In the dark of the Paris night, ensconced in her hotel suite with her lover sleeping in the next room, Addie knew an unexpected peace. Étienne had not asked why she had left him abruptly, and neither did he question why she had returned. He cared only that she was there and that when she left this time, she would return, again and again. It was the way of spirits, mysterious by nature and all-embracing of those they love.

———

A letter from the Red Clay law firm of Campbell, Stewart & MacPherson was waiting for Addie when she arrived home in New Orleans a few weeks later:

Dear Miss Parker:

We regret to inform you of the death of your brother, Mr. Claude Parker. Details concerning his death are enclosed as separate documents. As his sister, you are named in his will as a beneficiary of his estate. Details of the bequest are also enclosed . . .

Addie turned the letter face down on the desk in her parlor, stunned and unsure of what she felt. Her last encounter with Claude had been so angry, and she had left Road's End expecting never to see him again. Still, the finality of death had not been the way she had envisioned their permanent estrangement.

Through the window that faced the courtyard of her French Quarter home, she watched two hummingbirds battle over the blossoms in her flower gardens. They were small, but the birds' fight was titanic, and neither was willing to yield.

Addie read the document that informed her of the coroner's judgment of accidental death. Then she read the summary of the will. Claude's widow and children were the principal beneficiaries, along with small cash gifts to the church and to the school his daughters attended. To Addie, Claude had left a ten-acre plot of land along the creek at Road's End that had been passed down from their grandfather to their father and finally to him through their late mother. *My sister will know of my attachment to this parcel, but the land is hers to dispose of as she wishes*, the summary said.

Addie walked out of the room in search of Isabelle, whom she found in a back room, folding laundry. "Isabelle, please pack a bag for me," she said. "I am going to Red Clay." Then she walked to her bedroom, collapsed on the bed fully dressed and wept.

Seated at a long conference table in the book-lined library of the offices of Campbell, Stewart & MacPherson, the firm from which her father, her mother, and her brother had all sought legal counsel, Addie sipped tea and waited for the arrival of Robert MacPherson, the senior partner. As had her mother and her brother before her, she imagined how comfortable her father would have been here. The books, the dark paneling, and the heavy drapes on tall windows reflected his sensibility, and Addie fancied that she might be sitting in the same chair John Robert had once occupied.

"Miss Parker? I am sorry not to have been here when you arrived." The voice came from over her shoulder, a rich baritone, the accent shaped by a lifetime spent in the North.

Addie stood and faced Robert MacPherson. He was not as she had imagined him. As a petite woman, she rarely met men with whom she could speak without craning her neck to look up into their faces. In MacPherson's case, her eyes met his on the same level. He was in his midsixties and thick in the middle. His scalp shone through thinning gray-blond hair. He reached out to take Addie's extended hand and shook it gently before gesturing for her to take her seat.

"I have been well taken care of, Mr. MacPherson, and I appreciate the time you are giving me," Addie said.

"We could do no less," MacPherson said. "The Parker family and our firm have been associated for many years, and we are glad to be of assistance, even though this meeting is in the wake of your brother's tragic death."

"Did you know my brother, Mr. MacPherson?" Addie asked.

"I did not," he replied. "At the time of his death, I had just moved temporarily to Red Clay, and we had not met." MacPherson explained that he had headed the Philadelphia office until recently, and that the death of Angus Campbell, just six months after the passing of Andrew Stewart, had left him as the last of the named partners.

"I've come down here to oversee the restructuring of our firm and to eventually relocate the head office to Philadelphia. I knew your father, however. We were at school together at Princeton, and his untimely death was a great blow to me," he said. "We were good friends, and perhaps you know that I helped to set up the financial arrangements that I trust enabled your family to survive the economic turmoil at the end of the war."

"Yes," Addie replied, "and one of the reasons I am here is because I knew of the confidence my father had in you, and I hope that I may rely upon you as well. What I wish to do is an extension of my father's wishes, but it will require your expertise and your discretion."

"I am at your service, Miss Parker," he said.

Addie spent the next twenty minutes outlining her plan, and when she was done, MacPherson removed his glasses and squeezed the bridge of his nose between a thumb and forefinger. "I believe we can accomplish what you seek to achieve," he said as he replaced his glasses. "Would Thursday, three days from now, be acceptable?"

"Perfect," Addie said. "If this goes as planned, I can be on a train back to New Orleans by Friday."

The next afternoon, Felix was in his shop behind his home when a messenger arrived with a sealed envelope from the offices of Campbell, Stewart & MacPherson. "They say you supposed to open it right away and say 'yes' or 'no' to me," the messenger said. He was a small Black boy, perhaps seven or eight years old. *I was around his age when Massa John Robert shot himself in the wagon*, Felix thought as he opened the envelope.

> *Dear Felix Parker:*
>
> *We are writing to you at the request of Miss Adelaide Parker, with whom you are acquainted. Miss Parker wishes to meet with you at our offices tomorrow evening at 6:30 regarding the settlement of her late brother's estate. It is important that you attend this meeting. Please let the boy who delivered this note know if you will attend.*

Felix studied the note, which was signed by Robert MacPherson, for a long while before saying to the boy, "Tell them I said yes. I will be there."

———

Addie had hired a buggy and driver for her stay in Red Clay, and at the moment the note was being delivered to Felix, she was being driven away from Road's End, where she had met with Claude's widow.

"I am sorry to have arrived unannounced this way, but I am afraid that Claude's death has robbed me of my usual sense of decorum," she said when Carrie entered the parlor where Annabelle had seated her.

"I don't know why you have come here," Carrie said. She remained standing, with her arms folded beneath her breasts. "You are not wanted here, and I hope that whatever business you think you have with me can be resolved quickly so that you can be on your way."

Addie gave no outward sign that Carrie's rudeness affected her. "I have come here, Carrie, to ask about your intentions for Road's End now that Claude is gone."

"My intentions? My intentions are none of your business, but if you must know, I intend to sell the plantation and move to Huntsville, near my mother. I will be glad to be away from here, and it will be good for the girls to grow up near their grandmother."

"How are the girls, Carrie? I am their aunt, after all, and I would enjoy seeing them," Addie said.

"They are fine, or at least as fine as they can be without their father, no thanks to you," she replied.

"What do you mean?"

"I know about you and your bastard Colored baby. Felix was holding it over Claude's head, keeping Claude from fulfilling his destiny." Carrie's voice was shaking, and her face was flushed. "That's why he became un-balanced and why he drank so much. That's why your nieces will grow up without their father. Annabelle will see you out." She dropped her arms to her sides and stormed out of the room.

"Thank you, but I know this house well, and I don't need to be shown the door," Addie said when Annabelle appeared seconds later.

"Yes, ma'am, I know that," Annabelle said. She looked around to be sure they were alone, and then she closed the door. "Miss Addie, I want you to know something, and I wouldn't be telling you this if it wasn't important. Besides, I'm 'bout to be out of a job, and I'm movin' up North to get a job where my sister works. Now Mr. Claude, he wasn't no friend to Colored folks, but he always treated me fair, and I think it ain't right for Miss Carrie to put it all off on you.

"The thing is, Mr. Claude wasn't right in the head for a long time, and one time I heard Miss Carrie and her friend Miss Rebecca talkin' about how it would be a blessing if somethin' was to happen to Mr. Claude."

"What are you saying, Annabelle?" Addie asked in a hushed voice.

"I ain't sayin' nothin', 'cept the day Mr. Claude died, Miss Carrie give me the afternoon off, but I forgot my shawl 'cause it was such a nice warm day, and I come back to get it. I come in the house through the kitchen, and I was gon' let Miss Carrie know I was there, so I went into the parlor. The windows was open, and I heard her and Mr. Claude talkin' out front.

"I was gon' go out there, but I looked through the window first, and

I seen Miss Carrie helpin' him get on his horse. He wasn't in no shape to be goin' nowhere; he looked like he was 'bout to pass out. He tol' her he didn't feel good and didn't want to go, but she made him get on that horse anyhow. 'Jus' have another drink,' she say. I figured it wasn't none of my business, and I just went back out through the kitchen."

"Annabelle, have you told anybody else about this?" Addie whispered.

"No, ma'am, I ain't, and if anybody else was to ask, I'd tell them I had the afternoon off and didn't see nothin'," she said.

"Thank you, Annabelle," Addie said. "I think it is better for all, especially my nieces, if we leave things the way they are."

———

Felix was invited to have a seat after he was shown into Campbell, Stewart & MacPherson's library, but the legacy of slavery, the tensions created by the backlash against Reconstruction, and the encroachment of Jim Crow had left their marks on him. In this white-folks' domain, he couldn't relax until he knew more about what was happening. He paced until the door opened and Addie rushed in.

"Felix, I'm glad to see you," she said and extended her hand. He took it awkwardly and replied that he was glad to see her too.

"Felix, we have a few minutes before Mr. MacPherson joins us, and we get to the business of this meeting, so before he arrives, I want to tell you something," she said. "I appreciated your letter informing me that you had to use my secret, but I would like to know more about what happened to push you to that point."

Felix hesitated before responding. "Do you really want to know?"

"I do," she said. "It's important."

"All right," he said, and in hushed tones he told her about the way Claude had objected to their departure from Road's End, about his father's murder, and finally about the confrontation in the stable with Claude and Carrie. Addie reacted with expressions that may have been resignation or regret, it was hard to tell.

"I'm sorry I had to do that, but I had to protect my family," Felix said, "and I didn't have any choice."

"I understand, Felix. Thank you for being honest with me," Addie said.

A few minutes later, MacPherson entered the room. He studied both of their faces before placing a stack of papers on the table. "Mr. Parker," he said, "I understand that you are familiar with the ten-acre plot on the edge of the Road's End plantation, a parcel of land that was to have been signed over to your late father as the wish of the late John Robert Parker and subsequently as the wish of his widow."

Felix nodded, momentarily taken aback by the fact that MacPherson had addressed him as "Mr. Parker." It was the first time he had ever been addressed that way by a white man.

"Miss Adelaide Parker is aware of the history of this parcel, which she has inherited from the estate of the recently deceased Claude Parker, and she wishes to carry out the spirit of her father's request," MacPherson continued. "Mr. Parker, have you ever heard of the American Missionary Association?"

Felix shook his head. "No, sir."

"It is a group affiliated with the Congregationalist Church, which believes Colored people should have access to good education. The AMA is involved in starting schools across the South," MacPherson said. "Miss Parker proposes that the land be signed over to you with the understanding that you will donate it as the site of a new school for Colored children, developed by the AMA. A stipulation would be that the new school would be named the Plessant Parker Academy. I have exchanged telegrams with the AMA, and they are interested in pursuing this possibility."

Addie was watching Felix's face for his reaction to the proposal. "What do you think?" she asked.

"This is a lot for me to take in all at once," Felix said, "but I can tell you that my paw would sure enough be proud to have his name on a school."

"Good," Addie said. "I have to return to New Orleans tomorrow morning, but Mr. MacPherson assures me that we can complete the paperwork to assign ownership of the property to you before I leave. I have arranged for his firm to work with you to ensure that this project is completed."

"Thank you," Felix said.

"No, thank *you*," Addie said. "You know, when I was last in Red Clay, I thought it would be the last time I ever set foot here. I'm glad I had a chance to come once more. Many wrongs have been set right."

On Friday, when Addie boarded the train for New Orleans, there was only one other passenger who felt as happy and relieved to be departing as she. In a different car, Ray "Sharp" Stevens settled into his seat and adjusted the creases in his new trousers.

"Hey," he said to the man seated next to him. "Is it true what they say about New Orleans, that a man with a little cash in his pocket can have a mighty good time there?"

"Ain't nowhere else like it," the man said.

"Good," Sharp said. "Then I reckon I'll like it just fine." He patted his pocket to be sure his cash windfall from Claude was still there and scrunched down in his seat for a nap.

Chapter 49

RED CLAY, ALABAMA

SUMMER 1882

Albert Moore and his wife, Esther, sat quietly in their Third Baptist Church pew, second row, stage right of the altar, listening to the pianist playing devotional music as worshippers arrived. Next to them were their sons, Samuel and Walter, and the young men's wives and children—a daughter for Samuel and his wife, and two sons for Walter and his wife. The Moores were always among the first to arrive on Sunday mornings because Albert thought it his duty as a church elder to be on time as an example for others. Also, as one of the most prosperous congregants, he thought it vulgar to appear at the last minute and parade down the aisle with his family.

Albert checked the time on one of his most prized possessions, a gold Patek Philippe pocket watch. Eight minutes before the service was to begin, there was still no sign of Zilpha, her husband, and their new baby girl. The pianist was banging out the final chords of the last devotional hymn when the Parkers made their entrance, Felix in an exquisitely fitted frock coat, proudly carrying infant Mary, alongside Zilpha, who was wearing a forest green silk outfit that was sure to be the envy of all the other ladies that morning. They swept down the aisle and settled into seats across from the Moores, just as Pastor Ezekiel Jones stepped up to the podium. *About time*, Albert thought, annoyed by the timing and the high profile of their arrival. *Still*, he conceded as he nodded to them, *that boy has turned into a good provider, Zilpha seems happy, and they've delivered another grandchild for Esther and me.*

"I have an announcement to make before we begin," Pastor Jones said. "I would like to meet with all the elders downstairs immediately after the service. We have some important business to attend to, and I promise that it won't take too long."

When the service was over, Esther Moore cooed over her newest grandchild and carried her around the churchyard to show her off to all her friends with Zilpha trailing in her wake.

Meanwhile, the pastor closed the door to the meeting room in the church basement, where the elders, Red Clay's most prominent Black citizens, had gathered. "Gentlemen, we have received some disturbing news," Pastor Jackson said. "A white man who is a friend to our community has informed me that night riders are planning a raid next Sunday night. They plan to burn down the school that is being built in honor of our late Brother Plessant Parker, on land donated by his son, Felix."

There was stunned silence in the room.

"Has anyone told Felix?" Albert Moore asked. "I think he has a right to know and to be part of this discussion."

"No," the pastor said. "I just got word myself this morning before the service, but you are right. He should be told."

"I'll get him and bring him down here now," Albert Moore said.

The men all began to speak at once, and they quickly divided into two camps: baker Aaron Smith and farmer Thomas Jackson argued that they should stay out of it. After all, they contended, the school's construction and eventual operation was under the auspices of the Congregationalist Church and therefore no concern of theirs. Representing the other camp were barber Jesse Arnold and physician William Jefferson, who argued that they had a moral obligation to act on behalf of the Black community at large, especially since the school would be open to all children from the Black community, regardless of where they attended services. And besides, they said, it was to be named for Plessant, who had been one of their own.

They were still at it when Felix and Albert entered the room, unnoticed. They listened without interrupting until Felix slammed the door that had been left ajar, strode to the table where the men were seated, and hammered the tabletop with his fist.

"I don't care what you are going to do or not do," he said in a low quavering voice, "but I am not going to let them get away with it. They murdered my paw, and I will not stand by and let them kill his memorial too." Then he stormed out of the room ahead of a chorus of "We're sorry," "We didn't mean we wouldn't do anything," and "Come back; let's talk about this."

That evening, after Sunday supper dishes had been washed and put away, after children had been put to bed, and after husbands and wives were quiet together in the peace of another sunset, Felix, Jimmy, and Big Joe were hatching a plan in Felix's workshop in the low light of a kerosene lamp.

"You really think this can work?" Big Joe asked.

"I know it can work, if you and Jimmy do your part. It has to because, one way or another, I will stop them from destroying my paw's legacy."

The moon was a sickle in the night sky over the Plessant Parker Academy construction site, barely lighting the way for nine robed and hooded figures as they walked single file through the darkness, spectral figures on a mission. They let themselves into the fenced-in campus through the unlocked gate and methodically began to assemble a pile of scrap construction wood, twigs, and fallen tree branches in an open area between the recently completed red brick classroom building and the auditorium, which was still under construction. The foundation for a third building to house administrative offices and some additional classrooms had been dug.

One of the robed figures came forward with a five-gallon kerosene can while another produced torches and handed them around. They were soaking the rag-wrapped tips of their torches in the kerosene when they heard a voice from behind them.

"Good evening, gentlemen. I hope I'm not intruding on your evening's entertainment." The voice came from a tall man with a croker sack over his head with holes for his eyes. His brown hands clutched a torch of his own, which he lit and thrust into the faces of the surprised figures in robes. As they shrank from the light, the man in the croker sack pushed forward. "I'm sorry," he said. "Did the light hurt your eyes? Maybe it would help if you took off those hoods."

"What the hell do you think you're doing?" one of the robed figures blurted out. "Who are you? What do you want?"

"You don't need to know who I am," the man in the croker sack said. "All you need to know is that there won't be any school-burning here tonight, or any other night."

"What *you* need to know is that if you don't get out of here right now, you won't be getting out at all," the robed man shouted, and he rushed forward with his gang behind him.

"And you need to know you're about to be in a lot of trouble if you touch me," the man in the croker sack said. "Look around."

Jimmy and Big Joe had done their job. At least twenty-five men with croker sacks over their heads were emerging from the woods, lighting torches as they advanced. At least half of them were carrying shotguns.

"Now, I know you gentlemen will want to drop the guns I know you're carrying, because my friends will shoot you where you stand if you don't," the first man in the croker sack said. No one moved, but one of the men in a croker sack came forward and searched each of the robed men, each of whom had indeed been carrying a pistol.

"You'll pay for this," the night rider leader said.

"I'm tired of talking to someone whose face I can't see," the croker sack leader replied. He gestured to one of his companions, who yanked the hoods from the heads of each of the nine robed figures.

"Well, I might have known," Felix said when the face of the robed leader was revealed. "Seth Riordan, the best friend of the man who murdered my paw."

"Felix Parker. It figures," Riordan said.

"That's right," answered Felix. "You know, this bag is itchy. I think I'll take it off." He removed the croker sack to reveal his face.

"Look here, Felix, you might have gotten the best of Claude, but you won't have your way with me." Riordan looked to his cohorts, who grunted their agreement.

"At this point, I don't much care," Felix said. "All I care about is getting this school built and open with my paw's name on it. The American Missionary Association might be sponsoring this school, raising money and sending teachers down here, but *we* are building it. The students, the ones old enough, are working on it, and grown men like me are working with them. I helped build that classroom building myself. That's our future, Mr. Riordan, our future."

Riordan glowered at Felix.

Felix turned to one of his comrades. "Did you write down all their names? Do we know who they all are?" he asked. The man nodded.

"Okay, tie 'em up, and lay them out on that pile of wood they were planning to light."

When the robed men were secured and arranged on the kerosene-soaked stack of wood, Felix went to them one by one and put their hoods back over their heads. He saved Riordan for last.

"Look out in the woods. You see that torch burning out there? There's a man holding it. Look to your left and look to your right. You see the other torches in the woods? There are men holding them too. If you and your friends try to leave, those men will come in here and light this pile, and then they will leave. If I were you, I'd wait 'til workers show up and let you go in the morning."

"You won't get away with this!" Riordan shouted.

Felix leaned down next to Riordan's ear. "You need to understand something. I let Claude get away when he took my paw," he said, "but I won't let you get away with killing the only thing I have of him. If you try to come after me or mine, I will come to your plantation and burn it to the ground. If I am very lucky, you and your wife will be inside the house when I do it."

Felix moved closer to look Riordan in the eye. Riordan stared back, and he saw something in Felix's face that shook him, something cold and determined, and he understood why Claude had been afraid.

A couple of weeks later, Felix and Jimmy were at Jim Bibb's Saturday night bash laughing and talking when Big Joe walked up to them with a grin on his face and three drinks in his hands. He gave one to Felix, one to Jimmy, and kept one for himself. "Did you hear the news?" he asked.

"I guess we didn't," Jimmy said. "What's goin' on?"

Big Joe slapped Felix on the back and raised his glass. When Felix and Jimmy clicked their glasses against his, he said, "Seth Riordan put his plantation up for sale. He's leaving town."

Chapter 50

RED CLAY, ALABAMA

AUTUMN 1886

At midnight on a chilly October evening, Jim Bibb shut down his Saturday shindig in the woods for the last time. Standing by his stool at the entrance to the tent after the last customer departed, he pulled the collar of his coat tight around his neck. He reached into his cashbox and counted out two stacks of bills. "This here's for you," he said and handed the first stack to Big Joe. "Now you take this other money and pay off the boys and see that they shut everything down right. I need the whiskey brought over to the new place tomorrow, and see to it that the tent gets taken down and delivered to—"

"I been workin' for you for a while, Mr. Bibb; I know what to do," Big Joe said, interrupting his employer. "I'll take care of everything here, and I'll see you Monday at the new place." The "new place" was Jim Bibb's Pool Hall and Bar, set to open the following Saturday night in a renovated space on the main drag of the town's Colored business section.

Felix had overseen the renovation, and he had personally built the bar of dark-stained wood. In the front, there were six tables with four chairs at each, where Bibb planned to serve his signature fried chicken and fried catfish sandwiches. Two pool tables stood side by side in the rear. On the far side of the room, opposite the bar, there was an upright piano and an area for a drummer and a bass player, next to a postage-stamp-sized dance floor.

"All right," Bibb said as he climbed into his buggy. "I'll see you Monday morning. We still got a lot of work to do."

"Yes, sir," Big Joe said. "I'll be there."

Bibb looked past Big Joe to the scene of the men breaking down the tent and packing up food service equipment and the makeshift bar. "We worked hard to get to where we could open the new place, but it won't be the same, will it?" he said.

"No, sir, it won't be the same," Big Joe agreed, "but it's time to move on, ain't it?"

"I reckon so," Bibb said and clicked his tongue at the horse.

In the woods surrounding the clearing, where the trees had already shed their leaves in anticipation of winter, raccoons, field mice, possums, and other scavengers were watching, waiting for their chance to descend on the scraps of bread, chicken, and fish the men were sure to leave behind. They couldn't know that it would be the last time for them too.

———

At Jim Bibb's new place, Felix was a regular. Most Friday evenings after work, he could be found perched on the barstool farthest from the front door, holding court and drinking Bibb's good homemade whiskey with his friends before going home to dinner with his family. One Saturday night a month, he and Jimmy were among the first to arrive and the last to leave, just as they had been at the old operation in the woods.

"Looks like you got a good deal going on here, Jim," Felix said as he wrapped his fingers around another shot on a Friday night.

"Yeah, I guess so. The biggest problem I got is keeping enough whiskey on hand to satisfy you and your boys." Bibb allowed a sly grin to split his face. He worked the bar in the new place and charged for each drink and each plate of food, instead of a flat fee at the door the way he had in the woods, but some things remained the same: He still kept his club and an old shotgun close at hand under the bar. Bibb slapped Felix on the shoulder and winked before moving to the other end of the bar to serve a customer.

Zilpha wasn't happy that Felix spent so much time at Jim Bibb's place. "I didn't like it when he and Jimmy went out there in the woods once a month," she complained to Lucille. "But now he goes in that place once a week and comes home smelling like something somebody left out in a back alley. You would think that a man with a wife, a home, and two daughters—and little Margaret just two years old—would be more considerate."

"I know," Lucille said, "and you know Jimmy is right there with him most Fridays. But Zilpha, they're both good men, so we can't complain too much. Besides, they always come home, don't they?"

It was a Friday afternoon, and the women were in Zilpha's kitchen, canning tomatoes, corn, green beans, and peaches from Zilpha's gardens. The previous day they had been at Lucille's home to prepare her produce for winter. Mary, Zilpha's older daughter, sat on the floor playing with a doll that Felix had made for her. He had carved the head, hands, and feet from scrap wood and stained them brown. The hair was glued-on black yarn, and the legs, arms, and body were cloth stuffed with cotton. Zilpha had made a little dress for the creation. Margaret, the two-year-old, sat nearby watching, content to chew a piece of sugarcane.

"Sweet babies," Lucille remarked. "I guess it's not in the Lord's plan for Jimmy and me to be so blessed."

Zilpha saw the tears forming in her friend's eyes and walked across the room to embrace her. "It's all right," she said. "You and Jimmy have each other, and that's a blessing too, isn't it?"

Felix was working on his third drink. *The last one before I go home*, he told himself. The early Friday evening crowd had left, gone home to supper and sleep, and the late-night Friday crowd was arriving—young men and women, dressed to the nines, ready for a good time. He was about to toss down the rest of his drink and leave when a sultry voice spoke to him from over his shoulder.

"Hey, Felix." It was Edna Mae Daniels.

"Hi, Edna Mae," Felix replied, acutely aware of her nearness to him. He couldn't stand without brushing against her. Edna Mae's gray-green eyes were twinkling, and her thick cherry-red lips stretched into a broad smile that showed even white teeth. Her skin glistened with perspiration from her exertions on the dance floor.

"Jim Bibb got a good band here. Don't you want to come out and dance with me?" she asked.

"I'd like to, Edna Mae, but I got to be getting home. Zilpha and the babies are waiting for me, and I should have been there a long time ago," Felix said, growing more nervous by the second.

Edna Mae's response to Felix's brushoff was to move closer to him. "Maybe you got time for just one more drink?" She lifted herself onto the stool next to him.

Felix gestured to Jim Bibb for a round, and when the drinks arrived, Felix downed his in a single gulp while Edna Mae took a ladylike sip.

"This is nice," she said. "You know, I've wanted a chance to talk with you for a long time."

"Is that right?" Felix said.

"Yes, it is."

"I don't know what's so interesting about me. Seems like you have plenty of men to keep you company," Felix said.

Edna Mae took another sip of her drink. "Do you believe all the things they say about me?" she asked.

"I don't know. What do you think 'they' say about you?"

Edna Mae threw her head back and laughed. Her ample bosom rose and fell, and her butt jiggled where it hung off the sides of the barstool. She took another sip of her drink before whispering in Felix's ear: "They say I'm a bad woman, that I'm a whore who takes money from men when they get what they want from me."

"Well," Felix said, "is it true?"

Edna Mae stared directly into Felix's eyes. "Yes," she said, "and I'm good at it too."

Felix didn't know what to say. He felt dizzy, as if he might slip off the stool onto the floor. He tried to stand, but his legs felt wobbly. "Sorry," he muttered. "I think I've had too much liquor. I have to go home now."

"You could just come home with me now," Edna Mae said, her voice low and husky. "I told you I been wantin' to get to know you, Felix. Come on now, won't cost you nothin' this time."

Felix steadied himself. "I have to go home," he said. "I have to go home right now."

Edna Mae studied Felix's face. "Thanks for the drink," she said finally. "I'll be seein' you around. I think we'll be gettin' together soon." She slipped off her stool and sashayed back to the dance floor, where she was met by a young man with a smile on his lips and a hungry look in his eyes.

Felix stood by the bar and watched the couple dance until Jim Bibb came up to him. "It's time to go home, Felix," he said. "Go. Now."

Chapter 51

Few people around Red Clay, Alabama, in 1901, Black or white, re-membered a time when Jimmy Flowers didn't have the blacksmith shop on the edge of town. Jimmy shoed horses, fixed broken wagon wheels, forged tools, and worked on just about anything else made of metal. He was good at it, and customers came from miles away. Some-times they stayed to watch him work: Black Vulcan bending hot iron, six-foot-three, swinging his hammer, powerful muscles straining under ebony skin, sweat running off his bald head and down his bare back and across his chest, soaking the edges of his ancient leather apron. Even in winter the blacksmith's shop offered a glimpse of hell, as fire raged in the forge and sparks flew with every stroke of his hammer. It was too hot for most folks, and in the summer it became unbearable. On this summer day, there was only one other person in the shop.

"Jimmy, how long have you been doing this?" Felix asked from his seat by the front window of the shop. He had been there for nearly an hour.

"Man, how come you ask me that? You know how long I been doin' this—long as you been actin' like you know how to be a carpen-ter," Jimmy replied.

"I know. I just wanted to know if *you* know," Felix said with a sly grin.

"You ain't nothin'," Jimmy said and returned to his work.

Felix chuckled and nibbled the lunch he had brought with him, a dime's worth of crackers and sardines from the store up the street, along with a nickel bottle of Coca-Cola. When he finished, he wiped his mouth and hands with the handkerchief he carried in the back pocket of his denim overalls and stuffed the trash into a brown paper sack.

Now in their forties, Felix and Jimmy hardly needed to talk to communicate.

"What you doin' here anyhow?" Jimmy asked. "I thought you was supposed to be workin'."

"I was," Felix said, "but the new load of roofing shingles for that house we're building didn't come in, and we ran out of what we already had about eleven o'clock. So, the boss man sent us home and said to come back Monday morning. It's Friday, so I figured I'd come over here and make sure you were taking care of business."

"Humph," Jimmy grunted.

Felix pulled out his pocketknife, retrieved a half-finished wooden flute from his toolbox, and started to whittle. They were together that way for about half an hour, Jimmy working at his forge and Felix whittling his wooden flute.

"Jimmy, you ever think about the slavery times?" Felix asked, and without waiting for Jimmy to reply, he continued. "I've been thinking about it a lot lately. I've been thinking about when you and I were water boys on the plantation, and you got picked to go help in the blacksmith shop. I've got to tell you, I was jealous. I thought, how come he gets to do that and I'm still carrying this water bucket in the field?

"And then I got scared. I figured if they took you, they would take me too, but I was afraid they would take me to the field to pick, and you know how bad it was in the field. I didn't want to be picking cotton."

Jimmy listened while his old friend talked and waited for him to stop before speaking himself. "Why you thinkin' about this now?" he asked. "First, it didn't happen. You got picked to work in the carpenter shop just like I got picked to work for the blacksmith. We was chosen. We got lucky, and that's all there is to it."

"But how come it was us?" Felix interjected. "Why did we come out with a trade and no whip marks on our backs? How come we were lucky and not the others?"

Only the crackle of fire in the forge broke the silence in the blacksmith shop. Outside, there was no breeze, and dust hung in the air like red-brown mist. Jimmy walked across the shop, and the two old friends stepped outdoors.

"Sometimes there ain't no answer, Felix. Sometimes, a man just got to take life the way it come and hope he on the right side of things with God," Jimmy said. "Look at you. You got a pretty wife and four sweet little girls. You got a nice house, and you walk around town like you somebody and don't nobody mess with you. What else you want?"

Felix leaned against the building and closed his eyes, letting Jimmy's words hang in the air with the dust. "I guess I ought to be heading home," he said.

Jimmy studied Felix as he walked away. Something wasn't right. It wasn't like Felix to be unsure of himself, to worry about things a man couldn't control. Jimmy kept watching as Felix disappeared around the corner. Minutes later, as he was pounding the iron rim of a wagon wheel into shape, it occurred to him that Felix wasn't headed for home as he had said when he left the shop. He was headed in the opposite direction. *Where*, Jimmy wondered, *and to what?* Clouds rolled in, and Jimmy could hear thunder in the distance. A tempest was brewing, and he hoped his friend would find shelter and find it soon.

———

Felix walked aimlessly for a long while before his reverie broke, and he realized that he was on the road that ran past Edna Mae's house. He had not been inside it for years, and he was surprised to find himself staring at it now. The house, with its green curtains fluttering at a partially open window, seemed innocent, even charming, but it had been the site of events that led to one of the most painful moments of his life.

The wind was blowing harder since he'd left Jimmy's shop, and red dust eddies swirled along the edge of the hard-packed dirt road as he turned to head for home. He made it back into town just as heavy raindrops began to fall, kicking up dust like bullet strikes. Deep, muddy puddles were starting to form. Jim Bibb's place was just a block away, and he started to run toward it.

"Man, I ain't seen you in here on a Friday night in a long time," Bibb said and poured a whiskey for Felix as he shook the rain from his hat and collapsed on a barstool.

"Yeah, well I've been busy, you know with the kids and all, so I've been sticking close to home," Felix said. "Zilpha's happier that way too. You know how it is."

Bibb nodded and walked away to serve another customer. It was true. Except for the occasional Saturday night with Jimmy, Felix rarely stopped in the bar and pool hall anymore, and across the room, he spotted the reason for his absence: Edna Mae. She was sitting at a table with a young man who seemed intent on parting with a big chunk of his pay for an evening of her attention. She looked up and saw Felix. Their eyes locked for a moment, and then she turned away to focus on the young man across from her as if he was the brightest star in the universe.

Unbidden, a memory from fifteen years earlier surfaced in Felix's mind, the time when Edna Mae had whispered into his ear, "I think we'll be getting together soon," as he retreated from her offer to spend an evening with him. Felix had escaped that evening, but the next time he saw her in Jim Bibb's place, he succumbed, and he had become a frequent visitor to Edna Mae's cottage. That is, until several months into his dalliance with her, when he arrived home from work to find Zilpha sitting on the front porch with his suitcase lying beside her feet.

"What is this out here for?" he'd asked.

"I thought you might need it when you move in with your other woman," Zilpha had replied, rocking back and forth in her chair and gazing straight ahead.

"What are you talking about? What other woman?"

Zilpha stopped rocking. "Don't lie to me, Felix," she snapped. "The women at church have been telling me for weeks that you were up to no good, and I ignored them. I said they were wrong. I told them my Felix wouldn't do that. Then that hussy Edna Mae Daniels showed up here today, at my front door, brazen as anything, saying you told her she could get some pears from our tree and would it be okay if she just went out there and picked them herself. What else have you been giving her, Felix? Is that why we've been short on money lately?"

It had taken a couple of years for Felix to fully regain Zilpha's trust, and when he did, he vowed to never again risk it. Even now, after years of studiously avoiding close contact with Edna Mae, Felix shivered at the thought of how he had nearly ruined everything. He was still thinking about it when Edna Mae appeared at the bar next to him.

"Edna Mae, I don't think it's a good idea for us to be talking here," Felix said before she cut him off.

"Listen, Felix, I'm sorry about how things went. I feel bad that I messed things up for you and Zilpha," she said. "To tell the truth, I was just jealous. Don't think I never noticed how y'all are together and how you look at her when she's talking to her friends after church. Everything is good for y'all, and I know I'm never gon' have that, and I guess bein' jealous made me go up to your house that day."

"You got me into a lot of trouble, and it took a long time to get things right again," Felix replied, "but it never would have happened in the first place if I hadn't been messing around with you, so let's just say we're even and leave it at that."

Edna Mae slid onto the stool next to him. "Thank you, Felix. I appreciate it, but I got to tell you somethin' before you go. It's important."

Felix eyed Edna Mae, trying to read her thoughts. If he had learned anything from his experience with her, it was that there was more going on with her than she let on. Her gentlemen callers were often careless about what they said in front of her, and she had become a regular informant for Reverend Jones. The information about plans to burn the Plessant Parker Academy had been acquired in just that way.

"What's going on?" Felix asked.

"I was going to pass this on to Reverend Jones tomorrow, but you need to know now. Seth Riordan ain't never let it go about how you stopped the school burnin' and drove him out of Red Clay. What I hear is he been stewin' 'bout it all this time. You understand I cain't tell you where I heard it exactly, but he got friends here that been tellin' him 'bout how you turned out to be somebody, and I guess he just couldn't stand it no more. What I hear is he got plans to get you and get you good. So you be careful."

Felix swallowed the rest of his drink and motioned to Jim Bibb to bring one for Edna Mae. He laid some money on the bar and stood up to go. "Thanks, Edna Mae. I appreciate it," he said.

Felix was already out the door when Edna Mae noticed that he had forgotten his hat, and she rushed to the door to catch him, just in time to see three men in hoods grab Felix, throw him into the back of a wagon, and drive away.

Chapter 52

Felix didn't know how long he had been jostled around in the back of that wagon with his wrists tied behind his back and a hood over his head. They were moving fast over the bumpy road, and his head banged against the floorboards each time the wheels hit a hole. He could hear the horses' strenuous breathing and the swift staccato of their hooves striking the clay. His captors said nothing, but he could smell whiskey, tobacco, and sweat as the wind swept past them. He tried to sit up to ease the pain from the ropes restraining his wrists, but he was immediately knocked down by a blow from something heavy and hard. "Don't move, nigger," a disembodied voice said. "Move again, and I'll ram this shotgun down your throat and pull the trigger."

The wagon flew down the road, and for all Felix could tell, they had left the known world and were headed straight to hell. *I can't go now. Zilpha and the babies need me*, he thought. *I can't die, not now, not like this.* Suddenly the sound of the horses' hooves changed—muffled, slower—and the ride in the wagon seemed softer as it slowed to a stop. It was quiet but for the horses' snorting and the whine of a mosquito that had penetrated the hood over Felix's head and was feasting on the tender flesh of his ear.

Then he felt hands on him as he was lifted from the floor of the wagon and pitched through the air to land hard on his side on grass-covered soil.

More hands yanked the hood from his head, and as he blinked his eyes, trying to clear his vision, he saw a boot coming toward his head. Then there were more kicks, to his head, to his chest, to his belly and his back, and before he passed out, he heard a scream that he didn't realize was his own.

———

"Oh, Lord, oh Lord, oh Lord," Edna Mae exclaimed as she rushed back into Jim Bibb's with Felix's hat still in her hand. Her eyes were wild, and her face was slick with perspiration. Her gait was unsteady, and she had to grab the edge of the bar to keep from falling.

"What's the matter, Edna Mae?" Bibb asked. "You sick?"

"They got him, Jim. They threw him in the wagon and drove away," she replied.

"They got who? Who is 'they'?"

"Night riders. Night riders in hoods. They got Felix and took him away," she said, gasping for breath.

"Here," Bibb said and pressed a shot of whiskey into Edna Mae's trembling hand. "Tell me what happened."

Edna Mae gulped her drink, no ladylike pretensions now. "I'd just warned Felix about how Seth Riordan was back and how he was plannin' to get him somehow," she said in a rapid tumble of words. "Felix left his hat, and when I ran out to give it to him, I saw them men in hoods grab him and throw him in that wagon and drive off."

The alarm showed on Jim Bibb's face. "Big Joe," he shouted. "Get out here."

Big Joe poked his head out of the storeroom where he had been organizing supplies. "What you need, Mr. Bibb?" he said.

"Night riders got Felix," Bibb yelled. "Edna Mae saw them take him just now. We don't have much time. I'll round up some fellows and tell them to meet you at Felix's house. Somebody's got to tell Zilpha, and then we have to get him back. Edna Mae, where you think they took him?"

"I don't know," she said, "but the reason Seth Riordan left town was 'cause Felix and the rest of y'all stopped him from burnin' down the school and forced him to move away."

"That's good a place as any to start," Jim Bibb said. "Big Joe, when the boys meet you at Felix's house, the school's the first place to look." He reached under the bar and hauled out his shotgun and a box of shells. "Take this," he said, "and I'll tell all the fellows to bring whatever guns they got. Hurry."

Edna Mae drove her buggy faster than she had ever driven before, racing down the rutted dirt road to Felix's house, flying past stands of towering pines, the way lit by the glow of the moon filtering through thick cloud cover. She snapped the whip over the horse's back to urge him to ever greater speed. Big Joe was right behind her in Jim Bibb's wagon, pulled by a pair of mules that he drove to their limits to keep up. Edna Mae was already out of her buggy and climbing the steps to the front door when Big Joe pulled into the yard.

———

Zilpha was in the back of the house putting the girls to bed when she heard the pounding at the door, and when she opened it, the last person she expected to see was standing before her. "How dare you come to my house, Edna Mae Daniels! Felix isn't here, and you couldn't possibly have any business with me, so I will say good evening to you." Zilpha stepped back to slam the door.

"Wait, Miss Zilpha." Big Joe raced up the steps. "We're here 'cause Felix is in trouble, bad trouble."

"Can we come in, please?" Edna Mae implored. "It's serious. Night riders took Felix."

Big Joe saw Zilpha's eyes roll up into her head as she fainted, and he darted out to catch her before she could crumple onto the floor. "Go in the kitchen and bring a wet dishrag, Edna Mae." He lifted the limp form of Felix's wife, carried her across the room, and deposited her on the sofa. A minute later she came to and opened her eyes to see Edna Mae sitting beside her, holding the cold compress to her head.

"You fainted," Edna Mae said in response to the unspoken question in Zilpha's eyes. "Big Joe caught you and put you on the sofa."

Zilpha could hear loud noises from outside—men's raised voices, the horses snorting and stamping their hooves. "What's going on?" she asked. "Who's out there?"

"They the men Jim Bibb got together to go find Felix and take him back from the night riders," Edna Mae said.

"But why?" Zilpha asked. "Why did they take Felix?"

Edna Mae told her about Seth Riordan's revenge plans and how the hooded men had grabbed Felix and driven off with him in the back of a wagon.

"I have to go with them. I have to go get Felix," Zilpha said as she struggled to get up from the sofa.

Jimmy Flowers had arrived while Edna Mae was talking. "Zilpha, you need to stay here," he said. "We'll get Felix back."

"No," she insisted. "You know I can't stay here. I *won't* stay here." She looked back and forth frantically between Jimmy and Edna Mae. "Do you think Lucille would sit at home if you were in trouble?" she asked. "No," she said, answering her own question. "You know she wouldn't." Jimmy was silent, acknowledging the truth of what Zilpha had said.

Edna Mae broke the silence. "You go. You go get your man."

"My babies," Zilpha cried. "I need somebody to watch the girls. Jimmy, can we take them to Lucille?"

Before he could answer, Edna Mae took Zilpha's hands in hers. "I'll watch your daughters," she said. And, when doubt and suspicion clouded Zilpha's face, she added, "I'll take care of them like they was my own."

The two women's eyes locked, and an understanding that neither of them could have articulated occurred between them. "Thank you," said Zilpha, and she rose to walk out into the night.

Chapter 53

PLESSANT PARKER ACADEMY

SUMMER 1901

Felix's eyes were nearly swollen shut, and he couldn't breathe through his nose. It was broken, he thought, and he continually spat blood to keep his mouth clear. His arms, still tied behind his back, were numb, and he couldn't move his left leg. Insects drawn to the blood buzzed around his head, and he was pretty sure he had soiled his pants.

"Not so uppity now, are you?" he heard a voice say, and he turned his head from side to side to try to see who had spoken. "Yes, sir," the voice continued. "The last time we were together, you were the big man. Oh, yeah, you were the cock of the walk, strutting this way and that, talking big about what you would do if I got out of line."

The speaker was moving, circling Felix as he spoke. *I know that voice*, he thought. *I've heard that voice before. Who is it?* And then he passed out again.

A bucket of cold water tossed into his face roused him. "That's better," the voice said. "I want you awake. I want you to know what's happening to you. I want you to suffer."

That's Seth Riordan, Felix thought. *Edna Mae warned me, but I guess it was too late.* "I know it's you, Seth Riordan," Felix said as he gasped from the pain. Every part of his body screamed in agony.

"Well now, that's the best news I've had all night," Seth said. "I thought I might have to kill you without you knowing who did it. I didn't want you to die without knowing that I was the one who took you from your family, that I was the one to remind you that you're nothing but a nigger, no matter what airs you put on. You thought you could get the better of a white man and not pay a price? Well, I've got news for you: It's time to pay, and the price is steep."

Felix's eyes had grown accustomed to the dark, and through the slits of his swollen eyelids, he could see that he was at the Plessant Parker Academy, where he had foiled Seth Riordan's planned arson years earlier. "So, we're back here again, Seth? You're going to try to burn the place down again?" he said. His voice was raspy, emerging from his parched throat, pushing past broken teeth, through cracked, bloody lips.

"No," Seth said. "Nothing as simple as that. Look, Felix, you're going to die here, and I will make you one promise: Your death won't be easy. It will be long and painful. That will give me a lot more pleasure than seeing this school burn ever could."

A cool breeze blew through the woods that bordered the campus and swept across Felix's face. For a moment it seemed to ease his pain, and he thought he heard his father's voice telling him to be strong, a whisper on the wind that soothed his mind as he fell again into oblivion.

———

Zilpha was squeezed between Big Joe Miles and Jimmy Flowers as the mule-drawn wagon hurtled down the country road that led into Red Clay, through the town, past the courthouse square, and into the countryside again, toward the site of the Plessant Parker Academy on what had once been Road's End Plantation. A band of wagons and individual riders stretched out behind them, about twenty men armed with shotguns, rifles, and pistols, all with one goal: to save their friend Felix—if he was still alive. The knowledge of what could be happening to him spurred them on, and they were resolved to take their revenge if they found that the worst had occurred.

Zilpha kept her eyes straight ahead and tried to suppress her terror that Felix might be dead. The night was warm, but she was shivering, and Jimmy pulled a blanket from the back of the wagon and wrapped it around her shoulders.

"We're almost there, Zilpha. You sure you want to go the rest of the way?" Jimmy asked quietly. "We could get somebody to stay with you here while the rest of us go on. Maybe he's not even at the school, and we'll have to look somewhere else."

Zilpha continued to look ahead and shook her head. "I'm going. I have to be there when you find him."

When they were about three hundred yards from the campus, Big Joe stopped the wagon and signaled the rest of the party to stop. "We'll go the rest of the way on foot," he said. "We need to surprise them if this is where they got him. Fan out, y'all, and keep your eyes open."

They picked their way through the woods, treading carefully to avoid making noise that might give them away. They stopped when they reached the edge of the campus.

Jimmy whispered, "Big Joe, you take half the men and circle around to the other side and come in that way. Check everything. See if any of the buildings are open. If they are, search inside. If they're not, move on to the next one. We'll meet in the middle." He started to tell Zilpha to wait, but he knew that would be futile, so he said instead, "Zilpha, you stay close to me."

One by one, they checked the buildings. Unsurprisingly, because it was summer and the fall session was still more than a month away, they were all locked. "Looks like ain't nobody here," one of the men said.

"Let's try the old Riordan place," another man said. "He don't own it no more, but he mighta gone there anyhow."

Jimmy raised his voice to be heard over the group. "We need to be smart," he said. "Some of y'all go to the Riordan place, two or three more go down by the river. I need another group to go out the road to Demopolis, you know, out to the spot where they found those boys lynched last year. The rest of us will split up to cover everywhere else we can think of. Hurry."

———

Felix was regaining consciousness slowly. His eyes were open, but he couldn't see anything. He was in total darkness. *Maybe I'm dead*, he thought. *But I can't be dead; I hurt too much.*

As his head began to clear, he remembered what had happened. His captors had awakened him and beaten him into unconsciousness twice more before dragging him across the campus to the cafeteria building, where they opened the door to the coal chute and dumped him in. He could still hear Seth Riordan's taunts from the chute opening above: "This is where it ends for you, Felix Parker. You know this is summer, so nobody will be around to hear you scream. You'll die of hunger and thirst on a pile of dirty coal, and when fall comes and the school re-opens, the coal delivery will be dumped on your dead, rotting body, at least the parts left over after the rats get through with you. Maybe somebody will find the pieces when they shovel coal to feed the furnace when it gets cold." They slammed the door and walked away laughing.

Felix wasn't sure how long he had lain there, but he thought it might be the same evening. There was no light coming through cracks in the chute door. He could hear scratching noises around him, rats crawling around the coal bin. He was lying on his back, and he felt one run across his chest. He wanted to raise his arm to brush it away, but his wrists were still tied behind his back. He was thirsty, so thirsty. An insect, maybe a spider, walked across his forehead. He shook his head to get rid of it.

An image of Zilpha came into his mind, not as she was now, but as she was when she opened the front door of her father's business and found him there, an awkward teenager hoping to make a good impression. She had never been more beautiful to him than she was at that moment, and through all their years together that was the face he always saw. It was the face that would be with him as he lay there, fearing that he would never see her again. And what about the babies? What would they be like when they grew up? Would they be like their mother—beautiful, sweet, and gracious, and more forgiving than he ever deserved?

Then he heard sounds, footsteps and muffled voices above him. He tried to shout, "I'm here, I'm here!" But nothing came out. His throat was too dry, and the sound that came out was hardly more than a quiet rasp.

Felix listened. He knew those voices. They were friends, fellows he knew from Jim Bibb's bar. He listened some more, and he could tell that they were looking for him. *Don't go, don't go,* a voice screamed in his head. *I'm here!* And then it was quiet again.

All of the men were gone, looking for Felix in other places, except Jimmy and Big Joe. They stood in the center of the campus with Zilpha. "We have to go, Miss Zilpha," Big Joe said. "We looked everywhere 'round here, and he ain't to be found. We need to go and look somewhere else."

"Please," Zilpha replied. "Can't we look here just once more? Maybe I'm crazy, but I have this feeling that if we leave now, we'll be forever sorry."

Big Joe and Jimmy eyed each other sideways, then turned to face her determination.

"All right, once more," Jimmy said, "and then we have to leave."

They made their way around the campus, checking around each building carefully, testing the locks and looking for any other signs of disturbance. As they rounded the back of the cafeteria building, Jimmy said, "This is the last one, Zilpha. We've looked and we have to go."

Zilpha couldn't hold back any longer. Tears started to flow, and she let out a scream of such heartrending pain that Big Joe felt it somewhere deep in his soul, and he began to cry too, big shoulder-shaking sobs as the tears ran down his face. Jimmy shook his head, also on the verge of breaking down. Then they heard it, a tiny cry from beneath their feet.

"Zilpha," the voice said.

"Did you hear that?" Zilpha said. "I heard my name."

"Zilpha," the voice said again, barely audible.

They realized that it had come from the coal chute beside their feet.

Big Joe pulled the door open, and Jimmy held their lantern down inside. The flickering rays of light revealed a figure crumpled below.

"Oh, Lord, thank you. Thank you, Jesus," Zilpha shrieked as she scrambled down the chute to wrap Felix in her arms.

———

RED CLAY, ALABAMA

SUMMER 1901

Seth Riordan drove his wagon with his two henchmen in the rear up the old North Road, away from Red Clay and toward the crossroads, where a left turn would take them the last twelve miles to home. "We could be there by eleven o'clock if these damned roads weren't so bad," Seth said.

"That's all right," one of the men replied. "We took care of business, it ain't raining, and we got a jug, so it don't matter what time we get home. You want a swig?"

"Nah, I'm already feeling good," Seth said. "I'll wait 'til I get home and celebrate with a glass of good cognac. My wife might even join me. She hated that Felix Parker nearly as much as I did. She'll be happy to know he's gone."

The junction was coming into view, and the sky seemed to expand as the wagon emerged from a claustrophobic stretch of roadway lined with looming pines and thick underbrush. The clouds parted, and the moon's glow illuminated everything around them. Except for the *clip-clop* of the horses' hooves, the creaking of the wagon's undercarriage, and the occasional hoot of an owl, the night was still. They entered the crossroads, and Seth turned the horses left. He flicked the whip over their backs to urge them on. "Almost home, boys. Almost home," he said, and then, "Damn!" as the wagon bounced through yet another rut. There was no sound from the back of the wagon, where the contents of the jug had taken its toll on his cronies.

Then he heard something else behind him—men's voices and the beat of hooves, coming up fast. "There they are. Get 'em!" he heard one of them say. Seth looked over his shoulder to see three Black men on horseback barreling toward him. "Don't let 'em get away," one of them shouted.

Seth snapped the whip over the horses. "Giddyup!" he cried, and he snapped the whip again and again, urging the horses onward. The riders were closing in, and as he whipped the horses harder, the wagon swayed wildly, sending the men in back rolling around as the wagon hit bump after bump.

"Seth, what's goin' on?" one of them yelled.

"Niggers," Seth hollered over his shoulder. "They're after us. Grab your guns. Shoot!"

One of the men fired his shotgun, one barrel after the other, but the careening wagon made it impossible to get a bead on the pursuers. The other man fired while the first shooter reloaded. He missed too.

One of the riders was coming alongside, and Seth lashed out at him with his whip. He gave the horses their head and dropped the reins to reach for his own shotgun, but just as his fingers closed around the stock, one of the horses stepped into a hole. Seth heard the bones snap as the horse went down with an agonized whinny, taking the other horse and the wagon with him, pitching the driver and the two passengers overboard.

They landed hard. One of the men died instantly when his skull slammed against a boulder half-buried in the clay by the side of the road. The second man lived long enough to see their pursuers arrive and dismount from their horses before succumbing to his injuries.

Seth Riordan was barely conscious when the riders reached him. He was struggling to breathe, and he lay motionless, racked with pain, unable to move as the Black men advanced toward him, their elongating shadows reaching across his face until they surrounded him and blocked his view of the moon and the stars.

"I guess you a big man now, ain't you?" one of the pursuers growled.

"Naw, he ain't no big man," another one sniffed. "He ain't nothin', at least nothin' nobody gon' miss."

Gasping for breath, Seth managed to spit out a few words: "Go to hell, you black piece of shit." He forced his swollen eyes open, but all he saw was darkness—impenetrable, eternal darkness where there had never been, nor would there ever be, the light of God or man.

In the morning, passersby found the wreckage of the wagon in the middle of the road with one horse standing, still in harness, and the carcass of the second one resting in a heap with a broken leg and a bullet hole in its head. About one hundred feet off the road, three bodies lay in an unmarked grave deep in the woods, beneath underbrush that covered all signs of digging. The fate of their souls was unknown.

Chapter 54

Addie always took the same suite in the same hotel when she visited Paris, and in the summer of 1901, twenty years since she and Étienne had begun their periodic clandestine rendezvous, she arrived in the city she considered her second home with a feeling of unease. Nothing had changed—not the hotel and its accommodating, discreet staff, nor the street outside, nor the *chocolat chaud et croissant* from the hotel's kitchen each morning. Certainly the passion the two lovers felt for each other had not diminished. And yet, after three weeks, she still couldn't shake her anxiety.

She and Étienne had spent nearly all of that time together, strolling the streets and visiting galleries, people-watching in *les places*, and dining together in out-of-the-way bistros. It had been glorious, as it always was, and they had exchanged their doleful farewells the night before. Étienne's wife, Jeannette, was returning to the city in two days from a long visit to their daughter, Adélaïde, and her new baby in Lyon, and he needed to prepare for her arrival. Addie had practically finished packing, and she had spent the morning walking along the Seine before returning to the hotel to check out and go to her ship for an evening departure.

"Oh, madame," the desk clerk said as she retrieved her key, "the ship has sent word that your departure will be delayed for three days while unexpected repairs are made." It was not good news. She had said her goodbyes, and now she would be alone in a city where everything and every place would remind her of Étienne and the life she could never have with him.

"*Merci, monsieur*," she replied. "I shall remain here then. I assume that my suite will remain available to me?"

"*Oui, madame*. Of course."

Addie spent the next two days going through the motions, moving about the city in a fog, despite going to all of the places and doing all of the things that would normally have delighted her. On the third day, she arose feeling relieved that she would soon be on the ship and headed for home. She dressed and decided to go out for breakfast rather than eating at her hotel, a chance to say farewell to Paris—again.

She was on a bridge over the Seine when she encountered a sight that stopped her in her tracks. Coming from the other direction was Étienne, accompanied by a woman who must surely be his wife, along with an attractive young woman pushing a baby carriage next to an attentive young man. That must be Adélaïde and her husband and baby. They must have come to Paris with Jeannette.

Oh, my Lord, she thought, *what to do? If I turn and run away, I will draw attention to myself. If I keep going, I don't know how it will go when we pass each other.* The family was drawing closer, and frozen there, Addie decided to simply turn her back and appear to be absorbed by the sights of boats passing beneath the bridge.

She could feel her pulse throbbing in her temples, and her breathing became labored and irregular. Every nerve in her body vibrated as she struggled not to steal a glance at the family. She could hear their voices, lively and happy, clearly delighting in the beauty of the morning and of the new life in the carriage. A wave of dizziness swept over Addie, and her knees buckled. She started to fall, and she might have gone over the edge of the bridge had not a pair of strong arms caught her.

"Are you all right, madame?" Her eyes met those of her rescuer, Étienne's apparent son-in-law. "I thought you were going to fall," he said.

"Thank you," she said. "I was dizzy, but I feel fine now. Thank you so much. If you had not caught me, I fear that things might have turned out quite differently. I am grateful for your quick thinking and action."

"You are not French?" he replied. "Your accent is excellent, but I think you are not from here," he said. "Allow me to introduce myself. I am Gerard Bertrand. This is my wife Adélaïde and"—he gestured to the baby in the carriage—"our son, Pierre."

"You have a keen ear, Monsieur Bertrand. I am Madame Parker, an American from New Orleans. I'm visiting friends here in Paris, but this is my last day. My ship, which had been delayed, sails this evening—and but for you, it might have sailed without me."

"Madame Parker, may I also present my wife's father and mother? This is Professor Étienne Dupuis and his wife, Madame Jeannette Dupuis."

Until that moment, Addie had managed not to look at Étienne, but now their eyes met and despite their best efforts, a flicker of recognition passed between them, which was not missed by Jeannette.

"Have you met before?" she asked.

"No, Madame Dupuis," Addie lied, "but it is my loss not to have been acquainted with a fine family such as yours. You should count yourself as fortunate."

Jeannette said nothing, and in the awkward silence, Addie found her voice. "Thank you again, Monsieur Bertrand. You must go on your way now, and I must depart as well. Good luck to you all. I shall have quite the story to tell about my last day in Paris when I return to New Orleans."

A wave of emotions rolled over Addie as she watched them walk away—relief at having made it through the encounter, anger at herself for having failed to create a family of her own, resentment of Étienne, though for what she wasn't sure, and jealousy of all the families she saw strolling around her, taking delight in simply being together. *Damn them all*, she thought, and immediately felt ashamed of the notion.

RED CLAY, ALABAMA

AUTUMN 1943

More than four decades after the encounter on the bridge over the Seine, Addie still felt the pain of it as she told the story on the front porch of Felix Parker's house in Red Clay, Alabama.

Addie, Eileen, and Maybelle sat quietly, watching fat gray clouds roll in from the southwest. "I think it's time for me to go," Addie said. She stood slowly, leaning on her cane, then looked each of the other women in the eye. "Sharing these memories of Felix has been a precious gift that I shall cherish in the time I have left."

Maybelle and Eileen stepped forward, and one by one they embraced her. "It has been dear to us, too, and we are grateful," Maybelle said.

"I will go to Paris one day, and when I do, I will think of you," Eileen whispered into Addie's ear.

Addie smiled, and with the help of her chauffeur, descended the stairs and got into her car. When she was settled inside, she opened the window and waved before the car pulled out of the driveway and disappeared down the road.

Eileen and Maybelle remained on the porch, sitting together on the swing and enjoying the warmth of the early afternoon sun. "You know, Daddy and Mama loved this place, especially in the spring," Maybelle said, taking her daughter's hand and leaning back to share one last memory.

RED CLAY, ALABAMA

SUMMER 1915

Life was good for the Parkers. They owned their house and the fifteen acres surrounding it, and Felix was getting plenty of carpentry work. Zilpha delighted in working in her garden of herbs and flowers, a small plot surrounded on three sides by twelve acres of peas, turnips, corn, potatoes, peanuts, and yams that she worked with help from Felix and the occasional hired hand. There was also a small plum orchard with a massive solitary pear tree in the center.

At harvest time Zilpha turned the kitchen into a canning factory, putting up dozens of jars of produce for the family's dinner table when the cold fall and winter months arrived. She sold the fresh pears for a dime apiece, but she turned the plums into her legendary jam, along with the blackberries and muscadines from vines that grew wild around the perimeter of the orchard. Most years Felix raised a hog for slaughter in the fall. He also kept chickens that gave eggs and occasionally their lives for the family's table.

When it rained too hard to work in the garden, Zilpha would sit in her rocking chair on the front porch, reading and listening to the music of raindrops splattering on the tin roof overhead. Out on the lawn, earthworms slithered through the grass, forced above ground by rainwater seeping into the soil, soon to be a banquet for sharp-eyed robins perched in the magnolia tree that dominated the yard.

Zilpha liked the cool breezes that accompanied the storms. They felt good on her face, and she didn't mind that they ruffled the pages of the *Chicago Defender* weekly newspaper she often read. The Black-owned *Defender* found its way into thousands of homes across the South and the Midwest, featuring stories about the accomplishments of Black people in business, entertainment, and sports up North.

All of it seemed far away and vaguely unreal to Zilpha, more fantastic than wonderful to a formerly enslaved woman who had learned her letters in defiance of the law by listening in on lessons given to the master's children. Zilpha had served as a companion for the children, and she had listened intently to everything the tutor said, while pretending not to hear a word. At night, back in the slave quarters, she would practice saying the letters and scrawling them in the dirt floor with a stick, eventually learning to read with help from her father, who had also hidden his ability.

Still, there was no denying that Colored people were making progress, she thought. All four of her daughters—Mary, Margaret, Mattie, and Maybelle—had graduated from the Plessant Parker Academy, though sadly the two middle girls had died young, victims of a mysterious virus that took one and then the other in quick succession. They were gone before they had a chance to marry and have children, a tragedy made worse because they were so beautiful and so talented. Both had played the piano at church and had sung in the choir. Margaret and Mattie had been gone for years, but in the early morning hours before the sun chased away the dark, Zilpha, lying next to Felix in their brass bed, could always hear their voices singing in the gentle gusts that rustled the leaves of the chinaberry tree outside their window.

Mary had married a preacher from Birmingham and moved there with him, and Maybelle was a teacher at a Colored school in Birmingham, living with Mary and her husband. It was only a matter of time, Zilpha thought, before Maybelle was married too.

They were prospering, and Felix was well-thought-of around town. And didn't the Jewish man at the dry goods store let Felix bring home dresses for her to try on so she wouldn't have to hold them up in front of a mirror and guess whether they would fit, the way most Colored women had to make their purchases? A new midnight-blue taffeta dress with matching hat hung in her closet at that moment, waiting to be worn to church for the first time on Sunday. Felix had brought it home earlier in the week, along with three others, and she had tried them on right away, sashaying back and forth across the bedroom while Felix sat in a chair and admired the view.

"Uh-huh, you look mighty fine, Miz Parker," Felix had said, affecting the uneducated diction he had long since left behind. "Your husband better not let you outta his sight in that dress, 'cause he sho nuff don't feel like whuppin' all the Negroes that gon' come sniffin' 'round."

"You stop," she had giggled, but she knew that she had kept her figure at age fifty-six, and that the color of the dress complemented her smooth *café au lait* skin. She knew, too, that Felix liked it when she let her silky black hair, a legacy of her mixed-race parents, hang down her back to her waist the way it was now. It didn't matter that it was streaked with random strands of gray, and she couldn't wait to walk into Third Baptist Church on Sunday morning in her new outfit.

As much as Zilpha appreciated her good fortune, she was not a fool. The *Chicago Defender* also carried stories about lynchings happening all over the South, and everyone seemed to know a young man who had suddenly disappeared when he ran afoul of some white man or woman and whose family had spirited him out of town under cover of darkness ahead of a certain date with a lynch mob. Sometimes she worried about Felix. He was so cocksure, and he carried himself like he was somebody special. Ironically, the very qualities that had so drawn her to Felix right from her first sight of him were those that could endanger him. But there was no use in worrying about Felix. He was his own man, and he was not going to change—nor would she want him to.

The sound of the grandfather clock inside the house striking four reminded her that it was time to start making dinner. The sun was high in the sky so much later during these spring days, and she had lost track of the time. Felix would be coming home soon, and she had promised him his favorite dinner—fried pork chops with brown gravy, mashed potatoes, green peas, and hot biscuits—as a treat for finishing a new addition to an old house, a big job that had been fraught with problems.

Life with Felix was not always easy, she thought, but she felt blessed to be sharing a life with him, and as she took one last look at the late afternoon sky before going inside, she remembered a Walt Whitman poem she had read in a book that Maybelle left behind on her last visit:

> When lilacs last in the dooryard bloom'd,
> And the great star early droop'd in the western sky in
> 　　the night,
> I mourn'd, and yet shall mourn with ever-returning
> 　　spring.
>
> Ever-returning spring, trinity sure to me you bring,
> Lilac blooming perennial and drooping star in the west,
> And thought of him I love.

Afterword

My mother earned three advanced degrees, headed a university library, and was well-known for her involvement with local civic and social organizations before and after she retired. Despite her high public profile, however, she has always been intensely private about her personal life, even within the confines of the family.

Consequently, during a visit a few years ago, I was delighted when she began to regale me with stories I'd never heard about my late great-grandfather. I listened eagerly as she described a talented, honorable, and proud man who, despite having been born into slavery on an Alabama plantation, made a good life for himself and his family in the post–Civil War years. The revelation that brought me up short, however, was the way my decorous, then ninety-two-year-old mother gleefully described my ancestor as a fellow with a roguish streak, including a taste for good liquor and an eye for the ladies. "You should write about him," she said. "His story would be a good book."

Over the next several months, she sent me dozens of pages of handwritten anecdotes and other bits of information, and I visited South Alabama, where my great-grandfather had lived his entire life. I searched for documents in dusty archives and online. I conducted interviews with people who had known our family, as well as with local historians. I drove along backroads—past farms, through miles of woodlands and pastures—and cruised through little towns that seemed frozen in the mid-1950s. I stood on the land that had once belonged to him, and on which as a child I had romped with his daughter, my doting grandma. I breathed the air and watched puffs of ancient red clay dust swirl around my ankles and settle on my shoes as I walked.

Although there are no surviving photographs of my great-grandfather, and though he died six years before I was born, he was becoming ever more real to me, and I could imagine his face, his bearing, and the sound of his voice. I could see the landscape through his eyes, feel the wind on his skin, and hear the murmurings of Southern small-town life through his ears.

Then I realized something important. The forebear in my mind had become something more than just my ancestor. He had become the embodiment of all the Black men, and the women who stood beside them, who clawed their way out of the wretchedness of slavery, who rode the exhilarating wave of Reconstruction, and who navigated the dangers and uncertainties of Jim Crow to make something of themselves and to build lives for their families and their descendants.

My mission changed. When I told my mother about my plan to write a historical novel rather than the nonfiction narrative she had envisioned, I expected her to object. Instead, she endorsed it. Thus, *Red Clay* was born. A few given names and family anecdotes survived the transition, but the story—including the town of Red Clay and the Road's End plantation—is otherwise a product of my imagination and an expression of the truth in ways the book I'd originally planned could never have conveyed.

—Charles B. Fancher

Acknowledgments

I am grateful to many friends, family members, and others for their thoughtful, helpful comments and suggestions after reading drafts of the book, but a few need to be singled out.

My agent, Chip Rice, and his then assistant, Sydney Queen DeTellis, now an agent herself, were tireless champions of the novel and brought it to the attention of Marilyn Kretzer, Blackstone Publishing's senior acquisitions editor. Marilyn's enthusiasm and support for *Red Clay* were precisely what I needed at that time. I also appreciated the experience of working with the rest of the Blackstone team, notably editor Holly Rubino, senior publicity manager Sarah Bonamino, director of marketing Rachel Sanders, print editor Levi Coren, and designer Alenka Linaschke.

Many others were also critical to bringing this work to life. East Stroudsburg University English Professor-Emeritus Michael Liberman provided many constructive insights, and independent editor Carol Gaskin asked all the right questions as I polished the draft for submission. Others who provided helpful observations included Janice Berman, Sue Campbell, Joseph Dunn, Pamela Ice, Andrew and Carol Klyman, Julianna Padgett, Vicki Sanders, Jim Stovall, and Lisa Tracy. Few people were more supportive than the members of the weekly writers' group at The Older Adult Learning Community in

East Stroudsburg, Pennsylvania. They were unflagging in their support, and I will always be grateful.

I have quoted briefly from the following public domain sources: "No Progress Without Struggle" (1857) by Frederick Douglass; "When Lilacs Last in the Dooryard Bloom'd" (1865) by Walt Whitman; and the King James Version of the Bible, first published in 1611.

Perhaps it has become cliché to single out one's spouse for special thanks, but it is a fact that my wife, Diane, a fine writer and editor in her own right, read every word and provided invaluable opinions and suggestions to make the book better. I am also grateful to my parents, the late Dr. Charles B. Fancher Sr. and my mother, Dr. Evelyn P. Fancher, whose memories and hand-written notes provided the spark for what eventually became *Red Clay*.

Finally, there is one more supporter who must be mentioned here—Sammy, our rescued terrier mix, who camped out under my desk every day as I wrote and reminded me periodically that it was time to get up and go for a walk. He was there when the last words were written, and though he is gone now, his constant companionship made all the difference.